She wrote in English because it came naturally to her and because, anyway, the book would be published in London and New York long before it would be published in China. Her style was strong and vigorous, reflecting her personality. Years ago, when she had been a student at Wellesley College in the United States, her teachers had sometimes held up her prose as an example to the class.

"Now I will tell you something of our travels," she began. "To get here we used steamers, motorcars and aeroplanes. From Kiukiang I went by steamer to Chungking, which is in Szechuan, and is some 1,350 miles from Shanghai, and some 600 feet higher than Nanking. Really the steamer climbs up that height through the rapids of the Upper Yangtze. Up to Yichang the river is just a great body of water running strongly and eating its way into the fields on either side and carrying lots of good earth out to sea, making the ocean yellow for some 60 miles out, so strong is the current of the river, so great is the quantity of silt that it carries . . ."

She paused, casting her mind back to the day when she and the Generalissimo and their entourage had first arrived in Chungking, transforming that provincial town into the seat of government for the duration of the war. From where she sat now, in her private study in the Generalissimo's villa set high above the Yangtze, she had a clear view of the ravaged city on the other side of the river. How the people had suffered! Sometimes after a bombing raid she would visit the crowded hospitals, encouraging the nursing staff to yet more heroic efforts and comforting the wounded.

Today, however, Madame Chiang Kai Shek felt more cheerful than she had in a long time. Mr Roosevelt had sent a new man to replace that odious General Stillwell who had caused her husband so much trouble. Did Stillwell suppose that Chiang didn't know what the American was saying about him? What a fool the man was! Chiang Kai Shek knew almost everything that went on in Chungking and what he didn't know, Tai Li – the head of the Kuomintang secret police – told him. The Generalissimo had even showed her a copy of the poem that Stillwell had written the other day, the one in which he referred to Chiang as "The Peanut"! Even now as she remembered the poem's harsh vulgarity, her anger returned. With Stillwell's ignominious recall, they were at last having their revenge.

She allowed her mind to dwell for a minute on her recent visit to Washington. What a success that had been! She had enjoyed staying at the White House more than she could say. What was more, her personal diplomacy, her striking advocacy of the Nationalist cause during those five months, had been dramatically rewarded. US supplies were coming in increasing quantities over the Hump – 50,000 tons last month alone. Of course the Americans hoped and supposed that the Generalissimo would use these supplies – the planes, the tanks, the guns – for the war against Japan. But President Chiang knew better than that. Up here in the mountains of Szechuan, hidden behind the mighty Yangtze Gorges, he and his cronies were safe. Not once in ten years had Japanese troops ventured upstream beyond the mouth of the Gorges some 200 miles to the east. Naturally, their planes had done their worst, but there was a limit to the damage that even the heaviest bombing could do. And the fogs had helped too; those heavy white fogs that swirled up from the confluence of the Yangtze and Jialing rivers and for six months out of 12 enveloped the city in an impenetrable cloud which had proved most effective against air attack.

She permitted herself a small smile of satisfaction as she thought about the way America was becoming ever more irrevocably committed to the Generalissimo. It was strange how few of them understood the game that Chiang was playing. When the time came to use those American supplies, it would not be against the Japanese. No, the real enemies were the Communists up there with Mao in the mountains of Yenan. Notionally, Mao and Chiang were allies in the common effort to defeat Japan, but the whole world (except for the Americans, it seemed) knew that this was just "words on paper" – wasn't that what Mao himself had called it?

She gazed down at the river as it swept in a great bend beneath the Eagle's Nest, the name which Chiang had given to his hill-side villa. As she watched, she saw two or three fishing-boats, the traditional sampans, trailing their butter-fly-wing nets as they headed swiftly for the shelter of the bank. The sun was already low over the mountains to the west. The Japanese, if they came at all, would come at dusk.

After a few moments, she turned back to her writing, reliving the day when she and the Generalissimo had first arrived in Chungking.

"Just after leaving Yichang we came into the famous Gorges. The river has, through the centuries, eaten its way through the mountains, and sometimes the cliffs are over 1,000 feet high, some of the mountain tops being as high as 4,000 feet. How strong the river is; what power it possesses can be seen as the steamer drives up against it and one sees what mighty work the rushing water has done on the rocks. Sometimes they are just straight walls on either side, with the river rushing deep and menacing in between, making whirlpools and eddies and currents that are sometimes almost too strong for the steamer engines to work against. Some of the rapids roar in tumult and are very dangerous. These the steamer climbs, throbbing and panting – almost stopping. It is all very exciting, for one wonders if the steamer will manage to make the ascent, and it is a climb, one rapid having to be negotiated upwards some six or seven feet in fifty yards. Steamers often get wrecked because the savage river literally takes them and throws them against the jagged and cruel rocks, and woe betide any people who get thrown into the river. They are swept down in the great roaring whirlpools and are lost . . ."

She paused and once again looked out of the window. The sun had almost disappeared behind the mountains.

She wrote rapidly, anxious to finish her account before the light failed.

"Before the steamers were made to fight their way through this powerful water the junks had to be hauled by men, taking weeks to get through the Gorges alone. Twenty or 30 men hauling on great ropes made of plaited bamboo strips dragged the junks slowly and painfully, most times working like animals, with bare feet clinging to the rocks, and often wearing no clothes. Now that the steamers have come, the big junks are not used to go against the stream, but all the small ones have to be hauled – or tracked as they call it – against the strong current, the trackers having to struggle along a narrow path cut in the rocks of the Gorges. If they fall, they are lucky if they are not drowned.

"The Gorges are very beautiful in the sunlight and while in them one can fully appreciate the greatness and grandeur of nature."

She blotted the paper carefully, pleased with her work. It might not be great literature but she knew that the book would sell well in the West and later, after the war, when the Generalissimo had moved his capital back to Nanking, they would publish it in China as well. She was already famous as Madame Chiang Kai Shek; now she would be famous in her own right as Mayling Soong – the name she had before she married and of which she was still inordinately proud. After all, weren't the Soongs one of the most important families in China? Her sister had married Dr Sun Yat Sen, the founder and first President of modern China. Another sister had married H. H. Kung, the Finance Minister, and her brother T. V. – or "Teevy" – Soong was now the chief representative of the Nationalist regime in Washington.

She put the manuscript in the drawer, hiding the key in a small purse which she carried with her at all times. The Generalissimo could put tabs on Stillwell if he liked, but she preferred to keep her literary efforts to herself – at least until they were published.

As she stood up from the desk, her work completed for the day, she heard the familiar drone of the planes.

There were about a hundred of them altogether, many of them the newer Type 97 bombers which the factories in Japan were now churning out at a cracking rate. The rest were either Fiat BR–20s which the Japanese military machine had recently bought from Italy, or medium attack planes from the Navy. They came in waves every twenty minutes with about thirty planes in each wave, releasing a thousand bombs in a few seconds. Two years ago, when the raids on Chungking first began, the world had held its breath in shock. Long before Hitler's bombers filled the skies above London and Coventry, the Japanese had scored a macabre first by inaugurating massive bombing raids aimed at a civilian population. Now the outside world, with its own problems, had virtually forgotten Chungking.

As had been the case so often in recent months, the city was virtually undefended. Some scattered detonations came from the few anti-aircraft guns which were still functioning, but Madame Chiang noticed no visible impact on the waves of attackers. There seemed to be no defensive fighters, apart from one lone Chinese Hawk which emerged suddenly from the north-west to engage a Japanese monoplane. As she watched from the upstairs window, the Japanese plane seemed to stall in mid-air. The Hawk pulled round to return to the attack but, before it could do so, the monoplane went into a headlong dive, flames streaming out behind.

She stayed by the window as the Hawk circled twice over the city, dipping its wings in triumph, before once again disappearing behind the mountains.

Colonel Oliver Murphy, Deputy Head of SACO – the Sino-American Cooperative Organisation – looked out from his office in the SACO compound, situated four miles outside Chungking in an area ironically dubbed by the inhabitants, 'the Happy Valley', to observe that the fires which had been started by the air-raid were dying down. It was time to go. He stood up, a tall, spare man, with sandy hair which was beginning to thin at the crown. As he did so, he tightened his belt. There was not much danger of over-eating in this city; not now. Not with the current crowding and disruption.

11

Szechuan might be one of the richest of China's provinces, renowned in better days for the variety and interest of its cuisine, but there was precious little left of that.

Thinking about food, about the fine Szechuan cooking which he had known when he first was posted to China, Murphy realised that he was hungry. He looked at his watch. Should he grab a bite to eat first in the mess or go straight to the party which the British Ambassador was hosting that evening as a farewell gesture to General Stillwell? After a moment's reflection, Murphy decided that he could rely on the Brits to push the boat out tonight even if – like so many others – they had to go short later on.

Bending his head instinctively so as to avoid hitting it on the low ceiling, he left the squat and ugly SACO building and walked outside to the jeep. At once the noise of the drilling and blasting struck him. Goddammit, he thought, whatever view you might take of their leaders, the people themselves had guts. As soon as an air-raid was over, the Chinese were at work repairing the damage and carving out new caves and tunnels under the high cliffs of Chungking.

"Wu, are you ready? I'm leaving now."

The young Chinese – he was barely 18 years old – who had been dozing in the back of the vehicle jumped out and held the door open on the driver's side as Murphy got in.

"Come on in to town with me." Murphy pointed to the seat beside him. "I'll want you to guard the car."

"Okay, Sir. Very good!" Wu Canping jumped back in with alacrity. He had been with SACO almost twelve months now and had spent most of that time at Murphy's beck and call. The fact that he was only paid a pittance didn't bother him at all. What mattered was that he had a roof over his head, food in his belly and a job to do. He had arrived in Chungking two years earlier, fleeing into the mountains like so many others before the advancing Japanese. With the population of the city already swollen with refugees, he knew he was lucky to find work, particularly work with the Americans. His daily presence at SACO gave him both insights and access which he was not slow to appreciate.

Now that the all-clear had sounded, the road from the Happy Valley into the city was filling up rapidly. Murphy drove with one hand on the horn, weaving in and out of the potholes and bomb craters and avoiding, sometimes by a hair's breadth, the swarming crowd of coolies who struggled to manoeuvre handcarts piled high with debris up the steep narrow streets or else swarmed over the roadway with baskets slung from their shoulders on long thin poles.

From time to time he had to swerve round the corpses of those who had been killed in the recent air-raids. Nobody seemed to be making any effort to move the bodies. They had a strange view of death. He had seen old men just sit down in the street and die, almost as though they had decided that their time had come and they had better get it over with. On such occasions a small crowd would sometimes collect, but no one would try to intervene. Life here had its own rhythms and patterns, and dying was a part of it.

The British Embassy to the Chinese government, as currently represented by the Nationalist regime of Generalissimo Chiang Kai Shek, was a large building set in its own gardens on the banks of the Yangtze. It had miraculously remained unscathed throughout the years of bombing, a fact which provided the Ambassador, Sir Horace Seymour, with considerable satisfaction. When the rest of his diplomatic colleagues – the Americans, the French, the Swiss – heeded the Japanese warnings to transfer their operations to the 'neutral', supposedly bombardment-free, zone on the south side of the river, he had stayed put, upholding splendidly the tradition of Ambassadorial imperturbability.

It was, perhaps, Sir Horace's engaging idiosyncracy which had enabled him to establish, over the last couple of years, a surprising rapport with General Stillwell. Stillwell himself had scant respect for diplomats as a class and for British diplomats in particular. He disliked Britain's colonial posturings and regarded her China policy as being one of expediency, largely determined by a desire to regain her overseas possessions after the war; but he had come to exempt Sir Horace Seymour from the general criticism. In some ways they were birds of a feather. Horace Seymour was a lean, brown Scotsman with a keen, tough mind who appreciated Stillwell's waspish tongue and sometimes vicious wit. Stillwell in turn enjoyed the Ambassador's dry humour. Legend had it that the sobriquet 'Vinegar Joe' had in fact been coined at the British Ambassador's dinner table.

As he parked his own vehicle, Murphy noted that Stillwell, the guest of honour, had already arrived. The General's flag was flying on the open Studebaker in which he liked to travel when he was in town. He also deduced that Commodore Milton Miles, his immediate superior at SACO, was there ahead of him since the latter's jeep, inscribed with the legend 'US Navy Group', was parked next to Stillwell's car. A large area had been kept clear in front of the steps and four Chinese coolies were standing guard to make sure it stayed that way.

Telling Wu to remain in the vehicle until he came back, Murphy strode into the brightly-lit building. You had to hand it to the goddammed Limeys, he thought. They knew how to do things. White-gloved flunkies stood to attention on either side of the door; there was a silver tray on a lacquered table just inside the hall where guests were expected to place their calling cards. Murphy added his own to the growing pile. *Colonel Oliver E Murphy*, it read, *US Army Corps of Engineers, Deputy Head, SACO*.

"Why, hello! How are you-all getting along?"

The words were spoken with a distinct Oklahoma drawl, as distinctive in its way as the man behind them. Patrick J. Hurley, the new US Ambassador, was tall, well over six foot; he was craggily handsome with thick, silver-grey hair rumpled, possibly deliberately Murphy suspected, to give him a tousled, almost boyish look. Good looks, vanity, pluck – these were the qualities which people associated with President Hoover's former Secretary of War. And luck, too, thought Murphy. A great deal of luck. After all, Hurley had been born poor in rural Oklahoma; he had parlayed self-education, enthusiasm, a quick wit and a law degree into a full life and public recognition. It wasn't only Hoover who had liked the man enough to appoint him to high office.

Roosevelt too had been beguiled by his peculiar blend of charm, cunning and folksiness. After a stint as diplomatic envoy to New Zealand, FDR had sent him to visit Chiang and to report back. Now that initial contact was being followed by a full-scale Ambassadorial assignment.

"How are you-all getting on?" Hurley repeated his question and, as he did so, laid a long arm around Murphy's shoulders. "We've got to bring you SACO fellas into line, huh?"

Hurley spoke jocularly, but there was more than a hint of steel in his voice. America's new Ambassador had determined that now he had successfully engineered the recall of Stillwell he, and only he, was going to run the show in Chungking. First he was going to lick those Foreign Service bastards into shape so that the people in the Embassy did his bidding and nothing else. Next he was going to take on the freelance operations like SACO. If this meant lining up fairly and squarely behind the Generalissimo, well, so be it. He had long ago made up his mind where his own and America's interests lay.

Murphy tried unsuccessfully to disentangle himself from the US Ambassador's grasp. He was still enough of an upper-crust New Englander – fourth generation Boston Irish to be precise – to be wary of indiscriminate human contact.

"I guess we're getting on fine."

Hurley steered him to one side conspiratorially, while the party swirled on around them like a river by-passing an outcrop of rocks. "How can we help President Chiang Kai Shek deal with the Communists up there in Yenan?"

Murphy, taken aback by Hurley's abrupt question, considered how best to reply. With men like Hurley around, you were in danger of being taken for a Communist sympathiser or, worse still, a Commie pure and simple, if you showed the least hint of sympathy with the people up there in the remote North-West. Even if you believed that Mao's men would win out in the long run as sure as God made little green apples, while Chiang was nothing but a gangster building his own fortune on the backs of the people; even if you were convinced that America's long-term interests lay in making friends not enemies of China, it was no use saying so. There had been Foreign Service diplomats in Chungking who had sent back reports to the State Department along these, or similar, lines – men like John Service, for example – and they had rapidly found themselves transferred elsewhere with a black mark against their careers which no amount of subsequent scrubbing could erase.

Somehow he managed an honest, yet still diplomatic, answer. "Why don't you form your own judgement? Talk to Chou En Lai. He's here tonight, by the way."

Discreetly, he pointed out a tall slim Chinese, who stood by himself in one corner of the room, smoking a cigarette and surveying the noisy scene with a faint air of disdain. For two years now, Chou had represented the Communists in Chungking, acting as a kind of envoy to the Nationalist Government. He lived in a house in Jiefang Lu, high up on the cliffs above the Yangtze, observing and, as necessary, reporting. And he was in turn closely watched by Tai Li and his secret police. Ironically, Chou – who was notionally an ally – was far less free in his movements than many of the diplomats present on this occasion. When he wasn't in town, Chou lived with his wife, Deng Yingchao, and the rest of the Communist mission in a separate cantonment outside the city known as the Red Crag Village.

A brilliant, cultivated man and a long-time ally of Mao, Chou had joined the revolution early. He had spent four formative years in France where he had met up with other allies and had then returned to China to take up, along with Mao Tse Tung himself, the role of intellectual mentor of the nascent Communist movement. It was Chou, as much as anyone, who had insisted that though China and the Soviet Union might share a common heritage in the philosophy of Marx and Engels, the systems they developed would necessarily be very different. The life lived by the Communists in Yenan had already evolved its own distinctive pattern and organisation which was a very far cry indeed from the bleak, monolithic nature of Soviet Communism.

"Well I'll be darned!" Hurley had clearly not foreseen a

face-to-face contact with the Communists' representative so early in his mission. "Would you care to introduce me, Mr Murphy. I'd be much obliged."

They walked over together. Though Oliver Murphy had met Chou En Lai on several occasions, he was struck once again by the pallor of the man. The delicate, almost bleached, skin contrasted with the black bushy eyebrows which seemed to fuse above the bridge of his nose. Chou was wearing a grey suit with a high collar buttoned up under the neck. In the lapel was the small red star which the Communists had taken as their emblem.

"Comrade Chou," he saw no reason why he should not use the appellation which the Communists themselves preferred, "I have the honour to present the new American Ambassador in Chungking, His Excellency Mr Patrick Hurley. I don't believe you have yet made his acquaintance."

Chou shifted his gaze towards the tall Oklahoman, seeming to take every aspect of the man in at a glance.

"I'm delighted to meet you, Ambassador." He spoke in perfectly modulated English, the product of long nights of study over a camp table during the hard months of the Long March. Besides English and French, he had a passable knowledge of Russian as well, which he had on several occasions put to good use. Men like Michael Borodin, the Comintern's agent among the Chinese Communists, had quickly learned that Chou was quite familiar with the finer nuances of Soviet thinking and policy, his proficiency resulting in part at least from an ability to read the key documents in the vernacular.

Hurley seized Chou by the hand and pumped it vigorously up and down.

"So you're the man from Yenan. I hear you have quite a place up there."

"Perhaps you would care to visit us, Ambassador? We would be honoured."

Murphy held his breath, wondering what Hurley would reply. Surely the man was so committed to the Generalissimo that a visit to Yenan would, in fact, be impossible? But to his amazement he heard Hurley respond:

"I am at your disposal, Mr Chou. Name the time and the place. We are allies in a common cause which is to kick the goddam Japs out of China once and for all. If we can work together to that end no one will be better pleased than I."

Murphy left the two men talking. If Hurley was prepared to go to Yenan, he thought, maybe there was some hope yet.

On the other side of the room, he saw a pretty, auburn-haired girl talking to Milton Miles. The US Navy Group Commander looked flushed. As Murphy came up to join them, Miles said:

"Ah, Mr Murphy! I see you've been hob-nobbing, or should I say kow-towing, to our little friend, the emissary from Yenan. Commies are more dangerous than snakes!" He laughed hoarsely and turned to the girl. "Don't waste your tender loving care in that direction, my dear!"

"I'm a nurse, Commodore Miles," she replied simply. "I leave politics to the politicians."

Murphy looked at her with interest. It was the first time he had seen her. She must be one of the American Red Cross volunteers who had come to China at the beginning of the war with Japan only to retreat step by step with Chiang to this mountain fastness in Szechuan. She was wearing a gold W-shaped pin on the starched collar of her nurse's uniform.

"What's the pin for?" he ventured.

"Wellesley College."

Murphy laughed. "So you're from Wellesley too, are you? That's quite a coincidence. Have you met the college's most famous alumnus here in Chungking, or should I say 'alumna'?"

"Who's that?"

"Madame Chiang Kai Shek."

She shook her head, smiling. "I don't move in such exalted circles."

Milton Miles had witnessed the exchange with evident irritation. "When you've finished chatting up the ladies, Murphy, perhaps we can have a word about business."

"Will you excuse me?" Murphy bowed briefly to the nurse. "Perhaps we'll meet up later."

"I hope so, Colonel."

Experience had taught Miles that you were never safer from eavesdropping than when in a crowded room. The hubbub of conversation, the sound of laughter, the clinking of glasses, the rattle of ice – amazingly, the British Embassy in Chungking had managed to lay on a supply of ice – all this proved effective insulation against the curious. He steered Murphy to one side.

"Friday," he said. "We leave at dusk. It will take us two days to get down the river through the Gorges. We go in around midnight on Sunday."

"What abut the moon? It's full at the weekend." It was Murphy's job, as Deputy Commander, to make sure they didn't overlook the obvious.

"Nine times out of ten it's foggy downstream, just as it is up here," Miles responded irritably. "There may be a full moon, but who the hell's going to see it?"

"Friday it is then!" Murphy wasn't going to argue. The scheme might be harebrained and risky, with a high probability of failure, but at least it would give him a chance to do something which he had always wanted: to go down through the great Yangtze Gorges to where the river at last tumbled out into the vast central Chinese plains. He'd be able to take a look at the geology and topography of the area. Could it be done, or couldn't it? They'd built the giant Hoover Dam across the Colorado, a towering structure over 700 feet high. But of course the Colorado was a mere trickle of piss compared with the Yangtze. After the Nile and the Amazon, the Yangtze was the longest river in the world, and one of the largest too. When it flooded, the devastation was total. How many had died in those great floods of the thirties? One million, three million? Probably no one had even counted. The bloated bodies had been flushed downstream like so much debris and out into the South China Sea beyond Shanghai, where for several weeks they had clogged up the fishing nets and obstructed navigation. No, the Yangtze was not the Colorado. Those great Gorges soared not hundreds but thousands of feet into the air at either side of the chasm. He had read the literature, the tales the missionaries had told when they first penetrated up the river into the heart of Szechuan. He had seen the old photographs of the coolies, hundreds of them on the rocky precarious towpath dragging the boats upstream against the raging torrent. He had no illusions about the magnitude of the task or about the inherent dangers. But, once upon a time, before the present war broke out, he had been a professional engineer and he found that the idea of damming the Yangtze had an irresistible appeal. It was the ultimate challenge. Many of the world's great rivers had been brought under control but no one to his knowledge had ever produced a scheme for damming the Yangtze. Yet he was certain that the Yangtze Gorges, extending for hundreds of miles through Szechuan and Hubei Provinces, must offer the possibility of an extraordinary, ready-built natural reservoir of immense size.

But it was not just the technical challenge of the vast project which appealed to him. No one could live in China for more than a few weeks, for more than a few days, without being struck by the country's desperate need for development. Sometimes of an evening he would walk down to the docks in Chungking. The main dock was called Chaotianmen. It was here that ships of all sizes would put in after their 1,500-mile journey from the coast. It was here that any transhipment would be made of goods that were to carry on upriver, for Chungking was the last port of call for the larger vessels. If you wanted to get an idea of downtrodden humanity, of misery in its acutest form, of poverty and oppression, you just had to stand for an hour or two on the steep steps which connected Chaotianmen to the town. When a ship arrived to discharge its load of passengers or cargo, there was a chaotic rush as hundreds of coolies, many of them half-naked or emaciated, fought for whatever jobs were going. Sometimes you saw old men laden with goods struggling up the steep steps with such agony in their faces that you wondered whether they were going to make it. Once he saw an old boy fail when he had almost reached the top; his body, curled up like a football, rolled back down the stairs, to be trampled and kicked by the upward rush of feet.

Of course there were poor people in Boston too. Not all the Boston Irish lived on Beacon Hill. But the desolation, the destitution that you could find in China, was something else again. The missionaries came to win souls for Christ, but they learned the hard way. To win a man's soul, you must first offer him bread. Or rice.

Murphy was under no illusion that hydro-electric power was the answer to all China's problems. But as an engineer, he believed in the viability of engineering solutions. The energy that was spared from the daily grind could be used for other purposes. If one single factor had been responsible for America's industrial revolution, for the fact that America's factories now supplied the whole Allied war effort, it was the development of cheap and efficient energy sources. China might or might not have oil. That was something for the future, perhaps the distant future. But she was as well-endowed with hydro-electric power as any country in the world. On the Yangtze alone 960 cubic kilometres of water were discharged annually; that was 50 per cent greater than the discharge of the Mississippi. If that resource could be tapped, if it could be put to good use, if . . . Sometimes, in his most optimistic mood, Murphy foresaw a new, healthier alliance between the United States and China; an alliance which included – which indeed might be built around – Sino-US collaboration in the mightiest project of all time: the Yangtze River Dam! Generating unbelievable quantities of energy, while at the same time permitting the devastating annual flooding in the Yangtze valley to be controlled, the Three Gorges Dam would be a project mightier in scope than the great pyramids of Egypt and certainly more productive!

"We shall need guides," Miles said, interrupting Murphy's reverie. "Good men, who know the river, particularly the area above Yichang."

Murphy remembered Wu sitting outside in the jeep. "I have a young Chinese working for me who comes from

21

there. He told me his village is literally at the mouth of the Gorges. He and his family fled upstream when the Japanese occupied Yichang. He's a fisherman."

"Can you trust him?"

"If any man hates the Japanese, Wu does. He escaped but the rest of his family were not so lucky. Four men raped his sister, one after another, before bayonetting her. They wanted to rape his mother too. When she said she was too old, they rammed a stick up her . . ."

"The bastards!" Miles paused before coming to a decision. "We'll take him along. We'll give him a chance to get his own back. But tell him to keep his mouth shut. I don't want Tai Li sticking his nose in this one."

Before Murphy could reply, there was a sudden surge of laughter from the end of the room where the crowd which had gathered spontaneously around General Stillwell as soon as the party began, had grown considerably larger and more raucous.

"Give us the poem, General!" Murphy heard one of the guests call. Others picked up the refrain. "Let's have the poem, Joe!"

The laughter redoubled in intensity. The British Ambassador climbed up onto a chair, holding out his hands for silence.

"Ladies and gentlemen," Sir Horace Seymour began. "Tonight we say goodbye to one of America's most famous sons. We in Chungking are privileged to have had him with us for so long. Old Vinegar Joe . . ." As a roar of laughter went up the Ambassador added, "I hope you don't mind if I call you by your nickname, General?"

"Hell, no! Everyone else does." In spite of everything, Stillwell was clearly enjoying his last evening. If he had to leave China, at least it wouldn't be with his tail between his legs.

"He is one of those few men who are a legend in their lifetime, and we are glad to have known him. We say goodbye to him with real regret. China will not be the same without him."

As the Ambassador got down off the chair, Stillwell

climbed up in his place. For once he had discarded the
World War I battle dress complete with lace-up spats which
he wore on most occasions and was turned out in evening
dress. He was a fine orator and his remarks that night were
vintage stuff: coarse, earthy, often plain unprintable. The
soldiers among them had of course heard it before. But
there were diplomats of several nations present that evening,
smooth urbane men, whom Stillwell's down-to-earth allo-
cutions affected with the force of a powerful blow struck
directly between the eyes.

"The problem, my friends," he began, "is the Chinese
general staff. Through stupidity, fear and their defensive
attitude they lost a grand chance to slap the Japs back at
Toungee. So we lost Burma. And the basic reason was
Chiang Kai Shek's meddling. I told them so in plain words.
The army and division commanders had failed to obey, and
I had insufficient authority to force them to obey. Those
people are chizzlers and grafters. Chiang Kai Shek has been
boss so long, he's got so many yes-men, that he has the
idea he's infallible on any subject. It's patently impossible
for me to compete with the swarm of parasites and syco-
phants who surround him. So I'm going. I've been recalled.
That's the truth of it. Chiang Kai Shek says I refused to
obey orders. The real reason is that I know too much about
the conditions here. This whole place is a racket. The
Chinese Red Cross is a racket. Stealing and the sale of
medicines is rampant. The higher-ups in the army steal the
soldiers' food. The officers put sand in the rice they feed
the recruits. Do you know how many billions, yes billions,
of US dollars have come to China in the last few years and
how many billions more are in the pipeline? Well, let me
tell you one thing. That money came here all right. And do
you know where it is now? Back in Washington, or in
Switzerland, or anywhere else where Chiang and his bunch
of gangsters have been able to open a bank account..."

Standing next to the departing US General, the British
Ambassador was smiling nervously. It was all very well for
Stillwell. He was leaving. But some of them, most of them,

would have to stay on and work with the Nationalist regime whatever reservations they might have.

"The poem, General," he reminded him. "We want to hear your poem."

"Ah, yes." Stillwell's leathery face cracked into a grin as he pulled a piece of paper from his pocket. He looked down at the Ambassador and then at the guests who were standing with expressions of interest and anticipation on their faces.

"Go on! Read it out, General!" Murphy recognised the hoarse, excitable tones of Milton Miles. He wondered momentarily whether Miles wasn't, for reasons best known to himself, urging Stillwell to hammer yet another nail into his own coffin. Leaving Chungking was one thing; arriving in Washington and finding a decent job waiting for him was something else again. Murphy had no doubt that Miles – who like Hurley was no friend of Stillwell's – was already mentally composing his telegram to his cronies back home reporting on the evening's events.

Stillwell needed no more urging.

"There are five verses altogether, my friends, so you'll have to bear with me." He cleared his throat, looked around to make sure that he had their attention, then began to recite in firm ringing tones.

"I've waited long for vengeance
At last I've had my chance;
I've looked the Peanut in the eye
And kicked him in the pants."

A great guffaw of laughter echoed in the room as Stillwell came to the end of his first verse. He paused; he could see that his audience was with him now. Whatever nervousness and hesitation there might have been, had evaporated. Almost everyone present in the room that night knew that 'Peanut' was Stillwell's private nickname for Chiang Kai Shek, the sobriquet deriving – or so it was supposed – from the peculiar shape of the President's shaved head. Even Hurley was reluctantly smiling, and the British Ambassador, rubbing his hands together in amusement, had obviously

24

decided that he might as well be hung for a sheep as for a lamb.

So General Joseph W. Stillwell, Commander of the China-Burma-India theatre, but henceforth destined for redundancy if not obscurity, continued with his idiosyncratic vaudeville act on this, the eve of his final departure from China.

"The old harpoon was ready.
With aim and timing true
I sank it to the handle
And stung him through and through.

"The little bastard shivered
And lost the power of speech
His face turned green and quivered
And he struggled not to screech."

Again the laughter filled the room, even louder than before so that the glass of the chandeliers tinkled.

The line of cars swept through the town and out towards the high ground overlooking the river where the British Embassy was located. The sirens wailed on the lead car and lights flashed on the escorting vehicles. The Generalissimo looked straight ahead. He had no wish to observe the scenes of devastation on either side, or hear the lamentations of his people. He had come a long way since those early days when he had commanded the famous Whampoa military academy in Canton. He had waded through blood, smashing the warlords first, then turning savagely on his Communist allies, to drive them north on the Long March to Yenan. He should never have let them escape!

As the car swung into the Embassy grounds, he touched his moustache, smoothing the hairs with that nervous mannerism which those close to him had come to recognise as a warning signal. He placed his peaked cap back on his shaved head, fingering the six gold stripes and heavy, solid gold badge which denoted the rank of Generalissimo, or General of all the Generals. Let Stillwell try to equal that!

The car drew right up in front of the house where a space had been left clear. The Chinese guards, trembling with fear at the sight of the Generalissimo, held the door open for him. As Chiang Kai Shek walked into the entrance hall, he heard the sound of laughter and amusement from within, and then distinctly, unmistakeably, General Stillwell's voice.

By now Old Vinegar Joe had his audience in stitches. Standing there on the chair, glass of beer in one hand and the piece of paper with his famous poem in the other, the General was nearing the climax of his performance. He managed to give the last few lines an air of powerful melodrama.

"For all my weary battles
For all my hours of woe
At last I've had my innings
And laid the Peanut low.

"I know I've still to suffer
And run a weary race
But, oh, the blessed pleasure!
I've wrecked the Peanut's face!"

Suddenly Stillwell realised that no one was laughing any more. The British Ambassador had turned the colour of his starched shirt-front and several of the other guests were looking distinctly queasy.

Stillwell turned slowly round.

There were many present that night who had heard of, or even been witness to, Chiang Kai Shek's ungovernable rages. The Generalissimo's temper was legendary. Any man who unwisely crossed him when he had been provoked into anger was quite literally risking his life. What surprised the British Ambassador's guests on that famous occasion when *le tout* Chungking paid farewell to Vinegar Joe Stillwell was not that the Generalissimo lost his cool and went on the rampage, but that he did not. A deep and ominous calm came over Chiang as Stillwell stuffed the poem back in his pocket and climbed down off the chair.

"What a pity, General", said Chiang at last, "that your literary triumphs are not equalled by your victories on the battlefield."

Stillwell blanched beneath his battle tan, almost as though his very manhood had been called into question.

"A fish stinks from the head, Generalissimo," he hissed. Then, without another word, he nodded to the British Ambassador, bowed to Lady Seymour, and walked stiffly from the room.

As the American's footsteps died away, Chiang gave vent to a short tense laugh.

"I am so glad the air raids do not deter the diplomatic world from its traditional duties. Perhaps Her Ladyship would care to dance?"

He turned with a slight bow to the British Ambassador's wife, a tall handsome woman who had been standing uneasily at her husband's side for the last few minutes. With visible relief, Sir Horace gave a signal to the band leader. As the band struck up a tune, the Generalissimo took off his braided cap and handed it to an aide, revealing his yellow skull-like head.

Oliver Murphy sought out the American nurse with whom he had been talking earlier.

"I'm not much good at dancing," she protested.

"You don't need to be good. Just listen to the music."

It was the first time she had heard the Glen Miller sound; indeed, it was the first time the US band leader's score sheets had been played in China, since the music had only recently been made available by special arrangement to Forces in the CBI theatre. But somehow Seymour had managed to get hold of them for the occasion and have a local band rehearse the haunting tunes.

"Mood music, they call it," said Murphy.

The tall American was quick and light on his feet. He held her firmly by the waist and steered her through the

27

throng of couples on the crowded floor. She found the tension of the past few minutes evaporating.

"I guess I am getting in the mood," she smiled. "What's your first name, Colonel?"

"Oliver. Oliver Edward Murphy. What's yours?"

"Mary. Just plain Mary." She threw back her head and laughed, revealing the pearly whiteness of her throat. "You see, I'm just a simple old-fashioned girl!"

Wu Canping, standing guard as instructed beside the SACO jeep, had had a ring-side view of the evening's comings and goings. He had witnessed Chiang's arrival. He had heard the merriment from within as Stillwell recited his poem, and the silence which had followed the General-issimo's entry. He had observed Stillwell's rapid departure. Now he could hear the band playing and, through the open windows of the salon, could catch glimpses of figures moving on the dance floor.

Suddenly, a movement in the shadows at the side of the house caught his eye. Wu Canping recognised the tall spare figure of the Chinese Communist Party's chief diplomat in Chungking as he walked to the gate. He took a long careful look around the garden, letting his eyes range over the other vehicles which were parked there. Though the city itself, outside the walls of the Embassy, was swollen to bursting with refugees, Sir Horace Seymour's well-manicured lawns were deserted that night. Quickly and silently, he followed Chou up the drive.

Twenty minutes later a battered black Volga sedan, with a red star emblazoned on the bonnet, drew up in front of the British Embassy gates and Chou En Lai disappeared into the night. Wu Canping watched the tail-lights of the retreating car, then walked back to his own vehicle to wait for Murphy. Already guests were beginning to emerge from the residence as the party broke up for the evening. Down below in the crowded city, some of the fires started by the Japanese air-raid a few hours earlier were still burning fitfully as though no one could be bothered to put them out.

2

As he sat back in the leather seat of the Studebaker, looking at the green hills of China for the last time, Stillwell reflected on the events of the last few days. He had learned less than a week earlier that he was to leave China. In fact, it was only on Wednesday that he had heard officially that he had been relieved of command and was to emplane immediately for America. Thursday, there had been that farewell party at the British Embassy and the painful, ludicrous encounter with Chiang. Then, on the day before he was due to leave, amazingly, the Generalissimo had invited him to tea and offered him the Special Grand Cordon of the Blue Sky and White Sun, the highest Chinese decoration for which a foreigner could qualify. He had told the 'Gimo' in no uncertain terms what he could do with it!

Altogether, it had been an horrendous 45 minutes. Finally the two of them had saluted each other in a kind of controlled, tight-lipped fury. As he left, Stillwell had given the war slogan: *Tsui hou sheng li* – the traditional call for final victory – wondering what on earth the Generalissimo was playing at. What did the invitation to tea mean? What did the offer of the honour mean? It was almost as though Chiang Kai Shek was preparing some kind of alibi for himself, seeking to demonstrate that, in spite of all the insults they had exchanged over the years, he and Stillwell had parted on the best of terms after all.

A few minutes later, the car arrived at the airstrip. Glancing up at the sky as he got out, Stillwell saw that it was cold, cloudy and dark. The tops of the encircling mountains were lost in mist. Sometimes the fog was so thick that planes had to wait for days before taking off. Today they were lucky. As far as the weather was concerned, they were a notch or two under the limit.

He saw to his surprise that a large mud-splattered limousine flying the stars and stripes was drawn up next to his plane and that Ambassador Hurley was standing beside it.

Seeing Hurley there, Stillwell couldn't suppress a last caustic comment. After all, the Oklahoman had done as much as anyone to undercut him in Washington and turn the President against him.

"I guess I've been Hurleyed out of China!"

When Hurley, for once, had nothing to say in reply, Stillwell turned his back and strode over to his plane. A small squad of Chinese aviators, led by young Charlie Soong, Madame Chiang's nephew, was drawn up in front of the fuselage. Stillwell's mood lightened perceptibly. He had always had more time for Charlie Soong than the rest of the 'Chiang gang'. Soong had flair, style and courage of a high order. Stillwell knew that the list of his certified 'kills' – over forty Japanese planes accounted for in the skies above Chungking – wasn't one of Chiang's fake statistics, like the victories he reported in the Kuomintang-controlled press with such nauseating frequency. Just the other day, in a spectacular piece of flying, Soong had downed a Japanese bomber right above the city of Chungking itself.

"Goodbye Charlie. Keep your finger on the button and aim straight!"

The engines on the plane were already revving as Stillwell climbed aboard. He looked out at the dark grey skies.

"What are we waiting for?" The doors slammed.

The plane trundled through the sticky ruts to the end of the runway, where it halted. The field was bare; the clouds seemed momentarily to have cleared over the mountains. A lone figure in American uniform at the end of the runway waved the all-clear.

As Charlie Soong was walking back to the tin shack on the perimeter of the airfield which served as an officers' mess, the siren sounded. For Soong, as for most of the inhabitants of Chungking, it was a familiar noise. At the beginning of the war, the Japanese air-raids had taken them by surprise. Chungking had no radar network to give early warning of an impending raid. But as the months passed and the attacks continued, Chinese spies in Hankow, the main bombing base, learned how to splice into the city telephone system to report the news to Chinese radio transmitters hidden in the city almost as soon as the enemy planes had taken off – and certainly long before they were at cruising altitude. The alarm was signalled by the erection of immense paper lanterns on huge gallows-like poles on the highest hills of the city, and around its mountainous rim. One red lantern, put up when the first siren sounded, meant that the enemy planes were approaching but still an hour away. Two red lanterns meant the enemy was coming close. When both suddenly dropped, it meant 'Get inside the dugouts'. A long green paper stocking was the all-clear signal.

At night the lanterns were lighted. Chungking City Fathers wasted no time on brown-outs, dim-outs, or black-outs; when the Japanese were within fifty miles, the central switch on the power house was thrown and the city went dead – lights, radios, telephones, machinery. If a gendarme saw a lighted window, or a glowing flashlight during a raid, he simply shot at it.

As soon as Charlie Soong heard the air-raid warning, he quickened his stride and changed direction to head for the Operations Room next to the control tower.

The air of the small, untidy Ops. Room at Chungking air base was thick with the smoke of cheap cigarettes made out of the local Szechuan tobacco. As he entered, Charlie Soong was greeted with laconic humour by the handful of pilots who had heard the alarm and were already there ahead of him.

"Hi, Charlie! Another great and glorious day for us, no doubt!"

The speaker was Roberto Lopez, a tall handsome Argentinian, who – after Soong himself – was probably the ablest pilot of the bunch. He flew the somewhat ungainly Chinese Hawk as though it had the aerodynamic features of the Hurricane or Spitfire, those remarkable British planes which had recently won such signal victories in the Battle of Britain. But the total of Roberto's 'kills' came nowhere near that of Soong.

31

The truth of the matter was that, where Charlie Soong could ignore standing orders and engage the enemy in combat as he had done just the other day, Lopez and the rest of them had to stick to the rules. Because of his many links with Chiang, Soong was virtually untouchable: China's golden boy. But the others – men like Lopez and the brilliant Frenchman Guillaume Verbier, who had escaped from the Japanese in Indo-China to join Chiang's forces in Chungking – knew that they could take no such liberties. Though they might be the most famous international volunteer force to take the field since the Spanish Civil War, though they were individualists to a man, there was a limit to their ability to defy the rules of engagement which the Generalissimo had prescribed. So when the squadron scrambled it did so not to attack the enemy in the skies, but simply to avoid being blown to pieces on the ground.

Charlie Soong surveyed his colleagues with evident affection. He had got to know them well over the last few months, had come to appreciate their idiosyncrasies, their personal vanities, their superlative professional skills. Lopez had been a friend since the days when they had been undergraduates together at Harvard. In fact, they had shared a large house on the banks of the Charles River where they had been renowned for the generosity of their hospitality and for the constant stream of rich and beautiful girls who visited them. Like Soong, Lopez was rich, his family owning one of the largest ranches in Argentina. Before leaving for China, he had captained Buenos Aires's most famous polo team and could ride a horse as well as he could fly a plane.

Verbier, a short thick-set man with ginger hair worn *en brosse*, was a complete contrast to Lopez. He was a civilian pilot by trade, the scion of a bourgeois family which a generation earlier had left France to find fortune, if not fame, in Hanoi.

"Hello, Roberto! *Salut*, Guillaume! It seems the Japanese are coming in early for once. Don't you think that today we should give them a surprise?"

"What kind of a surprise?" Roberto Lopez asked, a broad smile breaking out over his bronzed features.

32

"This kind." Soong made a sudden chopping movement with his right hand, like a man punching a rabbit in the neck.

They timed their attack nicely, hitting the first wave of Japanese bombers from below as they flew over the Qutang Gorge, the first and most spectacular of the three great Yangtze Gorges. It was a superbly executed piece of flying. Charlie Soong led his squadron down-river, skimming a few feet above the surface of the water, until the Hawks snaked between the 1,000-foot-high cliffs at the entrance to the Gorge. Invisible, unless you happened to be flying directly above them, Soong's unit in effect ambushed the Japanese from behind and below. The six Hawks rose swiftly and suddenly from the depths of the Gorge where they had been lurking to subject the marauding bombers to quick bursts of cannon fire. They downed three planes, sending them cartwheeling into the mountains, while a fourth veered away with smoke streaming from the starboard wing. Soong doubted whether it would make Hankow.

The Hawks dipped down again into the shelter of the Gorges almost as quickly as they had emerged. Soong recognised that there was no point in risking a second pass since by now the bombers' gunners, fore and aft, would be fully alerted. So he gave the signal to break and scatter, knowing that within 20 minutes – or at most half an hour – his team would find their own way back to the airstrip.

He himself flew back upstream along the river the way they had come, before banking sharply to the right and climbing to 5,000 feet, when he was still ten miles from the city. Well, he thought, today they had been lucky. They had shot down four enemy planes without losing one themselves. He knew that if the skirmish had had a different outcome – if, for example, four Chinese Hawks rather than six were now returning to base – he would have had a lot of explaining to do as to why he and his squadron had disobeyed the Generalissimo's most explicit orders to keep their powder dry.

But Charlie Soong was a risk-taker and this time the risk

had paid off. His wheels bounced down on the rutted surface of the airstrip and he rolled to a halt, grinning broadly. He had added one more kill to his score that day.

General Tai Li, sitting stiffly upright at his desk in the underground bunker at SACO headquarters in the Happy Valley, was waiting impatiently for the message that would tell him that Stillwell's plane was lost somewhere over the Hump. For the last two hours he had been expecting confirmation that the American general had failed to arrive in India on his way back to the States, but so far there had been no word of any kind.

Even when he was seated as he was now, you could tell that Tai Li was a tall man. He was both thin and handsome, with a ramrod posture that he must have copied from the Chinese army's Prussian instructors. He took grotesquely long, quick strides when he walked, whether on or off duty. Those who knew him well could spot whether he was angry or in a good humour by the pace of his steps. By turns gregarious, efficient, cruel and cunning, he had set out to give Chiang's China a modern, up-to-date espionage machine, something which the country had never known before, and to a large extent he had succeeded. Tai Li's Secret Service lacked the integrity of the Communists' much smaller organisation but as far as internal security was concerned, it was more ruthless than any of its predecessors. Tai Li had learned much from interrogation techniques used in Nazi Germany and had added his own peculiarly Chinese embellishments. Some of his prisoners were known to have collapsed and died on the spot, rather than face interrogation. Few who were interrogated lived to tell the tale. Those that did survive carried the scars of their experience – both mental and physical – with them for the rest of their lives.

The minutes passed and still Tai Li sat there motionless. One hand rested on the top of the desk, the other on the hilt of the sword. It was a very special sword. It had once belonged to a Japanese samurai but had been acquired by Tai Li's grandfather on a visit to Kyoto 60 years earlier, and had been kept in the family ever since. It had a thick blade, about four feet in length, which swelled at the end rather like a meat cleaver. Precisely how many people it had beheaded in its day was not recorded. Tai Li wore it at all times, even when in the presence of the Generalissimo himself, a privilege which Chiang accorded no one else.

Suddenly Tai Li leapt to his feet and strode across the room. He flung the door open to confront a trembling Chinese orderly who held in his hand a message which clearly he was afraid to deliver.

Tai Li grabbed the paper and read it. "STILLWELL AND PARTY ARRIVED DELHI THIS AFTER-NOON". He looked at the signature and recognised the code name of one of his own agents in India. There was no doubt that the news was authentic. With an oath he crumpled the paper in his hand and flung it to the floor. The bomb which his agents had planted should have detonated at 20,000 feet. His Secret Service goons had bungled matters.

Once, ten years earlier, Tai Li had invented a new and devastatingly efficient way of killing Chiang's enemies. He had lined up some locomotives on a siding, got the fireboxes red-hot, opened their doors, tied down their whistles to shut out the screams, and one after another had thrown his living victims into the fiery furnaces. In this manner, thousands of labour leaders and students and intellectuals had been killed in a few days. As a result of this episode, he had earned the nickname of The Butcher.

Today, his vengeance was more immediate. He caught the messenger roughly by the shoulder and hurled him to the ground, screaming as he did so at the top of his voice the traditional command: "Prepare for beheading!"

The man whimpered and sank to his knees.

"Head up!" Tai Li shouted, still beside himself with rage. How could you behead a man properly if his chin was sunk on his chest? Then he shouted again: "Hands behind the back!"

The man knew there was no escaping his fate; knew that his soul must join the souls of his ancestors and that nothing now could be done to prevent it. Six thousand years of bitter-sweet Chinese history were enshrined in that single cameo: the man kneeling obediently, with the executioner standing over him poised to strike.

Tai Li pulled the sword from his belt with a single short two-handed motion. He measured the distance, whirled the blade once round his head, and struck with unerring force at exactly the point where the neck emerged from the spine.

Wu Canping pedalled fast, the hard burning anger inside him acting as a goad. It was strenuous work, since Chungking was a city of steep hills and valleys, hardly made for the bicycle. And the streets, for once, were crowded in the late afternoon. The bombers had already come and gone that day.

Wu barely noticed the other traffic on the road. He ignored the beggars and the pedlars, swerving grim-faced to avoid their outstretched or clutching hands. Though in his short life he had already seen much violence, not least the sacking of his own village, the scene which he had witnessed at SACO headquarters that afternoon had left him in a state of shock. Chen and he had grown up together in that quiet village at the eastern entrance to the Gorges; they had fled together to Chungking, huddled on a crowded junk which, with the help of a following wind – the wind always blew from the east in the Gorges – had inched its way upstream against the force of the current, at a speed that at times barely exceeded one knot an hour. Together they had found employment.

However hard he tried, he could not get those horrendous images out of his mind: Chen's head kicked like a football into the SACO courtyard, still spraying blood; his body unceremoniously dumped outside the gates of the compound.

Even Commodore Miles, who generally turned a blind eye and a deaf ear to Tai Li's excesses, had protested; but it had been to no avail. In this mood, Tai Li was unstoppable. Those screams, those dreadful screams, would cease when merciful death intervened; not before.

Notwithstanding the sudden swelling of its population as

a result of the influx of refugees, Chungking retained its mediaeval structure and pattern. The walls of the old city encircled the peninsula from its tip at the river junction where the Chaotianmen dock was located, to the crest of the spiny ridge where the city opened out into the back land. The wall had been built about five centuries earlier and in spite of the bombing it still stood largely intact, with its nine great gates channelling traffic in and out of the city. Eight of the nine gates opened out on the cliffs overlooking the river, but the ninth gave entrance by land. This was the Tung Yuan Men, the Gate Connecting with Distant Places. In the old days, Wu had learned, the imperial road left Chungking through the Tung Yuan Men and followed the valleys to Chengdu. After that, it climbed up over the northern mountains to Sian, the terminus of the Old Silk Road, and then wound its way on to Peking. Now, motor traffic had reached Chungking and they had constructed a modern road to western China which pierced the walls 100 yards from Tung Yuan Men. But the old archway was still open – a shadowy, sombre place where pedlars sold shoelaces and tangerines and beggars clustered on the worn stones.

Nearing the wall, Wu descended from his bicycle and pushed it, not towards the new gate where he could see that KMT guards were checking passers-by, but towards the disused entrance. It was not that he had anything specially to fear from the Kuomintang. His papers were in order. Indeed, since it was clear that he worked at SACO, where Tai Li held sway, it was not likely that any KMT patrol would make serious trouble for him. Still, they might ask questions. Where was he going? What was he doing? No doubt he could have given a perfectly acceptable answer. He could have said that he was off to help friends clear up after the bombing, or visiting a sick relative. But it was better to avoid such questions if possible.

Once inside the gate, he hid his bicycle among the rubble of a bombed-out house and proceeded the rest of the way on foot. His instructions were to wait on the corner of Xinhua Lu and Minzu Lu, two streets which intersected in the heart of the city about half a mile from the junction of the Yangtze and the Jialing. He had no idea who was going to meet him, nor had he been instructed to identify himself in any particular manner.

Wu Canping arrived at his appointed destination in good time. Chen's bicycle, which he had immediately appropriated before the Blue Shirts could lay their filthy hands on it, made all the difference to the journey into town from SACO headquarters at Zhazhidong. Going back, of course, would be a different story since it was uphill all the way and there were stretches where the road was so steep that you had to get off and push.

He had been standing on the corner of the street for about five minutes, pretending to be absorbed in contemplation of the wreck of the Japanese monoplane which had crashed there a few days earlier, when he felt a tap on his shoulder. A young man about Wu's own age quickly beckoned him to follow. Fifteen minutes later, after turning and twisting through a maze of narrow hilly streets, the two young men came to a small quay, about half a mile upstream from Chaotianmen, where a dozen sampans were moored. As they stepped aboard one of them, the guide produced a blindfold from his pocket, roughly bound Wu's eyes and pushed him into the small covered cabin which reeked of fish.

As he crouched inside the cabin, listening to the swish of the water against the side, Wu found that he was trembling violently. Partly, this was the result of sheer physical nervousness. In the months he had been in Chungking, working up in the Happy Valley, he had seen sights which made his stomach turn. Beatings and torture were the norm rather than the exception at SACO; those who survived – and some did survive – were thrown into the dank and venomous prisons where they languished in filthy pitch-dark cells. Wu did not underestimate the difficulties and the dangers of the path which lay ahead.

More important still to Wu's mood was the sense that he was approaching a climacteric in his life. In Sandouping, conditions were better than they were in many other Chinese villages. The fish in the Yangtze were plentiful and the vegetables grew well in the small terraced fields above the river. But even here, in relatively prosperous Hubei Province, they had known appalling famines, drought and pestilence, which the public authorities – such as they were – did nothing to alleviate.

When he had first come to Chungking, he had believed that things might be better. Here at least, as in most of Szechuan, the Generalissimo had won his battle with the warlords, or at least come to terms with them. But when he, with his young eyes, saw the grinding poverty, the searing corruption, the hopelessness which existed even here, the very seat of government, he had gradually come to the realisation that the system itself was at fault.

Chou's words that evening outside the Embassy, delivered as a father might speak to his son, had affected him deeply. The seed had fallen on fertile ground.

By shifting his position on the floorboards, Wu Canping was at last able to make himself moderately comfortable. The trembling had gone. He smiled beneath the blindfold.

When, an hour later, the bandage was removed and he was led into the small back room of a typical Szechuan village house, Wu recognised Chou En Lai immediately. He was sitting at a table with three other men, eating a simple peasant dinner. There was a bowl of rice in the middle of the table and next to it smaller bowls of fish and vegetables. Without interrupting his conversation, Chou waved with his chopsticks to a place at the table which was still empty. As he sat down, Wu realised that he was ravenously hungry.

"Eat," Chou En Lai ordered. "Revolutions are not made on empty stomachs."

Wu helped himself to the food. Szechuan cooking was different from that of his own province of Hubei. The peppers were hotter and the sauces were sharper and he felt as though his mouth was on fire when he crunched by accident a whole peppercorn. But he gulped down a mouthful of weak green tea and shovelled in some more rice and waited his turn, knowing that these were busy men, men who one day would rule China, and that he – the son of a

39

humble Yangtze fisherman – was honoured to be at the same table.

"Forgive me, Wu Canping," Chou turned to him at last, using the young man's full name in a formal but still friendly way. "We have been discussing the visit which the new American Ambassador, General Hurley, is to make to Yenan."

"In Zhazhidong", Wu said, referring to the site of SACO headquarters, "they call Mr Hurley *Ti Erh Ta Feng*, the Second Big Wind!"

Chou En Lai threw his head back and roared with laughter. "Oh, that's good!" he exclaimed. "I must remember that!"

He pushed the bowl of rice across the table. "Here, have some more. And have some fish."

So Wu Canping took some more fish, and rice and vegetables, and while he ate he told them all that he knew about life in SACO.

"Stay with us and you will reach the stars." Chou En Lai seemed delighted by what he had heard.

"I shall help in any way I can."

"We will work out a safe system for our communications," one of the other men said. "The Kuomintang must never suspect you are working for us and with us; the Americans must never suspect. Our interest in your safety is as great as your own."

"The truth of the matter", Chou added, "is that Tai Li watches every move. In theory, I'm a diplomat, head of the Communist Mission to Chungking at a time when the Communists and Nationalists are allies in name at least. But in practice I'm almost a prisoner in this city. It was probably as difficult for me to get here tonight as it was for you."

As Chou En Lai stood up to go, he laid a hand on Wu's shoulder. "We will meet again, Wu Canping. I must go now. Stay with these gentlemen for a while. They have some other questions to ask."

After Chou En Lai had left, Wu felt that some of the sparkle had gone out of the evening. The others could see that he was star-struck. "You're lucky to have met him like this," they told him. "Not many people have. He is a hero, but he is a human being as well. Do you know the story of Ye Yang Mei?"

"No, I don't."

"Ye Yang Mei is the daughter of General Ye Ting." This time Wu Canping nodded. Even an innocent village boy had heard of General Ye Ting, the legendary leader of the Red Army.

"Chou En Lai was flying from Chungking to Yenan. The plane ran into foul weather over the Qinling mountain range and began collecting ice on its wings, which added considerably to the payload. The plane was losing altitude fast, so the pilot ordered the baggage to be jettisoned and told the dozen or so passengers aboard to get their parachutes ready and wait for his signal to jump. Chou En Lai got up from his seat and put his own parachute on and helped others into theirs. Then he heard a young girl crying. It was Ye Yang Mei, who was eleven years old then. She was crying because there was no parachute under her seat. So Chou unfastened his own parachute and fitted it onto the child. He would have jumped without a parachute if he had had to, rather than let that young girl go without one."

"I would have jumped myself any day without a parachute for that man!" Wu meant it. He was conscious, as he spoke, that he had crossed a bridge that evening and that the world would never look the same again.

They talked for another hour. When they had finished, the man with the sampan blindfolded Wu a second time, and took him back to the city.

3

There were twenty Americans altogether, ten on each junk, each member of the assault forces hand-picked by either Miles or Murphy. For most of them, it was the first time they had been down-river. So for that reason if for no other the men were in high spirits. Besides, in recent months conditions in Chungking had grown so bad that almost any alternative seemed attractive. The daily bombings, the rampant disease and famine, the ubiquitous presence of rats – in the garbage, in the sewers, in the caves and cellars, or (as was so often the case) in broad daylight in the streets – all these had taken their toll. The SACO people fared better than most, having their own privileged sources of supply. Even so, the goods which were flown in over the Hump were for the most part confined to arms and munitions. If there were no picnic hampers among the cargo reaching the beleaguered city, it was – as the now departed General Stillwell used to remind them so pithily – because this wasn't meant to be a goddam picnic anyway.

They left before dawn. If there were Chinese spies in Hankow and Yichang, there were certainly Japanese spies in Chungking. Quite what conclusions the Japanese several hundred miles downstream might draw from the news that a score of Americans had boarded a couple of leaky Chinese junks at Chungking, Miles didn't know, but he wasn't taking any chances.

The junks sailed under cover of darkness with only the Chinese pilots and a load of innocent-looking cargo on board. The rendezvous with the Americans would take place at a point five miles downstream.

For Colonel Oliver Murphy, as for the others, the journey down the Yangtze was a novel experience. While his men kept out of sight, Murphy stood beside the pilot wearing a wide coolie hat on his head as a makeshift disguise, and admired the skill with which the man negotiated the hazards of the river.

He was a proud old boy, very much a local product, kitted out in a long white costume, immense moustache and a little hat to complete the ensemble. Murphy was astonished to see that he never spoke; never uttered his commands out loud; he just stood there watching the water, and moving his index finger from time to time as an indication to the helmsman.

Once or twice in the course of that first morning Wu Canping arrived on deck to offer them tea, or, around lunchtime, some rice and fish. Murphy could see that the young Chinese lad was in a state of considerable excitement. The previous evening he had participated in the final briefings, had inspected the equipment, had learnt – for the first time – the crucial role he was to play.

"Much water, Colonel Murphy, Sir," Wu had commented. "That is good, very good. When there is twelve foot of water at Chungking, we go easy over the rapids. When there is nine foot or less, big problem."

"That's good news then," Murphy said. You didn't live in Chungking long without realising that the water level in the Yangtze was on the whole far more important to the daily life of the city than, say, the colour of the sky or whether there was snow on the mountains. Boats could wait all summer at Yichang for the river to rise enough to give them passage up through the Gorges and the same was true if you were travelling in the other direction. But there were "false" rises as well as "true" rises and many a time ships had been left stranded high and dry as a sudden freshet, caused perhaps by the melting of the snow on the highlands of Tibet, came and as quickly went.

But now it was November and the river's flow, at least over the next few months, was relatively predictable. If a pilot could avoid the ultimate humiliation of running aground and having the river drop away 30 or 40 feet within a space of hours, the remaining difficulties were more manageable. It was a matter of knowing how to handle the rapids, how to avoid the whirlpools and the vortices, how to position one's vessel at the top of a channel and somehow back into the slipway to be bounced down-river like a cork floating on the waves.

From time to time Murphy walked to the back of the junk to check that the sampans were still being towed safely in line behind. If he ever got out of here alive, he thought, as he looked at the two craft swaying and bouncing in their wake, he would have a tale to tell which would surely go down in the annals of naval history.

For the first few hours after they left Chungking, the river flowed broad and brown, stretching almost a mile from side to side. Beyond the banks Murphy could see the green fields of Szechuan, and the lines of peasants bent double in the paddy. The sun caught them as they moved about their tasks, hoeing and weeding, plucking and carting. The cultivated land extended from the water's edge up the slopes of the mountains which, here at least, were still relatively gentle. Most of the fields ended a couple of hundred feet above the water level where the effort of pushing further upward usually outweighed the return. But occasionally, some more enterprising or possibly more desperate soul had extended the cultivated area still further, terracing what were virtually vertical surfaces in order to coax out of the unpromising rock some small squares or rectangles of till-able land.

He turned to Wu who had appeared silently at his elbow like a genie, bearing a pot of tea.

"How long before we enter the Gorges?" Murphy found it hard to imagine how this mighty river, now so wide, could be compressed into a channel a few hundred feet across.

"Tomorrow, Sir," Wu replied. "We shall tie up for the night at Wanxian; then, at first light, we will enter the first of the Gorges, Qutang Gorge."

It was a long day. The two junks made steady progress and by nightfall had covered a third of the distance. They tied up on the left bank of the river three miles from Wanxian. The Americans, who had been cooped up all day below decks, were glad of the opportunity to come up for air and stretch their legs. A gangplank was rigged up between the two boats and there was a good deal of to-ing and fro-ing as the men fraternised after a day of enforced inactivity. Morale, Murphy noted, was still good. He didn't know whether others believed, as he did, that Miles's scheme was harebrained at best and, most likely, downright perilous; if they did, they weren't showing it.

Commodore Miles himself was clearly in an ebullient mood. He beckoned Murphy over and the two men sat together in the stern of Miles's junk. Somehow he had managed to bring a crate of American beer along and he offered Murphy a frothing tankard.

"How are the fish, Colonel?"

"Mammals, actually," Murphy laughed in spite of himself. "The Yangtze river dolphin has tits just like any other dolphin."

"My mistake." Miles jerked a thumb in the direction of the sampans which, like the junks, had been tied up to the bank. "Whatever they are, are you sure they're all right?"

"As sure as I can be. For them, it's just another down-river journey."

Each sampan was fitted with special bulkheads to permit river water to enter the middle section, where the dolphin cages were situated, without at the same time flooding fore and aft. It had been a neat job. SACO's carpenters, assisted by the local work-force, had given full satisfaction.

Sitting there with the glass of beer in his hand and the sound of the river in his ears, Murphy reflected that the months he had spent helping to train the dolphins had been among the most rewarding of his time in China. They had rigged up an aquarium in the SACO compound. Most afternoons, he and his small team of animal experts would spend a few hours there teaching the animals tricks, including, of course, the ultimate trick, the trick to end all tricks . . .

"Sometimes I feel I'm betraying them," he found himself saying. Commodore Miles looked at him as though he was stark, staring mad. "They're expendable" he scoffed. "Just like any other bloody fish."

They entered the first of the Yangtze Gorges soon after sunrise the following day. Nothing Murphy had heard, nothing he had read, had prepared him for the spectacular nature of the sight which confronted them. The river narrowed to a rushing torrent, barely 150 yards across. The rock cliffs at either side of the cavern rose vertically for hundreds, thousands of feet. Looking up, Murphy could see the blue sky far above and the rays of the morning sun striking the tops of the mountains. The river twisted and turned and beyond each bend another chasm reared its head, more austere and cavernous than the last.

Steering a way through the Gorges with the river in flood was an art as much as it was a science. Once, as the junk pitched forward into one particularly turbulent stretch of water, Murphy observed that the pilot pulled up the long sleeve of his tunic and moved his whole arm, but that was the nearest he got to showing any sign of agitation.

"This is Qutang Gorge," Wu shouted above the roar of the rapids. "Look here!" As they passed dizzily close to the rocks, Wu pointed to two iron pillars nearly eight feet tall, driven into the cliff on either side. "In the Sung Dynasty time, they would block the river with iron chains."

Even now, Murphy knew, there were bandit groups in the mountains who, if a ship got into trouble, would kill the crew and pick its cargo clean. But what astonished him most was the noise as wind and water met inside this giant cauldron.

In spite of the obvious dangers, he found himself exulting in the thunder and the tumult of the place. He knew that, as long as he lived, he would never find anything else like it. Each peak, each crag, each bend in the river was a source of myth or legend. For the Chinese, the voyage through the Three Gorges was something like the pilgrimage to Mecca for the faithful of Islam. When he looked at the faces of the crew, he could see there a mixture of emotions: excitement, apprehension, even fear. But there was more than that. The men had tilted their heads back to look at the summit of the mountains towering almost directly above them and, as they did so, the wide coolie hats had fallen back onto their shoulders. In their upturned eyes Murphy saw the light of veneration.

It was another 20 miles to Wuchan, a small town on the north bank of the Yangtze, where the Daning flowed into the Yangtze. Standing on the deck of the junk, Murphy had a tantalising glimpse of a crystal clear stream that bisected the steep hills of Wuchan and debouched into the main stem of the river. Some other time, he promised himself, he would return at leisure to this magic place. Some day, when the present commotion was over, he would come back down-river again to explore the mysteries of the Daning river as it made a brief precipitous passage through its own smaller-scale system of gorges and rapids. He might even ask that nice American girl, Mary Cartwright, to come with him.

They spent the whole of the rest of the day on the Yangtze. Below Wuchan, they entered the Witches' Gorge – Wuxia – some 40 kilometres long. They had covered approximately half the distance when the Chinese crew gathered amidships and pointed excitedly up at the distant mountain tops. Even the old pilot forsook his station to join them.

"That is Shennu Peak – Goddess Peak," Wu told him.

Murphy could see, high up on the mountain ridge, a strange configuration of rocks, which seemed to resemble a gigantic statue, as large as the figure of Christ on Corcovado Mountain high above Rio de Janeiro. Except this statue was natural, not man-made.

"And they believe that that is the figure of Yao Ji herself, the Goddess who tamed the dragon!" Wu exclaimed. "That is why the Yangtze is known as the Dragon River!"

Murphy watched with fascination as the Chinese crewmen, vouchsafed a glimpse of a celestial figure whose shape was most often shrouded in mist, prostrated themselves in the scuppers of the boat.

Towards mid-afternoon of their second day, they entered the last and greatest of the three Yangtze Gorges, the Xiling Gorge, which began at the Xiang Xi and zigzagged for 76 kilometres down towards Yichang. It was the longest and

47

most dangerous of the Yangtze Gorges, comprising seven small gorges and two of the fiercest rapids between Chungking and Yichang. The larger boulders choking the channel had names such as "Big Pearl", "Monk's Rock" and "Chicken's Wings". Murphy had been amused, and a little alarmed, to learn from Wu that the deadliest hazard of all was known as "Come to Me".

The strike-force was allowed up on deck for the passage through the rapids. As the Americans emerged, blinking, into the daylight, the old Chinese pilot regarded them impassively. If he felt any surprise, he did not show it. He gave a barely perceptible nod of his wide coolie hat then, once again, returned his attention to the business in hand as the junk, sails furled, careered along a jagged, boulder-strewn passage which at its narrowest barely exceeded 50 yards.

That evening they tied up at the rotting quay of the now deserted village of Sandouping. Murphy noticed tears in Wu's eyes.

They walked together through the shattered streets. The bodies of the villagers still lay where they had fallen but the vultures had long since picked the bones clean.

"This was my house." Wu pointed to a building set back from the village, just where the land began to rise towards the mountain. The front door was half off its hinges, the roof had caved in and there were gaping holes in the walls. "Do you wish to come with me?"

Murphy shook his head. He had no wish to intrude on Wu's private grief. Besides, his attention was already elsewhere. It seemed to him that some 400 yards upstream from the village of Sandouping was the most perfect site for a dam on the River Yangtze. Looking at the topography with an instinct born of years of experience, he saw immediately how an arch-gravity construction – not unlike the great Hoover Dam on the Colorado – would fit perfectly into the configuration of the gorge, providing both maximum strength as well as maximum yield in terms of water stored and hydro-electric power generated. He clambered to a vantage point high up above the river, and sat with his notebook for over an hour that afternoon, sketching out then and there the basic elements of the project.

"Oh God!" thought Murphy. "I've found it! This is unbelievable, this is textbook stuff!" In his head he calculated the flow of the river in terms of cubic feet per second, worked out the fall between Chungking and, say, Yichang. Put a dam anywhere along here – the further down the gorge the better – and the hydro-electric yield would be fantastic.

He narrowed his eyes, gauging heights and distances. Just how high, technically speaking, could you build a dam? As far as he could estimate, here in the Three Gorges you could double the Hoover dam and still have room to spare. Imagine a dam 1,500 feet high! Imagine the water which could be stored behind it! Imagine the consequences if that dam burst! He had no idea, as he stood there, whether such a dam could or should be built. But one of the reasons why the US Army Corps of Engineers had been sent to China in the first place was to look for likely projects where the Corps' unrivalled experience and expertise could be put to good use while leading, of course, to some fat contracts for US companies. The outbreak of war had led to a reshaping of priorities and, in Murphy's own case, to his assignment to SACO as Deputy Commander. But that didn't mean his old interests were entirely supplanted. An engineer was an engineer was an engineer.

It was dark by the time he made his way back to the boats. Murphy felt exhilarated, almost light-headed. It was as though he knew that, whatever else he did in his life, this moment would outrank all others. The decision to build or not to build a dam on the Yangtze would not rest with him, but just to have discovered the potential of the site was enough.

Miles looked at Murphy angrily as he climbed back on board. He knew that the US Army Corps of Engineers was interested in possible dam sites on the Yangtze, but he didn't see why in hell army business should interfere with his plans.

"Finished your sightseeing, have you?" he snapped. "Then let's get on with the briefing, shall we?"

Around midnight, the two junks, still towing the sampans behind them, slipped their moorings and continued downstream.

4

Lieutenant Akio Nakamura could feel the pressure of sleep weighing on his eyelids. He had been awake since dawn, had come on watch around midnight and would not be relieved – in all likelihood – until the rest of the crew staggered back from their night on shore. Nakamura realised that he was paying the penalty for his own stand-offishness. When General Saburo had proclaimed a holiday in honour of the sixth anniversary of Japan's "famous victory on the upper Yangtze", Nakamura had been sceptical. He was tired of the war, ashamed that his countrymen had been ready to participate with such relish in all the senseless killings which had marked those six years. Time and again, he relived the terrible scenes which had occurred the day the Japanese armies entered Nanking. He recalled how two officers in his unit, Mukai and Noda, had competed with each other to see who could be first to decapitate 100 Chinese! Since they had both reached the target together, they had gone on to set a new figure – of 150. Noda in the end had won but only because Mukai's sword had been damaged in the contest.

He pushed his spectacles back onto the bridge of his nose, and looked up at the sky. There was no doubt about it, the clouds were clearing and the moon was beginning to break through. Nakamura's spirits lifted at the sight of the celestial body. Perhaps, after all, life was not so bad. Perhaps Japan would win the war; then they could all go home to their loved ones and he could forget the bitterness and the killing.

Ten miles upstream, Colonel Oliver Murphy looked up at the bright full moon suddenly emerging through the clouds and cursed. It was small comfort that he had previously warned Miles of the danger. The man had not listened then, and he would certainly not listen now. Full-moon or not, Murphy knew that Miles was hell-bent on seeing the action through to its finish.

"It's going to be like Broadway down there," Murphy told his men. "For God's sake don't stick your periscopes out of the water once you get within two miles of the target. Let the frogmen do the work. That's what they're for."

He turned to the two frogmen who stood fully kitted-out waiting to board the submersible and was rewarded by a gesture which looked remarkably like a V-sign.

Murphy smiled. "Keep that for the Japs, Saunders. Just get in there, do the job and then get the hell out of it!"

What Murphy didn't say was that the x-craft, forced to surface for the return run because of the limited capacity of the batteries, would be sitting ducks if anything went wrong. In theory, all the mines had fuses. They were timed to explode at 5 a.m. precisely; by then the midgets should have returned to base and the junks would be once more on their way upstream. But Murphy had been in the military long enough to know that the chances of a foul-up were always high on an occasion like this where technology was being stretched to the limit and where the human factor, so vital to success, was essentially unpredictable. Did Wu, for example, know this stretch of the river as well as he claimed? Could he guide the assault-team to the target? Could he bring them safely back again? Would Peterson be able to manage the dolphins, those unlikely beasts of burden? Would look-outs be posted on the Japanese vessels or, as their intelligence predicted, would most of the crews of the Japanese gunboats be roistering on shore?

He watched as they screwed the hatches down. His last glimpse was of Wu Canping smiling tensely through a port-hole, as the first of the two mini-submarines was lowered into the water.

It took Wu some time to get used to the angle of the periscope's eye-piece and to accept the fact that the images in the night-sight were being registered not directly by his own eyes but through the intermediary of prisms and refractions devised by some of the world's finest nautical engineers. But once he had grasped the principles involved, navigating under water with the hull of the boat submerged didn't seem very different from travelling on the surface.

As they neared Yichang, Wu signalled for the x-craft's engines to be throttled back. With the current behind them, they approached their target at a speed of a little over three knots.

Pete Peterson couldn't help feeling proud of his charges. Attached by ropes to the mini-submarines and each one of them carrying an explosive satchel, the dolphins escorted the x-craft as though they had been born to the task. Not only did they carry the mines, thereby lightening the load which the x-craft had to carry; they seemed to sense that speed was essential. Pulling together in harness, they managed almost to double the speed with which the x-craft passed through the water.

Lieutenant Nakamuru heard the dolphins spout.

"Ha!" he rose to his feet, walked across to the handrail, and stood there looking out at the calm surface of the Yangtze. Fifty yards away, he could see the silhouette of the next gunboat reflected in the water. "Ha!" he exclaimed again. There were several dolphins around the boats tonight, then. Perhaps a whole school of dolphins.

Wu Canping guided the x-craft in as close as he dared to the grey, silent hull of the Japanese gunboat. When a distance of not more than 300 yards separated them, he swung the midget's nose around until it pointed back upstream, let the engines idle so that the craft was just holding its own against the current, and gave the signal for the frogmen to move. In the second craft, Pete Peterson followed suit. There were four Japanese gunboats altogether and each one would receive two explosive charges, the limpet mines being attached both port and starboard, just below the waterline. Working under Peterson's supervision, the frogmen

53

unloaded the dolphins and then, each man carrying two mines, set off towards the targets.

When the frogmen had gone, Peterson himself passed through the valve and into the water. The dolphins recognised him immediately. They jack-knifed on their tethers and nuzzled him playfully, poking at him with their long spoon-shaped snouts.

"I'm sorry about this, old things," he murmured into his face-mask. Under any other circumstances, he would have cut the tethers then and there, so as to release the animals to the waters from which they had come. But there was still a war to be won and in the larger perspective the sacrifice, horrible though it was, had its point.

Peterson attached all four dolphins to a single ring at the side of his own x-craft. He would wait till the frogmen had safely returned and the submarines were once again heading up-stream before turning the animals loose.

Lieutenant Nakamura looked at his watch. It was almost 4 a.m. There had been something magical, he thought, about the hours he had just spent – the calm of the river, the moonlight on the water, the sound of the dolphins. The noisy return of his fellows would soon sour the atmosphere. He looked over towards the shore to see if there was any sign of the returning boat-party. All seemed to be quiet. The jetty which they used was about half a mile away; he could see the kink in the low dyke which marked the embarkation point. While he was standing there, squinting at the moonlit shore-line, a movement in the water, about 30 yards from the prow of the boat, caught his attention. At first Nakamura thought it was another dolphin, but what puzzled him was the fact that there was no spouting or spraying, no sudden commotion as the animal porpoised. What he saw instead was a steady stream of air bubbles rising to the surface and moving away from his vessel.

Lieutenant Nakamura took off his spectacles, wiped and polished them, before replacing them on his nose. This time he saw not one set of air bubbles, but three or four. The gap was opening up and the object, whatever it was,

was now 40 or 50 yards away. He hesitated for a moment, then quickly unslung his rifle.

The sound of gunfire broke the stillness of the night. The guard on the nearest gunboat called out to him: "What's the trouble? What are you shooting at?"

"Frogmen," Nakamura shouted back. "Three or four of them, perhaps more."

Following the drill, he ran to the bridge and pressed the alarm bell. The raw jangling noise cut through the night. At the same time the floodlights came on fore and aft.

Pete Peterson, waiting in the midget submarine for the frogmen to come back, saw the lights on the gunboats and made a quick mental calculation. Travelling on the surface, the x-craft could make it back to the mouth of the Gorges where the junks were waiting in less than two hours but this was a high-risk strategy. Following in hot pursuit, and using its searchlights, a Japanese patrol-boat could find and sink the submersibles long before they reached shelter. If, on the other hand, they travelled submerged, the journey-time would be doubled, and even so, they could be vulnerable to detection. He didn't know precisely what sonar equipment the Japanese Navy possessed, but it was a fair guess that they had some form of echo-sounder. The Yangtze squadron of the Japanese Navy was not confined to the river itself; it patrolled also the coastal areas and the waters of the South China Sea where it would be expected, amongst other things, to deal with the threat of enemy submarines.

Peterson looked at his watch. Over two hours had elapsed since the frogmen had left on their mission. According to the schedule, they should by now be well on their way back towards the rendezvous. He felt the prickles rise on the nape of his neck. What if the frogmen didn't make it in time? What if they were overtaken by the patrol-boats? What if the x-craft were forced to pull back before the divers had returned? Still watching through the periscope, he saw first one, then a second gunboat begin to move. He decided he would wait five minutes and no more. Ninety seconds later both gunboats were circling purposefully in mid-channel. Peterson wondered how long it would be before they picked up the scent and started heading upstream.

There were still 30 seconds to go by his watch when the two frogmen hurriedly entered the x-craft through the valve. Peterson didn't wait to hear a mission-report. As they stripped off their gear, he asked simply: "Are the others back?"

When they nodded, still winded from their rapid retreat, he started the motors and headed for home. As he did so he pulled the lever to release the last two dolphins which throughout the mission had stayed behind, tethered to the craft.

"Go, boys, go," he urged them.

The next five minutes were probably the most agonising that Pete Peterson had spent in his life. He no longer needed to look at the pursuing gunboats through the periscope; the thin metallic hull of the x-craft somehow magnified the under-water vibrations into a deafening cacophony of sound. Oh Christ! thought Peterson. If it doesn't happen now, it will be too late anyway!

Wu Canping, in the other submersible, felt the force of the explosion, stumbled and almost fell as the vessel rocked from side to side. For half a moment he imagined that the x-craft itself had been depth-charged by the pursuing gunboats.

Split seconds later there was another explosion, even more deafening than the first, and again the craft rocked violently. This time Wu noticed that the water was pouring in through one of the portholes which had cracked under the strain. Better to be blown to bits on the surface, he thought, than to be drowned like a rat. As instructed, he pulled the lever to shoot the x-craft into a rapid rising incline.

Wu Canping would never forget the sight which greeted him, as the tiny vessel bobbed up into the current of the great Yangtze river. Less than a quarter of a mile away, the two pursuing Japanese gunboats were blazing from bow to stern. Lifting the hatch, and poking his head out, he could see men flinging themselves off the decks into the water, and, even from this distance, he could hear the screams. He didn't understand who had dealt the enemy such a savage blow, nor the manner in which it had been delivered, but he didn't question his luck. In any case, there were two more gunboats berthed down there at Yichang and these had not yet been accounted for. As he started the engine and set the throttle to maximum speed – five fierce pulsating knots – he saw that Peterson's craft had surfaced nearby and was, like his own, now proceeding on the surface, exposed. If Peterson could risk it, then he could as well.

But then Wu realised, as the mines exploded against the sides of the remaining gunboats, shooting tongues of flame into the air, that even this last danger had been effectively dealt with. He let loose a long whoop of joy.

They had a party on board the junks that night. Somehow the news of the crippling blow the midget submarines had managed to strike against the Japanese had reached Commodore Miles even before the x-craft had returned safely to base. The message must have flashed up the river valley, village to village, hamlet to hamlet, home to home. The burning Japanese ships were in themselves a beacon signal and that signal had been relayed with staggering speed throughout free China. By the time the crew of the midgets dragged themselves wearily out of the craft and onto the deck of the junks, a throng had gathered on the bank. God knows where they had all come from, thought Wu, as he scanned their faces for anyone he might recognise. The excitement would, of course, pass as night turned into day. When dawn broke the skies would be clear for the Japanese fighters. Anyone caught out in the open, whether on the river or in-shore, could expect swift and sure retribution.

Using Wu as an interpreter, Commodore Milton Miles addressed the crowd. He was clearly in a state of high excitement. A hurricane lamp had been slung from the mast and Miles clambered up onto a packing case to stand beneath it. In the flickering light, his face shone with a kind of manic fervour.

"My friends," he began. "Today we have struck a blow against the Japanese from which they may never recover. The gunboats which have harassed you for the last five years have been destroyed. You may go back to your villages by the river; you may resume your traditional activities. The Japanese will trouble you no more . . ."

It was rubbish, of course. Four burnt-out gunboats could be replaced by other gunboats; the Japanese would not pull back from Szechuan and Hubei merely because of one unforeseen reverse. But it sounded good to Miles at the time. To tell the truth, it sounded good to all the SACO team on board and even the Chinese, who had suffered most from the Japanese invader, were prepared for those few hours at least to give the American the benefit of the doubt.

A cheer went up from the bank and the primitive tallow torches which some had brought with them were waved aloft in a mixture of joy and defiance. They were a ragged, emaciated bunch, these Chinese who had fled from their homes so many years before, to hide in the hills and ravines of the mountain valleys, scratching out a living where they could. Their clothes were in tatters and most of their shoes, where they had them, were made out of old bits of rubber or rope.

When Miles had finished, Wu climbed down off the boat and mingled with the crowd, still searching for faces he knew. Surely there must have been some survivors from his village. Working his way to the edge of the gathering, his eye fell on an old lady, hunched and way-worn, who seemed to be observing the scene with an air of blank incomprehension. Suddenly, the oil in one of the lamps flared up and for a second the light fell full on the old woman's face.

Wu pushed his way through the ragged crowd and threw himself at the old lady's feet.

"Mother," he said.

Her hand groped for his shoulder as he kneeled at her feet. Wu looked up to realise that his mother was blind.

*

In the cold dawn, they steamed slowly back up the Yangtze.

"They blinded her with the same stick . . ." Wu choked on the words. "She was left for dead. Some of the villagers took her with them as they fled and have cared for her ever since."

"You could have brought her, you know. We could have found a place for her at SACO." Murphy felt sure he could have arranged things.

Wu shook his head. "There would have been no point. She knows where she is. She is among her people. It is best for her to stay behind."

The war had never entirely halted the flow of traffic on the Yangtze – sampans, junks, fishing and transport vessels of various kinds had continued to operate at least on those stretches of the river which fell outside Japan's immediate reach. Miles had been convinced that they would blend in with the crowd.

Murphy himself had been less sanguine. It seemed to him that there was every chance of the Japanese, like angry wasps, sprinkling their cannon fire liberally on all and sundry. He had insisted that, at the very least, they should carry anti-aircraft weapons, capable of being fired in an emergency. So each junk had a nine-millimetre Bofors hidden beneath a tarpaulin in the prow. As weaponry went, the Bofors was neat and effective but, Murphy knew, it wouldn't be much use against a determined and prolonged air-attack.

They had covered some 40 miles altogether when they heard the sound of the Japanese planes coming up the canyon behind them. The Americans, who had been taking the air on deck, dived for cover. From above, the only people visible on each junk were the pilot and captain and a couple of coolies sitting on some coils of rope and idly smoking their daily pipe of opium.

There were three fighters altogether. They came fast and low, following the river up through the gorges. Murphy hid with two of the gunners under the tarpaulin and watched the enemy through a slit in the material. "This isn't going to work," he told himself. "We're still only 60 miles from

Yichang and we're going upstream. They're bound to wonder where we came from." He nodded to the gunners who crouched beside him. "You'd better get ready."

For a moment, Murphy thought he could after all be wrong. The Japanese fighters roared 60 feet overhead and followed the curve of the river out of sight. "Stay under cover," Murphy yelled as he saw some American faces emerging from the bowels of the vessel. "Get this thing ready for action," he told the gunners. "If they come back now, they'll mean business."

They did come back. And they did mean business. The Japanese planes must have pulled up out of the canyon to turn through 180 degrees, then dropped back down again in a piece of precision flying to zero in on the two junks with all guns blazing.

"Jesus!" thought Murphy. He could see the splash of the bullets hitting the water as the planes approached.

The gunners manning the Bofors knew their job. They were too late to hit the first two planes but, as the third screeched overhead, the nine millimetre shells ripped into the fuselage and the plane literally exploded against the side of the mountain.

In the sudden silence which followed, Murphy surveyed the damage. His own junk's mast had been cut in two by the hail of bullets and the old Chinese pilot was lying in a pool of blood, half his chest having been shot away. On Miles's vessel, as far as he could see, the situation was even worse. The junk was listing badly and seemed to be in danger of being swept by the force of the current against the walls of the ravine.

Even as he spoke, Murphy heard once again the sound of the Japanese fighters. They had turned round, even quicker than before, and were coming back up the river. This time, Murphy knew, they would be sure of their target.

As they prepared for the second round of the unequal contest, Murphy couldn't help thinking of that nice American nurse whom he had met at the British Ambassador's reception.

He was still thinking about Mary Cartwright as the

Japanese fighters – only two of them now – zoomed back into view. They flew lower this time, barely ten feet above the swirling brown surface of the Yangtze. As the gunners tried desperately to lower the elevation on the Bofors, Murphy noted out of the corner of his eye that Wu Canping had taken over the helm. The pilot's dead, Murphy thought, and the captain has probably jumped overboard, but that kid has got what it takes!

Seconds later, the cannon-fire ripped through the vessel, knocking out the Bofors while it was still pointing at the sky. One of the men was killed, the other thrown into the scuppers. Murphy felt a sharp pain in his shoulder as a bullet ricocheted off the hard metal of the gun and lodged below his collarbone.

When Charlie Soong, taking his turn at standby duty, heard that three Japanese fighters had taken off from Hankow on what was clearly *not* an escort mission (there were no reports of bombers leaving at the same time), he quickly put two and two together. Though Commodore Milton Miles firmly believed that his Yangtze mission was a closely guarded secret, the truth of the matter was that Charlie Soong, who knew most of what was going on in Chungking, had got wind of the plan at an early stage and had followed its subsequent evolution with considerable interest. If SACO wanted to engage in free-lance activities, that was no skin off his nose. He could understand Miles's sense of frustration.

They were airborne in less than three minutes, skimming the summits of the mountains in attack formation. Soong had the advantage of surprise and he made the best of it. He could hear the Japanese fighter-pilots talking to each other on their radios as they turned to make another strafing run on the junks. Then, as they came back upstream the second time, he took them from behind, neatly, viciously, like a hawk swooping on a rabbit.

After that, it seemed that everything happened at once. One minute the leading Japanese fighter was boring in on the junks, guns blazing. The next, it had veered crazily, one wing and half the fuselage shot away, to crash against the

61

side of the Gorge. Seconds later, the second Japanese plane met a similar fate.

Charlie Soong slid the canopy of the Hawk back, leaned out of the cockpit and waved his red neckerchief to the men on board the crippled junks.

"See you back at the ranch!" he shouted against the roar of the engines. By the time the squadron had wheeled for a slow victory pass above the junks, the surviving crew members – Americans and Chinese alike – were out on deck. Some of the men, recognising their saviour, cheered and whistled. It was not every day that they saw the Yellow Baron in action.

They spent three days hidden from view in an inlet some 40 miles upstream from Yichang while they repaired the damage to the junks as best they could. It was not an easy task. Apart from the shortage of material – wood, tar, nails, caulking fluid – they lacked some of the necessary skills. There were boat-builders and shipwrights among them – such men gravitated naturally to the Navy in times of war – but their experience of mending Chinese junks was limited! It took a good deal of ingenuity and opportunism and round-the-clock labour which left some of them prostrate with exhaustion before the vessels were once again ready to sail.

Murphy remembered very little of it. His shoulder-wound turned septic and delirium set in. For a week, Wu nursed him. There were American medicines on-board – sulphonamides, iodine, morphine – but Wu scorned these in favour of some traditional Chinese remedies – strange mixtures and potions – which somehow he managed to beg, borrow or steal from villages along the way. Murphy was vaguely conscious of their progress through the Gorges. Lying on his back in a makeshift shelter rigged up beside the mast, he had the impression of an endless series of mountain peaks, each one higher than the last. It seemed to him as though the Gods themselves inhabited those gigantic twisted forms.

*

When the repairs were finally completed, Commodore Miles decided to give the men an evening off.

"You can go ashore, if you like. Have a beer in the local cafe!" He laughed. "I'll come with you."

Before he left, Miles came to see Murphy. "How are you feeling? Anything we can get you?"

Murphy half-opened his eyes. He managed a crooked smile. "Don't worry about me. Wu's in charge." Wu, standing by solicitously, nodded in confirmation.

"We'll see you later, then," Miles said.

Around 6 p.m. Murphy felt a massive tremor which caused the boat to rock on its moorings. "What the hell's that?" he asked Wu.

"Earthquake, Mr Murphy, Sir. Somewhere upstream."

"Big earthquake?"

"Not too big."

"What's the worry then, Wu?" Murphy could see the young man standing anxiously on the prow of the junk staring out towards the mouth of the inlet and the main stem of the river. Suddenly, he jumped down and ran towards Murphy. "Quick, we go now! Big danger!"

"What are you talking about, Wu? The quake's over. I can't move anyway."

"Tidal wave coming, Sir. I hear it now. Sometimes earthquake cause landslide in the gorge. Whole mountain fall into river. Once three villages fall in."

"Oh my God!" Murphy could hear the roaring noise for himself now.

Wu picked him up bodily, and carried him across the gangplank as the tidal wave, approaching a speed of 70 or 80 miles an hour, crashed past the mouth of the inlet. The backwash hit the junk, literally catapulting it into the air before sweeping it downriver. By some fluke the second junk was hurled further up the inlet where it became lodged between two trees. As the water receded, the vessel was left high and dry 20 feet above the normal river level.

"Holy smoke!" Murphy was able to observe the whole scene from the place of safety to which Wu had brought him. A line of Shakespeare came unbidden into his mind:

" 'As flies to wanton boys are we to the Gods'," he murmured. " 'They kill us for their sport.' "

He repeated the words later that night, as he lay in a makeshift first-aid centre in a nearby village.

"Excuse me, Sir?" Wu looked at him with anxiety. The worst of the American's delirium seemed to have passed but they were not home yet. "Did you ask for something?"

"Don't worry, Wu. It's nothing." Mercifully, the potions and herbal remedies at last took effect and Murphy sank into a deep refreshing sleep.

5

When Commodore Miles, jubilant, went over to the Eagle's Nest to report the success of his mission, Chiang Kai Shek could barely contain his anger.

"These submersibles as you call them, where did they come from?" he asked icily. "Who authorised their delivery?"

Miles was taken aback. "These were SACO supplies, Generalissimo."

"SACO had no such authorisation. I have checked with Tai Li." The fingers of Chiang's hand were extended across the front of the military uniform which he habitually wore to grasp the jewelled hilt of his sword. "Those submersibles took up valuable cargo space. The planes which flew them in could have brought arms and munitions instead. Supplies we desperately need."

"We have struck a blow against the Japanese." Miles was having trouble controlling his own temper. "That's our mandate, Generalissimo. That's why the US Navy Group came to China in the first place."

"Pah! The Japanese! They are on the run anyway, why should we waste our weapons on them?"

"Are you disavowing the mission?"

Chiang glowered. "There will be no further activities of this nature without my express authorisation."

After Miles had stormed out, Chiang rang for his wife. Though they lived in the same house, it was several days since he had seen Mayling. Latterly, he had taken a new mistress – a young Szechuan girl whom he visited regularly and even, during Mayling's often frequent absences, invited to the great villa on the bluff overlooking the city of Chungking.

Madame Chiang knew perfectly well what was going on. It was not the first time her husband had taken a mistress and it would not be the last. She knew she was not the beauty she once had been, the fresh college girl Chiang had married 20 years earlier, divorcing his first wife to do so. But she was tough as nails, as hard-bitten in her way as the Generalissimo himself. She was damned if she was going to let a new furry kitten push the old tigress from her lair. She would outlast them all – she was quite confident of that. Chiang would tire of his paramours, as he always did, or else, she thought bitterly, they would tire of him. Familiarity bred contempt and the Generalissimo had several nasty habits which the intimacy of the bedroom quickly revealed. Oddly enough, one of the things she found most intolerable was the way Chiang refused to wear his false teeth for so much of the time when he was at home. Sometimes, when she found his decayed and smelling dentures lying around, she felt like flinging them on the ground and grinding them to pieces under her heel.

She entered the room in apparent good humour. The former Mayling Soong's smile had wooed Presidents and princes. It had appeared on the cover of innumerable magazines. Henry Luce, the founder and publisher of the immensely powerful *Life* magazine, had promoted her looks, her charm, her home-spun political morality (of the kind he himself favoured) on every possible occasion, and that smile had played a big part in her, and his, success. It was irresistible, honey-gold with just a hint of steel.

"Did Master call?" There was no mistaking the irony in her voice. Then she continued, sweetly, "How are you, Generalissimo?" She knew he liked her to address him by his title. "It seems ages since we last met!"

Chiang stayed seated at his desk while Mayling moved to the sofa which was placed alongside the wall. The view was one she knew well since she saw it also from her study window each afternoon, as she made the daily entry in her journal.

"I want you to see Chennault," Chiang said.

Madame Chiang was surprised. "In Kunming?" Kunming was the headquarters of China's Fourteenth Air Force and the place where General Claire Chennault, founder of the famous Flying Tigers, had his permanent headquarters.

"Where else?" Chiang snapped. And he added sarcastically, "The men should be delighted to see you. I'm told that they call him 'Mayling's poodle'!"

Mayling's smile never wavered but the lines around the edge of her mouth hardened imperceptibly. "I wouldn't pursue that line, if I were you." This time she dispensed with Chiang's title. "Not while your new little vixen is sniffing the front of your trousers!"

"Let's put it this way," he said irritably. "You are friends with Chennault. He will accept your advice, even your instructions. Go down to Kunming and talk to him."

"What about?"

Although Chiang had come to dislike any physical contact with his wife, he knew that a gesture of some sort was required. He came over and sat on the sofa, leaving an axe-length between them. Then, speaking quietly and in the clipped rather high-pitched voice which she knew so well, he began to explain what he had in mind.

"Chennault believes", he concluded, "that the Fourteenth Air Force will one day be called upon to bomb Japan. That's why he's hanging on here in China, waiting for his moment of glory. Your job is to persuade him that that moment will never come. The Americans don't need the Chinese bases any longer. Each day, the American Pacific fleet is getting nearer Japan. Bombers can fly from the islands; they can even fly from US aircraft carriers. Our spies in Washington have told us that the Americans have almost completed work on a new superweapon but even without that, Japan is doomed."

He stood and went back to his desk, opened a drawer and took out some papers. "These are the reports which have come in. One from T. V. Soong in Washington, another from an agent we have placed in Los Alamos, New Mexico, where the atomic bomb is being tested. Show them to no one except Chennault and return them to me personally. Chennault will recognise immediately that these documents are authentic and, once he has read them, he will realise that for him the game is over."

His tone, which up till then had been hard and impersonal, softened. "That will be your moment, Mayling. When Chennault sees one vision disappear, you must entice him with another. A different vision, a larger vision, a vision which will ensure Claire Chennault's place in the history-books far more surely than organising bombing raids against mainland Japan." And he told her then precisely what Chennault had to do.

She heard him out. When he had finished, she commented, "The Communist leadership never meets all at one time in the same place. Up there in Yenan, they have as many caves and holes and underground shelters as we do in Chungking. They'll all be dispersed."

Chiang Kai Shek smiled. "You're wrong. On this particular occasion, the whole Communist leadership *will* be gathered in one place."

"Why are you so sure?"

"Because" – his tone was almost unctuous now (after all she was still putty in his hands) – "the day Chennault does what we want him to do will be the same day that our foolish friend Hurley, the new US Ambassador, goes on his official visit up there."

Madame Chiang gasped involuntarily. "Surely, you don't mean . . . ?"

The Generalissimo interrupted her. "That is precisely what I do mean, my dear." Chiang's smile had turned into a leer of pure evil.

Even in November, Kunming – the key staging-post on the supply-route from Chungking to Burma – could be hot. Claire Chennault was perspiring gently on the veranda of his bungalow at the edge of the runway when his Chinese servant, bowing deeply, announced the presence of a visitor.

"Madame Chiang Kai Shek to see you, General!"

Madame Chiang! The Generalissimo's wife! Chennault leapt to his feet, blushing deeply. It was over seven years since he had first begun to work for the Kuomintang and throughout that time his relationship with Madame Chiang had been of the closest. It was she who had first persuaded him to come to China, ostensibly as an employee of the Bank of China (run by her brother, the ubiquitous T.V. Soong), but in reality with the objective of building up China's own Air Force. And he had been her favourite ever since. He knew, and enjoyed the fact, that Mayling boasted of all the breakfasts they had had together since she became head of the Air Force. Breakfast was one thing. Arriving without warning in the evening hours in his personal quarters was something else again!

"What can I do for you, Ma'am?" Chennault asked her somewhat incoherently, as she entered the room leaving both her driver and her bodyguard in the car outside. "Can I get you a drink? Have you had dinner?"

Madame Chiang laughed. "Don't look so flustered. Get me a Scotch and soda and then sit down and listen to what I have to say."

She took her time, chatting to him first about her hopes and expectations.

"Stillwell's gone, of course. Wedermeyer's replacing him as you know. There are changes in the air – you should be part of them, but you have to seize the moment." She leaned forward confidentially and placed a hand lightly on his knee.

"You've got 33 Lockheed Hudson and 30 DB–7-Douglas bombers sitting out there," she told him. "In addition, you've got a score of fighters to defend those planes against attack and yet you know and I know that your Lockheed Hudsons and your Douglases haven't flown for the last six months! Your 14th Air Force is a charade!"

Two things helped Mayling Soong gain her point that night. First, and possibly less important, was Chennault's deep sense of indignation, almost of betrayal, when he learnt from the documents she showed him, documents whose authenticity he did not question (he knew the real McCoy when he saw it), that the Fourteenth Air Force would play no part in Japan's defeat.

The second, and possibly more important reason, had to

69

do with the fact that Claire Chennault had been in love with Mayling Soong for almost as long as he had known her. He recalled the day in the summer of 1937, shortly before the outbreak of the Sino-Japanese war, when he had arrived in Nanking to take up his new job. Mayling had come out to the airport to greet him. Her beauty had struck him then and even though the years had passed, years of turmoil and suffering, in his eyes at least her charms were undiminished.

"You do understand, Claire, don't you?" In all the years he had known her, it was the first time that she had addressed him by his Christian name. In all probability, he would have agreed anyway to the request she put to him then. After all, she was the Generalissimo's wife and Commander of the Chinese Air Force. An order was an order. But when, almost as part of the bargain, she appeared already to offer him more, her mouth, her breasts, her body, it seemed churlish to refuse. During long lonely nights he had fantasised about this moment and the reality was better than the dream.

They had breakfast together in the cool of the morning.

"I heard some rumour", he poured her a cup of coffee, "that Hurley, the new US Ambassador, is thinking of making a visit to Yenan."

Suddenly, all her antennae were on the alert. "Out of the question", she snapped."The Generalissimo has strictly forbidden any visits by Chungking-based diplomats to Communist headquarters and that applies to the Americans most of all."

"I guess I got it wrong. We're out of touch with the news down here."

"Soon you'll be making the news, Claire." She flashed him her most winning smile.

"What turtle's egg do we have here?" Mao muttered to Chou and Marshal Ye as Ambassador Hurley bounced down the steps of the plane towards them, letting loose a wild Choctaw Indian war-cry which he had picked up in his boyhood on the western plains.

"In Chungking, apparently, they call him the Second Big Wind," Marshal Ye replied.

Mao pretended to cough to conceal his laughter.

Beginning with Mao, Hurley shook hands in turn with each member of the Chinese triumvirate. Though he frequently boasted of his farming background and of years spent on an Oklahoma ranch, the Ambassador's white and puffy palm was a marked contrast to the strong calloused handshakes of his hosts. Encircled by the Japanese, Mao's forces had learnt the hard way that they would only eat what they could grow. From morning to night, in the caves, in the fields, on the bare loess hillsides, Mao had taught his people by the sheer force of example that self-sufficiency was essential for long-term revolutionary activity.

Greetings over, Hurley thrust his stetson firmly back on his head and surveyed the desolate scene with some surprise. Apart from the US military transport plane in which he had arrived, and two or three battered vehicles of Soviet manufacture in which Mao's party had driven out to the airstrip on the plateau, there was almost no sign that this was the heart of Communist China. Apparently over 100,000 people lived here, in the Communist-controlled zone. Where the hell were they all, he wondered? He had heard that the Communists had a pretty rum show going on up there in Yenan. This half-assed reception seemed to prove it.

"What did you do with the dancing girls?" he guffawed. And then he let out a collosal belch. Ambassador Patrick Hurley's historic mission had begun.

They gave a reception for him in the Congress Hall. It was one of the few two-storey buildings in Yenan, and, miraculously, it had survived repeated Japanese bombings. The first floor was a large pillared room. The previous day Mao had been present there in person to receive Brigade No. 350 of the Eighth Route Army who were going south to reinforce the New Fourth Army. He had recited to them, movingly, one of his own poems – amid all the pressures of daily life in Yenan, poetry was an enduring consolation.

71

"Become like a pine or a willow.
The pine is evergreen, straight in wind or storm
(the pine has principle)
The willow grows anywhere it is planted,
In Spring its branches lengthen,
Numberless leaves move in the wind with beauty
(the willow has flexibility)."

Whether the battle-hardened veterans of the Eighth Route Army had absorbed all the poem's symbolism was not entirely clear, but it seemed to go down well. Mao had grown a little plumper in the face since those early days of the Long March – the diet was better now than it used to be – but even those who had not seen him for over a decade were able to recognise him instantly. His thick black hair was swept back from his forehead; his eyes were set surprisingly far apart; he had a wide, generous mouth which often broke into a smile as he exchanged pungent jokes with the Chinese peasantry whose lives he had moulded and redirected in such a comprehensive fashion.

That night the benches on which the soldiers had sat were removed and the room was prepared for a ceremonial banquet. The names of some of those who would attend the reception were almost as well-known as that of Mao himself. Men like Liu Shao-Chi and Lin Piao had been with Mao since the beginning and, like him, had already attained an almost legendary reputation among the rank and file. But there were others, too, like the wily Field Commander Deng Xiaoping or Quarter-Master Hua Gofeng whose influence in the movement, both at the practical and theoretical level, it was impossible to exaggerate.

In allowing the whole leadership of the Chinese Communist party to gather together in a single place, Mao knew he was breaking one of his own golden rules. Indeed in his Treatise on Conflict which he had written the previous year in the space of 96 hours, hardly pausing for sleep or refreshment, he had stressed the need to avoid all such acts of folly. But tonight was different. Hurley might indeed be what he appeared to be: a clown, a buffoon, a bag of wind, a turtle's egg! But the man's credentials were in order. He was the plenipotentiary representative of the greatest power on earth. They would put on a show for him, Mao decided, even if it were the last thing they did! Hurley should understand that he was not dealing with a gang of bandits but with men of stature who would soon be ruling the most populous nation on earth!

The tall, silver-haired Oklahoman who sat directly opposite Mao Tse Tung held his liquor well. Most of the toasts had been drunk in the traditional potent rice wine Mao Tai; but there had been a profusion of other drinks as well: sticky sweet red wine from the grapes which they had begun to grow on the hillsides around Yenan, Chinese brandies which somehow miraculously had been carried in the baggage-train of the Long March against just such an occasion as this. There was even a bottle of Scotch which a visiting American, Edgar Snow, had brought as a present for the Communist leader a few months earlier. Hurley stretched out a long arm to refill his glass with the precious brown liquid before rising to his feet for the second time that evening.

"Mr Mao, Mr Chou En Lai, Marshal Ye, you must forgive me taking the floor again, but I am told I already have a nickname here in China – the Second Big Wind – so I thought I had better live up to it!"

It took a while for the joke to be translated but, when it was, the laughter that followed was uproarious.

As Hurley, enjoying his moment, got into his stride, Marshal Ye allowed his grizzled head to droop towards his chest. It had been a long day and it was not over yet. On past form, the banquet would last well beyond midnight. Mao had written about that too, of course, in his essay "On Negotiations". Drink your enemy under the table the night before, then start talking early next day! He drifted off to sleep with Hurley's grandiloquent phrases - 'historic opportunity to compromise . . . President Roosevelt in person . . .' – ringing in his ears.

Moments later he found himself being shaken awake by an aide-de-camp, who leaned down and whispered an urgent message in his ear. As Marshal Ye listened, he blanched visibly. Then he snatched a paper napkin from a vase in front of him and wrote three brief sentences on it: "INTELLIGENCE REPORT JUST RECEIVED FROM CHUNGKING. FOURTEENTH AIR FORCE BASED KUNMING EXPECTED TO LAUNCH MAJOR BOMBING STRIKE AGAINST YENAN THIS NIGHT. AM ORDERING IMMEDIATE END TO BANQUET AND DISPERSAL TO SHELTER SYSTEM."

The aide was still waiting at his elbow.

"Take that to Comrade Mao at once." Ye didn't wait to hear Mao's reaction. Shaking his head to clear his brain of the fuddle induced by four hours of continous eating and drinking, he strode from the hall.

"Sound the air-raid alarms!" he snapped to his ADC. "Members of the Central Committee are to go to separate shelters in accordance with normal procedure."

"What about Hurley?"

"Screw Hurley!" Ye replied bitterly. Then he had second thoughts. After all, though the US Ambassador had obviously been used by Chiang Kai Shek as a stalking-horse – a way of guaranteeing that the whole Chinese leadership would be gathered together in one place at one time – he could hardly have colluded in the Generalissimo's plan, not if he valued his own skin which he patently did!

"Bring the Americans along too, damn them! Take them to the caves. They'll be as safe there as anywhere."

As he spoke, the alarm bells rang and the warning sirens sounded.

It took twelve minutes for the Congress Hall to be evacuated, and a further ten before the last Chinese had sought and found the shelter of the caves and burrows and bunkers which had been constructed over the years and whose efficacy against air attack had been proved time after time. Mao Tse Tung, honouring a long tradition of hospitality, personally escorted Ambassador Hurley and the members

74

of his team to his own cave dug deep in the hillside above the Communist stronghold. Less than 30 minutes after Marshal Ye received the warning that they were on their way, Chennault's long-range bombers arrived above Yenan.

They had flown with pin-point accuracy, profiting from the moonlit night and the fact that so much of China's topography was a navigator's dream. There was no mistaking the silver shimmering waters of the great rivers – the Yangtze, the Yellow River – as they flew over them, no mistaking the line of the Great Wall of China as it snaked past Sian; no mistaking the distant outline of the high Mongolian plateau as they neared the end of their journey. They came in waves of six, the Lockheeds first, then the Douglases, dropping their bombs and incendiary devices cluster by cluster, pod by pod, stick by stick.

To Ambassador Patrick Hurley, standing next to Mao Tse Tung in the mouth of the cave, which had served as the Communist leader's home for the last several years, the sight of the bombs falling was both awesome and baffling. Awesome, because – as he would later tell the folks back home – it was the "darn'dest Goddamn display of fireworks" he had ever seen. Baffling, because Hurley couldn't for the life of him understand where all the planes were coming from.

"Hell, I thought the Japs were leaving you people alone now that they're pulling back from the mainland of Asia," he said to Mao.

Mao looked at him with withering scorn. "Those are American-made planes, Ambassador, Chennault's planes, but dispatched by your loyal ally, Chiang Kai Shek!" Mao turned abruptly on his heel and withdrew into the far recesses of the cave.

"Jesus H. Christ!" As the implication of Mao's comment sank in, Hurley sputtered and fumed in rage and embarrassment.

"I just don't believe it . . ." he began, but never completed his sentence. There was a sudden deafening explosion and Hurley found himself literally flattened against the rock-wall as a bomb, loosed on some freakish trajectory, detonated in the mouth of the cave at precisely the spot where Mao Tse Tung had been standing seconds before.

It took three hours to dig the Ambassador free. When he finally emerged, bloody and bruised, but otherwise intact, Hurley's principal concern seemed to be for his distinctive headgear which had been crushed beyond recognition.

"Goddarn it," he swore, surveying the wreckage. "What am I going to do without a hat?"

"Have one of these, Ambassador?" Mao Tse Tung, looking none the worse for the night's events, handed the American one of the blue cloth caps which had become the trademark of the Yenan cadres. And then, to everyone's surprise, including Hurley's, he started to roar with laughter, holding his sides and swaying like a tree in the wind.

"A turtle's egg indeed . . . !" The tears streamed down his face, glistening as the first rays of the sun struck the devastated hillside.

6

After ten days in the hospital, Murphy was bored. But there was one redeeming feature of his stay – the presence of Nurse Cartwright. At first, she had been stern with him, rigorously respecting the boundaries of the nurse-patient relationship. It was almost as though she didn't remember, or didn't care to remember, the evening they had danced together to the strains of Glen Miller, while the Chungking big shots played politics around them. But latterly, as his health recovered, her attitude had softened.

She allowed him an almost daily visit from Wu Canping. Once he was firmly on the road to recovery, Murphy – somewhat to his surprise – found himself eagerly looking forward to those visits. Wu seemed to have an almost insatiable curiosity. Everything Murphy told him seemed to interest him, particularly when the American spoke about life in the United States, about America's role in the war and about his vision of post-war relationships.

"I see a grand alliance", Murphy had told him, "between China and America. Mark my words! Stalin and the Soviets may be our allies at the moment but the day peace breaks out, things will be very different. There's no way the Soviet system and the American system can go hand-in-hand together. A cold war between those two countries is in the making which will last for decades. But with China, Wu, things could be different. We must *make* them different!"

The relationship between the two men was not all one way. Sitting on a chair at the end of Murphy's bed, Wu absorbed everything he heard. But Murphy, at the same time, found that he too learned a lot. Within the framework of SACO, Americans and Chinese were of course constantly meeting. But this was a highly formal, structured relationship. The hospital provided opportunities for contact which quite simply didn't exist in the Happy Valley.

77

If Wu was interested in the wider world, what fascinated Murphy above all else was Wu's account of daily life in a Chinese village: the complex hierarchy of relationships within and between families; the struggle for survival; the rare times of plenty; the festivals and ceremonies which marked the progress of the year. Even in a language which was not his own, the young man had a gift for words, for choosing an apt image to describe a particular scene or event.

Then, one week, Wu's visits abruptly ceased.

"What's happened to your little Chinese friend, Oliver?" Mary Cartwright asked. Though she would have died rather than admit it, Nurse Cartwright was slightly jealous of the time Murphy spent with Wu and the close friendship which had grown up between them.

"I don't know." Murphy was puzzled and more than a little anxious. He tried to disguise his concern beneath a light, bantering tone. "No news is good news, I suppose. But next time you go dancing, Mary, and meet some of the boys from SACO, ask them about Wu!"

The following morning, she came into the ward with a long face. "Wu's been in prison for a week," she told him. "He may even be dead." Instinctively she took his hand. "I'm sorry, Oliver."

"Why?" The news came as a solid shock.

"It seems", she replied slowly, "that Tai Li has accused him of spying for the Communists."

She tried to restrain him as he leapt out of bed, but could not. The best she could do was insist on dressing his wound with fresh bandages and giving him a sling for his arm so as to keep the weight off his shoulder.

"I'll have to report you, Colonel, unless you're back by nightfall." She desperately wanted to kiss him.

Tai Li had not invented "the Aeroplane" but he had perfected it. As a method of torture, the Aeroplane fulfilled all the principal requirements. It was exquisitely painful; the agony could be prolonged almost indefinitely; it involved minimum effort on the part of the torturer as opposed to the torturee. In practical terms, moreover, the Aeroplane required very little by way of props. The victim's hands were bound behind his back, with a bamboo pole being placed under the shoulders and another behind the knees. He was then hoisted onto a hook in the ceiling where he hung suspended – hence the name "Aeroplane". Some practitioners of the black art believed that no further interventions were necessary. Sooner or later, death would occur and when it did it would be of a specially unpleasant nature. The vertebrae in the spinal column would crack one by one under the strain of the unnatural position, with the back arched backwards like a strung bow; the rib-cage would burst and the vital organs – heart, lungs, spleen – would literally fall out of the victim's chest. If all this didn't kill him, the poor bastard was in any case likely to drown or suffocate as the blood poured through throat and nostrils.

Tai Li himself was not a purist as far as torture was concerned. If he used the Aeroplane – and it was one of his favourite methods – he did so not primarily with a view to causing the victim's death (though this was invariably the result) but as a means of satisfying his own sadistic tendencies. He would stand, legs astride, in front of the naked prisoner and beat him on the ribs and back with a thin bamboo cane, slicing the flesh, inch by inch, from the bones until he managed to create a living bleeding skeleton jerking quirkishly beneath the current of blows.

For a week, Tai Li had been debating what to do with Wu Canping. As far as he was concerned, the case against the young man was clear enough. His agents in Yenan had informed him that Marshal Ye had been alerted – at the eleventh hour – about the impending raid and that the message had come from Chungking. He had strong positive evidence that Wu had been in touch with the Communists in Chungking. What's more, Wu was conceivably in a position to have known about the projected raid by the Fourteenth Air Force. (Madame Chiang's visit to Chennault in Kunming had been arranged through SACO channels and there would have been other signals which a sharp-eyed observer might have noticed.) Under normal circumstances, Wu would have been slung from the hook quicker than you

79

could kill a cornered rat and the odds were a million to one that, by now, he would have either confessed or died, or both.

But these were not normal circumstances. Strictly speaking, Wu was employed by the Americans and, somewhat to Tai Li's surprise, the Americans were kicking up a fuss about his imprisonment. As a result, Tai Li so far had refrained from using physical violence against Wu. He had tried bluff; he had tried cajolery, he had tried insinuation. Once, visiting the SACO dungeon in person late at night, he had suggested to Wu that all his problems would be solved and he could walk out of jail a free man if only he would name his contacts on the Communist side.

When Wu resolutely refused to cooperate, Tai Li lost his temper. He lashed the young man across the face with his cane. "Tomorrow I'll take you for a ride you'll never forget!"

By the time Murphy heard of Wu's plight, the young man was undergoing his third consecutive day of torture. The Americans had yet again protested vigorously, but Tai Li had brushed them brusquely aside. The Generalissimo himself had authorised the interrogation. If nice young boys like Wu Canping were going to start dabbling in politics, they had to learn what the rules were.

Nurse Cartwright was waiting for Murphy. She took one look at his tired, drawn face and knew immediately that the news was bad. Murphy flung himself down on the narrow iron bed at one end of the long ward, lit a cigarette (against the rules but for once she indulged him) and stared blankly at the ceiling.

"It's hopeless," he said at last. "Tai Li won't budge. The worst thing about it", he sighed, "is that up there at SACO Headquarters, quite a few people – Miles included – have doubts about Wu's innocence. Apparently he was seen leaving the compound the evening before the raid and returning, furtively, late that same night."

"What do you think?"

"I just don't believe it. Wu works for us. No matter what

he may or may not think about the Communists, American lives were at risk. Hurley almost got killed."

"Did you see Wu?"

Murphy shook his head. "We're not even sure he's still alive."

He puffed at his cigarette dejectedly for several minutes. She sat beside the bed and, tentatively, touched his arm. Though, as a nurse, she had bathed his body and cared for most of his essential needs, it was a suddenly intimate gesture.

"Perhaps I can help." She spoke reluctantly. Deep down she distrusted Wu, believing that Murphy had allowed too close a relationship to be established between them. Yet she recognised, too, how deeply Murphy cared about Wu's safety. And if Murphy cared, then she cared too.

He turned his head to look at her. How on earth could she be of assistance?

"I don't see . . ." he began.

"Madame Chiang is visiting the hospital tomorrow morning," she interrupted him. "She's President of the Chinese Red Cross. I might be able to talk to her."

"How the hell are you going to do that?" scoffed Murphy. "You can't just barge up to her. You need an invitation."

"I *have* an invitation." Mary Cartwright pointed to the W-shaped brooch pinned to the lapel of her uniform.

Madame Chiang was intrigued. "So you were at Wellesley, too? You must come and visit me one day and tell me about the old place. It's been quite a few years since I was last there." She smiled kindly at the young American nurse wearing the white starched uniform with the famous Wellesley 'pin' displayed next to the emblem of the Chinese Red Cross.

In spite of the confident manner she had adopted when talking to Oliver Murphy the previous evening, Mary Cartwright was nervous. She knew she did not have much time. When Madame Chiang visited hospitals and infirmaries in Chungking, these were usually whirlwind tours. Now, after the brief interruption, China's first lady was preparing to resume her rapid progress between the long rows of beds in the main ward, with a squad of doctors, matrons and nursing staff in dutiful attendance.

At the far end of the room Mary could see the American, Colonel Murphy, propped up on a pillow with his arm in a sling. He looked pale and exhausted, the exertions of the previous day having clearly taken their toll. The sight of him inspired Mary to seize her moment.

"Before you go, Ma'am, may I ask you one small favour?"

Madame Chiang's smile hardened microscopically. What kind of favour, she wondered, could this fresh-faced young woman be seeking?

"How could I refuse, my dear? We old Wellesleyans must stick together . . ."

Charlie Soong was intrigued by his aunt's request. If half of what he had heard was true, there was no earthly reason why she should want to save Wu Canping from a slow lingering death. Soong was well aware that the usual Chiang approach in such cases was "guilty even when proved innocent."

Later, when he heard about the little incident in the men's ward of Chungking hospital, he had chuckled out loud at the thought of smart, savvy Auntie Mayling being outmanoeuvred.

"Preposterous! You can have him when I've finished with him, not before," Tai Li fumed.

"He's not yours any longer. I want to see him – now!" Enjoying his moment (it was not every day he could put one over on Tai Li) Soong produced the letter of release signed by Madame Chiang and countersigned by Chiang himself.

Tai Li snatched the document from Soong's outstretched hand and examined it minutely. How in heaven's name, he wondered, had she got Chiang to put his name to that piece of paper?

He gave Charlie Soong one long vicious stare. "Take him then," he spat out at last. "If he's not dead already, he soon will be."

Wu had been on the Aeroplane for two full days and nights. During that time he had received two protracted beatings by Tai Li in person and a third administered by one of Tai Li's underlings. His face was covered with dried blood which had flowed from his mouth, nose and ears. Several of his teeth were missing and his right shoulder had been dislocated.

Yet, amazingly, Wu was still conscious when Soong entered his cell. Assuming at first that Soong was just another torturer in the long line of torturers, he had protested in a voice that was little more than the faintest croak: "I have nothing to say. I have nothing to say."

"I'd like to take another trip down the Yangtze, Sir."

"Good God, man, you're a glutton for punishment!" Miles had exclaimed. What an odd fish Murphy was, he thought. As far as he was concerned, his deputy's recall to Washington had come as a welcome relief.

What Murphy did not tell Miles was that he had invited Nurse Cartwright to join him. When he had been certain of her acceptance (she too had to apply for leave), he organised some fast river transport, several Chinese porters and ample supplies of food and drink. Four days after leaving Chungking, they were picnicking high up on the Daning River, the Yangtze tributary which Murphy had glimpsed a few weeks earlier as the junks passed Wuchan.

For Murphy it was a dream come true. The trip up through the ravines and grottoes of the Daning had in its way been every bit as spectacular as the journey down through the Three Gorges of the Yangtze. The Daning gorges were not, of course, of the same size or grandeur, but they possessed an extraordinary delicacy and beauty. To pass through them was to traverse a succession of magic caverns. Water, clear as crystal, flowed in limpid pools. The rocks shimmered green and blue. As they clawed their way up through the rapids, they noted an extraordinary abundance of wildlife. Birds, beasts, flowers – Murphy couldn't begin to name all the species, but he knew enough to realise that they were in a biological paradise.

On the sixth day, still following the river upwards through the mountains, they passed through the last of the gorges and emerged into an almost alpine meadow, full of flowers and long fragrant grasses.

"Let's stop here", said Mary, "and have a picnic."

The servants set up the table for them, and then tactfully retreated out of sight. Murphy opened a bottle of claret which he had saved for some special occasion. Nurse Cartwright took one sip, then another, then lay back with her hands behind her head. Through half-closed eyes she caught a glimpse of an eagle, circling high above the mountains.

Without moving his arm, Murphy leaned down and kissed her. A long lingering kiss. His first in four years. Hers too.

She surprised him with her response. He thought her reactions might be slow, starched – like her nurse's uniform. She had told him of her Methodist upbringing, her stern father and doting mother and the effective system of chaperones in the small New England town in which she had been brought up. But she clung to him passionately, warm and supple.

When she drew breath, she said, "I can't tell you how often, when you were on the ward, I wanted to do that. But they would have sacked me on the spot!"

She pulled him down onto the rug which they had spread in the shade of the giant fir-tree and they made love as the shadows rippled across the glade. He was not her first lover, nor she his; but both of them knew that this time was not like the others. She unbuttoned his shirt, noting that the wound in his shoulder was now almost completely healed. He fumbled with the hooks on her blouse.

"You need to be Houdini to get these things open!" he complained at the third attempt.

The whiteness of her breasts surprised him. Milk-white, he thought, like the Queen of Sheba. She smiled and leaned her head back. A shaft of sunlight, coming through the branches of the trees, bathed her neck and shoulders in gold.

Later they climbed up the slope behind their picnic site

towards a narrow saddle of land which provided the only break in the encircling mountains.

It took them half an hour to reach the col, but when they finally stood on the windy ridge and looked down upon the other side, their modest exertion proved to be most richly rewarded. For the mountain pass gave out over a deep saucer-shaped valley, an almost perfect circle whose diameter, Murphy estimated, was 15 or even 20 miles. The steeply sloping sides of the saucer were covered with the thick, luxuriant foliage of a pristine bamboo forest.

The clambered down the slope, eager to explore the mysteries of a lost world. As they penetrated the first thickets, Murphy raised a finger to his lips. "Look!" he whispered.

Mary Cartwright followed the direction of his gaze and saw, 30 feet away, an enormous panda sitting on its haunches, quietly munching a mouthful of bamboo. A spray of shoots and leaves was rapidly disappearing down its throat. As soon as it finished one mouthful, the animal leaned back casually to hook its paw round another clump. Mary watched fascinated as the creature, teeth and paws working together, peeled off the tough outer sheaths of the bamboo, leaving only the juicy centre.

They observed the scene for over half an hour. The first giant panda was shortly joined by another and then, to their delight, they watched a young cub, still barely able to walk, emerge from the thicket to be suckled by the animal they had first seen.

It was almost dark by the time they had climbed back out of the hidden valley and over the narrow saddle to descend to the place where they had picnicked. The guides and porters and coolies were bustling forward to welcome them, but there was still time for him to say what he wanted to say.

"Perhaps we'll come back here one day, Mary. Or perhaps our children will."

"Is that a proposal?"

"Of course it is. Will you marry me, Mary?"

She stood on tip-toe to kiss him. "Yes, Colonel," she replied. She had never been surer of anything in her life.

7

He passed the *Washington Post* over to his wife as they sat one sunny morning in May 1950, on the veranda of their newly-acquired home overlooking Rock Creek Park. In the garden below, young Preston Murphy, already two and a half years old, was building complicated structures from a pile of wooden bricks. Still further below, beyond the boundary fence where the trees dipped down sharply to the little river which had lent its name to the whole area, there was a flash of light as the sun caught the body-work of new cars being driven to work.

"So Tai Li finally got his come-uppance," Murphy commented with a short ironic laugh, pouring himself some more coffee. "A taste of his own medicine. He blew up enough planes in his time. I'm only sorry for the other people on board. As a matter of fact, I wouldn't be surprised if Chiang was behind it. Taiwan's a pretty small island and I guess Tai Li was getting too big for his boots."

Mary Murphy read the short piece with interest. "Serves him right," she said when she had finished. She pushed the paper back across the table, and began to clear away the breakfast. Murphy clipped the item and tucked it in his wallet, a small memento of the past.

As he lingered for a few moments at the table, his mind drifted back over the events of the last few years. Just as he had predicted all along, Chiang Kai Shek and the Kuomintang had lost the battle for the mainland. In spite of the logistic support which the United States had given the Nationalists – including the massive use of American planes to airlift Chiang's troops around the country – the Communists had achieved a total victory. The Red Armies had crossed the Yangtze River in April the previous year. Three hundred thousand men, using small boats, floats, rafts and junks had gone over in one night. After the Japanese defeat,

Chiang had returned to Nanking from Chungking, but Nanking fell on 27 April, 1949. The KMT flag was pulled down and the red flag hoisted. Shanghai was captured a month later. Chiang fled to Taiwan aboard a gunboat, taking with him a priceless treasury of China's fine art.

Sitting there that morning over the remains of his breakfast, Murphy remembered how – a few months earlier – he had dropped in at the cinema on M Street on his way back from work to see the newsreels of the foundation of the new Chinese People's Republic. On 1 October, 1949, standing on the terrace of Tien An Men – the Gate of Heavenly Peace – and flanked by the Politburo, the members of the Central Committee and even some ex-Kuomintang personalities (for he had indeed sought to unify the nation), Mao Tse Tung had spoken to the delirious crowd who filled the great square in front of him.

"The Chinese people have stood up ... nobody will insult us again," Mao had told what was probably the largest gathering of humanity ever to take place on earth. "This is only the first step ..."

"Day-dreaming about China, darling?"

"Yes, as a matter of fact." He smiled as he saw that his wife had brought Preston in from the garden to say good-bye to him before he left for work. Murphy held the tousle-headed boy in his arms and kissed him.

"Ni hao!" he said.

"What does that mean?" Mary asked.

"It means 'have a nice day' in Chinese," Murphy laughed.

She walked with him to the car. "Look after yourself," he said. "Don't overdo it." Though she was in the early months of pregnancy, she had a tendency to push herself to the limit.

"I will, darling." There was a soft mist in her eyes as he drove away. He was everything she had ever wanted.

The Senator from Wisconsin had been speaking for over four hours already. His voice had grown hoarse; he was red in the face and perspiring freely. He stood at his desk in the Senate Chamber, with his papers and files spread out in front of him. By now the Chamber was nearly deserted, but that didn't matter. The poison he had spread was already doing its work.

Facing the Senator, sitting in a carved chair on the dais, sat the Vice-President of the United States, Alben Barkley, serving as President of the Senate. As a former Senator, Barkley was horrified by McCarthy's performance that day. He had done his best to call the Senator from Wisconsin to order, to admonish him for abusing the privilege of Congressional immunity, for making charges on the floor of the Senate which he would never dare repeat outside Capitol Hill. In this he had been supported by some of the other Senators. Scott Lucas, for example, had interrupted 61 times in a futile effort to make McCarthy straighten out his mixed-up figures. Brian McMahon had made 34 vain attempts to have McCarthy submit to a testing of his claims against reason and evidence. Other Senators tried too, but it was useless. McCarthy would not explain, he would not amplify, he would not qualify.

"I am discussing a subject tonight which concerns me more than any other subject I have ever discussed before this body. It not only concerns me . . . it disturbs and frightens me. While I cannot take the time to indicate all of the men in the State Department who have been named as members of the Communist Party and members of a spy ring, I have here in my hand" – and here he waved a fistful of papers in the air – "a list of 205 that were known to the Secretary of State as being members of the Communist Party and who nevertheless are still working and shaping the policy of the State Department . . ."

By the time McCarthy had finished that night, the other Senators, terrified of what the reaction in their own constituencies might be if they were known to have opposed the Senator from Wisconsin, had agreed that a special congressional committee should be appointed to investigate whether there were Communists in the State Department or in other organs of government. Even the Democratic Majority Leader, Scott Lucas, had been unable to resist the pressure. Lucas had tried to make the best of a bad job.

"I guarantee that a Committee will be formed at once," he had stated, "and the Senator from Wisconsin will have an opportunity to come before the Committee to tell who these persons are. Before the Committee he will not be able to hide behind numbers. He will have to tell the facts and disclose the names of the persons . . ."

Watching from the gallery of the Senate Chamber, Charlie Soong smiled with quiet satisfaction. Friend would be turned against friend and family against family. In the great Offices of State and in the inner counsels of government, few would be safe from suspicion. The Federal Bureau of Investigation, under the leadership of J. Edgar Hoover, would seize on the opportunity provided by Senator Joseph McCarthy's accusations to increase dramatically its already extensive range of operations. Bugging, surveillance, interception of mail, the hounding (sometimes the hounding to death) of innocent citizens – the seeds of all these activities would be laid in the McCarthy era.

What interested Charlie Soong, of course, was not so much the general debilitating effect of McCarthyism on public life in America (though as a connoisseur of human frailties, the phenomenon was not without interest for him) but rather its specific impact in terms of the US-China relationship. For a large number of the names on McCarthy's famous list were those of Americans who had shown some interest in, and sympathy for, Mao Tse Tung and his cause. Some of the persons named served in the> Office of Far Eastern Affairs of the State Department in Washington. They were career diplomats, loyal to a great tradition and brave enough to write their adverse comments on some of the nonsense they received from Ambassadors like Patrick Hurley. Others on McCarthy's list had actually had field assignments in China. Men like John Carter Vincent, for example, who was a prime target of McCarthy's attack, had spent months in Chungking as First Secretary at the US Embassy there, doing his best to report accurately on the true situation, even if that meant being critical of the Generalissimo and his excesses. Men like Oliver Edward Murphy . . .

After Vice-President Barkley rapped with his gavel in the now virtually empty Chamber to wind up the Senate's business for that evening, Soong waited a few more moments, still lost in thought. He had put on weight since those Chungking days but he was still trim and fit. He had helped to form a private flying club in Westchester County outside New York City, had bought a flashy Cessna two-seater and, whenever he could, kept up his pilot's skills with dazzling displays of aerobatics above Long Island Sound. Once, just for the hell of it, he had done a high-speed mock strafing run down the Hudson River, mentally reliving the splendid days when he and his international team of flyers had chased the Japs up and down the Yangtze.

The trouble was – Charlie Soong couldn't spend half as much time in the air as he would have liked. Though he had only just turned thirty, he had already virtually taken over the running of the burgeoning Soong Empire. True, his father, T. V. Soong, and his wife Laura, had recently settled into a luxurious apartment at 113 Park Avenue in Manhattan, and his uncle, H. H. Kung, lived up there on the Hudson in Riverdale in the Kung Mansion at 4904 Independence Avenue, but neither Teevy nor H. H. were actually involved on a day-to-day basis in the business any longer. And what a business it was! The Bank of China, whose President Charlie Soong was, had branches in most of the major cities of the United States. The New York City branch was rated as one of the largest banks in town and the same was true of the Los Angeles branch. The Soong-Kung petroleum holdings included oil properties across Texas, Oklahoma and Louisiana, and Charlie Soong, personally, was a major share-holder. The links with the Henry Luce Empire, based on the *Time-Life* publications, which had been built up during the war years (even as she grew older, Luce retained his breathless admiration for Madame Chiang) had been expanded and consolidated in the post-war period. But Charlie Soong had looked beyond publishing to see the potential of the new medium, television, and uniquely, sat on the board of both CBS and ABC.

The Soong Empire was rooted in the United States, no doubt about that. Much of the money for the original investments had actually come from the United States with President Roosevelt's massive wartime financing of the Chiang regime at a time when Teevy had been Prime Minister and H. H. Finance Minister! But Charlie Soong knew one thing for sure and that was that the boundaries of the Soong Empire could in no sense be limited to the United States. They had made major acquisitions in London, Paris and Geneva. More important still, Soong was expanding his activities in Hong Kong. It was clear to Soong that Chiang, in fleeing to Taiwan, had – at least from the business point of view – made the wrong decision. Taiwan could never rival Hong Kong as a world commercial centre. Like his famous grandfather, after whom he had been named, Charlie Soong believed that a truly global financial operation had to straddle both East and West together. As far as the East was concerned, there could be no better centre than Hong Kong.

Of course, Hong Kong was dominated by the British. The island, as well as the territories on the Kowloon side, remained a Crown Colony and the Union Jack still flew from Victoria Peak. But already, Charlie Soong could sense the wind of change in the air. Month by month, year by year, he was building up his operations in Hong Kong. A few weeks ago he had been appointed a Director of Rowlands, the great British trading company whose fortunes had been built up in the previous century on the basis of opium and tea. The first non-British director ever to serve in that capacity, he had already attended his first board meeting in that fabled boardroom above the harbour, where pictures of the early, moustachioed directors of Rowlands were interspersed with paintings or, latterly, photographs of those elegant ships – the China clippers – which had graced the waters of the South China Sea. The day might come, Charlie Soong knew, when it would make sense to move from the United States to Hong Kong, not because the United

States would have ceased to be of interest, but quite simply because Hong Kong might be even more important. Here again it was a matter of long-term planning. One day the British would leave Hong Kong. There would be a vacuum waiting to be filled. Charlie Soong wanted to be in the right place at the right time. Quite apart from the advantages Hong Kong offered in itself, as a springboard for a return to China its location could hardly be bettered . . .

He walked slowly down the marble steps past the guards who were still on duty waiting for the last visitors to leave, and out to his car parked outside the East Wing. Yes, he thought, what with his financial and commercial interests in the United States, Europe and Asia, he had his hands full. And, on top of all that, there was the politics as well. Mayling, Teevy and H. H. might do some of the strategic thinking up there behind closed doors in Riverdale – and Charlie Soong did not underestimate the depth and breadth of their combined political experience – but still the day-to-day running of the China Lobby fell to him. He was the one who set up and financed the American-China Policy Association and the Committee to Defend America and ensured that big names like David Dubinsky of the AFL-CIO served on the Committee of Directors. He was the one who had organised the successful lobby to keep Communist China out of the United Nations. Above all, he had to deal with Congress itself. No less than 23 Senators, including William Knowland, Mike Mansfield, Everett Dirksen, and Jacob Javits, plus 83 Congressmen, could be counted on as supporters and now he had managed to bag Senator McCarthy himself! What a triumph! As he approached the car, Charlie Soong's face creased into a smile. The engine of the Cadillac was already running.

"Take me to the Occidental," Soong instructed the driver. He had booked a private room upstairs. Besides the Senator and Charlie Soong, there would be three journalists present; one from *Time-Life*, one from the Washington *Times-Herald* and one from the Hearst chain. If the campaign which had been announced that evening was to be properly orchestrated, it was essential that the media – or

92

at least those organs likely to be sympathetic – were brought in right from the beginning.

Apart from McCarthy, Soong's guests had already arrived by the time he reached the restaurant. The manager of the Occidental who knew the journalists well had served them drinks. When Congress was in session there was nothing unusual about midnight meetings over a pint of bourbon and a platter of oysters.

"Ah! Charlie, here you are!" Ed Rovere of the Chicago *Tribune* stood up as Soong entered the room. "We were wondering what had happened to you."

Rovere was a large, florid man who had been one of the first to sense the potential, in terms of the battle for circulation, of McCarthy's revelations. If he was present at the Occidental that evening, it was because he was determined that the Chicago *Tribune* should print the names as well as the numbers and he was relying on the Senator to supply them even in advance of the Congressional hearings. Rovere also, as it happened, served as a Director of one of the pro-Taiwan foundations which Soong had set up as a cover for his lobbying activities.

"Good to see you, Ed. Thank you for coming, gentlemen."

As Charlie Soong greeted his guests in the discreet panelled room, it was clear that he was as much at home in this haunt of Washington journalists and politicians, a stone's throw from the White House, as he was in say, a go-down on the waterfront in Kowloon. Indeed, as an Ivy League alumnus (and, incidentally, a major Harvard benefactor) Soong's American credentials were impeccable.

He nodded at the hovering waiter. "Bourbon for me too."

A few minutes later, McCarthy entered the room. "Sorry I'm late." The Senator seemed to be nervous. He ran his hand quickly through his receding hair, loosened his collar and drained his drink at a gulp.

"Bravo, Senator!" Soong patted McCarthy on the back of his wrinkled grey suit. "A great speech. Your constituents will love it. The whole country will love it."

McCarthy relaxed visibly. By the time the oysters arrived he was positively mellow.

"My people have been doing some research on your behalf, Senator," Soong said when the plates had been cleared away. He pushed some papers across the table. "You've got 81 names on your list. You're going to have to name those names before the Congressional Committee. You know and I know, Senator, that you can't make the mud stick without at least a minimum of fact. We've dug out all the circumstantial evidence we can find and a bit more and, let me tell you, there are some real lulus here!"

For the next 40 minutes Soong outlined some of the key elements in the dossier which he had put together.

McCarthy took off his rumpled jacket and hung it on the back of his chair. He loosened his tie, the better to concentrate on what Soong was telling him. There had been a lot of bluff in the speech he had made that evening for the Senate. He had cited 81 cases, but that didn't mean he had anything like a comprehensive dossier on 81 Communist spies or sympathisers. Far from it. In some instances, the only thing McCarthy had against a man was that he had served in the State Department's Office of Far Eastern Affairs or in the US Embassy in Chungking. Charlie Soong gave him some rich red meat to hang on the skeleton.

"How do you know all this?" McCarthy asked, amazed at the quality of Soong's information.

Soong gave an evasive reply, unwilling, even now, to reveal the extent to which Chiang and his Secret Police, under Tai Li, had spied on their American allies. Nor did he tell McCarthy, now or later, the extent to which the material in the files had been doctored to suit Soong's own particular ends.

When they came to the case of Oliver Edward Murphy, McCarthy was frankly incredulous.

"You mean to say this guy was linked with a Communist agent all the time he was in China?"

"The facts speak for themselves," Soong replied quietly. "Murphy brought Wu Canping into SACO in the first place. Already then, or certainly soon after, Wu had been

94

recruited as a Communist agent. We know that Wu met Chou En Lai on at least two occasions. When the Chinese Fourteenth Air Force bombed Yenan, Wu warned the Communists about the raid."

"And Murphy tipped him off?" McCarthy was like a ferret scenting a rabbit in a hole.

"The circumstantial evidence is overwhelming." Soong spoke confidently, knowing that they would believe him because they wanted to believe him.

McCarthy pulled the papers over and studied them. As he read the file, his indignation grew. His normally pale face turned a blotchy purple.

"Goddammit, if this isn't treason, I don't know what is!"

"Can you get this guy Wu to testify?" Rovere asked. "He's the key factor in the case against Murphy, isn't he?"

Charlie Soong chose that moment to play his trump card. He removed a stiff brown envelope from the breast-pocket of his immaculately tailored suit. Inside the envelope was a three-page document. He handed it to the Senator.

"That's a copy of Wu's signed confession. Of course, it's in Chinese, but the Congressional Committee will be able to have it translated officially. He gives names, dates, places – all the details you could ever want. It's quite clear from this that Murphy was far more than a Communist sympathiser. He told Wu categorically that he'd been actively recruited by the Communists even before the war. They were working in tandem."

McCarthy took the document. "Which way up do you read this damn thing?" he asked petulantly, unable to make head or tail of the hieroglyphs. Then he added: "Why did Wu confess anyway?"

Soong smiled, a slow, sad, totally insincere smile. "After the raid against Yenan failed, Tai Li had him arrested. He confessed under interrogation."

"You mean he was tortured?" McCarthy asked sharply. "The American public won't like that!"

"Good heavens, no!" Charlie Soong seemed genuinely shocked. "Look!" He jabbed his forefinger towards the bottom of the first page of the document which Senator

McCarthy still held in his hand. "It states clearly here that the prisoner has made his confession of his own free will and without duress."

As he spoke, Charlie Soong caught Ed Rovere's eye and winked.

McCarthy seemed convinced. He handed the document back to Soong. "Well, that clinches the case against Murphy. What happened to this guy Wu?"

"I don't know," Soong lied. "He may have died in prison; he may have escaped; or he may have been released. My guess is that, if he survived, he'll be making a career for himself as a loyal cadre. They owe him one, after all. He may have betrayed your boys but he certainly saved Mao's bacon."

"It's a humdinger." Beaming with satisfaction, McCarthy took another long swig of his bourbon and jerked his necktie towards half-mast. "We'll make Murphy our prime target. But we'll bide our time. We'll pick the right moment. If we can sew up the case against Murphy up good and proper – and it seems that we can . . ." A sudden thought occurred to him. "What's Murphy doing now, by the way?"

"Hell, Senator, don't you know?" Rovere said. "Murphy is Dean Acheson's right hand man. His full title is Special Assistant to the Secretary of State for Far Eastern Affairs!"

"Good God in Heaven!" McCarthy banged his hand on the table, rattling the now empty oyster shells. "Who appointed Murphy to a key job like that?"

"In the first instance, General Marshall." Rovere had all the facts at his fingertips. "When Marshall went to China to try to get the Nationalists and Communists together instead of fighting a civil war, he called in all the old Chungking hands. And later, when he took over as Secretary of State, he brought Murphy with him. Murphy stayed on under Dean Acheson as a result of Marshall's personal recommendation."

McCarthy groaned. "And this guy's still there advising the Secretary of State on a day-to-day basis. Christ! By the time we're through with the Congressional Committee hearings, the whole country could have been sold down the river!"

The silence which followed the Senator's remark lasted for well over a minute. Up till that moment, there had been an element of unreality in their discussions. They had been shuffling dossiers around, linking names with numbers, and files with names, but even so a certain immediacy had been lacking. But now, with Soong's revelations about Murphy, the whole picture had come into a sharper focus.

"Well?" McCarthy finally repeated his question. "Do we just wait for the Committee hearings before dropping our bombshell?"

Charlie Soong inspected the expensive gold signet ring which he wore on his left hand. He picked up a napkin and carefully polished the surface of the ring. He rearranged the cutlery on the table, then he looked Senator Joseph McCarthy straight in the eyes.

"Waiting for the Congressional hearings is one option, of course, but as you suggest, this could take a long time. And there's no way of being absolutely sure what the result of those hearings will be, however confident we are that we have a cast-iron case." He paused, raised the glass of bourbon to his lips and drained the final half-inch of liquid which it contained. "There could be other ways."

"What do you mean?" McCarthy was slow to grasp the point.

"Let's say we leave Murphy where he is now, act as though we know nothing about him."

"And then?"

"We wait for him to dig a deep pit beneath his own feet and when the moment comes . . ."

"Can the country afford the risk?"

"Senator," Soong rapped on the table with his knuckles for emphasis, "when you nail that guy, you've got to do it good. Murphy's a test-case. Win that one and you'll win 'em all . . . !"

8

The President of the United States had had a good day. Bess, who was often difficult to please, had agreed to his ideas of fixing up Grand View Farm with a fence and farmhouse roof. She had even agreed to spend more time in Washington once the White House had been fully over-hauled. Of course, she had exacted a quid pro quo.

"Harry," she had told him, "I'll come to Washington – once in a while at least – if you promise me you won't stand again. Come January 1953, we're moving back to Independence for good."

Well, he hadn't exactly promised her, he was too canny a man for that, but his reply had satisfied her and, to tell the truth, it had satisfied him too. He sat now in the little Library room behind the parlour in their home at 219 North Delaware Street, Independence, in his favourite wing-backed chair and enjoyed the sense of a decision well taken. He had known Bess since High School – the graduation portrait for the class of 1901 was on top of the piano in the living room – and he knew that what Mrs Truman wanted she usually got, even if that meant his giving up the Presidency of the United States! A smile played on his lips. For a poor farmer's boy, he reckoned he had had a good run anyway.

The house had a curving porch and heavy windows and it was calm as well as cool. Some fool had decided to rename the street outside Truman Road – couldn't they realise that some folks liked to be left in peace? – but on the whole it was a quiet thoroughfare. The sound of the traffic was more soothing than disturbing. Still smiling, the President closed his eyes and allowed his head to drop, while the book about James Madison which he had been reading lay still open in his lap.

President Truman had been asleep for about ten minutes

when, soon after 10 p.m., the telephone woke him. He frowned in annoyance. The book fell to the floor and he gave it a short irritable kick which sent it spinning across the polished floor of the parlour.

"Mr President," Truman immediately recognised the gravelly tones of his Secretary of State, Dean Acheson, "I have very serious news. The North Koreans have invaded the South."

The President swore under his breath. It was Saturday evening, and he had been hoping to spend a quiet Sunday with his wife and daughter before returning to the White House at the beginning of the following week. Bess would be furious, he thought, when she heard the news!

"Mr President, are you there?"

"Of course I'm here. Get on with it."

Knowing that Truman was a stickler for accuracy, the US Secretary of State gave the President the exact details. "The Duty Officer at State received a cable from our Ambassador in Seoul at 9.26 this evening. Muccio reported that North Korean forces invaded Republic of Korea territory at several points this morning. Action was initiated about 4 a.m. Onjin was blasted by North Korean artillery fire. About 6 a.m., North Korean infantry began crossing the 38th parallel. Kaesong was captured at 9 a.m. and North Korean forces were closing in on Chunchon."

"By God," Truman exploded into the phone. "I'm going to let those North Korean bastards have it!"

"Now, hold on a minute, Mr President!" Dean Acheson, like all good Secretaries of State, knew that sometimes it was as well to give the boss time to simmer down. "There's no need to rush back to Washington. Why don't I ask for an immediate meeting of the United Nations Security Council on the grounds that an act of aggression has been committed against the Republic of Korea? The UN will probably meet all night and by morning anyway we may have more news about events out there in the East. I'll call back before lunch tomorrow."

In the end, Truman decided that Acheson was right. There was no point flying back to Washington at once.

Better to let events take their course for the next few hours with the United Nations at the centre of the picture. Besides, if he delayed his return until, say, 2 p.m. the next day, there would be time for an early lunch with Bess. It was probably this last fact, as much as anything else, which determined the President's decision. This Korean business might keep him in Washington for weeks or months. If he waltzed out without even stopping for lunch, she'd never forgive him!

The Presidential plane, Independence, left the Kansas City Municipal Airport at 2 p.m., on Sunday, 25 June, 1950. It took just a little over three hours to make the trip to Washington. During those three hours the President had time to think. In his generation this was not the first occasion when the strong had attacked the weak. He recalled some earlier incidences: Manchuria, Ethiopia, Austria. The Communists were acting in Korea just as Hitler, Mussolini and the Japanese had acted ten, 15 and 20 years earlier. He felt certain that if South Korea was allowed to fall, Communist leaders would be emboldened to override nations closer to the Free World's own shores. What if the Russians intervened? Worse still, what if the Chinese – just across the border – decided to pour their millions into the fight? What would the American public, just recovering from the war, make of a President who embroiled his country in a full-scale conflict with China, the most populous nation on earth?

President Truman sighed and looked out of the window. Far below, he could see the homesteads of West Virginia and the foothills of the Appalachians. Young men who lived on the farms down there might once again be losing their lives in Asia. Only he could make the decision. The buck stopped at the Oval Office. He turned to the aide who sat next to him.

"Go up front", he instructed, "and tell the radio operator to send a message to Acheson. I want the Secretary of State and the top Defense chiefs to come to Blair House for a dinner conference as soon as we land."

100

Three hours later, dinner was served in the dining-room of Blair House to a party which included, besides President Truman himself, the Secretary of State, Dean Acheson, and Secretary of Defense, Louis A. Johnson, as well as the Joint Chiefs of Staff.

As the man with primary responsibility for foreign policy, Dean Acheson had brought with him his own personal delegation consisting of Under-Secretary Webb, Assistant Secretaries Dean Rusk and John Hickerson, and Ambassador at Large, Philip Jessup. He had also, brought with him his Special Assistant for Far Eastern Affairs, Oliver E. Murphy.

To his surprise Murphy found that he had been seated immediately next to Acheson in the middle of the long rectangular table where Robert E. Lee himself had once dined before accepting command of the Virginia troops following the outbreak of the Civil War. Thinking there must be some mistake (were there other Murphys among all the top brass present?) he began to sidle away down to one end of the table.

"Hold it, Murphy!" President Truman wagged an admonishing finger at him. "You're paid to advise the Secretary and that's what you're going to do!"

"Right, Sir!" Murphy snapped to attention. Officially, he was no longer a soldier but the President was still the Commander-in-Chief. Amazed that Truman should remember his name – he had met the President three or four times at most and always in Acheson's company – he took his seat as instructed. He wasn't exactly sure what he was expected to contribute that evening. There were others present far better qualified than he to offer the President advice, if that was what was required.

After dinner had been cleared and the Blair House staff had withdrawn, they got down to business in earnest. The President opened the proceedings by calling upon the Secretary of State to present the recommendations which the State and Defense Departments had hurriedly prepared.

"Thank you, Mr President," Acheson opened in sombre tones.

"First, General MacArthur, our Far East Commander, should evacuate all Americans from Korea.

"Second, MacArthur should be instructed to get ammunition and supplies to the Korean Army by airdrop and otherwise.

"Third, the Seventh Fleet should be ordered into the Formosa Straits to prevent the conflict from spreading to that area."

"Wait," the President interrupted. He turned to the Chief of Naval Operations. "Where is the Seventh Fleet at the moment, Admiral Sherman?"

"Nearing the Philippines, sir, two days out of Japan." Sherman had had a signal that evening from the Fleet Commander so he was sure of his facts.

"How long will it take to bring these ships to the Formosa Straits?"

"One and a half to two days."

The President snorted his displeasure. "Too long, damn it!"

As the President spoke, an aide entered the room with a message for the Army Chief, General Collins.

"With your permission, Mr President, I have here the latest message from General MacArthur."

Collins quickly read out the text which had been received some 40 minutes earlier in the Defense Department, decoded and rushed over by despatch rider to the meeting in Blair House:

ENEMY TANKS ENTERING SUBURBS OF SEOUL. GOVERNMENT TRANSFERRED TO SOUTH BUT SITUATION RAPIDLY DETERIORATING. SOUTH KOREAN UNITS UNABLE TO RESIST DETERMINED NORTHERN OFFENSIVE. CONTRIBUTORY FACTOR EXCLUSIVE ENEMY POSSESSION OF TANKS AND FIGHTER PLANES.

"So time is running out?" Truman questioned Collins. "MacArthur is telling us that the South Koreans are being overrun. Is that the case? What's more, it could be several days before we can send ground troops, yes?"

General Collins nodded glumly. "That's about the measure of it."

For the next 40 minutes the meeting, under the President's guidance, reviewed the situation in Korea and the options open to the United States or the United Nations, in the event the world body decided to intervene.

"We've had offers of assistance from Australia, Canada, New Zealand and the Netherlands," Acheson reported.

"And how close are *their* land forces to the scene of the fighting?" The President was clearly sceptical.

The Secretary of State was somewhat miffed by the President's reaction. He and his staff had worked hard most of the day lining up support. And he knew that in the long run, if there was to be any multinational effort in Korea under the United Nations flag to repel aggression, countries like Australia and Canada would have a crucial role to play. But he swallowed his annoyance.

"The Taiwan regime is offering assistance as well, Mr President. Chiang Kai Shek has instructed his Ambassador to tell us he's willing to send ground forces numbering 33,000 men to Korea!"

"Heck! Taiwan's right next door to Korea. Why don't we say yes to the Generalissimo's offer?"

President Truman caught Murphy's eye. "Mr Murphy? You have something to say? What's your view of the Generalissimo? Can he deliver?"

As the President spoke, Murphy had a sudden sense of foreboding. He was the only man present in that room who had seen Chiang at close quarters. The idea of encouraging Chiang, yet again, in his nefarious ambitions produced in him an almost physical revulsion.

"There's no doubt Chiang Kai Shek has the men," Murphy began. "And he has the weapons too. We supplied him with most of them!" In spite of the solemn nature of the occasion, there was a faint ripple of laughter around the table.

"It's the reaction of the Communist Chinese which worries me," Murphy continued quickly. "If we accept the Generalissimo's offer and we let the Nationalist troops enter Korea, that in my judgement is the one thing which will almost certainly guarantee that the Communist Chinese will enter the war in support of North Korea."

Murphy paused. "The latest estimates of the Central Intelligence Agency indicate that there may be as many as 200,000 Chinese Communist troops in Manchuria, and that's just the tip of the iceberg."

"And if we don't accept Chiang's offer?"

"My firm belief is that if you keep the Generalissimo out of this, you will keep Mao out of it as well." As he spoke, Murphy uttered a fervent but silent prayer that history would prove him right.

President Harry S. Truman removed his spectacles and thoughtfully polished them on his table napkin. Then he put them back on his nose and peered closely at Murphy.

"Mr Murphy, I hope to doggone goodness you know what you're talking about. We're going to say 'nuts' to Chiang. We'll find some other way . . ."

9

Less than three months later President Truman sat at his desk in his office early one morning, reflecting – with hindsight – on the wisdom of the decision which had been taken at the Blair House meeting.

For the first time in weeks, he felt relaxed, cheerful, optimistic. A few days earlier, on 15 September, 1950, in a daring amphibious landing, MacArthur had established a bridgehead at Inchon. The First Marine Division and the Army's Seventh Infantry Division had gone ashore and had moved towards Seoul to free the Korean capital. Resistance had been fanatical and the President grieved for the American lives which had been lost. But the operation had been successful. By 28 September the liberation of the city was complete. The next day Syngman Rhee had moved his government back.

General MacArthur, of course, was still gung-ho for action, constantly demanding more troops, more ammunition and urging the Joint Chiefs of Staff and the President himself to authorise operations not merely North of the 38th parallel, but up to and even beyond the Yalu River which formed the boundary with Chinese Manchuria.

It was absurd but he'd still not yet met MacArthur! The general had refused to come home for consultations, pleading that his job kept him in the field. Yet it was clear that more and more the man was out of touch with political realities back home. In the first place, he couldn't seem to grasp that it was a United Nations Force, not a United States Force that he commanded. Even if he had wanted to make the kind of decisions that MacArthur pressed him to make, the President could not have made those decisions without consulting allied countries – the British, the Australians, the Canadians, the Turks. And the President, in any case, wasn't sure that it was right to do what MacArthur wanted. MacArthur was confident that neither the Soviet Union nor Communist China would intervene in the Korean war. But how in hell could he be so sure?

Suddenly, Truman made a decision. War was too important to be left to the Generals. If Mohammed would not go to the mountain, the mountain would go to Mohammed!

He picked up his pen and began to write out in longhand the text of a message to be conveyed to General Douglas MacArthur.

"I know that I speak for the entire American people," he wrote, "when I send you my warmest congratulations on the victory which has been achieved under your leadership in Korea." He paused, lifting his head from the paper and staring out of the window at the White House gardens now bathed in early morning sunlight. It was important to hit the right note. Keep the sting for the tail, he told himself. "Few operations in military history," he continued, "can match either the delaying action where you traded space for time in which to build up your forces, or the brilliant manoeuvre which has now resulted in the liberation of Seoul. I am particularly impressed by the splendid cooperation of our Army, Navy and Air Force. . . ."

The President continued in the same vein for a few more lines before informing the General, almost as an afterthought, that he intended to fly to the Pacific within the next ten days to meet the US Commander and to exchange thoughts about the future conduct of the war.

"I realise," the President concluded, "that you will not wish to be too far from our Forces in Korea during these perilous days, but I'm sure that we can agree on a mutually convenient location."

Truman smiled as he concluded his letter. Surely, no one could accuse him of being high-handed! He had shown respect for MacArthur's feelings; at the same time there had been a hint of steel. He had no wish to go down in history as the President who started World War III. He knew that if he left MacArthur now to his own devices, if he allowed him to act as an independent potentate sur-

106

rounded by his own bunch of yes-men, that was the direction in which they might very well be headed.

He stood up from his desk and walked briskly across the room to the old upright piano which he had brought up from Independence, Missouri, and installed in the White House a year or two earlier. He chuckled as he sat down remembering that famous National Press Club dinner – he had still been Vice-President – when Lauren Bacall had climbed on top of the piano as he strummed out a tune and the picture had made the front page of virtually every newspaper in the nation. Bess had scolded him for that, no kidding!

He was still strumming away, when his secretary poked her head round the door.

"Good morning, Rose," he shouted without interrupting his playing. "You'll find a letter for old Brass Hat MacArthur on the desk. Let's get it out straightaway."

Rose Conway, a motherly woman who had been with Truman since his Senate days, smiled benevolently. She always liked to see the President in a good mood.

It was still dark when Truman, who had managed to snatch a few hours' sleep, went forward and sat in the second pilot's seat.

"The Hawaiian Islands will be coming up shortly, Sir," the pilot informed him. As the Independence droned on through the night, the lights of the ships stationed below could be seen at regular intervals. When the President commented on this fact, the pilot explained.

"Destroyers. They've been stationed there ready to pick us up if we go down in the drink."

"Well I'll be damned!" Truman exclaimed, not for the first time, marvelling at the efforts which went into each Presidential journey.

As morning broke they had a breath-taking view of the entire chain of Hawaiian Islands, rising slowly out of the western sky, tiny little dark points in a vastness of blue that Truman would not have believed if he had not seen it himself. Then slowly the specks of land took shape and became distinct islands. At last the plane passed Diamond Head, circled low over Pearl Harbor and came in for a landing at Hickam Air Force Base.

If the President had slept soundly on the long flight from California to Hawaii, the same was by no means true of Oliver Murphy, travelling on the same plane. Of course, Murphy's physical circumstances were not as comfortable as those of the President. The forward section of the plane had been curtained off for the nation's Chief Executive; a proper bed had been installed; the Air Force had laid on two pretty stewardesses to keep the President in good humour over the long trip. Murphy and other members of the Presidential party were not so fortunate. Even General Omar Bradley, whom the President had insisted on bringing along, had been relegated to a cramped seat behind the wing while the State Department contingent, including Murphy himself, were even further back.

But physical discomfort was not the only reason for Murphy's wakefulness. As he gazed out hour after hour into the blackness of the night, Murphy sensed that this mission could be one of his life's climactic moments. Though State had sent along both Ambassador Philip Jessup and Dean Rusk, Acheson had made it clear to Murphy before he left on the mission that, as the Secretary of State's Special Assistant for Far Eastern Affairs, he would be chiefly responsible for the foreign policy input.

"I wish to God I could have come with you myself," Acheson had told him, "but I've got the Senate hearings coming up and, I can tell you, McCarthy is out for blood."

The Secretary of State had been unable to conceal the bitterness in his voice. Though the President had given him as much backing as any man could wish for, the constant sniping had begun to take its toll.

It was odd, Murphy thought, still staring into space, that the McCarthy witch-hunt seemed to have by-passed him completely. There hadn't been the faintest suggestion that *his* name featured on that famous list. Yet he had been in Chungking along with the rest of them. It was almost as though McCarthy was biding his time, waiting for the right moment to pounce. He shivered . . .

The President and his party spent the day in Hawaii. Admiral Radford, the Commander of the Pacific fleet, escorted Truman on a boat trip around Pearl Harbor Naval Base, pointing out various relics and reminders of that tragic day in 1941 when the surprise Japanese air-attack brought America into the war. In the afternoon, the President visited the hospital and talked to some of the wounded who had been brought back from Korea.

The Independence finally left Hickam field a few minutes after midnight. The President once again managed to get a few hours' uninterrupted sleep and was up before dawn to breakfast with his bleary-eyed staff. At 6.30 a.m., just as the sun was rising, the plane rolled to a halt on Wake Island landing field. By crossing the international date line, they had gained a day. In Hawaii it would have been Saturday. Here on Wake Island it was Sunday, October 15th.

General MacArthur was waiting at the ramp as the President came down the steps of the plane. The general's shirt was unbuttoned, and he was wearing a cap which had evidently seen a good deal of use. The two men greeted each other cordially, though Murphy – a few paces behind – could detect a certain wariness in the encounter. For half a decade, MacArthur had played the role of Satrap, of supreme potentate, in his Far Eastern dominions; he must have resented Truman's sudden intrusion. By the same token, for the last two years at least, the President had found MacArthur's independent stance, his wilful obstinacy, increasingly difficult to tolerate. Murphy wondered whether there would be blood on the floor by the time the Wake Island meeting was over. If so, whose blood would it be?

After the photographers had finished, the two men got into an old two-door sedan and drove to the office of the Airline Manager where they talked alone for more than an hour.

A little after 7.30 President Truman and General MacArthur re-emerged into the sunlight. Both men seemed pleased by the way the discussions had gone. Together they walked over to a larger building where the President's entourage was assembled.

"Hold it a moment!" The President held up a hand. "I want to be sure that all these gentlemen understand precisely what it is that you're saying, General. You're telling us that you're now ready to pursue an offensive, to drive the North Korean troops back across the 38th parallel and the Chinese are not going to intervene?"

"I'm saying more than that, Mr President." MacArthur rasped out the words. "I'm saying that we can drive on North all the way to the Yalu River and reunify Korea under a free democratic regime and the Chinese won't lift a goddamn finger!"

President Truman turned to General Bradley. "Is that your assessment too, General Bradley?"

There was no mistaking the light of battle in Bradley's eyes. Patton, MacArthur, Bradley, Eisenhower – these had been the Titans of the Second World War and some of the old war-horses were still in harness. They seldom met together except at ceremonial parades on Veterans Day or, as most recently, at Truman's Inauguration as President in his own right; but – trusty steeds that they were – they knew when to pull together. Bradley had even heard it whispered that Eisenhower had political ambitions himself. Well, if that was the case, Ike knew where he could turn for support!

"General MacArthur's right, Mr President," he said flatly. "The Chinese will stay out of this one."

The President turned back to MacArthur, "What about the Russians?"

If General MacArthur was sure about Chinese intentions, he was doubly sure about the Russians. "There is no way, gentlemen, for the Russians to bring in any sizeable number of ground troops before the onset of winter." When no one appeared to dissent from this assessment, he continued, "That leaves the possibility of combined Chinese-Russian intervention, with Russian planes – after all, they have a few planes – supporting Chinese ground units. No danger

110

here, I submit. It just wouldn't work with Chinese Communist ground and Russian air."

MacArthur stepped back from the table, waiting for comments.

"What does State think?" the President asked. "Ambassador Harriman? Ambassador Jessup? Mr Rusk, Mr Murphy?"

Harriman, with his recent first-hand experience of Moscow, felt himself to be well qualified to speak about Soviet intentions. "They may use the Chinese as surrogates," he said. "They won't get involved themselves. They're more interested at the moment in the situation in eastern Europe and in Iran."

"Surrogates, eh?" The President smiled sardonically. It was obviously not the kind of word they used down on the farm in Missouri. He turned to Murphy. "You know China better than anyone here, Murphy. How do you read the tea-leaves?"

They were all looking at him now, he knew. In one small hut on a tiny Pacific island the cream of the nation's politicians, soldiers and diplomats had been assembled and were now waiting for his verdict.

"Mr President, gentlemen," he began slowly, weighing his words. "I'd love to give you a snap answer. You flatter me by saying that I know China better than anyone else here. That may be true, but it doesn't add up to very much. The fact is, Sir," and here he turned directly to the President, "for the last five years the United States has turned its back on China. We have built up walls between our two nations, instead of tearing them down. We have today no channels of communication. To put it bluntly, we don't know what they think. We don't even know *how* they think."

"Spit it out, man." The President was impatient with the preamble.

"I'm suggesting, Sir," Murphy quickened the pace of this intervention, "that now is the time to open up a dialogue with the Chinese Communists. To tell you the truth, Mr President, I believe we should have done it when first the

Communists took over. We should have had our man up there on the platform beside Mao, in Tien An Men square, the day they proclaimed the Chinese People's Republic."

General MacArthur banged his fist on the table. "Nonsense!" he barked. "It's worse than nonsense; it's treasonable. That guy's an adviser to the Secretary of State and you let him say that kind of thing!"

President Truman turned icily to MacArthur. "Steady now, General," he admonished. "You may do things differently out here – but in Washington we like to talk things through."

The President turned to his State Department team with a wide grin on his face. "Some unorthodox diplomacy, gentlemen? What do you say to that? Can we make contact with Peking without offending the Generalissimo?"

Before Harriman or his State Department colleagues had time to reply, Murphy interjected. "The way I see it, Chiang would never know. I'm not just talking about an unofficial communication with the Chinese. I'm talking about a *secret* communication. And we should move quickly, too, since the General" – Murphy nodded coldly in MacArthur's direction – "wants to get on with his offensive before winter sets in."

"And how exactly would you set up that kind of contact?"

"With respect, Sir," Murphy replied, "I would prefer to present my ideas to you in a more restricted framework."

There was a sharp intake of breath in the room. That's done it then, Murphy thought. He'd offended each and every one of them, and some of them were already gunning for him anyway!

But the President took his point. "The stenographer is to leave the room," he instructed. "No part of this discussion is to be recorded."

He paused; "On second thoughts, let's call it a day. I think I'll take a stroll on the beach. Would you like to come along with me, Mr Murphy?"

10

Old Vinegar Joe Stillwell, he remembered, used to talk about the place back in their Chungking days and, of course, he had seen photographs of the spectacular harbour with its splendid colonial architecture set against the backdrop of mountains. Even so, the sight of Victoria Peak catching the first rays of the sun as the US destroyer entered the narrow channel of water which separated Victoria Island from Kowloon filled Murphy with a sense of elation. Hong Kong might not be China, but it was pretty damned close! If you stood on the quayside in Kowloon, the border was a mere 20 miles away. Most of the refugees who had flooded into the city still had families on the mainland. The influence of the mainland – in food and dress, in the habits of day-to-day life – was all-pervasive. It was over five years since Murphy had been exposed to the sights and smells of a Chinese city. He recognised now, as he stood at the rail of the destroyer, watching the sampans laden with produce for sale cluster round the ship, what a profound impact his time in the Far East had had on him. He felt today almost as though he were coming home.

As he waited to disembark, he recalled that scene on the beach with the President. There had been something almost biblical about it, Murphy reflected. The long empty expanse of sand, fringed with palm trees. The roar of the surf. Two lonely figures walking together by the water's edge.

"Do you think you can handle it?" Truman had asked.

"I would like to have a go, Sir," he had replied quietly. And now here he was a few days later, taking the first step on the long road back.

He went ashore in the launch with half-a-dozen of the ship's officers. To all appearances, he was just one of the many American servicemen visiting this bustling entrepôt city as a break from the rigours of service elsewhere in the

Pacific. But while the others headed off into Tsimshatsui with its myriad shops and stalls, as well as other less salubrious attractions, Murphy waited by the quayside. A minute or two passed and he began to feel conspicuous. Half-a-dozen small Chinese boys gathered to stare at the tall American. Some of them held out their hands for money. Others, belying the innocence of their age, shouted rude enticements. "Fuckee, fuckee," they called. "You want my sister?"

He reached with his hand into his pocket, looking for some small coins to keep the crowd at bay.

"Ignore them, old boy. It's much the best way."

He turned round to see a middle-aged man, wearing a club blazer and smoking a pipe. He was carrying in his hand, as pre-arranged, a copy of the *South China Morning Post*.

"Sorry," the man spoke with the languid, affected tones which Murphy associated with the British. "I got held up on the way down. It's race day."

Murphy looked at him with a degree of scepticism. Bernard Crashaw had been Head of MI5's Hong Kong Station for the last three years. Ostensibly, he was a journalist working as the Far East correspondent of the London *Times*. In reality, his journalistic cover provided him with the excuse and opportunity to probe into aspects of the Colony's life which were largely inaccessible to the normal diplomat or official. It also served to justify, or at least camouflage, the somewhat eccentric *persona* which Crashaw projected. It was this *persona*, manifested by the striped blazer, the bow tie, the large smelly pipe and the thinning sandy hair parted precisely in the middle, which now added to Murphy's sense of unease. He knew the British could be engagingly different but in his experience, eccentricity was often a disguise for incompetence.

"I hope you placed your bets in time," he said coolly.

Crashaw bared his teeth at the crowd of small boys and gave a snarl like a Siberian tiger. As they scattered, half-amused, half-frightened, he took Murphy by the elbow and steered him firmly in the direction of the Peninsula Hotel.

"You'll be needing some refreshment, I'm sure. I don't suppose the US Navy lets you drink on board." Crashaw shook his head sadly, as though unable to understand how any fighting force could function without alcohol. "Still," he added, brightening, "plenty of time to make up for it now."

Though the days of its imperial splendour were over (the Japanese had seen to that), the Peninsula Hotel still managed to retain a certain solid grandeur associated with the fact that it was the terminus, in the most literal sense, of the Orient Express. Passengers arriving there from Europe stayed, sometimes for weeks, while suitable accommodation was found on the island opposite. And for those who had come in from the farther-flung points of the Colony, from Stanley or Repulse, for example, or from the New Territory which stretched beyond Kowloon towards that lowering monolithic giant, the People's Republic of China, the Peninsula Hotel was a convenient place to spend a day or two before finally embarking, late in the evening, on the train which would carry them back to the old country. Tea, and often something a good deal stronger, would be taken in the panelled rooms overlooking the harbour. Fond farewells would be said, an intrusive tear wiped away from cheeks already moist with the sub-tropical heat.

The restaurant was, for obvious reasons, called The Traveller. A table for two had been reserved in a secluded alcove. The maître d'hôtel, who clearly knew Crashaw well, welcomed him with an effusive display of interest.

"A late breakfast, Mr Crashaw? A drink? Or perhaps an early lunch?" The man bobbed and smiled, his eyes creasing at the corners.

"Just a drink, thank you, Foo. The usual for me. Whisky?" he asked Murphy.

"A beer will do me fine," Murphy said. Crashaw, he suspected, started drinking early in the day. The Colony was probably full of old soaks.

Crashaw gulped down half a tumbler of whisky in one go. "You'll be going in Wednesday night, around midnight.

Everything's organised. How you're coming out, though, God only knows!"

He took out a pen and sketched a rough silhouette of the coastline on a paper napkin. "Hong Kong and Macao straddle the mouth of the Pearl River. As the crow flies, the Chinese border is not much more than 20 miles away from where we sit. The train runs up through the New Territory to Lo Wu, but that's as far as you'd get if you tried that method of transport. The Shanchun River forms the boundary between the New Territory and the so-called People's Republic," – Crashaw clearly disliked the term – "and even for the Chinese themselves it's pretty impenetrable. The border has been closed ever since the new regime took over and so far there isn't a chink in the bamboo curtain. Not there, anyway."

"How do the refugees get here?"

"Mostly by boat down the coast. A lot of them, of course, are South Cantonese; people the Communists want to get rid of so they don't make too much trouble. The Chinese Communist Navy could sink those junk-loads of refugees any time they wanted to, but they usually let them go. On the other hand, return traffic is virtually nil; even the fishing vessels take good care to keep out of Chinese waters."

Murphy was obliged to concede that Crashaw, for all his exaggerated mannerisms, clearly knew his job.

"What *are* the options, then?" he asked.

Crashaw took his pipe out of his mouth and smiled benignly. There was a large gap between his two front teeth.

"The Pearl River to Canton. There's a good deal of traffic on the lower reaches of the river; yours will be one junk among many. The Chinese don't really bother to interfere with shipping until you get to The Bogue, which is only three and a half miles wide at its greatest point."

"What's The Bogue?"

"The Gateway to Canton. Nowadays the Chinese know it as Hu Men, or Tiger Gate. You're about 15 miles from the city of Canton itself at that point."

"How do we get through?"

"Our friends over here have friends over there."

Murphy wasn't exactly sure what Crashaw meant when he referred to 'friends'. In general terms, he knew that British Intelligence had, during the war, established some close links with the Chinese Secret Service run by Chiang Kai Shek and his henchman, Tai Li. He also knew that some of those contacts had been maintained in the post-war period. Tai Li's power had been founded on the Triads – the Red Gang, the Green Gang, the Black Gang – and even though Tai Li himself had met an unlamented end, the Triads had continued to prosper both in Taiwan – where the Generalissimo used them as effective tools of oppression – and in Hong Kong, where the scope for chicanery of every kind was, if anything, even greater. Murphy also understood that the Triads in some undefined manner still managed to operate in mainland China itself – particularly in areas such as the Province of Canton, which were relatively close to their power base in Hong Kong.

Had the British used such unorthodox channels to send to Peking the message that the Americans wanted to talk, or at least to talk about talks, and that Oliver Edward Murphy, engineer-turned-diplomat was on his way like the first swallow of spring?

"Don't you think . . . ?" he began.

Crashaw seemed to sense the direction of Murphy's thoughts. "Don't worry, old boy! You won't have your throat cut. Not by our side at least!"

He was about to order another round of drinks when he looked at his watch and thought better of it. "Good heavens! This won't do! I'm playing cricket at eleven, and I've got to change first."

"It's not going to last, is it?" Murphy had commented as they drove back down the hill to the cricket ground.

"What's not going to last?" Crashaw still had his pipe firmly clenched between his teeth, but he was now clad in white flannel trousers, held up by an old Free Foresters tie, and yet another striped blazer which looked as though it had seen several decades of use.

117

Murphy gestured at the splendid houses, the well-tended lawns, the magnificent flower-beds. "All this."

"You're probably right, old boy. But we may as well enjoy it while we've got it, don't you think? *Carpe diem*. Here, I'll show you."

Instead of continuing the descent, he swung left, following the contour. "This is a *cul de sac* called Prince Consort Road," Crashaw explained, "where the Big Boys live. You'll find that half the Executive Board of Rowlands, for example, have houses up here."

Murphy had seen ante-bellum mansions in the South which, in their size and elegance, had taken his breath away. But he had to admit that even those splendid structures could not stand comparison with the imposing architecture of Prince Consort Road. And it wasn't just the houses themselves, though these were spectacular enough, each one being set way back from the road and shaded from the noonday heat by trees which must, Murphy supposed, have been imported over a century ago from the nurseries of England's stately homes. It wasn't just the setting, with its unrivalled view over the harbour and the Outer Islands; it wasn't just the fragrance of the air, the cool scents of the mountain tingeing the breezes with balm. It was a combination of all these things – and more.

As they turned back, Murphy noticed that a new house was being built, some distance from the others, on a piece of ground which commanded an even more magnificent view of the scenery than was enjoyed by the rest. This new house, Murphy noted, was clearly modelled on the White House and it appeared to be about almost as large. There were fountains on the lawns in front of each wing and rosebushes were being planted by a squad of Chinese gardeners in a pattern which replicated that of President Truman's own Rose Garden.

"Who does that belong to?" Murphy waved towards the building. "The Maharajah of Bengal?"

Crashaw laughed. "The Maharajah of Bengal couldn't hold a candle to the man who is building that house. Not in money. Not in terms of real political influence. Charlie

118

Soong's going to live there when it's finished. He's the first Chinese to own a house on Prince Consort Road. They didn't want to let him in at first but, once he joined the board of Rowlands, there was no stopping him." Crashaw chuckled. "Charlie's getting his own back for that slight to his dignity by making sure that his place is twice as big as anyone else's! I expect he'll store his treasures there. You name it, Charlie's got it. Qing, Han, T'ang, Ming – apparently just about every dynasty is represented in his collection. As you probably know, Chiang Kai Shek took a lot of the good stuff off with him to Taiwan; but that still left more than enough for Charlie. Porcelain, jade, *lapis lazuli* - there are pieces in Soong's collection which the British Museum, or the New York Metropolitan, would pay a fortune for! I've even heard that he's got crated up somewhere the most unbelievable collection of terracotta figures from the first century. The Communists are hopping mad about all the looting the Nationalists did before they fled!"

As he listened, Murphy couldn't help recalling the daredevil young flyer who had been such a prominent feature of daily life in wartime Chungking. His abundant energies had clearly been put to good use since. Charlie Soong was, it seemed, an all-pervasive force, pushing like an incoming tide into every nook and cranny of Hong Kong life.

"He's a kind of taipan already, isn't he?" he commented.

"Give him a few more years", Crashaw replied, "and he'll be the taipan of all the taipans."

An hour later, Murphy sat in the pavilion watching the Hong Kong press corps, under the surprisingly able captaincy of Bernard Crashaw, take on a competent eleven fielded by the Hong Kong Civil Servants Association. Crashaw, using the captain's privilege, had put himself in third wicket down. He padded up and came to sit with Murphy while waiting for his turn at the crease. He carried a cricket bat in one hand and a striped cap in the other.

"Helps me to keep my eye on the ball." He waved his hand at the crowded Chinese tenements which rose higgledy-piggledy behind the bowler's arm. "Once you start

119

looking at all the washing hung out of those windows, you've had it."

"From privilege to penury." Murphy couldn't help contrasting the teeming Chinese ant-heap with the cool and spacious mansions they had just observed on the Peak.

"Oh, don't worry!" Crashaw sought to reassure him. "Those tenements are not going to stay there long. The Hong Kong authorities are putting up public housing all over the place. All those Chinese families will be relocated."

"And what will happen to the land?"

"Skyscrapers, American-style," Crashaw replied matter-of-factly. "The banks have moved in already – Standard & Chartered, the Shanghai Bank, the Bank of China. Those are just for starters, of course. There are plenty of others waiting in the wings, including American banks like Chase and First Boston. Business will follow the banks. Not just old-established trading companies like Rowlands, but new multinational enterprises based on modern technologies – "

He interrupted himself to applaud a smoothly executed late cut. "Good shot, there!" He turned to Murphy to explain. "A beautiful stroke if you can get the timing right."

Murphy watched the small hard red ball race across the emerald surface to resound with a satisfying thwack against the railings. "And if you don't?"

"You tend to get caught in the slips. Cricket's like life, isn't it?" Crashaw said.

Having received the firmest instructions from London not to let Murphy out of his sight for one minute, Crashaw insisted on taking him out to dinner that evening. The Head of MI5's Hong Kong Station was in a mellow mood. His team had trounced the opposition and he personally had scored a nimble 52.

"You've got every variety of Chinese cooking here," he said as they hailed a rickshaw on the Kowloon side. "But in the end I find that the Cantonese is by far the best. Or would you prefer Szechuan? You must have had some of that in Chungking, surely?"

"Supplies were pretty thin in those days. You were lucky if you got a bowl of rice with your soup."

"Well, you'll do better than that tonight, I can assure you!"

As they descended from the rickshaw, Crashaw stuffed his pipe firmly in his pocket. "Spoils the flavour of the food," he said, licking his lips in anticipation.

They ate in a crowded smoky restaurant on Nathan Road, sandwiched between a brothel and a household goods emporium.

"It's not the swankiest in town," Crashaw told Murphy, "but it's one of the best. You can eat dogs, cats, rats, ants, snakes and snails if you like."

"A little porcupine will do fine!"

While Crashaw ordered, Murphy sat back and observed his surroundings. They were, as far as he could see, the only Europeans in the room. For the most part, the clientele seemed to be made up of prosperous-looking Chinese seated at round tables, six or ten at a time; and all of them firmly engaged in the serious business of eating. A great variety of dishes was piled up in the middle of each table – meat, fish, rice, fruit – and each diner wielded his chopsticks with great dexterity to pluck choice morsels from the bowls of food in the middle before his fellows, equally agile, could anticipate him.

"What happened to all the women in Hong Kong?" asked Murphy. There wasn't one to be seen.

Crashaw, having made a satisfactory selection, pushed the menu aside. "The Revolution stopped short of the border. Here in Hong Kong the Chinese still do things in the old way. A woman's place is in the kitchen, or out in the fields."

"Were you ever married?"

"Good heavens, no! No time for that! What about you?"

"Yes, I'm married," Murphy told him.

"Any kids?"

"One three-year-old. Another on the way."

"Lucky man!" Crashaw raised his glass.

Murphy wasn't sure whether Crashaw was being totally

121

sincere. He wondered, momentarily, whether he had a Chinese mistress tucked away down the road somewhere. Then his thoughts turned to his own home back in Washington. How was Mary managing, he wondered? She must be puzzled, he thought. He had sent a message from Wake Island advising her that his mission had been prolonged but naturally he couldn't go into details.

The two men embarked with evident enjoyment on a typical Cantonese dinner. Watching Murphy pile his plate high, Crashaw warned him: "Take it easy, old boy. There's a lot more to get through before we're finished! Be selective!" Casual tourists might associate Cantonese cuisine with such staple fare as chow mein, chop suey or sweet-and-sour pork but Crashaw had lived in Hong Kong long enough to know that such dishes were carefully avoided by the Chinese themselves. Faced with a choice between roast sucking pig, fried milk, salt-baked chicken, dogmeat casserole, in addition to roast duck, chicken, fish and pork, the true gourmet ended up by trying them all. Not that he would eat the whole of every dish, but he would certainly taste each one and, in between mouthfuls, comment on the taste, texture and fragrance.

"This could have fed a platoon back in the old days!" Murphy finally pushed his bowl aside and laid his chopsticks on the table like a soldier surrendering his arms. "That was gluttony. sheer gluttony. But I loved every moment of it." He paused as he heard the siren. "What the hell's that?"

"Fire alarm!" Crashaw pushed his chair back with alacrity. "Let's get out of here!"

As he spoke, the smoke began to billow from the kitchen of the restaurant.

They fought their way to the door in an undignified scramble as the flames burst through to engulf the room in which they had just been sitting. Murphy had a brief glimpse of an elderly Chinese gentleman, the restaurant's proprietor, who a few minutes earlier had been so solicitously supervising his guests' entertainment, standing silhouetted against the fire and wringing his hands in despair.

Outside in the street, they joined the growing crowd to

122

watch the fire engine arrive with much clatter and noise. The Chinese crew, incongruous in fire-helmets and khaki shorts, climbed down to stand in front of the burning building.

"Look like they've just arrived for dinner, don't they?" Crashaw was clearly amused.

"Why the hell don't they turn the hoses on?"

"They'll negotiate with the owner first. If he wants to save his business, he'll have to pay any price they ask. That's the way it goes. You pay them to turn the water on – and you pay again to get them to turn it off! Look!"

Murphy watched fascinated as the owner emerged from the building, his clothes smouldering, to engage in a fierce discussion with the fire-crew. The man shouted, begged, pleaded and – finally – capitulated, accepting whatever terms were offered. Seconds later, the fire engine's jets arced into the building.

The two men stood watching until the flames began to die down, then they began to walk back along the road towards the ferry. The pavement, as always, was crowded and the shops even at this late hour were still open.

"I imagine a firework fell in the deep-fry oil!" Crashaw side-stepped a one-armed beggar sitting in the middle of the pavement. "It's an old family business, occupying a choice location. I remember Wen Shi from before the war. He has refused to be bought out on more than one occasion. It looks as though they're trying more persuasive tactics."

"Who's they?"

Crashaw shrugged. "The people who count in this place; the men with the money; the Big Boys."

"Like Charlie Soong?"

"You said it, not me," Crashaw replied.

When the US Navy destroyer which had brought him to Hong Kong left harbour early the following morning en route for the Philippines, Murphy notionally still formed part of the ship's complement. In reality, he kept out of sight at Crashaw's house most of the day, reading and writing, and only emerged after nightfall to be driven by Crashaw round the Island to Aberdeen.

The road was rough and pitted and once or twice it degenerated into little more than a track.

"It was pretty bad even before the war," Crashaw commented, "and the Japanese occupation didn't help. But you'll see changes. The Colony's heading for a boom. In a few years, little fishing-villages like Aberdeen are going to become major tourist attractions."

Even at night, Murphy could see what Crashaw meant. Between the village of Aberdeen itself and the small island opposite, was a stretch of water which formed a natural typhoon anchorage. As they bounced down the hill towards the shore, Murphy could see that the whole expanse was alive with twinkling lights.

"Boat people," Crashaw explained. "They've been living on these waters for centuries. Half of them are Tanka, which means the 'Egg people' because they pay their taxes in eggs rather than money; the rest are the Hoklo. They're great boat-builders too. They can make an 80-foot junk from teak logs in less than three months without blueprints. Most of the boat-building is over there on the island, which is where we're going."

They took a sampan across the water, weaving in and out of the streets and alleys of what was in effect a floating city. The aged boatman steered a sure path, guided by the dim lights of the kerosene lamps which flickered on board a thousand small boats.

Crashaw addressed the man in passable Cantonese.

"*Yiu gei noi*? How long will it take?"

The boatman nodded vigorously. "*Yih-sahp fan.*"

"Twenty minutes," Crashaw repeated. "That means anything between ten and 60."

In the event, the old boatman had gauged the distance accurately. Exactly 20 minutes later the sampan pulled alongside a junk whose motor was already quietly churning.

"This is where we say goodbye." Crashaw held out his hand. "Good luck, Murphy."

Murphy climbed on board, lugging his shoulder-bag

behind him. You asked for this, you idiot, he said to himself. It was your idea. No one else's. Foul up now and nobody, but nobody, is going to bail you out. He stuck his head above the gunwale. The deck of the junk appeared to be deserted. "Is there anybody there?" he called, sounding about fifty times more confident than he felt.

11

Ko Fenghua had piracy in his blood, both his father and grandfather having practised the profession in the China Sea with considerable success. A dark swarthy man of great physical strength, Ko himself was not averse to the occasional foray against unsuspecting prey. Recently, the flood of refugees coming out of China as a result of the turmoil created by the Civil War had provided some lucrative pickings. On more than one occasion, open boats had been found drifting and abandoned at the mouth of the Pearl River, halfway between Hong Kong and Macao. Ko Fenghua, hearing tell of such incidents as men gathered along the waterfront at Aberdeen, would shake his head sadly and point out how unwise it was to brave the force of the frequent typhoons in such tiny craft.

More recently, and in particular since the end of the war with Japan, Ko had 'gone straight' in the sense that he had abandoned piracy in favour of more conventional activities, such as the smuggling of contraband into the People's Republic. The truth of the matter was that, even though the Revolution of 1 October, 1949 had theoretically inaugurated an era of spiritual and physical purity, in practice – particularly in relatively cosmopolitan cities like Canton and Shanghai – there were some hold-outs from the past. The market for, say, a good bottle of scotch whisky or Gordon's gin still existed and Ko was ready to ensure that supply and demand stayed roughly in balance; at a price, of course.

That price included the element of danger. Ko, and his crew, ran considerable risks in sailing their junk up the Pearl River into Communist territory. Ko never, of course, penetrated into the narrower waters beyond The Bogue. That would have been altogether too hazardous. His practice was to rendezvous by pre-arrangement with some South Cantonese of like persuasion. Usually they chose the sheltered waters of one of the many small deserted islets which dotted the estuary. There, under cover of darkness, the trans-shipment would take place. The Cantonese fishermen would return with the contraband, while Ko would be amply recompensed either in cash or kind.

It was not a foolproof system. Once, a Communist patrol-boat had intercepted Ko just after he had unloaded his cargo and challenged him with violation of China's territorial sea. Ko had wriggled out of that precarious situation only by pleading navigational error on his part, an argument he strengthened by offering a financial bribe since he was, at that moment, fortunately, flush with cash as a result of the transaction which he had concluded successfully shortly before.

That narrow escape had not deterred Ko from further adventures. In the twelve months or so that had elapsed since the Communists took over to the north (Ko knew they referred to that event as the 'liberation' but it was not a term he could bring himself to use), his clandestine activities had proved so profitable that he was able to place an order with the boat-builders on Aberdeen Island for not one, but three, new junks. Optimistic as always, Ko reckoned that simply increasing the size of his fleet would increase his profits proportionately.

This projected expansion of Ko's business activities did not escape notice. Crashaw, who had inherited Ko when he took over as Head of the Hong Kong Station, had warned him in a friendly way to do nothing conspicuous. As far as the British were concerned, things were perfectly well as they were. From time to time they needed to send supplies into China, the cargo varying according to the needs of the agents who were still left behind. But Crashaw knew that once the trickle turned into a flood, things would not be the same.

Ko heard him out politely enough but it had been clear that he was unimpressed by Crashaw's arguments. To own one junk was already something; to own several was, for a man like Ko, unimaginable wealth.

"We still very careful, not worry!" Ko had beamed reassuringly at Crashaw when the latter, at Ko's invitation, had visited the Aberdeen boatyard one day.

Crashaw realised then and there that Ko's usefulness as a clandestine conduit was rapidly nearing an end. He decided that if the operation was going to be blown anyway, it might as well be well and truly blown.

"We want you to take a man in for us this time," he told him.

Ko had looked alarmed. "My friends, the fishermen, won't agree to that. It would be too dangerous for them."

"It will be a pleasure trip." Crashaw had spoken with conviction. "The red carpet treatment, I'll guarantee that!"

In the end, the assignment had appealed to Ko's sense of humour as well as his love of money (Crashaw promised to up the normal fee considerably). The crafty old pirate liked the idea of transporting, however unusually, a man whom Crashaw had represented as being an honoured guest of the Chinese State. So when he heard Murphy clambering over the gunwale, he emerged smiling from the cabin.

"Welcome, Mr Murphy, sir! Welcome on board my humble vessel. We trust you will have comfortable journey." In another age, Ko's wide gleaming teeth would have been clenched on a cutlass.

The junk set sail almost as soon as Murphy arrived. He was directed to a cabin and invited to remain there, out of sight. Though all the lights had been doused, it was a clear night with a half-moon shining strongly and there was always the chance, Murphy supposed, that the shape, if not the features, of a non-Asiatic might attract interest.

There was a mattress on the floor and, after a while, Murphy stretched himself out. Through the open doorway he could dimly see the figure of Ko at the wheel and he could hear the click and rattle of dice as two of the crew squatted on the bare boards to play a seemingly endless game of chance. After a while, he drifted off to sleep.

"Get up! On your feet." Murphy was shaken awake roughly by two soldiers dressed in the olive-green uniform of the

Chinese People's Liberation Army. Binding his hands behind his back, they thrust him unceremoniously onto the deck where he saw that the crew of the junk were already under guard. Tied up next to the junk was a grey coastguard cutter flying the red flag of Communist China. God in heaven! Murphy thought, what the hell has gone wrong?

Ko Fenghua was being vigorously interrogated, most of the questions being posed by a thuggish PLA captain who looked as though he might have served his apprenticeship in pre-Liberation days as an odd-job man for one of the nastier Triads. He apparently knew Ko well since he punctuated his interrogation with insults of a highly personal nature.

"You scum! You peacock-turd! This time you've gone too far!"

"You're the one who's making the mistake, you fool," Ko shouted back with withering scorn while at the same time ducking his head to avoid a hail of blows from the PLA captain's cane. "This time you've caught the wrong fish."

"Who's this, then?" the PLA man hissed as Murphy emerged blinking into the sunlight. "You know the penalty for smuggling illegal agents into China, Ko, don't you?"

"Now hold it a moment!" Murphy addressed the PLA thug directly "I don't know who you are or what you're doing, but I can tell you Ko's credentials are in order. So are mine."

"I can confirm that!" Wu Canping had timed his intervention nicely. He stood on the gangplank which had been placed between the junk and the cutter and surveyed the scene with an air of mild amusement. "Thank you, Captain. End your interrogation now, please."

As the PLA Captain, scowling, walked away, Wu turned to Murphy.

"Please forgive us, Mr Murphy. My people thought this good opportunity give Ko little lesson. Sometimes Ko is big nuisance to us! Sorry for inconvenience you personally." Wu shouted for Murphy's hands to be untied at once.

Wu motioned to Murphy to follow him back across the

gangplank. Almost immediately the cutter's captain started the engines, turned in a short fast circle and roared away up the river. As he looked back, Murphy could see Ko standing on the deck of his junk waving cheerfully.

"Please be seated." Wu motioned him to a chair. "Some tea? A cigarette?"

While Murphy, still overwhelmed by surprise, watched, Wu unscrewed the cap of a flower-painted thermos to pour some weak green tea into a porcelain cup. Wu's movements had an air of self-confidence and his voice a ring of authority which the PLA soldiers, even their brutish leader, clearly respected. Physically, too, Wu had filled out over the intervening years. His neck and shoulders had thickened; his face was full without being fleshy.

Murphy took a long pull on his cigarette, the first Chinese cigarette he had tasted in years. For a moment, he hardly knew what to say. He had thought of Wu so often, wondering what had become of him.

"Were you were working for the Communists all the time, then? Was Tai Li right, after all?" he finally asked.

A frown flashed across Wu's face as, having finished pouring the tea, he seated himself in a second chair on the other side of the small cabin where he could both talk to Murphy and, if necessary, shout instructions to the crew.

"All that is past history. We have different job to do now." He paused to sip his tea. "Yours is historic mission. Some very important people want to talk to you. They permitted me to tell you this already so that you can be prepared."

"Where are we going, Wu?"

"To Beijing."

Murphy looked out of the window of the cabin at the grey-brown waters of the Pearl River, the placid surface now whipped into a froth by the passage of the boat. Pick your way gingerly, he told himself. Keep the conversation in neutral.

"Remember that time we went down to Yichang through the Three Gorges?"

Wu smiled for the first time. An enigmatic smile, as

130

though that particular journey had been both an end and a beginning.

"Ah, Dragon River! How could I forget?" Wu leaned towards him, puffing urgently on his cigarette. "One day I shall go back home."

It was then that Wu began to talk, telling Murphy about how – after he had recovered from the injuries he had suffered during his torture and imprisonment – he had returned to Sandouping and tracked down his aged mother, though she had died shortly thereafter.

"And after that?" Murphy asked quickly. "What did you do later?"

"The Party helped me. With Revolution, our systems of production were reorganised; that included transportation systems. They put me in charge of all the shipping on the Upper Yangtze from Yichang to Chungking." He smiled. "Remember those shoals we had to avoid as we descended the rapids through Wanxian and Qutang Gorges? Well, we have blasted them away. We deepened channel where it was too shallow. We put in navigation lights on difficult stretches. Traffic on the river – both goods and people – has doubled and trebled in last three or four years. By the way," he asked casually, "you ever finish report?"

"What report?"

Wu smiled. "Surely you not forgotten? You so excited by it. Report on a possible dam-site in Gorges."

Murphy had a distinct feeling that he was being pumped for information. Of course, Wu was interested – particularly if he had professional responsibility for navigation on the Yangtze. And of course the question of the feasibility (or otherwise) of a dam across the Yangtze was of crucial concern to the new regime since the project could play a central part in the modernisation of China. But the truth of the matter was he had only very recently – just before leaving for the Pacific in fact – produced his final (qualified) recommendations. The US Army Corps of Engineers and the Bureau of Reclamation (to whom he had copied the report) would have had no time to assess his conclusions. Wu could hardly expect to have a personal preview!

He gave a partially true (and partially untrue) answer. "It's taken me a hell of a long time. I've been pretty busy since returning to Washington – just as you have here – but I'm getting there slowly." He changed the subject. "Are you still working on the river or have you moved on?"

Wu smiled modestly. "Party told me I did good job. They ask me to go to Beijing. Now I work with Central Committee. With Chou En Lai in person. That is how I knew you were coming. That is why I ask to be sent here to meet you."

Murphy was touched.

"As far as I was concerned, Wu," he said quietly, "you always did a good job." As he spoke he remembered how Wu had carried him to safety, weak and delirious, when the backwash of the tidal wave threatened to overwhelm them.

Later, as they approached Canton, Wu asked: "How is Nurse Cartwright?"

"She's Mrs Murphy now."

The young man's face seemed to light up with genuine pleasure. "That is good news, very good news!" Then he added, on a less exuberant note, "She never liked me, did she? I sensed that!"

These were murky waters which Murphy preferred to avoid.

"I don't know why you say that, Wu. Mary helped to get you out of gaol. She talked to Madame Chiang who in turn spoke to Charlie Soong – you know the rest."

Wu gave him a blank uncomprehending stare. "Soong? Charlie Soong? What does he have to do with it? I know nothing about Soong!"

"Surely . . . !" Murphy began to protest but Wu, rising abruptly from his seat, had already left the room.

'26 October, 1950. Canton, China'. Murphy wrote the date and place in a firm legible hand on a clean page in his journal. 'It has been a long day but a fascinating one. I came up the Pearl River this morning on board a Chinese Communist coastguard cutter escorted by a posse of po-faced soldiers of the People's Liberation Army and my old

132

friend Wu Canping who seems now to have an important official assignment in Peking, now renamed Beijing. We had some time to talk together and I have been trying to work out in my mind whether, and to what extent, Wu *was* involved with the Communists and with men like Chou En Lai – Mao's emissary in Chungking – during the time he worked for us at SACO. Not that it changes anything, of course. Whatever his position was then – did he, for example, tip them off about Chennault's raid on Yenan? – it is clear that he is very much associated with the regime now. The squad of soldiers on the cutter treated him with great deference and I guess he must be a rising star in the Party hierarchy. All this is odd, of course, when you consider that Wu probably owed his life to Charlie Soong's intervention and, indirectly, to both Mary and me! I mentioned this to him *en passant*, and without ulterior motive, to be rewarded by one of the blankest stares I have seen in a very long time. I think that Wu, for obvious reasons, is engaged in some selective rewriting of his personal history!

'Before he went to Beijing for his present post, Wu was involved with improving navigation on the Yangtze. He remembered I was writing a report about a possible dam in the Three Gorges, and asked me whether I'd finished it. I was a bit cagey in my reply. The fact is I more or less finished the report just before I left for the Pacific – it's taken me long enough in all conscience. After some final polishing, I'll keep the fair copy in the safe at home, having sent carbons to the Corps of Engineers and the Bureau of Reclamation. It will be interesting to know what they make of it . . .

'I'm sorry to say I didn't see much of Canton, not as much as I would have wished; we moored at a wharf in the heart of the city; there was a reception party waiting for me as I stepped down on to Chinese soil for the first time in five years; some quick handshakes all round while I practised some of the Chinese which I remembered from Chungking days, and then I was whisked away in a Russian-made car to the airport.

'Even that short journey was revealing. In terms of the

major landmarks, the Canton I have been looking at today is probably not much different from the pre-war city. We drove past Shamian Island where the 'foreign devils' had their concessions. Wu pointed out to me one great white building which had been Rowlands' headquarters and another which had been the seat of the Hong Kong & Shanghai Bank. For the time being, both establishments are boarded up, providing a convenient site for wall-posters of every kind. But Wu explained that the enterprises would soon be opening under new management, by which he presumably meant that some Committee would take control. What has changed most, it seems to me, are the habits of the people. On the surface, at least, the pimps and the prostitutes, the beggars and the vagabonds, which were so characteristic of any large city in China, have disappeared. In their place there are disciplined crowds doing physical fitness exercises to the blare of uplifting music which is broadcast from loudspeakers at every street corner.

'I'm meant to be taking a China Airways internal flight with Wu to Beijing. I'm told that the plane is coming down from Nanking and has been delayed by engine trouble. As I write this in the waiting-room at the airport, I can see that I'm not the only "European" to be flying today. There are three Russians – technicians, I suppose – standing to one side looking rather bad-tempered. China and Russia have recently signed some fairly substantial agreements relating to scientific and technical co-operation, as well as to general programmes of industrial rehabilitation, but I'm not sure that either side is very happy about the way things are working out. The Chinese suspect that Stalin is just using them for his own purposes, while the Russians seem to feel that the Chinese Communists are more interested in being Chinese than Communists. I must break off now as we have just learned that our plane is at last arriving and Wu is beginning to agitate . . .'

An hour later, as they were flying at 15,000 feet above the plains of central China, Murphy re-read what he had just written, then put his diary away. Usually he made entries on a daily basis but he realised that the next few days might be specially hectic.

The plane was a Dakota, flown into China originally under Lend-Lease for Chiang Kai Shek's airforce and captured from them on the ground by the Communists in one of the later engagements of the Civil War. Over the years, Murphy thought, he must have spent almost 100 hours of flying time in DC3s, to give the Dakota its proper classification. They were solid, serviceable machines. If the Chinese kept it in a good state of repair, there was no reason why this plane shouldn't fly for another 20 years or more. And, by God, they certainly needed every plane they could get! Looking down, Murphy saw the colossal sweep of country beneath him. Of course, there were the great rivers – the Yangtze and the Yellow River in particular – providing lines of communication east-west; there was a fledgling rail network linking some of the principal cities like Canton, Shanghai, Nanking and Beijing. But if the Communists truly wanted to unify the country and haul it into the twentieth century, they would have to build an internal airline capable of linking every city of, say, one million inhabitants with the rest of China. What a challenge that would be!

It took them 18 hours altogether to reach Beijing. They made two scheduled stops to re-fuel and one unscheduled stop to change an over-heating engine. On each occasion the drill was the same. Passengers and crew would disembark, file into the airport building – usually a fairly primitive hut on the tarmac – to be served tea from huge thermos-flasks and, if they were lucky, a bowl of sticky glutinous rice. There was one improvement which Murphy couldn't help noticing. Compared with his experiences five years earlier, the amount of hawking and spitting which went on was mercifully reduced. When he commented on this, Wu told him, "Spitting is a relic of a feudal regime"!

Murphy wasn't sure whether Wu believed what he was saying or whether, as a good functionary, he was merely parroting the official line.

*

135

They flew over the Yangtze at Hanchow. Murphy had a glimpse of the airfield which, during the war years, had served as a base for Japanese bombers raiding Chungking. He wondered how many of the pilots who had strafed them that day had made it safely back to base. How long ago it all seemed! Japan now was no longer the enemy. On the contrary, under General MacArthur's tutelage, a new nation was rising whose qualities were all the more remarkable for being tempered by defeat.

As they went north, the weather worsened.

"Wow!" Murphy exclaimed as the plane made one particularly dramatic lurch. As several of the passengers vomited into the paper bags provided, he turned to Wu. "Do you get scared in planes?"

Wu shook his head. "When you been in prison with Tai Li as your gaoler, you not scared of anything any more! He tortured me three days. Wanted me to confess. I told him nothing. Less than nothing!" He poked a finger towards his mouth. "See there. Lost teeth. Almost blind. Half my ribs broken. No skin on back. But still I did not speak. You believe me?"

"Of course, why shouldn't I?"

"That is good." Wu turned away to stare out of the window.

But apart from those few moments Murphy found Wu unwilling, or unable, to talk. Murphy regretted it, but there seemed to be nothing he could do about it.

They spent the night, uncomfortably, at Zhengzhou, the capital of Hunan Province. Though the Dakota was equipped with night-flying instruments, the system of ground-based navigation aids left much to be desired. When Murphy applauded the wise decision to put down on terra firma during the hours of darkness, Wu shrugged it off. He had no wish, or so it seemed, to admit that there could be any shortcomings in the new heaven and new earth which the Liberation had inaugurated.

"It is for the comfort of the passengers," he told Murphy unconvincingly.

So they spread themselves out where they could on the

hard floor of the passenger building. The soldiers on board laid their army greatcoats on the ground and pushed their hats with their fur ear-pieces firmly down over their eyes. Murphy, hotfoot from Wake Island via Hong Kong, shivered for much of the night. It would be even colder in Beijing, he realised, at this time of year.

"I'm going to buy a big, thick overcoat made out of quilt when we get there," he told Wu as he roused himself the next day, stiff, bleary-eyed and short of sleep.

"If you have time," Wu replied, leaving Murphy wondering, not for the first time, what kind of welcome was being prepared for him in the city where Kublai Khan had once held sway.

Next morning as they flew onwards on the last leg of their journey Wu disappeared towards the rear of the plane to talk to some of his fellow-passengers, leaving Murphy to himself. Sitting there with his nose glued to the scratched and pitted window of the Dakota, he found it hard to believe that he was finally approaching Beijing, a city which he had dreamed about for much of his adult life. For him, perhaps more than any other place in the world, it was the city of mystery and magic! During those long years in Chungking, he had read all the books about China, and Chinese history, that he could lay his hands on. At almost every period over the last 3,000 years, the role of Beijing had been preeminent. It had changed its name at least eight times. It had been sacked by the Mongols under Genghis Khan, demolished by earthquakes, occupied by foreign armies; yet, somehow, it had always managed to survive. It contained, still, some of the world's most sublime architecture, architecture which – as travellers from Marco Polo onwards had found – beggared description. It had been the seat of government for most of the major dynasties, and the Emperors associated with them. Yet today, Murphy reflected, this ancient city was home to a regime – to a political structure – which was unique in the annals of mankind.

As the plane lost height, dropping under the clouds on its final approach to the capital, Murphy leaned forward in

137

his seat, looking through the whirling propellers for a first glimpse of the city below.

Wu Canping, returning to his seat, interrupted the American's thoughts. "Fasten seat belt, please." Wu nodded in the direction of the illuminated sign. He seemed glum, unhappy.

"What's the matter?"

"Bad news," Wu replied gruffly. "Could make things difficult for you. Some people back there heard radio this morning at Zhengzhou. Pyongyang, North Korean capital, captured by American forces under General MacArthur. MacArthur still coming north even further."

Murphy noted that Wu studiously refrained from referring to the United Nations' role in the fighting. As far as the Chinese were concerned, MacArthur's activities in Korea were not to be seen as part of a United Nations' peace-keeping operation, but as the illegal actions of 'imperialist hegemonists'.

"Good grief!" Murphy couldn't suppress his surprise and shock. "What on earth is MacArthur playing at?" Capturing Pyongyang was provocative enough, without threatening to advance on Manchuria!

For a few moments Murphy stared despondently out of the window. He could see the pattern of fields clearly now, mostly rice paddies with the water lying on the surface and peasants stooping to tend the crop. To the west, as they continued to lose height, he could make out the first sprawl of Beijing. The weather had cleared and it had turned into a bright autumn day. In the far distance he saw, or at least imagined that he saw, the sun glinting on the roof of the Temple of Heaven.

Murphy turned back to his companion. "Tell me, Wu, as a friend," he said quietly, "how do you read the situation now?"

Wu shook his head. "What I think is no matter. Back there" – he gestured towards the rear of the plane – "officers talk of need for Chinese intervention."

Wu Canping sat in tight-lipped silence for the rest of the journey. It was almost as though Murphy's presence had become an embarrassment to him, given the latest turn of events. Murphy felt a sudden stab of unease. If China intervened in the Korean War, then his own situation could become highly precarious. Instead of being a messenger of goodwill, he could be seen quite simply as an enemy agent. Once upon a time the dungeons in the Forbidden City had been full of enemy agents. What were the guarantees of safe conduct worth if, overnight, the United States of America found itself at war with China?

They landed with a jolt and a rattle on the rough surface of the runway at Beijing airport, some 20 miles outside the city. The facilities on offer would have been more appropriate to a small town in the Mid-West, rather than one of the most populous places on earth. There was just one airport building, a low brown structure whose façade was largely obscured by a gigantic portrait of Mao Tse Tung. On a balcony, beneath the portrait, stood a party of Chinese officials wearing heavy greatcoats and fur hats in anticipation of the colder weather yet to come. Murphy walked with Wu the two or three hundred yards from the plane to the building. As far as he could see, there were five or six other planes, all of them Russian. Most of them, he imagined, would have been bringing technicians or equipment as part of the massive programme of Sino-Soviet collaboration which had been launched when the Communists came to power. How far did the Russians call the shots here, he wondered? All the signs were that at the technical level at least, their influence was massive. Russian engineers were building bridges, constructing highways and designing dams. Soviet-made machinery was being imported to build up China's industrial base and transform it, hopefully, from a backward rural nation into one of the world's leading economies. But Stalin was a hard taskmaster. Mao and his soul-mates might have read Marx and Engels but that didn't mean the Soviets would bankroll them just for the hell of it. They certainly didn't behave that way in Eastern Europe anyway. Murphy had no doubt that the Russians would be demanding a high price for their aid. Would that price include sending Chinese armies into Korea? As he followed

139

Wu into the airport building, Murphy decided that the only sensible course of action was to keep his eyes open, his wits alert and in general to play it by ear. Not a profound strategy, but the best he could think of.

The inside of the airport building was larger than it had appeared from the tarmac. One wall of the Arrivals Hall was decorated with a gigantic poster of three bright-eyed, black-haired Chinese women. One was in aviator's uniform in the cockpit of a plane; the second bore a sheaf of golden corn in her arms, while the third, wearing a white coat and trim cap, was operating some complicated scientific instrument with gloved hands. Huge Chinese characters had been painted in bold red brushstrokes across the empyrean blue background of the sky.

"What does that poster say?" Murphy asked Wu. Wu translated for him. " 'Times have changed. Men and women now equal. Criticise idea that men are superior to women'."

Murphy nodded. He knew the new regime had abolished the ancient practice of foot-binding, but that was obviously only the tip of the iceberg. His own experiences in China had brought home to him the position of total subservience in which most of China's womanhood was still kept.

"I guess you've got a long row to hoe there," he commented.

"But we make progress, yes." Wu smiled, and to Murphy's surprise introduced him to a young Chinese woman with thick dark hair and wide pearly-white teeth who had been waiting for them at the barrier.

"Please meet my wife, Wang Wen-chuan. Wang Wen-chuan is Senior Interpreter at Foreign Languages Institute in Beijing. She will be with you during your time here. My own English", he sounded apologetic, "still not good enough."

"Wu never told me he was married." Murphy took the young woman's hand in his. How small and delicate it seemed! "I would have brought a wedding-present if I had known."

She laughed. "Why should Wu have told you? He has his job; I have mine."

She thrust out her small chin in a determined but pretty way. "Please follow me now." Wang Wen-chuan led them across the crowded floor of the airport building and outside into the sunlight.

Chou En Lai took the small pot of Tiger Balm and rubbed it into his forehead. Apart from two catnaps, he had been on the go for over 30 hours. Not that this was anything unusual. Ever since he had been appointed – on 1 October, 1949 – Premier of the State Council, he had been used to burning the candle at both ends. One of the reasons he worked as hard as he did, concentrating on the day-to-day issues, was to leave Mao time for the broader perspective. They made a strange contrast – Mao, the earthy peasant from Hunan with his homespun philosophies which were rapidly acquiring the status of received wisdom (the State Publishing House was even preparing a book of the Thoughts of Chairman Mao); and the almost mandarin figure of Chou, a man whose intellect dominated most conventional horizons, and whose elegant and sophisticated personality charmed and impressed almost all those who encountered him.

The Tiger Balm oil, stowed in a battered leather briefcase which he had carried with him on the Long March and held on to ever since, came in handy when, unusually, Chou En Lai felt his age – he would be 53 next March – beginning to tell. Another man would have cracked beneath the load he carried. He was not only Premier of the State Council – China's Cabinet; he was concurrently Minister of Foreign Affairs. His was the name, almost as much as that of Mao himself, which was known to the outside world. He was the man who received the diplomats who were accredited to the new government of the Chinese People's Republic. And it was his responsibility, too, to travel the world tirelessly in an attempt to win international understanding for the new China. His most fervent hope was that some day soon China

141

would be admitted to the United Nations in place of that renegade fascist regime in Taiwan!

Like other leaders of the Revolution, Chou had chosen to live in a quiet section of the Forbidden City called Zhongnanhai, in the Park of the South Lake. His was an old house set within a walled compound which in turn was surrounded by imperial cedars and pines. His wife, Deng Yingchao, lived there with him, as well as their adopted daughter, Sun Weishi, an orphaned child whose parents has been killed by the Kuomintang. Sun Weishi's arrival (after an earlier miscarriage, Deng Yingchao had been warned against further pregnancies) symbolised their more settled way of life. Whenever he could, Chou came back to Zhongnanhai in the afternoon to be with his family or, at least, in the same house since, even when he was at home, the rhythm of his work was barely interrupted.

He stood up stiffly from his desk to reach for the lacquered box of cigarettes which he kept on the mantelpiece. He had started smoking seriously in the Chungking years and he had never managed to shake the habit. As a matter of fact, he had hardly tried. In spite of his stupendous workload Chou felt as fit as he had ever been. If anything, he was leaner, sleeker than he had been in Szechuan. There the bad diet had caused, sometimes, a certain puffiness in his otherwise dark, handsome face. Now things were better, at least on that score. Whatever other deficiencies there might be in the system, the rural communes had been keeping Beijing splendidly supplied with produce of every kind.

For the next few minutes, China's Premier stood by the window of his study, gazing absent-mindedly at the splendours of the Forbidden City – the arches, the cornices, the lacquered tiles, the mouldings created by more than 1,500 years of the finest craftsmanship. Then he looked at his watch. By now, the American should have arrived. Was there still time, he wondered? Or was it, even now, already too late? He was a powerful man, but he was not all-powerful. The generals were already flexing their muscles and it was clear that some of them were itching for a fight.

*

142

They drove at high speed along the winding country road which connected the airport with the city. The chauffeur kept his hand on the horn as bullock-carts laden with paddy scattered before them. Tall poplars grew at either side of the carriage-way and through them Murphy could see the long lines of workers toiling in the fields. He remembered a speech by Mao which had been circulating in the State Department just before he left Washington. What had Mao said? "Revolution plus Production will solve the problem of Population"? Perhaps he was right. There was no doubt that these people knew how to work.

They entered the city from the north-east, followed the line of the old walls south, then turned west on Changan Avenue. Five minutes later, they passed the massive façade of the Beijing Hotel and entered Tian An Men Square. On the right stood the Gate of Heavenly Peace.

"Could we stop a moment?" Murphy asked. "I may not get a chance to see this again."

Wang Wen-chuan seemed reluctant to authorise on her own responsibility any departure from the planned time-table. She consulted her husband, speaking so rapidly that Murphy, whose knowledge of the language was in any case rudimentary, was unable to follow.

"Thirty seconds only," Wu told him. "We have an appointment."

"With whom?"

"Please wait to find out."

So, for precisely half a minute, Murphy sat back in the car looking at the mighty arch which had become so much the symbol of modern China. How old was Tian An Men? Four centuries old? Five centuries old? He looked at the towering structure, the five doors and seven bridges, and tried to wrap his mind around the paradox which the Gate of Heavenly Peace represented. More than any other piece of architecture in Beijing it symbolised the power of Imperial China. In the vast square in front of the Gate the masses would gather to hear the Imperial proclamations. The Emperor himself would appear on the terrace above the crowds and receive the tribute of his people. Scrolls containing the Emperor's 'divine decrees' would be flung down to officials kneeling humbly below. Yet that same Gate, that same terrace, had been invoked by the new regime in a manner every bit as compelling as anything to be found in the Imperial traditions.

"Time to go." Wu Canping tapped his watch and nodded to the driver. The big car nosed forward along Changan Avenue, pushing through the crowd of afternoon bicyclists. It rolled past the Gate of Heavenly Peace, past the entrance to the Sun Yat Sen Memorial Park until it brought them to the western edge of the Forbidden City.

"This is Xinhuamen – Gate of New China," Wu explained. "Is entrance to Zhongnanhai."

Murphy saw the soldiers of the People's Liberation Army guarding the gateway, and the flagpole with the Red Flag flying. He felt a thrill of anticipation. He knew that Zhongnanhai was China's new forbidden city. This was where the highest-ranking members of the Communist Party lived: Mao Tse Tung, Chou En Lai, Lui Shao Chi; all of them had their houses in this 1,000-year-old compound, which once had served as a playground for the Emperors and their retinues.

"You are the first American ever to set foot in Zhongnanhai," Wang Wen-chuan told him. "It is a great honour."

"It is indeed." As the car swung right-handed under the gate, the PLA guards saluted.

"So you see," Chou En Lai continued, "our intentions are peaceful. China has no wish to engage in foreign adventures. We have too much work to do at home. We seek friendship, not enmity, with all nations of the world, including the United States of America – particularly the United States of America." He paused, choosing his words with care. "But if you push us beyond a certain limit, we shall retaliate. We have no other option."

"What limits are you talking about?" Murphy asked quietly.

Chou lit a foul-smelling cigar and blew smoke in the

direction of a Chinese Communist Party Class of '49 group photograph which was propped on the mantelpiece.

"I want you to listen very closely to what I'm going to say, Mr Murphy, so that there is not the slightest chance of any misunderstanding between us. If MacArthur's armies continue to occupy Pyongyang, if your troops continue to advance towards the Yalu and Chinese Manchuria, then I tell you categorically that China will intervene in this conflict."

As Chou finished speaking, the door to the study opened and a short powerfully-built man of around 65 entered the room. Murphy instantly recognised the face from the photographs which he had studied over the years. Chu Teh! The man who, virtually singlehandedly, had welded the Red Army into a modern fighting force. Veteran of the 20-year struggle against the Kuomintang, Chu Teh was now the top-ranking marshal in the Communist armed forces as well as Vice-Chairman of the Government.

"Ah, Chu Teh! You have come at a good moment," Chou waved his colleague to a seat. "As you know, we are lucky to have with us today an emissary of President Truman. I have been trying to make our position clear regarding any further advances by so-called United Nations' forces. But perhaps you would care to add a word yourself on this subject."

By way of reply, Chu Teh, a man whose exploits both on the battlefield and in the bedroom were legendary, hawked up a great gob of phlegm from the deep interior of his throat and, ignoring all the new restraints, spat with unerring accuracy into a spitoon which stood in a corner of the room.

"If MacArthur's forces come within 100 miles of the Yalu," he growled, "my armies will wipe them off the map."

Three days later, having flown from Beijing to Moscow and from Moscow to Paris (where he filed an interim report with the US Embassy with instructions for it to be encoded and transmitted to the State Department), Oliver Murphy landed in Washington, DC. He was met at the airport by a man from the office.

145

"You have a meeting with the President and the Joint Chiefs at noon. Acheson wants to see you first." There was something in the man's tone which made Murphy, tired though he was from his non-stop journey around the globe, glance at him sharply.

"Anything wrong?"

"Well, actually, yes," the man replied awkwardly. "You've been named, personally, by Senator McCarthy as a principal Communist agent. The papers are full of it."

He held up a copy of the day's Washington *Post*. Murphy read the banner headline with a sense of anger and despair: 'TRUMAN ENVOY IS COMMUNIST DUPE'. The article, syndicated across the nation, was signed by one of Washington's best-known columnists, Edward Rovere.

12

The Secretary of State looked up from his desk as Murphy entered his seventh-floor office in the new State Department building. From his window he had an uninterrupted view across the Potomac into Virginia. On this bright autumn morning, the sun accentuated the whiteness of the Lincoln Memorial and cast into relief the graceful arches of the Arlington Memorial Bridge. Dean Acheson's mood, however, was in marked contrast to the external surroundings. In the whole of his public life, he had seldom felt gloomier.

"Sit down, Murphy. Welcome back, though that's hardly the right word in the circumstances." He walked across the room to a red leather couch while Murphy pulled up a chair. "You've seen today's papers?"

Murphy nodded. "Most of them. Enough, anyway."

Acheson picked up a bulky dossier from a table next to the couch and handed it to Murphy. "All the reports you made from Chungking during the war years are in here. The complete dossier was circulated today to the House Committee on Un-American Activities and the Senate Investigating Committee has received it too. McCarthy's timing could hardly have been better – from his point of view."

"There was nothing subversive about those reports."

"I know that; you know that; but that's not the way it looks to people who are engaged on a witch-hunt. Besides, McCarthy and his crowd have been briefed on your relationship with this fellow – what's his name? – Wu Canping."

"What about Wu?" Murphy was suddenly wary.

Acheson looked embarrassed. "McCarthy maintains that Wu was a Communist agent even when he was working at SACO. He has a copy of a signed confession. What's more,

Wu alleges that you told him that you yourself had actually been recruited by the Communists before the war."

Murphy was flabbergasted. "Wu said that? That's palpable nonsense. Besides, Wu never made any confession."

"How do you know?"

"Because he told me."

"Do you believe him?"

"Why shouldn't I?"

Acheson sighed. "Can you explain to me – or to anyone else for that matter – why Wu Canping, who – as I understand from the telegram you filed from Paris – occupies a position of some influence in the Chinese Communist hierarchy at the present time, should have wished to discredit you?"

When Murphy had no response to make, the Secretary of State continued, lowering his voice: "We're in a bind, I have to tell you. It isn't just McCarthy. It's MacArthur too. The General's got a lot friends on the Hill who think he's on the right track; who believe that this is the moment to carry the fight to the enemy and teach the Communists a lesson they won't forget. Whether they're Soviet Communists or Chinese Communists, they don't really care."

Acheson leaned forward. "The rats have been getting at this one, Murphy, and we've got to salvage it if we can. What makes the whole thing doubly difficult is that the bastards are using you to get at me and the President – and anyone else who may feel that the time has come to do a deal with China."

"So who's going to listen to me now?"

"Much will depend on how convincing you personally are in the account you give of your meeting with Chou. They'll give you the third degree, Murphy; I hope to God you can come up with the answers."

"I'll tell them the truth, Goddamit." The anger that had been building up inside him had been replaced by a wave of nausea and that in turn was followed by a stab of fear.

The top brass had turned out in force. There were the three Chiefs of Staff – Collins, Vandenburg and Sherman;

148

there was General Bradley and two or three other people in military uniform whom Murphy did not recognise. On the civilian side, Vice-President Barkley had obviously decided that, though his job on the whole wasn't 'worth a pitcher full of warm spit', this was one meeting he was not going to miss, while all three Service Secretaries – Frank Pace for the Army, Francis Mathews for the Navy, and Thomas Finletter for the Air Force – has also decided that their presence was essential. The President himself sat in his high-backed chair in the middle of the long rectangular table; opposite him, a portrait of Thomas Jefferson, recently cleaned and restored, surveyed the scene with an air of considerable disinterest.

"Sit down, gentlemen." The President coughed irritably and looked around the room, peering at each one of them in turn over his thin-rimmed spectacles. "Let me make one thing absolutely clear at the outset of this meeting" – this was plain ole Harry speaking – "nobody's loyalty is on trial here today. What you may have read in the Press has no bearing on our present business. Mr Murphy was my personal emissary to China. I have the fullest confidence in him. I'm now going to give Mr Murphy the opportunity to give an account of his mission, though many of you will, of course, have read the telegram which was sent via our Embassy in Paris."

As far as he knew, Murphy omitted no material fact in his 12-minute presentation; at the same time he endeavoured to recall not merely what was said, but the manner in which it was said, recognising that – when you were dealing with the Chinese – nuance could be as important as anything else. At the end of his talk, he summed up his impressions:

"I have to tell you, gentlemen, that I believe that this is probably the most important message the Chinese have conveyed to the United States since General Marshall left that country in 1946. And if you will permit me, Mr President, to give an indication of my own personal opinion in this matter, I should say that it behoves us to act on this message, and to act *now*."

"Thank you, Mr Murphy." There was a noticeable coolness in the President's tone. "As to your last remark, I think we had best let some of the highly qualified persons present here today contribute to the discussion before jumping to conclusions."

Murphy felt the flush spread from his collar to his face while the sense of nausea returned stronger than ever in the pit of his stomach.

He caught the Secretary of State's eye across the table but Acheson, as though embarrassed, looked away. Murphy suddenly realised that by coming out with such a clear statement about his own personal beliefs, he had probably confirmed the meeting's worst suspicions.

Down at the far end of the table, General J. Lawton Collins raised a hand. As Army Chief of Staff, and as the man who was in almost daily contact with General MacArthur, Collins's view would, Murphy knew, carry a great deal of weight. He was a bluff, corpulent man who had of necessity learned to live with MacArthur's prima donna act out there in Asia and who was quite ready to back MacArthur's judgement (and, for that matter, his own) against the opinions of some trumped-up Colonel from the Army Corps of Engineers who had somehow wangled an appointment to the State Department, an institution which he, like others of his kind, suspected was at best a club of effete amateurs and at worst a nest of traitors.

"I'm going to be blunt, Mr President," he rasped. "If you fall for this one, you'll be falling for the oldest game in the world: Chinaman's bluff! Let's look at the facts." He paused. "Perhaps it would be easier if I use a map for those who are not familiar with the geography of the Korean Peninsula."

While an aide unrolled a large wall-map, looked around for a hook to hang it from and finally settled on the portrait of Daniel Webster at the far end of the room, General Collins armed himself with his swagger stick and proceeded to give them a brief lecture on recent military developments.

"In the last few weeks," he said, "the tide has turned dramatically in our favour. On September 15th, as you know, UN forces under General MacArthur made an

150

amphibious landing at Inchon and at the same time, forces in the Pusan perimeter attacked north to join them." He prodded at the map with one end of the stick. "Less than a week later we recaptured Seoul. By the end of last month, organised Communist resistance collapsed in the Eighth Army sector. Encircled North Korean forces, representing more than half the original North Korean invaders, where taken prisoner. On October 1st, the ROK 3rd Division pushed across the 38th Parallel and drove up the east coast. On October 20th, that is, ten days ago, we captured Pyong-yang, the capital of North Korea. Today, October 24th, the US 9th Corps and the 1st Marine Division are advancing towards Hamhung and the Changjin reservoir. At this time, it is probably true to state that the Korean Communist army has practically dissolved, and that the elements which remain have headed for the mountainous borderlands adjacent to Manchuria and Siberia."

General Collins could tell that he was making an impression on them all. In terms of the ground covered, MacArthur's successes in recent days had been dramatic. The United Nations' offensive had progressed to within 100 miles of the Yalu River and new advances were being made hour by hour.

"We have a chance now, gentlemen," continued Collins, speaking with conviction, "to pursue this matter to its logical conclusion and unify the Korean Peninsula and the Korean nation once and for all under a single, democratic flag. I am not going to advocate here, today, Mr. President" – he spread his hands as though making a magnanimous concession – "that we press on *beyond* the Yalu River into Chinese Manchuria although, as you know, General MacArthur has for some time now been urging you to authorise such action. I recognise that incursions of this kind might indeed result in increased Chinese Communist effort, and even the Soviets might contribute in response to what they might well construe as an attack on Manchuria. However, I am firmly of the view that General MacArthur is correct in his current assessment of the situation. As long as our operations are limited to the Korean peninsula, there will be no, repeat no, Chinese intervention. With respect, Mr President, Chou En Lai seems to think he can bluff us into retreat at a time when total victory lies within our grasp. I say – let's call his bluff!"

Collins stamped back to his chair and sat down heavily, while a chorus of approval ran around the table.

"And Marshal Chu Teh is in on this game of bluff too, is he? I knew diplomats like Chou could be devious buggers, but I didn't know you soldiers were as well!" The President was clearly recovering something of his good humour. A small ripple of laughter greeted this sally.

Secretary of State Dean Acheson could see the way the tide was turning, and he made an effort to hold it back. "There are power-plants on the Yalu River, Mr President, which serve China although they are on the Korean side. They were built by the Japanese when they occupied the region. You received, on October 20th, a memorandum from the CIA reporting that the Chinese Communists would move in far enough to safeguard the Suiho electricity plant and other vital installations along the Yalu River."

The President took the point reluctantly. "We'll have General MacArthur issue a statement to the effect that he does not intend to interfere with the operations of the Suiho and other power plants."

"But, Mr President . . ."

For once Truman ignored his Secretary of State, giving the floor instead to the other Chiefs of Staff and to the three Secretaries of Defense present, each of whom had his own contribution to make to what was clearly a gathering consensus.

Half an hour later, the meeting was over. Truman had summed up by drawing some clear operational conclusions. For the time being at least, MacArthur's advance would continue up to, though not beyond, the Yalu River.

"Goddamit!" the President said as he walked from the room. "We have no evidence of any Chinese forces coming over the border; no indications of troop movements, as I understand it, of any kind." He had caught sight of Murphy sitting glumly in his seat, contemplating the wreckage of his career. "I don't think we need send a message back to Mr Chou En Lai, gentlemen. General MacArthur can do that for us!"

Back in his office, Murphy sat staring at the wall. He felt drained, exhausted and embittered. In his view, what they had decided that morning was madness, complete and utter madness. There was no way China would tolerate further advances by UN troops. The Red Army would be thrown into the Korean conflict. The price of that morning's stupidity would be paid in American lives.

Standing up, he walked wearily over to the safe which stood against the wall of his office to put his papers away. To his surprise he couldn't make the combination number work, so he called the security guard, a cheerful black Marine who was stationed at a strategically-placed desk along the long corridor of the seventh floor.

"Number's been changed I'm afraid, sir."

"On whose instructions?"

"Security reasons, sir." Visibly embarrassed, the Marine Sergeant saluted, turned on his heel and left the room.

Murphy went back to his desk and sat with his head in his hands. Good grief, he thought, had it come to this already? Then, as if in a daze, he pulled the telephone towards him and dialled his home number.

"Mary? It's me. Sorry I couldn't call you earlier. I got back this morning, but it's been non-stop ever since."

"Oh, Oliver. I'm so glad to hear you. What on earth's going on? Did you see the papers? *You* a Communist agent? It's laughable!" He could feel the wave of relief sweeping over him. As long as Mary stood by him, he could face them all down.

"Of course it is," he said. "But this town is full of poison. We have to fight it – all the way. And we will, too. Thank God I've got you, darling. And Preston." He didn't want to alarm her unnecessarily but he felt bound to tell her to be careful.

"Keep an eye on him won't you?"

"What do you mean?"

153

"Just look out for him. That's all I mean. Better not let him play in the front unless you're there. And, Mary . . ."

"Yes, Oliver?" She felt anxious then, knowing that Preston was at that very moment playing with a couple of his friends in the road outside.

"You know I love you, don't you? It's been a grim home-coming – and things may get worse – but if we stick together, we'll survive."

She fought to keep the tears from her eyes. "I love you too, darling. Come back soon."

"I'm coming now." Murphy stepped out into the corridor, closing the door of his office quietly behind him.

The two men who sat in the car parked beside the kerb heard the telephone ring in the house. One of them was a large pock-marked Chinese who looked as though he could have emerged from some opium den in the backstreets of Shanghai. The other, sitting behind the wheel, was a smoother customer altogether. He was dressed in a dark suit and white shirt with starched collar and cuffs. His shoes had been carefully polished that morning and his dark hair, slicked down with brilliantine, contrasted sharply with his olive-yellow complexion.

"Let's do it now, while she's busy." The driver shoved the car into gear and moved slowly along the kerb to where the boy was playing with his friends.

Big Tu, sitting in the rear seat, held the door open and in one single flowing movement scooped the child inside, clamping a large gnarled hand over the boy's mouth as he did so.

"I've got him. Get going!" The car accelerated rapidly down the road towards Connecticut Avenue and disappeared in the early afternoon traffic.

Two minutes later, Mary Murphy – having finished her telephone call – emerged onto the porch of her home to discover that Preston was no longer where he had been. She ran into the street and asked the other children who were still playing on the lawn where her son had gone.

154

"He went in the car" – one of the boys, older than the rest, pointed down the road.

"Oh my God!" Mary cried. As she dashed back towards the house to telephone the police, she caught her foot on the kerb and slipped. By the time she reached her front door, she could feel the pains in her stomach. Fifteen minutes later, when Murphy arrived home, he found the ambulance as well as the police.

The baby was born dead. While his wife remained under sedation in the hospital, Murphy stayed by the 'phone at home. For two days there was no news. The police, it seemed, had been unable to trace the car or its occupants. The information gleaned from the other children had not helped. The vehicle had been described as being large and black and the men inside it were 'foreign-looking' but in a cosmopolitan city like Washington this was not much help.

Murphy pressed the police daily, sometimes hourly, for a report on police, but he got nowhere. It was cold comfort to recall that they had been unable to solve the Lindbergh kidnapping either, but at least in the latter's case they seemed to have tried. As far as he was concerned, Murphy had the strong suspicion that the police had put the matter firmly on the back-burner. One day he had heard one of the police officers say to a colleague: "Murphy's that Commie guy, isn't he? The one who was in the newspapers." And the colleague had replied: "Serves the bastard right, I say."

On the evening of the second day, he visited Mary in hospital and sat by the bed, holding her hand. She was still heavily drugged but she understood from the look on his face, even before he had spoken, that Preston was still missing.

"Wu Canping ..." she rambled incoherently. "You trusted Wu, Oliver. Shouldn't have. Betrayed you."

Murphy grieved to hear her. He could see that for her, in the aftermath of the double-shock (the kidnapping of her son and the loss of her baby), Wu – whom Mary had never really liked anyway – had become a kind of ogre, a baleful force affecting all their destinies.

155

"No, it's nothing to do with Wu . . ." he began to say.

"The police said they were foreign, they could have been Chinese."

Around 10.00 p.m. that night, soon after he had returned home from visiting Mary in the hospital, the telephone rang. It was the call he had been both expecting and dreading.

"We have boy," the voice said. Murphy noted that the accent was nasal, high-pitched, oriental. Dammit, perhaps Mary was right! "Drive to lookout point above bluff at Great Falls. We there. Come alone. If anyone with you, if any car follow you, we kill boy. And bring report. You give us report; we give you boy."

"What report?" Even now, Murphy played for time.

"Don't fool us, Murphy," the voice snarled. "You know report. One you wrote about dam."

"I understand." In a daze Murphy replaced the receiver.

For a few moments he stood beside the telephone, debating what to do. How had they known that he had finished his report on the Yangtze River Dam project? How had they known he was even writing any such report? Why were they interested? Who were they anyway? Goddammit, Murphy suddenly remembered, perhaps he had said something of the sort to Wu! As they travelled up the Pearl River that morning en route to Canton they had spoken of the Yangtze, and of Sandouping – Wu's home village which was also the natural dam-site. It came back to him now. He had mentioned his report to Wu, en passant, though he had not, as far as he could recall, given any indication as to the nature of his final recommendations.

He walked towards the door, then once again stopped in mid-stride, still trying to work it all out. What conceivable links could Wu possibly have with the men in Washington who had kidnapped his son? The Chinese in Washington, in New York, in Los Angeles, had nothing to do with the Communists. At a political level, they were Chiang supporters or, more likely, part of a Charlie Soong's all-pervasive network (for Soong had effectively replaced Chiang as the real focus of power). Or else they were the criminal class, the gangsters, the thugs, whose original links

156

had been with the Triads and who now continued abroad their nefarious activities – opium, drugs, gambling – which they could no longer prosecute at home.

He shook his head, baffled. There was no time to work it out now. If they wanted the report, they could have it. Anyway, he'd already filed a copy with the Corps of Engineers and another with the Bureau of Reclamation.

Murphy looked at his watch, then went to his study at the back of the house, unlocked the safe, took out the fair copy of his report on the Yangtze River Dam project, closed the safe again and then walked quickly to his car. As he started the engine, he wondered whether he shouldn't, after all, have called the police. But then he remembered the threat the man had made over the 'phone; "If any car follow you, we kill boy." Some risks were just not worth taking.

It took him about three-quarters of an hour to reach the great rocky bluff overlooking the Potomac at Great Falls. He sat in his car with the lights dowsed and window half open, listening to the sound of the rapids far below. His report on the Yangtze River Dam – the Three Gorges Project as he had come to call it – lay on the seat beside him.

Big Tu knew a hundred ways to kill a man without leaving a mark on his body. He crept soundlessly towards the car in which Murphy sat.

Murphy looked at his watch. It was 11.30 p.m. Any moment now, he imagined, they would be bringing Preston to the rendezvous. He glanced to his right. There was plenty of room for another car to park beside him on the lookout area. As he opened the door and got out of the car to stretch his legs, Big Tu pressed the knuckles of two enormous thumbs into Murphy's temples.

At six o'clock the following morning, Preston Murphy was found by neighbours alive and unharmed on the porch of his parents' house.

When the neighbours sought to open the door, they found it locked. They also observed that Murphy's car was missing. One of them, quicker off the mark than the rest, rang through to the hospital with a message for Mrs Murphy that her son was safe.

The police found Oliver Murphy's car, with Murphy inside it, two hours later that same morning. Murphy, it seemed, had driven off the cliff onto the rocks hundreds of feet below. His body had been badly damaged in the fall but a subsequent post-mortem produced no evidence to contradict the theory that he had taken his own life. On the contrary, the police pointed out at the Coroner's inquest that Murphy must clearly have been in an unbalanced state of mind. His wife had been hospitalised and had lost her baby; his son had been kidnapped and up to that point had not been traced. In addition, Murphy's own professional career was in ruins. The police reported that several newspapers of recent date had been found in the car, all of which ran stories about Senator McCarthy's attack on Murphy. Most significant of all, the car contained a copy of the latest issue of *Time* magazine which amounted to a wholesale condemnation of both Murphy the man and of his recent mission to China, and concluded by urging the President to disavow his envoy and to reject any deals proposed by the Chinese which would involve ceding one inch of territory so far gained in Korea.

In the event the Coroner returned an open verdict but the media and the general public spoke freely of Murphy's "suicide". The McCarthyites had a field-day. What was suicide, if not an admission of guilt?

Mary Murphy was well enough to attend her husband's funeral. She stood, heavily veiled, beside the open grave in the Chevy Chase cemetery with Preston's hand clasped tightly in hers.

"When will daddy come back?" the young boy asked as the coffin was lowered.

"Daddy's gone away for a long time." It was hard to fight back the tears.

There were flowers from colleagues in the State Department and a personal wreath from Dean Acheson whose

158

aide Oliver Murphy had been. But there were few mourners besides the immediate family.

The police stayed in the background. Though they indicated that their investigations into Murphy's death were complete, there remained the issue of Preston's kidnapping. They questioned the boy on three separate occasions without success. For Preston the event had clearly been traumatic. Odd bits and pieces of information could be coaxed from him – he spoke of things being "all dark" and remembered "funny voices" – but on the whole a heavy metal grille seemed to have descended across his memory. An eminent child psychiatrist, consulted by Mrs Murphy, explained for a 50-dollar fee that such forgetfulness was perfectly normal.

"Mental trauma is not very different from physical trauma," the learned doctor confided. "Amnesia is itself a form of healing."

Mary Murphy remained, of course, quite unaware of the telephone call which her husband had received on the night of his death or of the fact that he had taken with him to the rendezvous on the Potomac his report on the Yangtze River Dam. However, even without this information, she was personally convinced that Preston's kidnapping and Murphy's death were linked and that in any case Murphy was not a suicide.

One day, after coming home from play-school (where something must have been said by a teacher or a fellow-pupil) Preston asked her outright:

"Did daddy kill himself, mummy?"

She knelt in front of him, put her hands on his shoulders and looked him in the eyes.

"Your daddy was not that kind of man, darling."

"Who killed him, then?"

"I don't know, son. Maybe one day you may be able to find out for yourself."

A few months later, shattered and sickened by her husband's death and by the strain of the kidnapping which had preceded it, Mary Murphy sold the house in Washington and moved with Preston to Great Barrington, an attractive town in New England, where she occupied herself with raising the child while at the same time carrying out part-time nursing duties at the local hospital. She took with her many of her husband's effects, including the safe in which he had kept several mementoes of his years in China. These included the journals which he had begun in China and had continued, more or less regularly, up to the time of the kidnapping.

As she installed herself in her new house, Mary Murphy debated for a time what to do with all these documents. It was not that she was uninterested in what they contained. It was simply that she had her own memories of her husband and was happy to leave the diaries unread. In the end, she locked the safe up again and asked the odd-job man to store it in the attic. In other ways, Mary kept the memory of her husband very much alive. Just as she resolutely refused to believe in his suicide, so she continued to dismiss as far-fetched fabrications, the McCarthyite suggestions of his "treachery". She found every justification for her belief in her husband's essential patriotism in the dramatic events which took place less than a month after his death. For in mid-November 1950, the Red Army shuttled units across the Yalu at a rapid pace and as soon as they moved out of Manchuria, others moved in from central and southern China. By mid-November, there were 850,000 Chinese soldiers massed on both sides of the border. On 26 November, 1950, the Chinese attacked MacArthur's forces with fourteen divisions, swamping the over-extended UN positions and outflanking its armies. They moved at incredible speed through the most difficult snow-covered country and, while keeping up the pressure along a wide front, put in a series of powerful left and right hooks which bewildered the opposition. On New Year's Day, to the usual cacophony of bugle calls and hysterical screaming, the Chinese hurled themselves forward in what the press colourfully described as "human waves". Massed infantry slammed into the UN positions which were either over-run or cut off. On 4 January, 1951, the Red Army entered Seoul, the third time

160

the capital had changed hands during the war. General MacArthur was recalled in disgrace by President Truman.

Two years later, the Korean armistice was signed along lines which had previously been offered by the Chinese and rejected by the Americans. By then, McCarthyism was on the wane. Eisenhower had succeeded Truman in the White House and golf courses were being built all over the country. As her son grew older, Mary Murphy was able to tell him that his father had not only been a good man and a brave man but that his political judgements had been correct as well.

One evening soon after the armistice had been signed, she knelt by Preston's bed.

"They should have listened to your father, Preston. They could have saved themselves a lot of trouble." By then Preston's memories of his father had begun to dim, but he took comfort from his mother's words.

"Was daddy a hero, mother?" Her son's question took her by surprise. She had never thought of Murphy like that.

"He is for us, darling,"she whispered. "That's for sure."

As the years passed, Mrs Murphy's hair turned a steely grey but she became, if anything, more, not less handsome. She played a full part in the life of the local community, not just in the hospital where she worked (first as a nurse, then as matron, and finally as deputy administrator), but also in the affairs of the township as a whole. She was on the board of several local charities, served as a governor of one of the schools (even though her own child had been sent else-where), and had, on more than one occasion, refused invitations to run for elective office in the area. In turning such invitations down, Mary Murphy was not insensible to the compliment they implied. It meant that she had, in the public mind at least, clawed her way back from those McCarthy years.

In the eyes of the world, then, Mary Murphy had succeeded in re-establishing herself and her family in American society. She was not a rich woman; the money she earned from her job was money she needed for day-to-day living;

but she was respected, and even loved, by most of those who came into contact with her. In a land where the remarriage of divorcées and widows was becoming increasingly common, the fact that Mary remained faithful to her husband's memory made her, paradoxically, the more attractive. Somehow she turned grief into strength and that strength shone in her face.

Book Two

1

They had walked about 80 miles altogether from Cortona to Assisi, and Preston Murphy had enjoyed every minute of it. There had been a sense of purpose and camaraderie as they progressed from one ancient town to the next. They had spent five nights en route, sometimes sleeping in tented accommodation which had been provided by the organisers of the march, sometimes laying their sleeping bags out in the piazza of whatever little town they happened to be in. They had passed by Lake Trasimene, where the Romans had fought Hannibal; and rested the next night at a thirteenth-century Benedictine Abbey where, according to legend, Saint Francis took refuge after escaping from Assisi. Now they were on the last leg of the journey. Assisi itself – the object of their "pilgrimage" – lay only a few miles ahead.

The late afternoon sun, slanting across the dusty plain, cast a golden glow over the sheer façade of the great monastery, the home today – as it had been for the past 15 centuries – of the Franciscan order. Above and behind the monastery, silhouetted against the backdrop of Mount Subasio where Saint Francis himself had once preached to the birds, Preston could see the vast Basilica di S. Francesco, its splendid campanile soaring clear of the surrounding buildings.

Though it was calm down on the plain, where the marchers had come to a halt, a strong wind was gusting up there on the mountain-side. Banners, attached to the sides and roof of the Basilica, streamed energetically across the ramparts and parapets, adding to the fairy-tale atmosphere of the place.

A ragged cheer broke out among the ranks now that the end of the journey was in sight. Some of the marchers waved the flags and placards which they had been carrying since they set out from Cortona several days before. Others broke into song, chanting the hymns and canticles which had been the intermittent accompaniment of their journey.

After a short break, the procession began to move forward again. Preston found himself walking alongside a small delegation of Chinese who, like hundreds of others, had come from their distant land to participate both in the pilgrimage and the multi-faith service which would take place in the Basilica of St Francis the next morning. Unlike most of the other pilgrims, whose garb varied according to their individual tastes – some wore jeans and T-shirts, others long flowing robes; some wore climbing-boots, others went barefoot – the Chinese team had a certain disciplined uniformity, at least as far as outward appearances were concerned. There were three men and one woman, but all of them were clad in the same loose-fitting grey suit and soft grey cap. Each one carried a banner with Chinese characters on it indicating the name or title of the organisation which they represented. The banner carried by the Chinese woman was inscribed with the legend "WOLONG NATURE RESERVE". In the middle there was a picture of a giant panda. For a Chinese, she was rather tall, Preston thought, and the Mao-style cap perched precariously on top of a mass of thick dark hair served only to accentuate her height.

"It's a helluva long way from Wolong, isn't it?" He fell into step beside her while the other Chinese dropped back. "I'm Preston Murphy, by the way. Good to meet you." A tall confident young man (he was approaching his thirty-sixth birthday), Preston stuck out his hand as though he was running for office.

He thought for a second she was going to turn away from him – he had noted that for most of the journey the Chinese contingent had stuck together without fraternising with the other marchers – but, after a moment's hesitation, she took his hand in hers, bobbing her head as she did so.

"My name is Lilly Wu." She smiled, showing a row of small pearl-white teeth. "Who are you with?" She nodded at the crowd of banners.

"I'm not with any group in particular," Preston admitted. "I work for a firm of consulting engineers based in New York. I was vacationing in Tuscany and joined the march more or less on a whim."

That intrigued her. "We don't often do things like that in my country."

"Where did you learn English?" he asked. He was surprised at how well she spoke the language.

"My mother is an interpreter; she used to teach me in the evenings when she had time, which wasn't very often. And, of course, nowadays we learn English in school."

"Does your father speak English too?"

"Not so well as my mother, but well enough."

"Are you an ecologist by training?"

"I am a biologist. I am in charge of the scientific work at the Panda Research Station at Wolong."

"My father was in China during the war. So was my mother. As a matter of fact, according to the story my mother tells, they actually saw some pandas in the wild and I guess that's pretty rare."

She was puzzled. "Was your father at Wolong?"

"No, he was based in Chungking, with the American mission. He met my mother there. They went on a boat-trip down the Yangtze one day. That's when they discovered the pandas."

"There aren't any pandas downstream from Chung-king."

"Maybe there were then."

She shook her head vigorously. "Not then, not now. The Giant Panda is only to be found in the western part of Sichuan, where the land rises towards the Tibetan plateau."

She spoke so dogmatically that Preston decided he must have remembered the details wrong. His parents had obviously gone upstream, not downstream – west, not east. "I'm sure you know far more about it than I do." He turned on all his Irish charm and was rewarded with another dazzling smile. They continued talking as the procession wound on up the hill. Suddenly, Lilly Wu looked at her watch.

"I must go now," she told him. It was as though she had

been playing truant and would get into trouble if she delayed any further.

"See you later, I hope," Preston said. "Will you be at the ceremony?"

"I'll be there."

"I'll keep an eye out then. Ciao!"

"Goodbye, Preston."

She gave him a quick wave and dropped back to rejoin her companions.

Preston Murphy sat in his seat in the Upper Church of the Basilica of St Francis of Assisi waiting for the procession to arrive. Every place was occupied. Chairs had been brought in to cram the aisles and transepts, leaving scarcely an inch of free floor space. The sun streamed in through the great open doorway where, in a few minutes, the leaders of the world's five great religions would enter the church to begin the historic multi-faith service which the World Wildlife Fund had decided upon as the most fitting way to celebrate its anniversary.

It was a warm autumn day. Preston was glad he had left his coat behind in the small *albergo* where he had lodged the previous night. Even if the ambient temperature had been less than it was, the television arc-lights which had been erected for the occasion inside the church, taken together with the heat generated by the solid mass of the congregation, would have ensured a more than adequate degree of warmth inside the building.

It was 10.15 and the service wasn't scheduled to begin for another fifteen minutes. Preston had time to reflect on his surroundings – the splendid Giottos lining the walls, the magnificent illuminated vaults which arched over the congregation, the marble floors and columns, all of which made the Church of St Francis one of the wonders of Italian art and architecture.

His thoughts were interrupted by the high, pure note of the organ sounding the first thrilling bars of Bach's Canticle of Creation. The members of the congregation, more than 1,000 strong, rose to their feet and Preston Murphy stood with them. In the piazza outside the church they heard the sound of the Assisi trumpets, followed by the deep rumbling notes of the Swiss and Tibetan mountain horns.

The service which followed was, to Preston's surprise, strangely moving. Though it was a mishmash, a hodge-podge, an act of liturgical virtuosity which drew on the traditions of five of the world's major religions, somehow it worked. The message came across loud and clear. For far too long mankind had been busy subduing the earth and exerting dominion over it (and engineering firms like Wilmers and Friendly had played their part in that, hadn't they?) Now, the world's ecologists and the world's churchmen seemed ready to forge a new alliance based on the mutual interdependence of all species, including of course man himself.

The high point of the ceremony came with the so-called Procession of the Symbols. Preston watched, fascinated, as one after another the banners of the world's great religions were paraded down the central aisle of the Basilica high above the heads of the watching crowd. The Menorah was followed by the Buddhist Prayer-Wheel which was in turn followed by the Cross of Christ, the Crescent of Islam, and a large Hindu hieroglyph whose meaning he could not decipher. He picked up his programme from the seat, ready to follow the now united banners on the next scheduled event which, according to the day's agenda, was supposed to be a ceremonial ascent of Mount Subasio.

Others in the congregation, like Preston, thought that the service was over and were mentally preparing themselves for the exertions to come when late, but not too late, a sixth enormous banner was carried in through the portals of the church. A huge Giant Panda! Christ, what *chutzpah!* Murphy thought. The organisers of the event knew a thing or two about showmanship!

She still wore the Mao-style cap, marking, he supposed, her solidarity with the Revolution and its secular basis even as she participated in the present exercise. But she had exchanged the drab grey uniform for a dramatic canary-

yellow trouser suit of the softest silk. The garment accentuated her lithe figure, small pert breasts, trim waist, shapely
ankles. As she walked up the aisle, Preston could imagine
the television cameras zooming in on the improbable, yet
stunning spectacle.

Mentally, he cheered her on, feeling as he did so the
stirring of lust. Then, remembering where he was, he gave
himself a sharp, though silent, rebuke. "For God's sake,
Preston," he told himself, "keep yourself under control."

But still he was more than pleased when Lilly Wu passed
the place where he was sitting and gave him an almost
imperceptible nod of her head. Entranced, Preston watched
her mount the steps of the altar, before turning to face the
congregation, her banner held triumphantly aloft like the
others.

Preston Murphy saw Lilly Wu again later that day. She was
sitting on a dais in the Assisi Conference Centre together
with other notables, answering questions from the press.
Next to her was Ben Bradman, the golden-haired idol of
the screen with two Oscars already to his name. Bradman's
conservationist philosophy was simple. If you want to protect
the view, buy it! The Bradman Foundation, which he had
set up with the money he had made in Hollywood, owned
several hundred thousand acres of mountain and forest in
Washington State, in America's scenic North-West.

"I don't believe," Bradman told the audience, "that it *is*
always possible for man and nature to co-exist. Most times
the odds are stacked in favour of man. I'm just trying to
redress the balance a little."

Some of the journalists in the audience were clearly sceptical. One of them, a corpulent correspondent from *La
Stampa* who had found the ascent of Mount Subasio hot
and tiring, challenged him. "In your country, Mr Bradman,
college kids take their over-powered cars to drive-in movies.
If they didn't, there wouldn't be any profits for your Foundation. Don't you need the system as much as anyone?"

"Hell, yes – I used to go to movies myself before I started
making 'em!" Bradman flashed his famous grin in the gen-

eral direction of the questioner. "I'm just saying we should think about changing the system now, before it's too late." He turned to Lilly Wu, sitting next to him: "Let's ask our Chinese friend what she thinks. She's working at the sharp end, after all."

How easy it would be, Preston thought, for her to score an easy point off capitalism! Deng Xiaoping's tornado of change might have blown away some of the political cobwebs but the political party was still in charge in China. Lilly Wu's minders (that was how he thought of them) seemed to be as interested as he was in Lilly's response. They were sitting near the front, a few seats along, with notebooks in hand and pencils poised.

"Thank you for passing the buck." She laughed, removing her cap and sweeping her hair back. Then she said, in a quiet voice so that those sitting to the rear of the auditorium had to strain to hear: "I believe nature needs all the help it can get, no matter what the country, no matter what the political system may be."

"Bravo!" Bradman led the applause and the audience joined in.

When the press conference was over, Preston caught her alone for a moment. "Great job, Lilly." He glanced towards the other Chinese as they advanced protectively. "There's going to be a party tonight in the piazza – probably an orgy!" he joked. "You ought to try one of our orgies before you go back to China."

She seemed delighted to see him again. "I'll try to be there," she whispered. She found it hard to explain, even to herself, why this tall American with his easy confident manner so attracted her, why she felt so comfortable in his company. It was almost as though they were old friends . . . She giggled, glancing quickly at her colleagues who were having a hard time following the conversation. "I may have to climb out of my hotel window."

The party began late and it continued until the early hours of the morning. They lit a bonfire in the middle of the great square in front of the Basilica and sat around talking and laughing and drinking. An impromptu band

171

established itself beneath the ramparts and those of the 'pilgrims' who still had enough spring left in their step after the day's events danced to the music by the light of the flames.

He began to think she wasn't coming after all, began to suspect that he had misread the tea-leaves, then recognised in himself a sudden and surprising sense of anguish. What if she couldn't make it? What if she'd packed up and departed . . . and he didn't even have her telephone number? Maybe she didn't have a telephone over there . . .

He felt a tug at his sleeve. "Hello, Preston, I'm sorry I'm late. I fell off the rope!"

For Preston, it was a magic memorable night. He'd been to the best schools – Groton and Harvard – thanks to his mother's diligence and the support of some loyal friends; he'd lived – and lived to the full – the life of a well-heeled New York bachelor. His contemporaries had gone into Wall Street or business whereas he had pursued a more practical trade but, after working hours, his life-style did not differ markedly from theirs. He had had a succession of girl-friends and more than once had seemed to be heading for marriage. He had spent months in exotic places and counted himself rich in insight as well as experience. Yet somehow all this seemed insignificant.

"Jesus!" he held her closely to him as they danced. "I don't believe this! How can this be happening to me?"

Later, as the fire in the square began to die down, they walked up onto the ramparts to look at the dawn breaking on the vast Umbrian plain.

"Are you married?" She questioned in that direct, frank manner which he found so attractive.

"No, as a matter of fact I've just broken off with my girl-friend."

"How long ago?"

"About ten minutes ago, actually. When we were dancing back down there." He pointed, laughing, to the piazza below. "What about you?"

"In China, professional women like me marry late – 30, 32, even 34 sometimes . . ."

172

"Wait for me, Lilly!" He made it sound like a joke. For a time, they sat in silence as the day began to lighten. Then, suddenly, Lilly started to sing – a low plaintive song which seemed to flow on and on . . .

Preston had never heard anything like it before. "I wish I could understand what you're saying. Who wrote it? Who composed it?"

"I did," she replied simply. "I wrote this song in the mountains of Sichuan . . . one day last month, before I left for Europe. I sing when I work sometimes."

"I want to kiss you," Preston said, "You're so clever, so beautiful. I've never met anyone like you."

She turned up her face to his. As he held her to him, feeling her body against his, her lips against his lips, her mouth sweet and joyous, he thought – for a moment – that things could just conceivably work out for them. Maybe she would come to America, maybe he would go to China . . .

The bell, tolling its early morning message from the top of the campanile, brought them back to their senses.

"I have to go." Lilly disentangled herself gently. "I have a breakfast meeting with my colleagues. I must be there, otherwise they may go to my room to look for me."

"Breakfast meetings! I thought we were in Italy, not New York!"

Around lunch-time, hoping to see her again, he called her hotel, only to be told that the delegation from China had checked out.

173

2

He spent the afternoon seeing the sights and trying, in vain, to put Lilly Wu out of his mind. It was the last day of his vacation. Tomorrow, he told himself, he would be on a plane to New York. Things would be different then.

When he returned to his hotel, he found a message asking him to call his office.

"Ah, Mr Murphy! Glad you called back. Mr Wilmers has been trying to reach you all morning." The switch-board operator sounded agitated, which was not surprising. Jim Wilmers, President, Chief Executive and Senior Partner of Wilmers & Friendly – a big burly man who in the space of 15 years had pushed his company into the top rank of international consulting engineers – liked his senior staff to be accessible by telephone, telex or telefax at all times.

"Preston, what the hell are you up to?" Wilmers came on the line.

It only took one telephone call, Preston thought, to puncture the euphoria. Reality was an irate boss concerned not with tomorrow's world, but today's. He realised there was no point in trying to explain what Assisi meant. Not now, anyway, with Wilmers about 6,000 miles away and the clock ticking.

"I'm on vacation, actually," Preston tried unsuccessfully to mollify his employer. "I'll be in the office next week."

"You aren't coming back to the office."

"What . . . ?" For a moment Preston thought he might have been sacked just for going on holiday at the wrong moment.

"You're booked on the afternoon plane tomorrow from Paris to Beijing. You'll get your visa on arrival."

"What am I doing exactly?" China! Preston could hardly believe the coincidence.

"You'll find a detailed telex waiting for you at the Air

174

France departure desk. I can tell you now that we've got big trouble."

"Three Gorges?" Most of Preston's work in recent years had been in the Americas, especially in Brazil where he had been trying to sort out the problems which had arisen with the massive Itaipu hydro-electric system. But as a partner in the firm, he of course knew that Wilmers & Friendly's single most important commitment at the present time was in China, where they had been retained as the overall consulting engineers on the Three Gorges Project, the massive dam on the Yangtze River which politicians and engineers had dreamed about for decades and whose construction was now finally nearing completion. For the last five years, work had been proceeding steadily. Water was already being impounded behind the massive barrage which had been built near the town of Sandouping at the mouth of the Three Gorges. The turbines were in the process of being installed at both ends of the dam with a planned capacity of 15 million kilowatts. The benefits, in terms of irrigation and flood-control, were estimated to be equally gigantic. The Three Gorges Dam had become the very symbol of modern China, the central plank in the programme of modernisation inaugurated by Deng Xiaoping in the 1980s.

"Of course, I'm talking about Three Gorges!" Wilmers snapped. "We're not just in trouble, we're in double trouble. Bill Friendly's sick. He's on his way home at the moment and he won't be returning to China."

"Hell, I'm sorry to hear that!" Preston's concern was genuine. Bill Friendly, the other half of the roadshow, was in many respects the opposite of Jim Wilmers. Whereas Wilmers hustled for business, browbeating and arm-twisting, Friendly's job had been on the technical side. Getting the business was one thing, but there was no substitute for actual performance in the field. If a firm of consulting engineers was linked with a dam that burst, or a road that washed away in the first flood, or a bridge that collapsed, then it was dead in the water. Consulting engineers were normally engaged on a percentage basis in addition to the flat-rate fee they charged for their services. The larger the

175

project, the more money came in. But Friendly had always been scrupulous, perfectionist in his approach. If he thought a project was flawed, he said so. He'd insist on changes and, if the changes weren't made, he'd walk away from the job. His partner's attitude sometimes irritated the hell out of Wilmers who, on the whole, believed that corners were made for cutting. But in the last analysis, Wilmers had always been wise enough to respect Friendly's point of view. He knew that if he didn't, his firm wouldn't stay in business for very long.

"Yes, it's bad news," Wilmers agreed gruffly. "But we've got to concentrate on the present. I want you to take over from Bill. You're the best man we have available. Itaipu may not be as big as the Three Gorges but, dammit, we all thought it was big enough when we started! You'll be on that plane tomorrow then?"

"You bet!" Preston couldn't keep the excitement out of his voice. To build one big dam in a lifetime was more than most engineers hoped for. To build the two biggest dams the world had ever seen exceeded his wildest dreams! "You said double trouble. What's the other problem?"

Sitting in his office half a world away, Jim Wilmers hesitated. For the last three hours, ever since he had heard the news that the World Bank had called a press conference in Beijing for the following Thursday on the subject of the Three Gorges project, he had been on the telephone trying to find out what was up. He had called Harry Christiansen, the World Bank's Senior Vice-President in charge of operations and a personal friend, but Christiansen had, for once, been evasive, conceding merely that it was more than a normal progress statement.

Wilmers had called other friends and contacts in Washington: in the Treasury, in the US Agency for International Development, in the State Department; but either they didn't know, or they weren't saying.

"My own guess," Wilmers spoke slowly in reply to Preston's question, "is that the World Bank is going to spring some kind of surprise next Thursday. It might be a pleasant surprise. Or again, it could be a nasty one. That's why I want you there. You can go on down to the site after that."

Exactly 12 hours later, Preston Murphy was sitting in the departure lounge at Charles de Gaulle International Airport at Roissy outside Paris. With ten minutes to go before boarding, he walked over to a telephone booth, took out a credit card and placed a call to a number in the United States.

"Mother, this is Preston. I'm in Paris. I'm on my way to Beijing."

Mary Murphy had long since given up trying to keep track of her son's movements. Engineers were like soldiers. They went where duty called. "That's great, darling. What will you be doing?"

Keeping an eye on the indicator board and an ear open for any announcements, he told her briefly of his conversation the previous afternoon with Jim Wilmers. "I'll be responsible for supervising the whole project. Basically, that means it may be quite a few months before I get back home. The official inauguration of the dam is meant to be on October 1st next year, that's the Fortieth Anniversary of the founding of the Chinese People's Republic."

Mary Murphy had been delighted to hear her son's news. "I'm going to mail you a package tomorrow, darling." He was about to hang up but instead, he paused, intrigued. Something in her voice told him she wasn't talking about socks or candy.

"What is it?"

"A surprise."

As she replaced the receiver, Mary Murphy smiled. For years she had been waiting for the right moment to give Preston his father's diaries but somehow it never seemed to arrive. Preston had always seemed too busy leading his own life to dwell in the past. Or maybe, she thought, he simply didn't want to dig down too deep . . .

On the long flight to Beijing, Preston had plenty of time to put his thoughts in order. Here he was, he reflected, an

177

American citizen jumping on to a plane to China at the drop of a hat without even a valid visa in his passport. Yet only a few years earlier, such a journey would have been unthinkable. What a long way US-China relations had come since the doldrums of the past! Roosevelt, Truman, Eisenhower, Kennedy, Johnson – no less than five successive US Presidents had been either unable or unwilling to build bridges between America and China. How ironic it was that the breakthrough had been achieved by that most maligned of leaders, Richard Milhouse Nixon. Whatever his other failings might have been, President Nixon had initiated not only a new diplomatic relationship with China, but also the whole process of trade, exchange and investment which – ten or 15 years later – had grown to be of such importance. In many ways, Preston thought, the Three Gorges Dam was itself the gigantic symbol of this collaboration. US engineers had designed the project, with Wilmers & Friendly in the lead; US companies played a major role in the international consortium charged with the construction. True, much of the money had been provided by the World Bank, but there too the United States was a major shareholder.

They spent about an hour on the ground in New Delhi, then flew on to Beijing. Preston slept most of the way and when he woke up to see the green fields of China beneath him, he felt a sense of elation which he had never experienced before.

3

Preston Murphy's first glimpse of China was of a large bill-
board fixed to the front of the modern airport building:
ROWLANDS-SOONG: ASIA'S LARGEST BANKING
AND TRADING COMPANY. Beneath the legend was a
picture of a soaring gleaming skyscraper, set against the
background of Hong Kong Harbour.

Somehow the image confused Preston. He had anticipated a smoother landing, involving less of an immediate
culture shock, though in this case the surprise lay in finding
the garish symbols of capitalism so prominently displayed
at the very portals of Cathay.

Inside the airport building, quarantine forms were handed
out. "Should passengers", Preston read, "develop any
symptoms, chills, acute skin rash, jaundice, diarrhoea,
vomiting, or swelling, please contact quarantine offices
immediately." He took out a pen, ticked what seemed to be
the relevant boxes and handed it back. What the Chinese
were terrified of, he suspected, was the spread of AIDS.
So far, amazingly, there had only been one authenticated
case and that had been some student from Zaïre who had
entered the country on an exchange programme. If the
incident was repeated, he imagined the authorities would
soon clamp down by insisting on blood tests.

For a second he wondered whether the pretty Chinese
health official sitting behind her stack of yellow forms was
going to whip out a needle and plunge it into his arm. But
the girl merely smiled at him, taking in his sober suit and
clean-shaven appearance, and waved him through.

"Next stop customs!" she nodded in the direction of the
desks immediately behind her where a row of immigration
officers, smartly-dressed in green denim uniforms and
peaked hats complete with ear-pieces to be used in cold
weather, waited to process arriving passengers.

179

The other side of the barrier the usual forest of placards greeted the arriving traveller. He spotted a man carrying a sign with his name on it.

"Wilmers and Friendly?" The man nodded his head enthusiastically. "Welcome to Beijing, Mr Murphy! I am Fen Huashi, Wilmers and Friendly's Beijing agent. Driver waiting in car. We go Lido Hotel now! Lido Hotel is Beijing's Holiday Inn. Best hamburger bar in town! Twenty-four-hour telex too!"

Twenty minutes later, the car drew up in front of the Beijing Lido.

"You have free day tomorrow," Fen saw him into the lobby. "Visit Great Wall of China. Tonight you have dinner with Mr Friendly. Meet him 7 p.m. in Jakarta Lounge. Then you eat in hotel restaurant. Best Peking Duck in town."

"Good Heavens!" Preston exclaimed, "I had no idea Friendly was still in China."

"Mr Friendly leaving tomorrow."

Fen Huashi beckoned to the doorman to fetch the bags. He saw Preston reach into his pocket. "No tipping in China," he warned. Then he smiled. "Not yet, anyway."

Shortly before seven, having showered and changed, Preston Murphy was waiting in the Jakarta Lounge of the hotel for Bill Friendly to come down and join him for dinner. It was a large room, furnished – as the name implied – in exotic style. Cane chairs were interspersed with long leather couches and an intricate fountain, illuminated from within, cascaded over a large glass and metal sculpture. In front of the fountain, a Chinese quartet played classical music. Still jet-lagged, Preston shut his eyes and leaned his head back in the chair.

"How are you? Good to see you!" Preston felt a hand on his shoulder and looked up to see Bill Friendly standing beside him.

"Bill! This is great! I hadn't expected to see you." As they shook hands, Preston noticed that the flesh on Friendly's face seemed to have shrunk and there was a noticeable pallor beneath his professional tan (you couldn't build dams without going out in the sun). Friendly was a tall man, well over six foot, but his shoulders had a stoop to them now which Preston didn't recall seeing before.

"Sit down, Preston." Friendly pushed him back into his chair and pulled up one of his own. "Don't look so shocked, I'm not dead yet!" He laughed hoarsely and leaned forward so that Preston could see the greyish-yellow tinge to his eyeballs. "I had hepatitis but I'm over that now. The trouble is, there's something else they can't pin down. I'm going back for tests."

He leaned back in his chair and beckoned to a waiter.

"What'll you have?" he asked when a smartly-dressed youth arrived to take the order. "I'm sticking to fruit juice."

"Scotch and soda, please." After eighteen hours in the air, Preston felt he needed something long and cool and definitely alcoholic.

Over drinks, Bill Friendly revealed the full extent of his disappointment: "I'm an engineer of the old school, you see. I grew up believing that structures like the Hoover Dam represented the ultimate in civil engineering, until the next one came along, of course. We hadn't heard when I was at school that 'small is beautiful'. That went for your father, too, Preston. He and I trained together, as you know. I couldn't have been more delighted than I was the day I heard Oliver Murphy's son was going to join the firm."

He paused, sipping his fruit juice. "I wish I'd seen more of you over the years. We always seem to get posted to different parts of the world. There's something I've wanted to say to you for a long time. I guess now is as good a moment as any." He looked Preston straight in the eye as he continued: "I was abroad at the time of your father's death – we were working on some Marshall Plan projects in Europe – but I didn't believe a word of the stories I read. Your father was no more a Communist than I am. If he committed suicide, and I say 'if' because I was never convinced, then they drove him to it.

"It must have been hell for you as a child," he added, sympathetically. "Not only had you lost a father; you had to grow up with the knowledge that, in the public mind at least, he was next best thing to a traitor. Alger Hiss and Oliver Murphy, I remember that people used to couple the two names together like Sacco and Vanzetti . . ."

"You say, *if* my father committed suicide . . ." Preston spoke quietly.

"They found a copy of the latest issue of *Time* magazine in the wreck of your father's car, next to his body. That issue had a cover story on Communists in the State Department in which your father featured prominently. It was written by one of Henry Luce's bum-boys, a journalist called Ed Rovere – long since dead. Many people believed that the *Time* feature was one of the reasons, if not *the* reason, for the suicide, but to me, that was plain nonsense. Your father died, as far as they could establish, around midnight on a Thursday. His body was found around 9 a.m. the next morning. When I was back in New York, I went to the Reading Room in the Public Library on 42nd Street and looked up the issue of *Time* magazine. I wanted to see the story. That issue was dated Friday, November 30th, that is to say the very morning your father's body was found. So I checked with the publishers and I was told that on the whole the magazine doesn't hit the bookstands until around noon on the Friday. If you're lucky, you might get it an hour or two earlier in New York – after all that's where the Luce Empire had its headquarters – but it certainly wouldn't be available in the Washington area until lunchtime at the earliest. On the other hand, someone with access could have picked up an advance copy and flown down to Washington with it. Do you see what I'm getting at?"

Friendly was wracked by a sudden fit of coughing. "Too many cheap Chinese cigarettes," he spluttered. When he finally recovered his breath, he came straight to the point.

"I always thought your father might have been murdered. Someone could have pushed him over the edge of the cliff in his car, possibly when he was already dead, but – before they did so – they could have placed a copy of the magazine inside the vehicle, knowing that it would be found together with the body."

"Why didn't you say so at the time?"

182

"I did. I wrote to the Coroner and to the police. They simply weren't interested. It was almost as though the public authorities took the view that whatever happened to Murphy served him right and it certainly wasn't sensible to stir the pot. I wrote your mother, too, Preston, just as I was leaving for another overseas assignment. I didn't hear from her for several months but when at last her reply reached me – I was in Iran at the time – she too seemed to feel that it was pointless to drag the whole business into the open again. She was starting a new life, she said, and she had to think of the future, not the past. I think she felt that nothing but trouble could come if she tried to track down your father's murderers, if indeed he was murdered. For all I know, she may have been right. Only someone who's lived through them can realise just how dark those days were. Remember you yourself had been kidnapped. To your mother it seemed like a miracle that you had been returned unharmed."

"My father never knew that," Preston said. "He was dead by the time they gave me back." He paused, marshalling his thoughts, trying to fit all the pieces together. "Why should anyone have wanted to kill him? Hadn't they destroyed him already?"

Bill Friendly rose unsteadily to his feet. "Let's go into dinner."

They ate in the Marco Polo Restaurant. It was strange, thought Preston, how the Venetian traveller lived on seven centuries later. The Chinese had fought their first, losing, battles against the Japanese at the famous Marco Polo bridge outside Peking. Henry Kissinger's secret trips to see Chou En Lai before Nixon's 1972 visit had been code-named Polo One and Polo Two. And now the old boy had lent his name to what was probably the best establishment for international cuisine in the city.

"They cater for all tastes, I believe," Friendly said as they took their seats. "If you're an American and feeling home-sick – which is true of quite a lot of us – you can choose between a Venison Burger, a Sea Food Burger, a Farmer's Burger, a Chicken Burger or a plain old Hamburger. Alternatively you can try the international menu. Calamari from

Greece, Wienerschnitzel? Something tasty from Malaysia with curried prawns and steamed rice?"

"Nothing Chinese on the menu?" Preston asked. "Shouldn't I be calling for chopsticks and noodles?"

Friendly laughed. "By the time you go home, you'll be so sick of Chinese food – you'll be eating it for breakfast, lunch and dinner down at the dam site, I can tell you that – that you'll be longing for a hamburger and french fries. Put one in the bag now, that's my advice, you never know where the next will come from."

In the end they both ordered the Chef's Salad with a bottle of white Chinese wine, marketed under the Dynasty label which cost at the official exchange rate around 25 dollars. New York prices, Preston thought, but in a way the Beijing Lido was little more than an outpost of Manhattan.

Half-way through their meal, Preston reverted to the question which was uppermost in his mind. "Who might have wished to have killed my father?" he asked.

Friendly chased a piece of lettuce round his plate with a fork. "I don't know, son. It's all so long ago now." He sounded tired, drained. "At the time, of course, it was a question I asked myself as well, as you may imagine. Undoubtedly, Murphy's apparent suicide helped the McCarthyites. In the circumstances, it was seen as an admission of guilt. It was the next best thing to a verdict of the courts. Or even better, perhaps, when you come to think of it. Suicide was neater, quicker, and there was no danger that the other side of the story would have to be told, as it would have been if there had been an open trial. And if the 'suicide' helped the McCarthyites, it helped the China Lobby too. For a time at least, the pro-Taiwan faction in Washington had a field day. But as for saying precisely who might have had your father murdered . . ." His voice trailed off.

They sat at the table over coffee for another half-hour. Friendly took the opportunity to give Preston a quick briefing about the situation he would encounter when he reached the dam-site.

"Things are going well," he concluded. "Work is on

schedule. We began impounding water four months back. The planned operating level is 180 metres and we should reach that in a few months."

"Then why are they calling this special meeting on Thursday? Wilmers sounded unusually uptight."

Friendly shrugged his shoulders. "I'm as much in the dark as everyone else."

Later, they went for a leisurely walk in the streets near the hotel.

"I've got to take it easy," Friendly explained. "Too much exercise knocks the hell out of me! I would never have let Jim pull me off the project, not now with the end in sight after six long years, if I had felt I could still do my job. But the truth of the matter is, Preston, I couldn't get around any longer. You know as well as I do that you can't just sit in the office. You've got to be able to walk and climb. I couldn't even crawl."

They turned the corner of the block. The Beijing Lido was situated some way from the centre of the city and the streets were already deserted. Friendly felt a chill in the air. In a few weeks' time winter would have set in with a vengeance.

As they reached the lobby of the hotel, Friendly turned to say goodbye. "It's done me good talking to you, son. I've been feeling pretty low recently." He paused. "There's one thing I'd like you to do for me. You're going to Xian on Friday, aren't you?"

Preston nodded. "Xian first, then Chungking."

Friendly reached into his pocket. "I want you to give this computer disk to a friend of mine. Professor Zheng Fushun. He runs the seismology programme at Xian's Jiaotong University. I'd put it in the mail normally," he added, "but I'd prefer to send it with you, since you're going that way." He laughed. "As a matter of fact, you may get to see quite a bit of Xian. I was once stranded there for three days while we waited for the fog to clear in Chungking!"

"No problem." Preston took the disk and turned it over in his hand. "What's on it?"

"Seismic data, collected during the period of impoundment. We've got no facilities down at Sandouping, so it all goes to Zheng. He has some of the most powerful computers in China and the best brains to go with them." A shadow crossed Friendly's face. "The Chinese showed us all the data before construction began. In that part of Sichuan you've never had quakes of more than five on the Richter scale. The way we've built the dam, you'd need a quake much larger than that before the structure even began to rattle!"

"Why does Zheng need the disk, then?"

"Heaven knows! But I told him I'd help in any way I could. Will you do it, Preston?"

"Of course." Preston slipped the disk into his pocket. He held out his hand. "Goodnight, Bill."

"Goodnight, son, look after yourself." Friendly picked up his key at the desk and walked to the elevator.

After Friendly had gone, Preston sat for a while by himself in the lobby of the hotel. How strange it was, he thought, that a few words from Bill Friendly had once again brought to the surface his longing to find out the truth about his father's death. He had his childhood memories, of course – of a tall, solid, comforting figure, playing with him in the sun-dappled yard; of family walks along the old overgrown Chesapeake and Ohio canal; of perching on his lap as they drove through Rock Creek Park in their shiny new car. But the shadow of doubt remained. The act of suicide, if such it had been, was an act of rejection, the ultimate rejection. If, on the other hand, his father had been murdered, if there was indeed a link between his own kidnapping and his father's death . . . As a three-year-old, he had not been much use to the police in their inquiries. He had been able to point out the kind of car that had picked him up, confirming what the police already knew from other witnesses. But he had never been able to describe the men involved nor where they had taken him. It was as though someone had pressed the erase key, blanking out that particular file. One day, Preston thought, maybe something might jolt his memory . . .

Earlier that evening a string quartet had played Haydn

186

and Mozart for the benefit of the guests, but the musicians had long since disappeared to be replaced by canned music of the kind typical of high-class international hotels. It was the sort of music you didn't bother to listen to but you noticed if it stopped. Preston was about to go to bed – it had, indeed, been a long day – when the tune of the muzak changed and he found himself listening, not to synthetic pap, but to the most haunting melody he had ever heard in his life.

He stood stock-still in the middle of the lobby, noting to his surprise that he was not alone in his reaction. Almost all the Chinese staff on duty – the receptionists, the cashiers, the bell-boys, the waiters – had gathered in front of the loudspeaker. When at last the song ended and the waves of sound fell back, dying into a slow tragic silence, the little crowd burst into applause.

Who was the singer? Preston wondered. What was her song about?

Later that night, as he tried to sleep, he found he could not put the sounds and rhythms of the song from his mind. What the singer had done, he realised, was to clothe an identifiable melody of a kind which would not be out of place amid, say, the Top Ten in the United States in the traditional garments of a Chinese vocalist. He slept at last to dream of forests and mountains, of a lake building up behind a great dam, and of a Chinese girl, looking remarkably like Lilly Wu, singing in the thin morning air.

4

Preston came down to the hotel lobby early the next morning to find that Fen had not only produced a car for him but a guide as well. The little man excused himself with a smile.

"Guide look after you very well," he explained. "She bring you back to hotel this evening. I meet you tomorrow morning, same time – yes?"

The guide, a studious bespectacled lady who told Preston she was employed by Luxingshe, China's tourist agency, was determined to make sure he had his money's worth. "Today we visit Great Wall. I think weather is not too bad, right? But maybe cold at Wall. Please take your jacket."

They drove out of the city in a north-westerly direction. The streets were full of people on bicycles. High-rise buildings, some with washing hanging from the windows, dominated the roadside. The architecture was uninspired.

"Beijing divided into ten districts and nine counties. Population more than nine million, five million in suburban area, four million in city area. In 1911, Beijing became cradle of new Chinese Democratic Revolution; main fight against feudalism began here. On October 1st, 1949, Chairman Mao proclaimed to whole world the independence of China. From then on Chinese people stood up . . ."

Preston absorbed the scenery while he listened to his guide with half an ear. They could never dethrone Mao completely, he thought, any more than the Russians could disown Stalin. They might topple some of the statues but you could never rewrite history entirely.

They crossed over one motorway, then another. "Second and third ringroads are finished. Fourth and fifth ringroads are under construction. Two sections of the subway are completed. One, opened in 1959, goes from railway station – seventeen stops altogether. Second section, opened two years ago, encircles city. You pay ten Fen on subway, no matter how far you go."

"How many Fen in one Yuan?"

"One hundred."

"And how many Yuan for one US dollar?" He asked the question deliberately. At the official exchange rate, the Bank of China would give him two Yuan for one dollar, but he wanted to hear her answer.

For the first time that morning she smiled, her eyes lighting up behind the thick black glasses. "You change dollars for foreign exchange certificates, please, Sir."

By now they had left the city area. The road was still crowded with cyclists and pedestrians and commercial vehicles of one kind or another, but the land had opened out at either side. The guide kept up her steady stream of commentary: "Two hundred ninety-six people's communes in Beijing area. First introduced in 1958. Now Chinese people have responsibility system so production has gone up." She pointed at agricultural produce piled by the wayside. "Main crops in Beijing area are wheat and rice, two crops a year. Main fruit crops are apples, peach, pear and grapes."

"Ask the driver to stop, would you, I'd like to take a look."

They walked among the wayside stalls. The goods, Preston observed, were plentiful and varied. "This is free market," she explained. "Farmers must sell part to government market, rest they can sell here."

"What's that?" He pointed to a huge poster which had been fixed onto the wall of a building at the edge of the market. It depicted a smiling Chinese man and woman with a placid well-fed child standing between them.

"That is family planning message," the guide explained. "It says 'one child, one family'. In city area if you have second child, you pay 1,000 Yuan fine or maybe 2,000 Yuan. Minority peoples in remote areas, they can have second and third, maybe fourth child, but for Han people in city, just one child!"

"Sounds a bit hard."

189

"Population problem very big problem." She sounded defensive. "Today China have over one thousand million people. How to feed them, how to clothe them, how to educate them and many more millions still to come! Family planning is basic national policy in China!"

As they drove on, the air became perceptibly clearer. When they left Beijing that morning, the city had been enveloped in a sharp acrid mist. Preston had remarked how many of the inhabitants, young and old, went around with white gauze face-masks.

"Big pollution problem in Beijing," his guide had explained. "All big cities in China have air pollution problem. Power plants burn dirty coal, industry burns dirty coal. People burn coal in their houses. Necessary to keep warm."

"Where did you learn English?" Preston asked, thinking of all the wonderful clean life-transforming hydro-electric power which would be generated by the Three Gorges Dam.

"In Middle School. During Cultural Revolution, most of the schools closed for almost two years. Children had nothing to do. They just stayed in their house. In 1976, many students went to study in University, but no chance for me. You stay in China long?"

"Six months, maybe more, I'd like to learn Chinese."

"Best way to learn Chinese you marry Chinese girl!" she laughed.

"Why not?" Preston laughed. "Do you think the rules about having only one child would apply?"

"Depends whether you marry Han woman! Depends whether you live in rural area!"

Preston had a brief mental glimpse of a new little nuclear family, consisting of himself and some smiling Chinese bride, infant on hip, walking across a golden plain towards distant sunlit mountains.

They were silent for a while and the driver turned the radio on.

"There's that song again!" Preston exclaimed, as the strange melody which he had heard in the hotel the previous evening filled the car. "What's it about?"

190

"About Yangtze river as it flows through Sichuan Province," the guide told him. "About how all forests are being cut down in mountains, about how animals are disappearing, about how river itself is swollen with mud and sediment. It is song about how we are destroying own country through thoughtless acts."

"No wonder it's Top of the Pops!"

She missed the irony in his tone.

"Singer is Lilly Wu," she continued. "She wrote this song, sang it one day on Chengdu radio station. Everyone is singing it now. Of course," the guide added, "She is lucky. Minister Wu Canping is her father. That helps, you see. Otherwise, could be problems. In China, we not used to pop stars like you have in America. Elvis Presley, Bob Dylan, Janice Joplin . . ." She laughed.

"I met her once in Italy," he told his guide.

"How wonderful! What was she like?" For a moment she was transformed from being the studious, overworked, underpaid interpreter into an avid member of the growing Lilly Wu Fan Club.

She left him to his own devices when they reached the Great Wall. "Come back in two hours," she instructed. "Car will be waiting. Today you are lucky. Not many people."

Preston looked up at the vast structure which towered above him, then snaked and zigzagged over the distant hills. This section of the Wall had been carefully restored. The parapets were in good order; the flag-stones had been cleaned; the battlements which crowned each succeeding section had been repaired where they had crumbled or collapsed. He was pleased. After the long flight it would do him good to stretch his legs.

As he got out of the car, he felt the stiff cold breeze, saw a vendor selling fur hats with earpieces at the foot of the wide stairs which led up to the first parapet, and decided to buy one. Thus equipped, he waved goodbye to his guide and bounded up the steps, two at a time.

Ten minutes later he overtook a group of soldiers. They were ambling along the top of the wall, five abreast, in their

191

bottle-green uniforms clearly enjoying their break from the usual monotony of military life. One of them carried a transistor radio and Preston recognised the now familiar voice of Lilly Wu.

As he climbed up the ladder inside the observation tower towards the platform at the top, Preston looked up to see a man of medium height wearing a tartan hunting jacket and a golfing hat peering down at him. The face was familiar.

Preston smiled. "Ben Bradman! I saw you in Assisi. My name's Preston Murphy." He held out his hand.

"Good to meet you, Preston." Bradman flashed him the rugged smile which over the years had charmed millions into the box-office. "Welcome to the Middle Kingdom!" He waved his arm at the chain of mountains which stretched ahead of them and at the Wall which ran like a switch-back from crest to crest until it shrank at last to a thin golden-grey line blending into the distant sky.

"What are you doing here?" Bradman asked, as they started back. "Tourist?"

Preston explained the reasons for his visit. "And you?"

Bradman answered the question with another. "Did you ever hear about Père David's deer?"

"No."

"Well, we've got plenty of time. Père David," Bradman explained, "was a French missionary and explorer turned naturalist. He travelled in China and Mongolia in the nineteenth century and his chief claim to fame lies in the fact that he managed to persuade the Emperor to send a few specimens of a kind of reindeer which survived only in the Imperial Park to zoos in London and Berlin. In 1894 a flood destroyed parts of the Imperial Park wall, which meant that most of the deer escaped into the countryside, where of course they got eaten. A few years later, in 1900 actually, the few breeding specimens which remained were slaughtered by troops during the Boxer rebellion. That meant that the deer was now totally extinct in China which was its native home and it wasn't found anywhere else in the wild. In fact, Père David's deer would probably be extinct, period,

192

if the eleventh Duke of Bedford, one of those eccentric English aristocrats, I guess, hadn't bought up the animals from the zoos in London and Berlin, put them in a 3,000-acre park on his vast estate at Woburn and began to breed from them. The whole of the present herd of Père David's deer springs from a gene pool of around eighteen animals! You've got over four hundred deer at Woburn today. What's more, they've even managed to reintroduce then into China ..."

They paused as they reached the end of one stretch of wall before embarking on the next. Preston gazed curiously at his companion. "And you want to do the same for the Giant Panda?"

"How did you guess?" Bradman grinned. "There are probably less than a thousand of them left and many of these are in isolated clumps in inadequate environments. In my view, the last viable gene-pool is at Wolong, and even that is under threat today. People are encroaching on the reserve all the time. The pandas are on the retreat but there's nowhere else left for them to go. If you go any further West, you hit the Tibetan plateau and that's not panda country."

He turned to face Preston directly.

"My Foundation owns a mountain-valley in the Pacific North-West – Washington State actually. Terrain and climate are not dissimilar to that of Sichuan. For the last fifteen years we've been growing bamboo there. Every damn type of bamboo that pandas eat. If one kind flowers and dies, there's another kind to fall back on. I want to build up a viable panda population in the United States, based on a nucleus of pandas taken from China. The moment the Chinese demonstrate they can protect the habitat, we'll return the stock with interest. Not all of it, of course. The Foundation will still keep its own little colony as an insurance policy."

There was a gleam in Bradman's eyes. Each man, Preston thought, has his own intimations of immortality. You could build a giant dam, you could save a Giant Panda – was it all, in the end, an ego trip?

"Did you talk to Lilly Wu when you were in Assisi?"

Bradman frowned. "She just laughed at me, told me the place to save the panda was in China, not America! Apparently they've introduced the death penalty for killing or stealing pandas. I told her I wasn't ready to take 'no' for an answer and that I'd come and talk to the government officially."

Preston shot a quick sideways look at the actor. There was, it seemed to him, something almost maniacal about Bradman's enthusiasm. Did the man really expect the Chinese to surrender a sizeable chunk of the fast-dwindling panda population so that it could be transported to some mountain-park in the United States on a speculative breeding venture?

Bradman sensed his silent criticism. "Top scientists have vetted the scheme, Preston. The President's interested. WWF's people have gone over every detail. They've even chewed the bamboo!"

Preston saw his guide waiting as they reached the base of the wall. "Can I give you a lift?"

"I'm taken care of, thanks." Bradman nodded in the direction of a long black limousine, flying the red flag of the People's Republic of China.

How strange the pattern of things was, Preston reflected, as he watched the film-star being driven away. Forty years earlier his parents had stumbled upon a mountain valley which, according to his mother's account, had been a veritable paradise for wildlife. He had recounted the whole story to Bradman during the course of the afternoon, much to the man's excitement.

"Hell, do you think they could be still there?" Bradman had asked eagerly. "That could solve all our problems!"

"No hope at all, I'd say." Preston had hated to prick the man's enthusiasm. "Remember the population of Sichuan is over one hundred million people today. There are precious few wilderness areas left in China anywhere. Forty years ago, of course, it was a different story."

*

194

On the way back to the city, they stopped for half an hour at a wayside tea-house where Preston made brave attempts to improve his chopstick technique. The secret, he realised from studying his fellow diners – all of them Chinese – was to lift the bowl to one's lips, tilt it at a 45-degree angle and, literally, shovel the food in. It wasn't elegant, but it worked.

Small pieces of stewed fish lurked among the tangled strands of noodle and at one point Preston found himself chewing on a round, rubbery object which inspection showed to be the actual eye of whatever finny creature had been dumped into the broth.

"Enjoy your meal?" The guide came to join him at the table.

"You bet." Preston burped in the approved fashion and washed down the last noodles with a glass of beer. He'd had better Chinese meals on Second Avenue but they'd cost about 500 times as much!

An hour and a half later, they were back in Beijing. As they drove down Changan Avenue and into Tien An Men, the Square of Heavenly Peace, Preston asked his guide to drop him off. "Thanks for everything. I'll find my own way back to the hotel later."

Left alone, Preston walked towards the middle of Tien An Men Square and then turned to face the Gate of Heavenly Peace. By now, it was late afternoon. To his left, the sun was already dropping behind the Great Hall of the People so that the shadow of the gigantic building was projected across the square. It was here, Preston recalled, that President Nixon had been given the colossal State banquet which had set the seal on China's new-found friendship with America. He remembered how he had cut classes that day to watch the event live on television and even now he could recall the words that Nixon had used: "There is no reason for us to be enemies. Neither of us seeks the territory of the other; neither of us seeks domination over the other; neither of us seeks to stretch out our hands and rule the world."

He walked in a slow semi-circle. On the south side of the square stood the vast mausoleum which they had con-

195

structed virtually overnight to house the mortal remains of Chairman Mao. Even now, nearly 15 years after his death, a long line of people waited to pay their respects to the lost leader. They would shuffle, two by two, past the open coffin where Mao's body lay embalmed before rejoining the throngs which, at almost any hour of the day, seemed to collect spontaneously in the vast square. Tien An Men was the very heart of modern China. Five times larger than Red Square in Moscow, it covered almost a hundred acres and could hold a million people!

As he walked on, it seemed to him that he was able to look at the surrounding scene with a heightened awareness, almost as though he had taken some mind-expanding drug. The people who were with him – families with children, soldiers on leave, minority people from far-away places like Tibet in their bright national costumes, peasants with white kerchiefs round their heads – seemed to have stepped straight out of the smiling, simplified wall-posters onto the street. Some of them carried cameras and transistor radios. One or two even had Walkmans.

When Preston returned to his hotel, he was surprised to find that his room had been disturbed. He was a methodical man and it didn't take him long to realise that his luggage had been searched and that someone had riffled through his papers. As far as he could tell, nothing had been taken.

Was it standard official practice, he wondered, to give new arrivals the once-over? Or was this a free-lance effort by some local entrepreneur, demonstrating that at least the petty criminal class had absorbed Deng's message about the need for individual initiative?

As he hung his jacket in the cupboard, he felt in the pocket the weight of the computer-disk which Bill Friendly had given him the previous evening.

When he went to bed that night, he locked and chained the door and next morning, as he went down to breakfast, he made sure that he carried the disk with him.

5

Successive Emperors had decreed that no building in Peking should ever be higher than the halls and palaces of the Forbidden City – they were averse to being looked down on by their subjects. As Premier, Chou En Lai had sought to maintain the old imperial rule, though for different reasons. He realised the danger that injudicious building might pose to the city's sublime architecture. On the whole, he had been successful. Around Tien An Men, at least, the skyline still remained relatively uncluttered. If you climbed up to the top of the hill in Beihai Park, just to the north of the Imperial City, and stood at the base of the great white Dagoba Pagoda which crowned its summit, you could see that even now, more than a decade after Chou's death, relatively little high-rise construction had taken place in the area which lay within the old city walls.

But outside those limits, it was a different story. From where he sat, in the Conference Room on the 14th floor of Beijing's newest skyscraper, carefully positioned just south of Qianmen Gate in the outer suburban zone, Preston had an uninterrupted bird's eye view of the magnificent layered roof of the Temple of Heaven and of the great park beyond. Was it here, he wondered, that Père David's deer had browsed in antediluvian bliss?

His reverie didn't last long. Harry Christiansen, Senior Vice-President of the World Bank, came into the room to take his seat at the top table. He was followed by a thick-set Chinese of medium height who sat down in front of a name-card marked WU CANPING – MINISTER FOR ENERGY AND NATURAL RESOURCES. So this was Wu! Preston eyed him curiously seeing as he did so not only China's Senior Vice-Premier, but Lilly Wu's father. There wasn't, he reflected, much physical resemblance between the two. He remembered – how could he forget?

– Lilly as lithe and supple, whereas Wu Canping had clearly thickened up with age. But perhaps they had certain character traits in common . . . Was Lilly, deep-down, as tough as her old man?

The last person to take his allotted place was Horst Klarfeld, boss of the giant West German construction company, DeutscheWerk. Klarfeld was a solid, broad-shouldered man in his early sixties who had, over the last few years, become the de facto leader of the international consortium of firms engaged on building the giant Yangtze Dam.

Preston himself, together with others closely involved on the Yangtze project, sat in the front row of the stalls. Behind them an area had been set aside for journalists. Preston was surprised to note that more than a dozen members of Beijing's international press corps had decided to attend that morning's event together with a small handful of Chinese newsmen representing, Preston supposed, the main newspapers or wire services, such as Xinhua, the official Chinese press agency.

Christiansen, whose sand-coloured hair and fair complexion betrayed his Scandinavian origins even though he had lived for the last thirty years in the United States, glanced to his right towards the end of the table.

"Perhaps we should wait a few minutes more," he announced. "I'm sure Sir Charles is on his way."

The minutes passed. Christiansen looked at his watch and appeared to be about to start the meeting anyway when there was a small commotion at the back of the hall.

"Ah! Sir Charles has arrived!" Christiansen pushed his chair back and rose to his feet to greet the powerful, fit-looking gentleman who was now walking firmly down the middle of the room towards the dais, his face wreathed in a broad smile.

"So sorry to be late," Charlie Soong muttered insincerely, as he shook hands with the World Bank official. "I hope you haven't been waiting for me!"

Christiansen merely raised an eyebrow, and introduced Soong quickly to the other occupants of the dais.

"Have you met Minister Wu, China's Minister for Energy?" Soong said something in Chinese which Christiansen was clearly unable to follow.

"I have not yet had the pleasure, but I have long looked forward to this moment." Soong reverted to English for Christiansen's benefit. As the cameras flashed, the two men – Soong and Wu – shook hands in what seemed to Preston to be an almost perfunctory manner. Wu's face remained impassive throughout and even Soong's natural bonhomie seemed to wilt under the pressure of the moment.

As Sir Charles Soong took his allotted seat on the dais, the small group of people who had entered the room with him found their own places in the body of the hall. Preston, sitting at the end of one row, stood up to allow a Japanese gentleman to occupy an empty chair next to him.

"Excuse me, very sorry." The man whispered his apologies as he pushed by. Two other Japanese, who appeared to be the first man's aides, immediately occupied seats in the row behind. Preston decided to introduce himself.

"My name's Preston Murphy, I'm working for Wilmers and Friendly, the supervising engineers."

"Very pleased to meet you." The Japanese half rose in his chair, a movement which was immediately imitated by the loyal duo sitting behind. "I am Akio Nakamura."

As Harry Christiansen called the meeting to order, Preston glanced at the card which the Japanese businessman had immediately thrust at him. Nakamura, he saw, was the chief executive in Japan of Rowlands-Soong International; he was also President of Sufimoto Bank, one of Japan's largest financial concerns. The plot thickens, Preston thought, as he tucked the card into the breast pocket of his jacket. What new developments could bring together Mr Nakamuru from Japan, Sir Charles Soong from Hong Kong, Mr Harry Christiansen from Washington DC and Minister Wu Canping from Beijing, China?

The World Bank man seemed to read his thoughts. "Some of you", Harry Christiansen began, "must wonder why we have called this meeting in the form of an open Press Conference. The reason is quite simple. Today, the

World Bank is pleased to announce that, in agreement with the government of China, we are cancelling the last four billion dollars of the ten billion dollar loan which we made to China to enable the construction of the Three Gorges Dam to go ahead. The reason we are taking this unusual step", he smiled briefly in the direction of the Chinese Minister for Energy, "is not that we are unhappy about the way the project is being carried out. Far from it. The Bank is of the opinion that all the conditions of the loan have been adequately fulfilled. Indeed, they have been more than adequately fulfilled. I take this opportunity to pay tribute to the dedication with which the Chinese authorities and, if I may say so, Minister, you personally, have pursued your task. We believe that the project will be completed on time and that it will produce the intended benefits as far as irrigation, flood control and energy production are concerned.

"You may be sure", Christiansen continued, looking this time first to Sir Charles Soong, sitting at the end of the dais, and then towards the second row of chairs in the body of the hall where the Japanese banker was polishing his spectacles on a large silk handkerchief, "that there are others ready to step in and take the Bank's place. I'm authorised by Minister Wu to announce that Sir Charles Soong, whom many of you will know as Hong Kong's pre-eminent financier, will, together with his Japanese associates, be purchasing an equity stake in the Three Gorges Project in an amount exactly equivalent to the financing shortfall which will be created by the World Bank withdrawal, namely four billion dollars or its equivalent in convertible currencies."

There was an audible gasp from some of the financial journalists present. Both the London *Financial Times* and the *Wall Street Journal* published daily Asian editions and their Beijing correspondents had, like everyone else, been speculating about the purpose of the day's meeting. *The Economist*'s Hong Kong correspondent, briefed in advance by Soong, had flown in specially. But none of these men, familiar though they were with most forms of financial wizardry, had fully anticipated the nature of Christiansen's announcement. For the World Bank to stop disbursing on a project as big as the Three Gorges Dam was a matter of considerable interest, particularly given the magnitude of the sums involved. For private investors to pick up an equity share in what was essentially a public-sector operation was even more remarkable. And when you considered just who those private investors were, the mind boggled! For over 40 years the Chinese government had been vilifying Chiang Kai Shek's "renegade clique" and their finely-developed and widely broadcast contumely extended not just to the Generalissimo's entourage on Taiwan, but to all who directly or indirectly supported his cause. However clever Sir Charles Soong might have been in distancing himself from more extreme nationalist propaganda, nobody – up till that moment – had had much doubt about which side of the political divide he stood.

Veteran Soong-watchers had generally assumed that Sir Charles would pull out of Hong Kong either on or before 30 June, 1997, which was the day Hong Kong would become a Special Administrative Region of the People's Republic of China. Between now and then, so the speculation ran, Soong would milk the situation for all it was worth. The great trading and financing house of Rowlands-Soong would of course have to leave its spectacular offices over-looking Hong Kong harbour but everyone knew that there were plenty of alternative locations – places like Singapore, Seoul, Bangkok or even Tokyo itself – where Soong's arrival would be greeted with enthusiasm and, the more cynical observers suggested, an attractive package of financial inducements. The race to succeed Hong Kong as Asia's prime financial centre had already begun and there was no doubt that attracting Rowlands-Soong megabucks could be considerably more important than being chosen as a site for the Olympics.

As for Soong's Japanese partners, personified that day through the presence in Beijing of Mr Nakamura, this too was a startling development. Not that Japanese investment in China was new. Far from it. Recent years had seen the

201

increasing involvement of Japanese firms in both trade and manufacture, particularly as Deng Xiaoping's economic reforms began to bite. Some people suggested that the Four Modernisations – to use the fashionable phrase – really stood for Honda, Toyota, Mitsui and Mitsubishi! But trade and manufacture was one thing. Letting the Japanese participate as major equity shareholders in the most important economic development project of modern China was something else again. The Chinese were a long-lived race. There were tens of millions of people still alive who remembered the Japanese occupation of Manchuria in the 1930s. There were hundreds of millions still alive who remembered the Second World War.

In the event, it was not one of the financial journalists who put the first question. It was David Burns, the *New York Times* Beijing correspondent. Burns was a bearded, grey-haired man, 50 years old, whose knowledge of China and all things Chinese was probably as profound as that of any other Western journalist currently on assignment in the capital. Burns had already been in Beijing over fifteen years. In fact he had been part of that great posse of pressmen that accompanied President Nixon to China on his first famous visit in 1972. But whereas the rest of them filed their stories, had their photographs taken on the Great Wall, and then jumped on the first plane back home, Burns had stayed on.

"Can you confirm" – Burns rose to his feet from his place in the front row, a tall, gangling figure – "that dividends will be paid on Mr Soong's investment?"

"That's not a question for the World Bank", Harry Christiansen parried, "but I'm sure Minister Wu will be able to reply."

Wu Canping, who had been smoking steadily since his arrival, stubbed his cigarette out in the ashtray in front of him. He glanced at Burns, who had resumed his seat. "China's policy is very clear," he said. "Please note what Premier Zhao Ziyang said in Beidaihe last August. Our aim is to make foreign investment in China more competitive than anywhere else in the world. Premier Zhao confirmed that favourable treatment could also be given overseas investors who do not take their profits out of China but spend them buying Chinese goods."

"So you are expecting the dam to show a profit, Minister?" Burns pressed him.

"I am sure Mr Soong and his associates would not be investing four billion dollars under other circumstances!" Wu smiled for the first time, showing a row of broken yellow teeth.

"Sir Charles, do you have anything to add?" Christiansen asked.

"Yes, I do, as a matter of fact," Sir Charles Soong replied quietly. He glanced quickly at the other occupants of the dais. "I want to thank the Chinese Government and in particular Minister Wu for the marks of confidence which they have shown. For me, speaking very personally, this is a great occasion. From where I sit today I can see the roof of the Temple of Heaven. I have to tell you, Ladies and Gentlemen, that is a sight I have not witnessed in over forty years." There was an audible catch in his voice as he added: "Thank you, Minister, for making it possible. Four billion dollars may seem like a large sum of money but, believe me, we are convinced this project is worth every cent! I am sure Mr Nakamura, who is also with us today, will be ready to confirm this view."

Nakamura rose to his feet, clasped his hands together as though in prayer, and bowed quickly to the right and left. "One hundred per cent correct!" As with Soong, it was more than 40 years since Nakamura had been in China. But he thought it was wiser not to recall the circumstances.

Half an hour later, Preston Murphy found himself standing in the street next to David Burns, as the bigshots drove off. Wu and Christiansen departed in the standard black Mercedes, a vehicle, Preston reflected, which had become almost de rigueur for a high government official in a developing country. Sir Charles Soong had gone one better. A gleaming gold Rolls-Royce was waiting by the kerb with Sir Charles' own personalised numberplate – SOONG I. The chauffeur was already at the wheel with the engine running, while a huge ugly man with a pock-marked face, whom Preston took to be Soong's bodyguard, held open the passenger door for his master. As the Rolls-Royce pulled away, Preston had the curious sensation that somewhere he had seen the bodyguard before.

"We're not going to find a taxi here. Do you have transport?"

Preston dragged himself back to the present to see that Burns was addressing him.

"I thought I'd walk. Care to join me?" He'd been impressed by the journalist's questions that morning. Burns could be a useful contact.

The two men introduced themselves, then – as they headed towards Qianmen – Burns put his own gloss on the morning's events.

"Bloody charade, wasn't it?"

"What do you mean?"

"The fact of the matter is," Burns said, "the World Bank is desperately overlent in China. Their outstanding loans here amount to over twelve billion dollars. What's more, back in Washington the environmental lobby has focussed on the Three Gorges Dam. They're saying that the Bank is financing the destruction of one of the world's greatest landscapes and displacing over one million people into the bargain. Which, by the way, is partly true. Have you been there yet?"

"Next week."

"You'll see what I mean, then. Now that the water is backing up behind the dam the whole character of the place is changing. It's as though you started flooding the Grand Canyon. That's why Soong's intervention couldn't have come at a better time. The Bank can pull out of the Three Gorges Project, saving money and pacifying the eco-nuts at the same time!"

"That's not exactly how Christiansen put it," Preston commented.

"Bloody right! If the Chinese want to plug the Yangtze, that's their business. But it'll be a different story back in Washington!"

204

Preston shook his head. "There's got to be more behind it than that."

Burns looked at him sharply. "Funny you should say that. I had the same impression myself. It was all too neat, too pat, wasn't it? And I'll tell you something else. Soong maintained that he'd never met Wu before but I was up there in the front row and I could swear I heard him say in Chinese something like, 'How are you, old friend? It's been far too long since we last met.'" He looked at his watch. "I live near here and was going home for lunch anyway today. Come and take pot-luck."

Burns turned off the main avenue into a maze of narrow streets, each one of which seemed at first sight to Preston to be bounded by uninterrupted single-storey grey walls.

"These are the *Hutungs*," Burns explained. "There are doors set in these walls and each one of these doors opens onto an inner courtyard. The typical Chinese house is built around that courtyard. There are no windows onto the street."

Most of the doors were shut but, once or twice, as they walked, Preston had a glimpse through an open doorway into the space beyond. An old lady sewing a sack, an equally old toothless man with a long wispy beard sitting on a straight-backed chair staring into space, a child, dressed like a miniature soldier, playing with a bucket by a water-trough.

"Here we are!" Burns turned a corner, crossed over the street, walked 20 yards down the other side and opened the door set in the wall in front of him.

What struck Preston straight away was the size of the place. When he stepped through the doorway, he had been expecting to find a cramped living-area, cluttered with the bric-à-brac of daily life and reflecting the stresses and strains of urban living. What he discovered, instead, was a small oasis, an inner courtyard in which trees and ornamental shrubs had been planted and in whose centre a small square pond was graced by a handsome stone fountain.

"This is beautiful!" Preston exclaimed, as he stood at the edge of the courtyard.

"I was lucky," Burns said. "Ya-Mei's family have lived here for generations and somehow they managed to hang on to it in spite of all the upheavals. Mind you, quite a lot of us live here," he laughed. "My wife's parents are over there" – he pointed to the room behind the fountain – "and we used to have her grandparents too until they died. And then there always seem to be hangers-on – uncles, aunts, nephews and nieces." He laughed. "You get used to it. When I want to work, I go to the office!"

"Is your wife at home?"

"I hope so. It's supposed to be her day off. She's a doctor at the hospital." He led Preston across the courtyard towards the main living area, a large comfortably-furnished room which opened off the kitchen. Ya Mei emerged from within to shake Preston's hand, smiling in a way that softened her otherwise austere features.

"I'm afraid my English is not so good. Welcome to our humble abode!"

"Perfect!" Burns hugged his wife delightedly. "Professor Higgins would be proud of you!"

They sat at a round table in the living-room. David Burns took a chair opposite his wife, while Preston found himself sandwiched between an aunt and a grandmother. There was not much conversation – most of them were too busy with their chopsticks to talk – and what there was took place in rapid, staccato sentences which Preston would have been hard pressed to follow even if he had spent months studying the language.

"Are you OK?" Burns called out in English to him across the table.

"Never enjoyed myself more!" Preston stretched out to grab a mouthful of steamed fish before it all disappeared.

Later, when the family melted mysteriously away, Burns poured out some Chinese brandy and they sat together, glass in hand, in front of the fire.

"What I don't understand", Preston said, "is why, if the dam's going to be the sure-fire money-spinner that Soong obviously anticipates, the big boys didn't get in on this one earlier. There's a lot of venture capital sloshing around nowadays looking for a home. Of course, I'm an engineer not a money-man."

Burns refilled the brandy glasses. He had caught the first faint whiff of a good story.

"Charlie Soong's a shrewd operator, otherwise he wouldn't be where he is today. I've interviewed him a couple of times in Hong Kong over the last few years. You should see the place he has there, up on the Peak! Maybe he's done some deal with Minister Wu Canping. Wu comes from Sichuan originally. In fact one of his first jobs before he went into politics was improving navigation on the Yangtze. Perhaps Soong's got permission to run his fleet of giant tankers and passenger liners all the way up into Chungking after the dam is built. Apparently once the Gorges are flooded there will be virtually no limit on size of ships. Is that correct?"

"Not quite." Preston was familiar with the salient facts. "To get enough draught at Chungking for the really big passenger ships or cargo vessels, you'd have to raise the height of the dam at least 20 metres above the 180-metre level."

"Is that technically possible?"

"Not impossible, but highly inadvisable. Every dam has its design limits which are dictated by considerations of safety as well as economics. The structure you select for a dam is one that is suitable for the particular geological configuration you're dealing with. One hundred and eighty metres is the limit for the Three Gorges which is pretty high anyway, if you come to think about it. Higher than Hoover, higher than Aswan, higher than Kariba!"

"Oh!" Burns sounded disappointed. "I guess Soong reckons it's a good moment to make a friendly gesture towards Beijing. From what you're saying, it could be a pretty expensive investment if they can't use the full potential of the Yangtze."

"That's how I see it," Preston confirmed. "That's why I didn't really understand this morning's performance. Not Soong's. Not Wu's. But, hell, I've only just arrived in China. I'm still wet behind the ears . . ."

207

6

It was one of those peculiar Chinese compromises, not quite an official reception, but more than just a private dinner. There was no doubt who was the guest of honour; it was less clear whether Sir Charles Soong was a guest of the State or of China's Minister for Energy and Natural Resources acting in a personal capacity.

They had curtained off a corner in one of the lesser banqueting rooms in the Great Hall of the People. Wu Canping, who presided, had waited for the *pièce de résistance* to arrive in the shape of a steaming, lacquered Peking Duck before offering the first toast.

"We shall not talk politics tonight," he smiled reassuringly at his guests. "Friendship is sometimes more important than politics and today, Sir Charles, we welcome you as a friend of China." He raised his glass of Mao Tai, the clear, powerful rice-alcohol which had been served liberally throughout the meal. "Canpei! Good health!"

Wu's words of greeting found an echo around the table as the guests, following the Minister's lead, drank to the success of Soong's visit. To what extent some of those present might have had inner reservations about the welcome, official or otherwise, being given to Chiang Kai Shek's nephew, was not obvious. But when Minister Wu hoisted the sticky liquid to his lips, even the sceptics did the same.

"Welcome back!" they murmured. And one or two – was it boldness or merely irony? – went further and called out across the table, "Welcome home!"

When Sir Charles Soong in turn rose to speak, his eyes glistened with tears. He was wearing a conventional dark suit tailored not in Kowloon but in London's Savile Row. His starched white shirt-cuffs protruded the regulation half-inch from the sleeves; solid gold cuff-links glinted in the light of the Chinese lanterns which decorated the table. Except for the rasp of emotion in his voice, Sir Charles might have been about to address the Rowlands-Soong Annual General Meeting. He chose his opening remarks with care.

"This afternoon", he began, "I visited a house here in the city which I had not seen for fifty years or longer, since I was a boy, really. It is a beautiful house, set to the north of Lake Shishahai. I am sure that many of you know it. It used to belong to my aunt, Soong Qingling, the wife of Sun Yat-Sen. Now, of course, it has been transformed into a museum, dedicated to her memory and to the the memory of Sun Yat-Sen, the founder of the Republic of China. Still, I wanted to see the old place and to pay my respects."

He paused to allow his audience time to applaud. Most of them, of course, already knew about Sir Charles' well-publicised pilgrimage that afternoon to the home of Mayling Soong's elder sister, Qinling, the plain serious girl who, like the other two Soong sisters, had been educated in the States but who, unlike them, had remained faithful to the Republic which her husband had founded.

Many of the guests at the dinner had even seen the pictures which had been broadcast on the news bulletins that evening of Sir Charles Soong stepping out of his Rolls-Royce to be greeted with evident joy by the staff at Soong Qinling's former residence, including a toothless old couple who had stayed on as caretakers and who recognised, or at least pretended to recognise, the prodigal nephew returning after half a century's absence.

So they applauded the neat gambit, the finely-judged sense of showmanship, but there was more to it than that. By alluding in this way to his aunt Qinling and the very special place she occupied in the history of twentieth century China (when she died less than a decade earlier she had held the position of Vice-Chairman of State), Charles Soong was reminding his audience, gently but firmly, that the debts were not all on one side of the balance-sheet and that there were people, including Soongs, who had contributed to the building of a nation even before Mao and his comrades took the first steps on their Long March.

For the next few minutes Sir Charles Soong talked in a very personal way about what it meant to him to be back in China after all these years. He spoke briefly of the Yangtze Dam Project and of the great sense of honour and satisfaction he had at being able to participate in this scheme.

"I pay special tribute to Minister Wu." He looked across the table to where his host sat, beaming with evident pleasure at the way the evening was going. "Without Wu Canping's determination, without his passionate advocacy, it is possible that the Three Gorges Dam would not now be nearing completion! I salute you, Sir! And I salute all those who over the years have worked together to make this great project possible!"

The dinner ended well before 9 p.m. Beijing was not a nocturnal city. People went home after nightfall and tended to stay home. It was not like the great cities of the South – Shanghai or Canton, for example – which by night as well as by day had a life and vitality of their own. Partly, this was simply a reflection of Beijing's northerly climate. The cold winds blew down from the steppe and by this time of night at this time of year the sensible place to be was indoors or, better still, in bed.

"Are you coming?" The Minister for Energy was waiting by the door where he had said a firm goodbye to the rest of his guests, thereby making it clear that any further conversation with Sir Charles Soong was to take place on a one-to-one basis.

"I'm so sorry." Soong rose quickly to his feet and followed the other man out of the room. The cars were waiting outside.

"Let's walk," Wu said. "It's not far." He cast a glance at Soong's chauffeur and bodyguard, both of them waiting patiently by the Rolls. "Why don't you give them the evening off? I'll organise a government car to run you back to your hotel."

"What a good idea!" Sir Charles responded with forced enthusiasm. He was not sure he wanted to let his men loose

210

on the town. Big Tu in particular, in spite of his advancing years (he was well over 60 and had been in Soong's service since those first early days in Hong Kong), could sometimes be carried away by an excess of zeal...

As the Rolls drove off into the night with Big Tu sitting up front next to the chauffeur, Wu and Soong crossed the north-east corner of Tien An Men Square and walked east a short way along Changan Avenue. The wide boulevard, which in daytime was crowded with cyclists and pedestrians and street-vendors of every kind, was now virtually deserted. The lights, lining both sides of the avenue, were still illuminated and the only shadows were those cast by the fast-growing trees which the authorities had in recent years planted by the thousand along the city's sidewalks in an at least partially successful attempt to improve the micro-climate.

They turned right at Xinhuamen – the Gate of New China – to enter Zhongnanhai, China's new Forbidden City. The guards on duty recognised Wu and saluted. Once inside the compound, Wu took Soong's arm.

"You haven't changed, Charles. You'd still fit into the pilot seat of a Hawk Fighter!"

"Only just, I'm afraid!" Soong laughed. "You've put on a bit of weight yourself, Wu. You were a skinny streak of nothing when I first knew you!"

They walked along the shore of the lake, across a long narrow bridge and down a quiet road where a row of villas hid behind a screen of willow trees.

"As Senior Vice-Premier I get to live in Chou En Lai's old house," Wu said. "It may sound foolish, but sometimes I think I can still feel his presence here."

They entered the old villa by the lake, substituted slippers for shoes and went on in to Wu's private den which had once been Chou En Lai's own retreat from the cares of State. For a few brief seconds the two men stood, heads bowed, before a faded wreath of flowers which had been hung in place next to a signed portrait of the great man himself.

"Read out the words of the inscription," Wu requested.

Sir Charles Soong pulled out his spectacles from the breast pocket of his dark suit and then, peering closely at the faded lettering, intoned the words of the eulogy: " 'He left no inheritance; he had no children, he has no grave, he left no remains ...' " When Soong turned round, he saw the glint of tears in Wu's eyes.

Later, when they had settled themselves down at either side of the fire-place, Wu said, "I'm not sure it was wise to speak to me like that at the Press Conference. Someone might have heard."

Soong scoffed. "My experience is that most of them can't even order a meal in Chinese and, heaven knows, they get enough practice! By the way," he added, "do you think Christiansen smelt a rat?"

"Don't worry about the Bank. They're only too happy to bail out."

Sir Charles Soong rose to his feet and walked over to the window. It was a clear cold night. Outside, the moon had risen and its reflection could be seen in the still waters of the lake. Half a mile away, the roofs and pinnacles of the Imperial City were silhouetted against the bright back-drop of stars. He took a cigar from his pocket, clipped its end and placed it between his teeth.

"I meant what I said this evening, Wu. I want to move the headquarters of the Rowlands-Soong empire from Hong Kong to mainland China. And I want to do it now, not in 1997. I may not be around in 1997!"

An odd expression came over Wu's face, a mixture of cunning and disdain. "Three billion dollars, four billion dollars, doesn't get you that return ticket, Charles. Not by itself. Even if I were Premier, which I'm not, I don't think I could swing it. Let's face it. You're going to be making real money as it is out of Three Gorges."

"We're all going to make money, aren't we?" Soong reminded him acidly.

Wu chose to ignore Sir Charles's remark but adopted, nevertheless, a more emollient tone. "Don't get me wrong, Charles. You know I'll do anything I can." He glanced down at his gnarled and wounded hands. "But you want us to roll out the red carpet, let bygones be bygones, put the Soongs back on the pedestal. You want a seat on the Central Advisory Committee, maybe even a vice-premiership. However much influence I may have, I would find it hard to put all that through unless . . ."

Sir Charles Soong kept the lid on his anger. Damn the man! he thought. For almost the first time in his life, he was being squeezed and didn't like the sensation. "Unless what . . ."

Wu Canping stood up and placed the empty whisky bottles back in the safe behind the portrait of Premier Chou. It wouldn't do to have the staff finding them in the morning. He turned back to face Soong with an ironic, expectant smile on his face. "Come now, Charles . . ."

"You don't want all of them, surely?" Sir Charles Soong did not want to surrender without a fight.

"Well, they are a series, aren't they?" Wu walked over to his desk and picked up a sheet of paper which he handed to his guest. "Have I listed them correctly?" he asked.

Soong studied the document with care before handing it back. "You certainly did your homework."

"All thanks to you." We found it hard to keep the amused, almost patronising note from his voice. "I had the most luxurious convalescence as you may remember!"

Sir Charles knew when he was beaten. He lurched unsteadily to his feet. "It's a deal," he said. And then he grinned. "You learned fast, didn't you, even then?"

Wu came with Soong to the door and watched until the car was out of sight. Then he turned to go back into his house. How odd it was, he reflected. That evening the debt had been cancelled, the slate wiped clean. Both sides of the ledger were in balance. And yet that was not the end of the matter. Not by any means. He sat down at his desk, opened a drawer and took out a pile of faded newspaper cuttings. Several of them carried a picture of a crumpled car lying at the bottom of a ravine . . .

As he looked at the photographs and re-read the captions, Wu's face tensed with anger. Murphy's death had never been part of the bargain he had struck with Soong. Keeping quiet about the so-called "confession" had been hard enough. He had never said a word to Tai Li, not a word!

He pushed the drawer shut with a bang and picked up the telephone. "I want the report today, this morning if possible," he ordered. "The chauffeur and the bodyguard: where they went; what they did; who they saw – above all, who they saw. Friends; family; I need to know it all."

He replaced the receiver and for the next 20 minutes sat at his desk without moving, watching the sun rise over the lake.

7

Preston joined the scrum of people in front of what he took to be the check-in desk for CAAC flight number B1201 to Xian. Accompanied by the invaluable Fen Huashi, his firm's local agent, he had spent an hour the previous afternoon at the CAAC office in down-town Beijing, trying to confirm his reservation.

"You must go to airport," the clerk had informed him when finally he reached the head of the line.

"But am I on the list?"

"No list here. You must go to airport."

Now, as he looked around, Preston realised that he was one of the lucky ones. As a foreigner, he was waved to the front of the queue together with three senior officers in the Chinese army who looked as if they too were used to being given preferential treatment. While the crowd of would-be travellers waved their tickets behind him, contributing to the general uproar and confusion in the hall, Preston was relieved to be handed a boarding-pass.

Half an hour later they were in the air. Preston sat with his nose glued to the window, watching the densely populated plains give way to the dry upland landscape as they flew west towards the mountains of Shaanxi. He could see that the plateau was deeply-eroded. Gulfs and ravines had been formed in the wind-blown loess soil and, from the air at least, the signs of habitation were few and far between – a track curling around a hill-top, a small barrage here or there with a pond of water behind it, some half-hearted terracing.

Once, the stewardess tapped him on the shoulder to offer him an orange from a red plastic bowl and a packet of biscuits. He ate the biscuits and put the orange in his jacket pocket, checking as he did so that he still had the tape Bill Friendly had asked him to deliver.

*

215

Preston was sitting in Professor Zheng's office in Jiaotong University's Institute of Seismology, a grey concrete building two storeys high, situated on the northern edge of the campus next to the Department of Architecture and Structural Engineering. Computer print-outs, several inches thick, were stacked on a table against the wall and the bookshelves bulged with scientific journals and text-books.

Unlike many of his colleagues who still wore the traditional Mao-style tunic, Zheng was smartly dressed in a well-cut suit, white shirt and flower-patterned silk tie which looked as though it could have been bought at Bergdorf Goodman. He had studied in the United States and spoke English impeccably.

"The Institute of Seismology," said Zheng, polishing his spectacles on his tie, "was created in 1976 soon after the Tangshan earthquake. You remember the event of course – 240,000 people died, 160,000 were seriously wounded. Ninety-seven per cent of all the buildings in the city were shattered and the rest were unusable. The roads, the railways, the bridges, all the public utility installations were put out of action. The damage, in so far as it was possible to estimate, exceeded three million Yuan. And do you know what was almost the worst aspect? The fact that the people had no warning, no warning at all. The scientists failed totally to predict the Tangshan earthquake!"

Professor Zheng poured himself another cup of tea from the large thermos which stood on the low wicker table in front of him. "Let's face it" – he raised the cup to his lips – "China is the most earthquake-prone country in the world. I've studied the records. Did you know that in Shensi in 1556, an estimated 830,000 people were killed in an earthquake? That was the worst catastrophe in the world up to that time. In this century alone, China has suffered one earthquake after another. After Tangshan the government decided that no major earthquake should go unpredicted. That is why they set up the Institute of Seismology here at Xian. That is why they have given us all the money we need for equipment and for personnel. And that, finally," he smiled modestly, "is why I was appointed Director. Come, let me show you round."

The Seismic Laboratory, on the ground floor of the building, was a large, light room with an array of computers, seismographs and other monitoring and recording equipment. Half-a-dozen white-coated technicians were present, some of them at the keyboards of computers, others apparently absorbed in their own calculations.

"Two associate Professors work here full time." Zheng paused by the door as they entered. "The graduate students also work here on a rotating basis. Xian is linked to WWSSN – that's the World-Wide Standardised Seismograph Network, headquartered in Edinburgh, Scotland. We are contributing our own measurements of seismic events occurring outside China and thus helping to establish the global picture. But the bulk of our work is concerned with the national and regional scene. Here in this room we are assessing on a day-to-day basis data collected in almost every part of the country. We are looking for signs of movement in the tectonic plates, evidence of fracture zones or transform faults, or other geological events which may help us predict – and thus prevent – the kind of catastrophe that occurred in Tangshan."

He guided Preston slowly through the laboratory. From time to time they stopped in front of a VDU and watched while the technician worked on the data. Once or twice, the Professor asked questions in rapid-fire Mandarin and then nodded in apparent satisfaction at the replies he received. "We've begun to calibrate some new laser-generated data which show the changes in topography in sensitive areas," he explained.

At the far end of the room a large bronze instrument was displayed in a glass cabinet. As they approached it Professor Zheng told Preston: "This is a model of the earliest known instrument for detecting earthquakes. It was invented in A. D. 132 by the Chinese philosopher Zhang Heng. The original was about two metres in diameter – also in bronze. What you have here is a modern reconstruction made from contemporary descriptions."

Preston gazed with interest at the object. Zhang Heng's earthquake detector looked like a huge, decorated wine bottle. The bronze vessel was elaborately carved and ornamented with eight dragon heads, spaced equally around its sides.

"Each Dragon," Zheng explained, "holds a ball in its mouth. Below the dragons, as you can see, are metal frogs, with their heads tipped back and their mouths wide open to catch the balls suspended above them. Inside the vessel is a hinged rod with the weight at the bottom arranged so that, if it swings far enough to one side, it strikes a dragon's head and dislodges a ball."

Preston laughed. Looking around the room, with its flashing screens and busy benches, he commented: "You're quite sure you can do better today?"

Though Preston had spoken lightly, Zheng replied with deadly seriousness. "We can't afford to fail, Mr Murphy."

Preston was about to pull the computer disk from his pocket and present it to the Professor when Zheng, seeming to sense his intention, abruptly suggested that they might profit from the sunshine to do a little sightseeing.

The old Imperial Park was situated just beyond the campus boundaries. One of its principal features was an ornamental lake where pleasure-boats could be rented by the hour. In spite of the cold, a group of people were waiting on the jetty for their turn. Preston looked at them with interest. For the most part they were young marrieds, he suspected, or else courting couples looking for an hour or two's privacy. He was surprised when Zheng suggested a brief outing.

The Professor proved himself to be a competent oarsman. He manoeuvred the boat smartly away from the jetty and propelled it with sure strokes towards the middle of the lake, some 300 yards away from shore, where a graceful Chinese pavilion stood on stilts in the water. When he reached the pavilion, Zheng rested the oars.

"It's always best to take precautions," he said. "Even if people are not suspicious, they are curious. And it is not

218

inconceivable that my office is bugged. You have something for me, I think?"

Preston passed over the disk. Zheng placed it quickly inside the zip-pocket of his jacket. For a moment, Preston wondered whether the Professor was simply going to leave the matter there, row back to the shore and call it a day without a word of explanation. Zheng, indeed, seemed to be in two minds. He fidgeted with the oars, sending up a small flurry of water. Then, suddenly, he seemed to make up his mind.

"The problem is, you see, the data we are getting from the Yangtze region near the dam-site don't seem to make much sense. I don't know what's been going wrong. Some fault in the transmission lines, perhaps. I mentioned this to Mr Friendly the last time I met him. I told him what we really needed was the raw data, as recorded on site, in its pre-transmission mode." He smiled. "We ought to be able to sort things out now."

The Professor was waiting for him early the next morning in the lobby of the Xian Hotel.

"I have been able to borrow the Institute's car," he explained. "Bring your luggage now; we can go straight to the airport later."

Preston paid the bill for his one night's stay, picked up his bags and followed Zheng outside. As they got into the battered Land-Rover which was waiting at the kerb, the Professor outlined the programme.

"First, we shall visit the tomb of Qin Shi Huang."

"Great! Who was Qin Shi Huang, by the way?"

"Qin was the first Emperor of a unified Chinese people. He built the roads from Xian to the other parts of the Empire: he introduced a national currency and system of writing; he ordered the building of the Great Wall."

"Quite a guy, eh?"

As they drove northwards down the wide avenue past the Big Wild Goose Pagoda and the Bell Tower before passing through the old city walls at the Great Northern Gate, Zheng warmed to his theme. "They used to teach the

219

children in schools that Qin was a despot, a tyrant, a man who burned the Confucian tracts and put scholars to death whenever he could. Nowadays, he is being increasingly held up as a symbol of China's greatness."

Zheng kept his eye on the road as he talked, weaving skilfully among the hand-carts and bicycles and overtaking slower vehicles with a blast of the horn and a firm kick at the accelerator. Occasionally, he would swing out into the centre of the road to be confronted by an on-coming bus or truck. After a couple of hair-raising misses, Preston found himself admiring the Professor's split-second timing as he jinked and swerved with confident precision.

An hour later, they stood together on the huge mound of earth which covered the tomb of China's first Emperor. It was like being on top of the Great Pyramid of Cheops, Preston thought. The Qin Emperor had been far more powerful than the Pharaohs of Egypt. Ramses and Akhenaten had ruled a country, but Qin Shi Huang had ruled a continent.

"Has the tomb ever been excavated?" he asked.

"No. And the Chinese government has no plans to do so at the present time. Qin Shi Huang's grave has been undisturbed for over 2,000 years; it can wait a bit longer. Besides," Zheng added, smiling, "the place is meant to be booby-trapped with an elaborate system of crossbows lined up to fire automatically at any intruders! And don't forget," he pointed to the east, "down there, a mile and a half away, a whole army stood guard."

"The terracotta army?"

"Exactly. Come on, let's walk there. We can pick up the car later." Zheng set off at a brisk pace down the steep slope of the pyramid, still talking as he leapt agilely from step to step.

"So far they have uncovered more than 1,000 life-size warriors and horses, 20 wooden war chariots and 10,000 bronze weapons. They estimate that when the excavation has finished there will be over 7,000 warriors, as well as some 600 clay horses and a massive quantity of real weaponry."

220

"How was the place first discovered?" Preston had to break into a jog to keep up with the Professor.

"Peasants digging a well for irrigation back in 1974, when the commune movement was still at its height. Simple peasants. Not one of them could read, yet they knew they had stumbled on one of the greatest finds of history!"

They walked east along an undulating track which followed the gentle contour of the plain until they came to the huge dome which had been erected over the pits. A crowd of sight-seers stood behind ropes, gazing down on the columns of clay figures assembled in battle array. The vast bulk of the sight-seers were Chinese, though there was also a sprinkling of other nationalities including a group of Japanese tourists who were audibly disgruntled by the prohibition on photography.

Zheng pulled a card from his wallet and showed it to the guard at the entrance. The man nodded and unhooked the rope to let them pass. "Even in China there are special privileges," the Professor smiled.

As they walked down the long ridge between the two columns, Zheng filled in the background. "The first pit was discovered in 1974. Number two and number three pits were discovered in the summer of 1976, about 25 metres to the north of the first pit. At the same time, they found another pit just between the number two and number three pits, but we don't usually include it when we talk about the archaeological complex here."

"Why not?"

"It was a small pit," the Professor explained, "and when they excavated it they found that it was empty. Whatever once had been there had been removed. Or else there was never anything there in the first place. Frankly, it's a mystery."

Preston was intrigued. "What *might* have been there? Do you have any idea?"

Professor Zheng stepped over a pile of rubble towards a vantage-point at the far end of the chamber from which they could survey the whole weird, spectacular scene. He pointed to some terracotta figures standing at the front of the battle-formation. The group included a larger-than-life charioteer, a team of four horses, and, standing behind the chariot itself, two stern-faced warriors.

"Look at the extraordinary detail of these figures," Zheng said. "The man in front, wearing the long robe, is an officer. See how the tips of his shoes turn up, his long cap, the fine and delicate features. What you are looking at is not a stylised representation but the real thing. Look at the general standing just behind him. Of course there are some standard features, the cap adorned with pheasant's feathers, the long coat with its plate of armour, the hand on the sword. But here again this is, it seems to me, a very personal rendering of the commanding officer."

"You mean each terracotta figure represents an actual soldier in Emperor Qin's army?"

"Whenever I have had a spare moment, I come out here. It's been more than a hobby; it's been a passion. I've studied the faces of the charioteers, of the cavalry men, of the foot-soldiers, of the petty officers, of the middle class military officers, of the generals themselves. Each and every one of them is different. It's almost as though these were real individuals. They were moulded in yellow clay and baked in a kiln over 2,000 years ago, but even now the realism, the subtlety of the carving is frightening. You look at these statues and you think they could almost march away."

Zheng paused. "But if this is the real-life army of the Emperor, from General down to foot-soldier, there is surely something missing. Where is the Emperor himself? Where are the Empress and the Principal Concubine? Were these figures buried in that now empty vault? If so, when were they removed?"

They walked back along the northern edge of number one pit, past the second and third pits which had not yet been excavated, towards the site's eastern exit. Half-way to the door, Zheng pointed. "Number four pit – the empty pit – was here. They filled it in again when they discovered there was nothing in it." He turned to Preston: "It could have been robbed any time over the last 20 centuries. My own hunch is, though, that it happened in the relatively recent past. Why was the site first discovered? Because men were actually digging a well deep into the ground. I've looked up the records. When the workers from the Yanzhai Rural Commune found the army in 1974, they were in fact working on the extension of a system which had been started, then abandoned, *forty years* earlier. I reckon that, some time in the thirties, some Shaanxi villagers found and robbed pit number four, and lived comfortably ever after on the proceeds!"

"Elementary, my dear Watson!"

Zheng laughed. "I prefer Miss Marple to Sherlock Holmes!"

Outside the site, there was the usual crowd of hawkers, thrusting products of various kinds – agricultural or artisanal – under the noses of the tourists. Row upon row of miniature soldiers, perfect replicas of the terracotta army, were being sold for a few Yuan each.

Preston pulled a five Yuan note from his pocket. "I'll have a general," he pointed to one of the statuettes, "and I'll take a horse as well."

"For five Yuan he'll sell you a kneeling archer too," Zheng laughed.

They stopped for lunch at the Hua Qing Hot Springs, about eighteen miles from Xian, close by the slopes of Black Horse Mountain.

"This is where Chiang Kai Shek was arrested by the Young Marshal, the local warlord, in December 1936, in the notorious Xian incident. Chiang was still trying to make up his mind whether to fight the Japanese or the Communists!"

"What happened?"

"Madame Chiang and T. V. Soong, her brother, flew into Xian from Nanking, in a plane piloted by their aviator nephew, Charlie Soong. At the same time Chou En Lai flew in from Beijing. The upshot of it all was that on Christmas Day, 1936, 13 days after his arrest, the Young Marshal took the Generalissimo with his wife and advisors to the airport for the return journey to Nanking."

"Why did he let them go?"

Zheng shook his head. "It's very hard to say. Some people suggest that the Young Marshal acted out of respect for Chiang as his former military commander. Others believe that some kind of a deal was struck, involving both Chiang and Chou. The most extraordinary part of the whole story was what happened at the airport itself. The Young Marshal, as I have said, came to see the Generalissimo off, but at the very last minute he either got on to the plane of his own accord, or was forced on to the plane, with the result that he effectively became Chiang's prisoner for the rest of his life. Even when Chiang fled from China in 1949 he took the Young Marshal with him, and he continued to keep him in prison for the next 25 years in Taiwan. The Young Marshal actually died in Taiwan in 1976, still under house arrest!"

Frowning, the Professor dabbed at his tie to remove a fragment of fried pork. "Talking about the Young Marshal," he said, "reminds me that we should have time to stop at Banpo on the way to the airport. It's the largest and best preserved Neolithic settlement ever to be discovered in China. The Young Marshal was responsible for first unearthing it."

Six miles before they reached the outskirts of Xian, they turned off to the right and drove down a dirt road.

"The settlement lies in a square of fertile table land between a river and a hill," Zheng explained. "It covers nearly 50,000 square metres altogether. So far about 4,000 square metres have been fully excavated."

For the next hour Preston accompanied the Professor on a tour of Banpo village. Zheng, as erudite as ever, kept up a running commentary as they walked around the area on the raised platforms that had been constructed so as to permit visitors to have a better view of the remains.

"It is in villages like this that Chinese civilisation was born. We estimate that there were 43 houses here, crowded together, some square, some round. All the dwellings opened towards the south and had a hearth in the middle.

224

Bones were used as tools and it is clear that these people knew how to spin and to weave. They had learned how to use steam to cook food; they caught fish in the river."

Just outside the village, they came to an area which was occupied by a series of gigantic urns, each one standing over two metres tall and well over a metre in diameter at the widest point of the circumference.

"What's in those?" Preston asked, pointing.

"This whole area is the burial ground – the cemetery," Zheng replied as they walked slowly along the line of jars, like generals inspecting their troops. "The Young Marshal, back in the thirties when they first discovered the village, unsealed some of them and found that they were full of human remains. The archeologists of the day surmised that this was the response of primitive man when confronted with unknown or infectious diseases. If you weren't sure what the problem was or if you knew there was no cure or containment possible, you took the people concerned out-side the village and stuffed them in these urns! Anyway, the Young Marshal, fearing that there might still be some noxi-ous bugs present, had the urns resealed and put out an edict, absolutely forbidding anyone to open them again, upon pain of execution. That edict has never been rescinded."

"Just as well they don't deal with unfortunate AIDS suf-ferers like that nowadays!" After a full day in the Professor's company, Preston felt he knew Zheng well enough to risk an off-colour remark. "There wouldn't be enough pots to go round . . . !"

8

The plane from Xian, a twin-engined Ilyushin of indeterminate vintage, after waiting several hours for fog to clear at his place of destination, had finally left at 6 p.m. Details of Preston's arrival had been forwarded to Chungking by the Wilmers and Friendly Beijing office and Preston was both pleased and surprised to find someone was still waiting for him at the airport.

"I am Tsen, from the Sichuan Department of Transportation." The speaker was a serious-looking young man, wearing blue jeans and a leather jacket. As he steered Preston to the car, he asked: "How many people in your group?"

"Just me."

"Then you are a group of one!"

They sat together in the back of the car for the journey into the city. The front seat, next to the driver, was occupied by a young woman, about the same age as Preston's escort.

"This is my friend Ru-jie."

Ru-jie turned round and smiled at Preston. "Do you like pop music?" she asked. "David Bowie, Mick Jagger?"

Preston laughed. "Personally I prefer Lilly Wu." And he made a dismal attempt at humming her latest hit. The girl was convulsed with amusement at his efforts to catch the rhythm and lilt of the song.

Tsen's father joined them for a meal in a small crowded restaurant near the dock. "My father is a very busy man," Tsen explained. "He is the director of the Port of Chungking."

"I am delighted to meet you." Preston shook hands with the new arrival, a man of around 60 years of age who, judging by the way the waiters treated him, was clearly a big-shot. But Tsen Senior's English was less fluent than his son's.

"Port of Chungking one day bigger than the Port of

226

Shanghai! Once dam is built, biggest ships in world possible to come here!"

Preston was amused by the man's use of the superlative. "Not the really large ships, surely?"

His reservations seemed to take the man by surprise. He talked rapidly with his son in Chinese.

"My father says even a 500,000 tonne tanker will be able to reach Chungking. They are building the new dock facilities already."

Preston let it pass but he couldn't help recalling what David Burns, the *New York Times* man in Beijing, had said a few days earlier. What the hell was going on?

Tsen Junior called for Preston early next morning at his hotel to escort him to the dock. Though it was still dark, the wide steps leading down to the river were already crowded as travellers made for the waiting boats bearing – or so it seemed to Preston – half their worldly goods with them.

The quay-side at Chaotianmen was illuminated by flood-lights and the three-decker ferry which would make the run down-river was itself lit up from prow to stern. Music blared from a loud-speaker, hooters sounded, capstans creaked and stevedores shouted as the final preparations for departure were made. It might have been a water-front scene at any sea-port in the world, thought Preston, yet here they were in the very heart of China over a thousand miles from the ocean.

The younger Tsen came on board with him. "My father has arranged for you to have cabin, first-class. Breakfast today will be at 8.30 in dining-room. You like English breakfast or Chinese breakfast?"

"I'll take whatever's going." Preston had been prepared, if necessary, to sit on a packing-case for the next two days.

Tsen seemed to read his thoughts. "We are trying to upgrade transportation service on Yangtze. Three new luxury ferry-boats will be ready when dam is finished."

"For foreign tourists?"

"Also for Chinese people. People come from all over

China to visit Yangtze Gorges. Especially honeymoon couples. At least on boat, they can be alone together!"

Disappointingly, a thick fog rolled down over the Yangtze almost as soon as they left Chungking. Standing on deck with his fur cap pulled down over his ears, Preston had the occasional tantalising glimpse of a pagoda looming through the mist on the river bank, beyond the swirling brown water. Later, feeling the cold, he went inside to the observation deck below the bridge, and found a seat next to an elderly Chinese gentleman.

The man, Preston discovered, had visited Sheffield in England during the war to learn steel-making, had returned to China after the Liberation and, after a career in different parts of the country, was now employed in a senior position at the large steel mills in Wuhan, some 500 miles downstream. He introduced himself as Mao.

"Mao is a very famous name," Preston smiled.

For some reason, the man appeared to find Preston's remark hilariously funny. His hearty laughter was only interrupted by a fit of coughing linked, Preston didn't doubt, to a lifetime's consumption of cheap cigarettes. After that, since the ice was broken, Mao took care to ensure that, notwithstanding the poor visibility, Preston did not lack for information.

"Yangtze River largest in our country, third largest river in the world. Extends 6,300 kilometres. Flows through nine provinces from source to sea. Very old river. Seventy million years old. Formed when mountains squeezed each other. Sometimes people call it Dragon River because dragon caused earthquake which made river rise. You know how many people live today in Yangtze Valley?"

Preston shook his head. "How many?"

"Three hundred million people. Almost one third of population of China! Yangtze Valley extends over 1.8 million square kilometres. Much of China's food grown here – corn and wheat and rice. Down below Yichang, below dam they are building, where river enters plains –"

"I'm going to work on the Three Gorges dam," he told Mao. "It's a great project, don't you think?"

Mao stared into the mist a long time before replying. "Chinese government approve project." He shook his head. "But I say, this dam is not a good idea. Too big, too dangerous. Too many difficulties. Why not many smaller dams on different rivers? Why one big dam on Yangtze? When I was boy, before I went to England, I remember what old people used to say."

"What was that?"

"You cannot tame Dragon River." The man rose abruptly to his feet, and, bowing briefly, shuffled off towards his cabin, leaving Preston to stare reflectively into the gloom.

Preston rose the following morning while it was still dark and went up on deck just as they were about to enter the eight-kilometre-long Qutang Gorge. The mountains seemed suddenly to have closed in on the river leaving only the narrowest passage. Search-lights were mounted on the top deck and as he observed their powerful beams cutting through the blackness to play on the sheer rock-face at either side, Preston realised to his relief that the fog had not returned during the night. As the sky lightened with the dawn, he could glimpse the outlines of the immense cliffs towering hundreds, thousands of feet above the river. If he lived to be a hundred, he doubted that he would ever see another sight as spectacular as this.

Below Daixi, a small town at the eastern end of the Qutang Gorge, the river widened and for the next 15 miles the ferry swept through a mountain valley where small villages clung precipitously to the hillsides and terraced fields inched their way up the slopes so as to gain every last square metre of cultivable land. As far as Preston could see, no roads linked these tiny villages to any larger centres of civilisation. Whatever contact they had with the outside world was via the mountain tracks, negotiable only on foot or on horseback, or else by water.

His new Chinese friend, Mao, stood on the deck next to him and pointed up at the cliffs. "Last year was big landslide here. Whole village fell into river. Many people killed. Navigation blocked one month."

"What caused the landslide?"

"Earthquake. Many earthquakes here."

"Small earthquakes?"

The man laughed, incongruously. "Sometimes big earthquakes too. Big enough to destroy village."

Half an hour later, they came to Wuchan, a small town nestling on the north bank of the Yangtze against a background of mountain peaks. The ferry stopped for an hour while cargo and passengers were discharged, the dock being situated at a point where a tributary river joined the main stream.

"This is Daning River," Mao told him.

The name rang a bell, though for the moment Preston couldn't remember why . . .

The next few hours were among the most magical that Preston had ever spent in his life. A bright sun streamed down, tempering the cold wind and delighting the passengers who now crowded on deck and craned their heads backwards to observe the landmarks which for generations of Chinese, including this latest, most secular generation, had long been the stuff of myth and legend.

Mao stood by the rail, looking up at the rim of mountains and at the distinctive silhouette of Shennu or Goddess Peak and, with a note of genuine reverence in his voice, recited the famous lines:

"See Goddess Peak from afar,
Her form is true loveliness.
Reflected in water is long knot of her hair
Sun-filled clouds caress her flowing robes."

As he listened to the words and absorbed the sights and sounds of Wuxia Gorge, Preston felt suddenly overwhelmed with emotion. All his sensations seemed to have been compressed, distilled, somehow rendered more acute. Just as the mighty waters of the Yangtze were now being channelled through the narrowest of Gorges – "a thousand seas poured into one cup" as his friend Mao had described it quoting the famous poet Su Dong Po – so his life, his thoughts, his very identity seemed to be concentrated in this one moment of illumination.

Later that afternoon they traversed the third and longest of the Yangtze Gorges – Xiling Gorge – 50 long miles of cliff and chasm where the slightest error of navigation spelt disaster. As the ferry rounded the last bend in the ravine, a gigantic wall seemed to block out the sky. The height of the dam was, Preston calculated, well over 1,000 feet. And it was twice as wide as it was high. Put the Hoover and the Grand Coulee together, he thought, and then add on 50 per cent for good measure, and you might come somewhere near describing the sheer scale of the Three Gorges project. The ferry seemed to be totally dwarfed by the immensity of the structure.

Since impounding had begun, the ship-locks were already functioning, so the Chungking to Wuhan ferry on which Preston was travelling had to take its turn in the queue. Half an hour later, when one set of gigantic hydraulic gates had been shut behind them and another set had opened ahead of them, the ferry passed through the lock to pull into the dock at Sandouping. What had once been a small fishing village had, over the past decade, been transformed into a vast construction site. Though the nucleus of the old village remained, with its cluster of white houses rising up the hill from the water, a whole new settlement had been built around it. At the peak of the activity, thousands of workers had been employed on the project and even now several hundred remained to complete the installation of the turbines and to erect the transformers and transmission facilities which would in a few months ensure that the vast quantities of electricity generated by the dam would be able to reach the farthest-flung corners of China.

Looked at from the east or downstream angle, the face of the dam seemed even more overwhelming than it had been from the upstream side since the the great vertical wall of masonry was exposed from the crest almost to the foundations.

As he stepped down from the boat, Preston realised that on this side the sun which had warmed their passage through the Gorges had been totally blocked out by the dam-face. Though dark was still several hours away, the deep shadow of night seemed to have descended already.

9

The Project Engineer's house was situated, together with most of the other purpose-built dwellings, on the left bank of the Yangtze exactly half a mile down-stream of the dam. No expense had been spared by the Consortium to ensure that the staff engaged on the project were properly looked after. The spacious bungalows which had been constructed at Sandouping, Preston's included, were equipped with all the latest conveniences, such as television and hi-fi and large well-stocked refrigerators. Not that the Consortium believed in pampering its personnel. Far from it. The Chinese drove a hard bargain and there was never much fat left in a contract when the time came to sign on the dotted line. Certainly not enough for firms like Deutsche-Werke to indulge in any unnecessary extravagances. No, if the expatriate engineers and surveyors and hydraulics experts were well supplied with food and drink with equal attention being given to their psychological and even spiritual needs, it was simply because the hard-headed people who had invested money in Three Gorges knew very well that when you asked a man to spend several years in a single place working on a single scheme, morale was crucial. A discontented engineer was a bad engineer and bad engineers were the ones who made mistakes. On any given day the Consortium helicopter which made the milk-run between Sandouping and Yichang was quite likely to be carrying boxes packed with the latest videos or crates of Black Label whisky.

At first, Preston had been embarrassed by the air-conditioned luxury in which he spent his off-duty hours. His Chinese counterparts, he soon found out, had no such privileges. They lived in a communal compound on the other side of the village where frugality and discipline were the order of the day. Whereas the Consortium had provided senior expatriate personnel with Jeeps and Land-Rovers, the Chinese seemed invariably to be crowded into battered minibuses which shuttled according to a precise timetable between the compound and the dam-site. Insofar as any fraternisation occurred between the two sides, it was on a professional basis – at the dam itself or at the site-offices.

Preston's opposite number on the Chinese side was a short, apparently jovial man known to the expatriate community as "Sammy" Wong. Strictly speaking, Wong's title was "Chairman of Revolutionary Committee Overseeing the Construction of Three Gorges Dam so as to Achieve New Spectacular Advances for Heroic and Peace-Loving Chinese People." In practice his title tended to be abbreviated, at least by the "expats", to Chairman Wong. Though Preston had met the man two or three times on the site, his first extended interview with Wong came a week after his arrival when he was invited or, more properly, summoned late one afternoon. Wong's office was in a modern bungalow built on the hillside above the old village of San-douping and commanding a spectacular view of the dam and its ancillary works. Preston had the use of one of the Consortium's Jeeps for the duration and he drove himself up the rough dirt road for his appointment.

"Ah! Come in, Mr Murphy. Very pleased to see you. How you like China?" Wong's face was wreathed in smiles as he greeted his guest. "How you like Three Gorges Project? Chinese build biggest dam in world. Very good, yes?"

He motioned Preston to a sofa, offered him tea and cigarettes, and spent the next half-hour in small-talk as though he had all the time in the world on his hands and getting a dam finished on schedule was the least of his concerns.

"You visit Beijing yet?"

"Yes," Preston nodded. "I flew to Beijing from Paris."

"Air France plane? You stop in Delhi?"

"Just for an hour or two. Have you been to India your-self?" Preston wasn't sure where the conversation was leading, but he was prepared to prattle on until it was clear what game they were playing.

234

"Maybe one day," Sammy Wong laughed. "First we get job finished here. Very hard work for engineers, yes? By the way," the question seemed deceptively casual, "you see Mr Friendly in Beijing?"

Here we go, thought Preston. "Yes, I did. But very briefly. He was leaving China the next day. Do you have any news?"

Sammy Wong shook his head and pushed the thermos-flask across the table in Preston's direction. "More tea?"

"No, thank you."

Sammy lit another cigarette. "After Beijing, you travel to Xian and Chungking? Business or just tourist?"

"Neither," Preston replied sharply. "I wanted to come down through the Gorges to see how it all looks."

Wong stared at him across the rim of his tea-cup.

"Mr Friendly talked about friend of his in Xian. At Jiaotong University. Professor Zheng. You see Professor Zheng?"

"Indeed, I had a very pleasant meeting with Professor Zheng," he smiled. "China is a land of a thousand million people, and when you first arrive you can feel very lonely. It's good to have some introductions."

"Mr Murphy, please come here with me." Sammy Wong stood up and beckoned Preston to the window. From their vantage-point on the shoulder of the hill, they were able to observe both the upstream and the downstream sides of the great dam. Looking to the west, Preston could see the water backing up through the Gorges and, in the distance, the towering peaks of the mountains of Sichuan. Looking to the east, he could see the dizzying drop of the dam-face, the power-houses and transmission facilities and, filling the middle ground of this spectacular tableau, the widening Yangtze as it began its journey through the great plain of central China.

"My God, what a fantastic view!" he said.

"View not important, Mr Murphy. China too poor country to bother about scenery." Wong was suddenly curt, official. "We want projects that work. Value for money. That's why I here." He pivoted on his heel to face Murphy directly. "I instructed to tell you that Chinese Government

235

revise specifications of Three Gorges Dam. Dam will operate with water-level of 200 metres, not 180 metres level. This necessary" – it was almost as though he was now parroting some official decree – "not only in interests of power generation, but also to permit extension of navigation facilities on Upper Yangtze."

"How can you operate with a 200 metre water level! That's higher than the dam itself!"

"Very observant," Wong smiled thinly. "You have done homework, I see. Of course, you speak about original blueprints. In view of factors mentioned, Chinese Government raise final height of dam by 20 metres. Come, Mr Murphy, why you look so surprised?"

"The design height is the design height!" Preston protested. "You can't just add 20 metres on!"

"Mr Murphy," Wong's tone was very cool, "you forget this is China project only. China have own design experts. Chinese people designing dams while buffalo were still leaving turds on North American Plains. Consulting engineers have right to be informed of design changes to project. Have right to comment on changes. Have right to go home now, if they want! Don't forget, Mr Murphy, who is paying bills. I buy plenty Chinese experts for one American! Think about that, please?"

Sammy Wong steered Preston firmly in the direction of the door.

Preston was up before dawn next morning. The first hint of spring was in the air. The warm weather, he knew, came early in central and south-western China. Indeed, come the summer, the place could be altogether too warm. The Chinese colloquially referred to Chungking, Wuhan and Nanking as the "Three Furnaces" – not without good reason.

He decided to leave the Jeep behind and set off on foot. As he began the long haul up the road which would take him to the crest of the dam, he heard the low rumble of heavy-duty trucks. He moved to the side of the road to let a convoy of vehicles pass, gear-boxes grinding noisily as the drivers took the uphill bends. Preston looked at his watch: 6.30 a.m. They had begun on the dot and he knew from experience that they would keep at it until nightfall. He had learned just the other day that Chairman Wong's new plan was to work a 24-hour shift and now he understood the reason. If they were trying to put another 20 metres on the dam and still get it finished on time, they would be working against the clock.

An hour later, Preston stopped to admire the view. The road he had been following led along the crest of the dam itself linking the north and south banks of the Yangtze and providing, in effect, the first bridge across the river downstream of Chungking. Since the dam was arched with its convex face bearing the weight of water, the road along the crest naturally had the same configuration. Preston paused at mid-point. All around, he could see that preparations were already being made to extend the height of the dam and, even as he watched, a steady stream of trucks carrying concrete-mixers passed him ready to dump their loads in the appropriate place.

He walked to the outer edge and, with the sun behind him, looked upstream. The water was already beginning to rise in the Gorges behind the dam. Indeed, he reckoned that at its present elevation the dam was already half full. From where he stood, it was easy to envisage just what a crucial difference that extra 20 metres would make. Given the topography of the Upper Yangtze, the added height could ensure not only that the narrow passages of the Gorges were effectively enlarged (though the cliffs seemed vertical when you went through them, the opening at the top was still wider than at the base), but that the vital reaches below Chungking would even at times of low-flow be assured of adequate draught.

At the base of the dam, over a thousand feet below, he could see the power-units which housed the turbines. The Chinese had decided to go for "state of the art" technology. To generate that stupendous output of 16 gigawatts they would be using 24 turbines rated at 750 megawatts each. The last units were now being installed. The spillway too was finished. He leaned over the guard-rail for a better view, imagining as he did so the man-made Niagara – the mist and spray and spume – which would occur when the spillway was in use.

He walked slowly on across the top of the dam towards the farther shore. The mountains on the south side of the river were lower, the cliffs less precipitous. Substantial grouting and filling had been necessary at the higher levels to ensure that the dam was anchored firmly to the adjacent rock.

When he reached the far side, Preston spent about an hour examining the cliff-face against which the extended dam would have to rest. His research was necessarily perfunctory. He was looking for fissures or fractures visible to the naked eye while recognising that hidden flaws would need to be detected by other means. Had the Chinese, he wondered, gone over the ground inch by inch as they should have done? Had they tested the inner strength of the pillar against which so much pressure would be brought to bear? Where were the X-rays? Had there been any? Would the Chinese make them available? As he scrabbled up the abutment, he swore out loud.

"Bloody lunatics! Mercenary fools!"

Preston was already on his way back down when he saw a Jeep carrying a party of Chinese soldiers driving along the dam-crest towards him at considerable speed.

"Hey you! What are you doing? Come on down!" One of the soldiers jumped out as the Jeep came to an abrupt halt. He pointed a machine gun menacingly in Preston's direction.

"Hold it now, hold it!" As he climbed rapidly down, Preston felt in his pocket for the official I.D. which the Chinese had issued when he first took up the job.

The soldier looked at the card, and at Preston. "Come with us," he ordered roughly.

Preston found himself being bundled into the Jeep and driven back at high speed toward Sandouping. Twenty minutes later he was engaged in an angry dialogue with Sammy Wong in the latter's office.

The short stocky man was in a foul temper. "No unauthorised visits allowed to dam-site," he shouted.

"Now hold on a minute!" Preston tried to keep cool. "I've got a job to do the same as you have, Mr Wong."

"I told you yesterday, Mr Murphy. This is our project. We do it our way."

"You've no right to change the specifications unilaterally. The World Bank is funding this project. They have a right to be consulted, and they'll never agree."

Wong smiled icily. "World Bank finished disbursing on loan. You must know that. Cost of extension – up to 200 metre level – will be fully covered by private finance."

"You mean Charlie Soong?" Suddenly Preston understood, only too clearly, what was happening. "You'll never get away with it," he said as he stormed out. "I'll make it my business to see that you don't!"

As he left Wong's office to return to his own quarters, Preston decided to send a full telex of explanation to New York that day. Maybe Bill Friendly had been too sick to notice what was happening, but Preston knew he himself had no such excuse.

He had lunch alone in the works canteen, spooning noodles with one hand while, with the other, he drafted his report in pencil on a yellow legal pad. He had just about finished when he heard someone say, "Mind if I join you?"

Preston looked up to see a familiar face. "David!" he exclaimed in surprise, "I didn't expect to see you here!"

"I was in Wuhan on a story, so I thought I would come on up-river." The tall bearded journalist pulled up a chair and joined Preston at his table. Preston put his pen away and tidied up his papers. "The Chinese have sprung a last-minute design change . . ."

"It figures, doesn't it?" Burns said after Preston had given him the whole story. "I felt sure that Soong had something up his sleeve when he suddenly came through with over four billion dollars."

"How long do you think they have been planning this?"

"Heaven knows! They play a long hand, these buggers!" Preston managed a half-hearted laugh. "And what do you think I should do? See no evil, hear no evil, speak no evil?"

"That's your problem, not mine. I don't envy you! I think you should file your report and see what your head-office says. They may say nothing, of course. The fat cats are in on this. You've got Wu and Soong and heaven knows who else. New York may simply tell you to keep your nose clean and pocket your pay-cheque."

Though the room was virtually empty, Burns dropped his voice: "Even if you have to pretend to play ball with the Chinese, while they throw an extra 20 metres onto the pile, you ought to dig around a bit. Get your hands on the geological reports, look at the early feasibility studies, do some basic research. Wilmers and Friendly may not have the guff on Super-Dam. The Chinese, if they have data, won't want you to see it. But that doesn't necessarily mean the cupboard is bare. Just keep poking around." He stood up and held out his hand. "Let me know if I can help."

"Are you going to write a Super-Dam piece? I was just telling you what Sammy Wong told me. It may not be official yet."

"It is official." Burns fished out of his pocket a crumpled press release. "That's why I came up from Wuhan."

"Thanks for letting me know." Preston felt vaguely irritated that he had been led on.

Burns smiled into his beard. "I wanted to hear your side of it."

Two days after Preston had sent his long telex to New York, he received an anodyne reply signed Jim Wilmers advising him that his job at this stage of the project was purely consultative and that he was not, repeat not, to raise questions which might be thought to reflect on Chinese sovereignty or competence as far as matters relating to the design and execution of the Three Gorges Project were concerned. Preston crumpled the flimsy in his hand and threw it in the waste-paper basket. Just how much, he wondered, did Jim Wilmers know? Could he have pulled Friendly out of China, not because of Friendly's illness, but because of the engineer's Triple-A personal rating for professionalism and integrity, whereas Preston was seen as a relative "tyro" who could be relied upon to keep his head safely below the parapet . . . ?

But as the days passed, and as the crash programme of construction continued, Preston began to wonder whether he wasn't perhaps making a mountain out of a molehill. There were plenty of other foreign engineers at Sandouping and none of them seemed to be as worried as he was about the Chinese change of plan. The big German, Horst Klarfeld, whom Preston had first met in Beijing at the Press Conference and who had now returned to the site, had been positively scornful when Preston divulged some of his fears.

"What is your problem, man?" Klarfeld had exploded. "If the Chinese want to build a bigger dam, that's good news! More work for all of us!"

Then, one evening, as Preston's mood swung erratically between anger and despondency, he received a telegram: "VISITING DAM-SITE AT SANDOUPING NEXT WEDNESDAY STOP HOPE TO SEE YOU". The telegram was signed simply BEN.

10

Preston was about to leave his office and head for the power-house complex, for a routine tour of inspection, when he heard the familiar whirring, clattering sound of a helicopter. Looking up, he noticed that it wasn't one of the usual Consortium Sikorskis, but a snappy silver Augusta, operated – as he read from the inscription on the fuselage – by China Tours Inc., Beijing and Seattle, a wholly-owned subsidiary of Bradman Enterprises. Behind the perspex windscreen he could see the familiar shock of fair hair and the broad smile of the American film-star.

As the Augusta touched down on the heli-pad, Bradman jumped out like a Green Beret hot for action. "I'm late." Bradman ducked under the still revolving rotor-blades. "Some fucking bureaucrat tried to foul up my flight-plan at the last minute!" He shook Preston's hand warmly.

They spent two hours together that afternoon in Preston's bungalow, poring over maps. "People have been concentrating on the western parts of Sichuan," Bradman explained, "and of course that's where the known panda reserves are. Apart from Wolong itself, you've got scattered groups in other districts." He jabbed a finger at the map. "There may be some pandas left, a few dozen or so, at Tangjeihe and a handful more at Dafengding. But just look how far apart these surviving groups are. There are no connecting corridors of land between them, no way the gene pool can be enlarged. And look at the size of the areas involved! Apart from Wolong, you're really talking about insignificant pockets of land, a few hundred square kilometres at best. Now I'm not saying these populations are unimportant. Of course they are and we've got to do what we can for them. But no matter what happens in western Sichuan, and even if they do manage to breed a few pandas in captivity, the species is still doomed to extinction."

Bradman paused. "That story, Preston, about your parents seeing pandas on the Yangtze during the war set me thinking. So, since I last saw you, I've been doing some research in the library of the Academica Sinica in Beijing. Helluva job, I can tell you! I got someone to translate for me the classic work on pandas by a couple of fellas known as Chu and Long. Even as recently as the 18th and 19th centuries, Chu and Long cite numerous historical records of pandas being present in eastern Sichuan and the western parts of Hubei Province." He pulled out a sheet of paper and spread it on the table in front of them. "I photocopied this from the Chu and Long article. Look at the clusters here and here! If you trace the curve of the Yangtze you can see that one of the main areas where pandas historically existed outside the present known reserves is in the mountains north and south of the Three Gorges! That could be the place where your parents spotted them!"

"But most of those records are over a hundred years old – 1774, 1860, 1865 – anything could have happened between then and now. Besides, my parents travelled upstream on the Yangtze, towards Tibet, not down-stream towards Yichang."

"Are you sure?"

Preston paused. After the conversation he had had with Lilly Wu on the road to Assisi, he had assumed that he had simply got his facts wrong in believing that his parents had travelled east, not west on the Yangtze. And yet, now he came to think of it, hadn't his mother mentioned the Daning River . . .

"Call your mother, dammit. She'll remember!"

"From here? You must be joking! No, wait, I've got a better idea."

Preston strode over to a side-table and picked up an unopened package. "My father's diaries, including his time in China. They arrived yesterday."

The first volume was labelled CHUNGKING; the second, WASHINGTON. Murphy, a methodical man, had produced a rough contents page for each volume.

243

"You'll have your work cut out to read all that!" Bradman commented.

"That's for later!" Preston knew that it would take him far more than an evening to examine and absorb these relics of the past. "Here, look at this!" He ran his finger down the Contents page of the first volume. "See what it says? JOURNEY UP DANING RIVER."

Quickly he turned the pages of the book until he came to the right place. "Jesus, father's even drawn us a map . . . !"

With the wind behind them, they averaged 80 knots. Bradman flew the helicopter 100 feet above the surface of the Yangtze, following a course which took them more or less up the centre-line of the river. Preston, of course, had been through the Gorges before but for Bradman it was a novel experience and, as he deftly manipulated the Augusta through the towering ravines, he kept up a running commentary.

"This is unbelievable!" he exclaimed. "No wonder the Japs stayed in the plains. How could you ever get an army through here?"

They passed through the Xiling Gorge, then through Wuxia Gorge and at Wuchan, where the Daning came down and cut through the mountains to join the Yangtze, they swung abruptly right-handed to follow the course of the tributary river. Deep clear emerald pools alternated with foaming rapids. Wild duck flew up as the helicopter passed overhead and more than once they glimpsed a troupe of the famous Golden Monkeys of Sichuan.

An hour later, having landed the helicopter in an upland meadow where the headwaters of the Daning dwindled to a trickle, the two men started to climb towards a saddle of land lying almost due north. The pass was further away than it seemed and, though they had started out early, it was well past midday before they finally mounted the last slope and were able to look down into the valley beyond. For a moment, Preston felt like Moses.

For beyond the saddle on which they were standing, the land dropped away sharply, opening out to form a complete saucer-shaped valley whose diameter, Preston calculated, must have been 20 or 30 miles in extent and whose circumference was determined by an unbroken ring of mountains. The only entrance to the valley appeared to be via the pass which they themselves had just traversed. In the centre of the saucer and on the sides of the steep slopes which led down into the bowl of the valley they could see the thick luxuriant groves of bamboo.

"This has got to be it!" Preston exclaimed.

Bradman shrugged. "Yeah, it looks good. But even if they're here, all we may find is a pile of turd!"

They unpacked two hand-held video units they had carried from the helicopter.

"We won't get the first prize at Cannes, but by God they're practical!" Bradman passed Preston one of the cameras and showed him how to work it. "It's got a built-in zoom and exposure metre. All you have to do is put your finger on the button." He looked at his watch. "We can't risk flying down the Gorges after dark. How long do we have before sunset?"

Preston glanced up at the sun. "Three hours. Three and a half if we're lucky."

"Hell! That's not enough time! We'll camp here tonight. Go back tomorrow in daylight."

"What about your flight-plan? The Chinese will find out we never landed at Wanxian."

"Fuck 'em!"

Preston didn't need much persuading. "I'll go back to the helicopter and fetch the sleeping-bags," he volunteered.

"We don't need sleeping-bags!" Bradman sounded scornful. "Tonight we'll build a fire and have ourselves a barbecue!"

Bradman heaved the pack from his shoulders and Preston noticed for the first time the stocky butt of a hunting rifle.

It seemed to be the camp-fire which brought the animals out of the dense bamboo thickets. First one panda came shuffling up to the fire, almost singeing its paws, then there were half-a-dozen of them, not counting the cubs.

"Hell, if there are that many here, just in one spot,"

245

Bradman whispered as they filmed the scene from a make-shift hide which they had constructed earlier that evening, "how many must there be if you take the valley as a whole?"

Next morning, when all the nocturnal visitors had departed, they inspected the area around the camp-site.

"Christ almighty, you'd think a herd of elephants had been through here!" Preston commented. The piles of dung and the crushed and bruised vegetation indicated the extent of the commotion which had taken place the previous night.

Before they left, Bradman looked through the view-finder at some of the film which they had taken. "This is fantastic!" he crowed. "Better than Walt Disney!"

For a few minutes, he stood there with his eye glued to the video-camera, before packing the equipment back in its case. They raked over the now cold ashes of the fire, took a last look round and then, as the sun's first rays hit the surrounding mountains, began the climb back up the hill towards the col.

There were six of them guarding the helicopter, all soldiers of the People's Liberation Army. Preston's heart sank.

"Looks like we're going to have to tough this one out," muttered Bradman.

The soldiers raised their rifles.

"Where you been?" asked one. "That is forbidden area." He pointed in the direction of the pass. "What you doing?" Then his eye fell on the cameras. "Give us film! Now, at once!" Almost before they had time to realise what was happening, the soldiers seized the cameras.

"Hold it!" Bradman shouted. "That's our equipment! You leave that alone!"

As he tried to grab one of the cameras back, a soldier hit him hard in the stomach with a rifle-butt.

"Goddammit, you little fucker!" Bradman brushed the rifle aside and drove his fist into the man's solar plexus. He followed the blow with a solid upper cut and looked like he was preparing to deliver the *coup de grace* when Preston intervened.

"Hey, cut it out, for God's sake, Ben." He grabbed Bradman's arm and pulled him roughly back.

"Destroy the film!" The PLA leader ordered his men to remove the cassettes from the cameras. For a moment he held the tapes in his hand as though contemplating what to do.

"That's my property!" Bradman gritted his teeth. "I warn you, you'll be in big trouble if you mess around with it."

As Bradman pulled himself free of Preston's restraining grasp and lunged for the cassettes, determined to wrest them back, the PLA leader side-stepped neatly and hurled them one after the other into the turbulent waters of the Daning.

They flew back to Sandouping under guard, two PLA soldiers crouched behind them in the cabin of the helicopter. Once they had landed at the heli-pad, they barely had time to stow their bags in Preston's bungalow before a military Jeep arrived to take them down to the police station in the Chinese compound for questioning.

Their interrogator was a hard-faced Police Captain of about 50. He gestured to two wooden chairs which had been placed in front of his desk.

"I want to lodge a formal protest." Ben Bradman had clearly decided that attack was the best form of defence. "Your men destroyed our films!"

"Why did you not stick to the flight-plan you had filed? Why did you not visit Wanxian? Why did you enter a forbidden area? Why did you not cooperate with Chinese people?" The man spat out the questions in quick succession.

While the Police Captain was still in the middle of his tirade, the door opened.

"Ah, Wong!" the Police Captain snapped. "You too must bear the responsibility for this deviation!"

The momentary diversion of the policeman's interest gave Bradman a chance to interrupt. "What the hell is the matter? We just went on a sight-seeing detour up the Daning and camped the night because it was too late to get back here in daylight."

"What exactly were you filming?" the man snapped.

247

"Mountains, trees, the military installations," Bradman replied sarcastically. "You could look at the stuff yourself if your moronic men hadn't thrown it in the river!"

It was a point Sammy Wong seized on with alacrity. For the next few minutes, the two Americans witnessed a splendid altercation between their interrogators as one branch of Chinese officialdom berated the other for dereliction of duty. If the loss of the cassettes had not been so tragic, Preston thought, the situation would have been comic.

It was dark before they were finally released. In the end, the Chinese seemed to have been convinced that the excursion into a forbidden zone was wholly accidental, an understandable error which could be overlooked, particularly in view of the significant benefits which Bradman's tourist investments promised to bring to Sandouping and the surrounding area. Indeed, by the end of the interrogation, the Chinese Police Captain seemed to become positively jovial. Glasses of Mao Tai were produced and toasts drunk to present and future prosperity.

"Up yours," said Bradman softly, as he raised his glass.

"I don't understand," Preston shook his head. "Why would the Chinese be trying to hide the pandas? Are they trying to keep them secret because they're afraid that too many people will come along and turn the place into a picnic site?"

"I'm afraid not." Bradman emptied his tumbler of Black Label and helped himself to another.

"This is where we went . . ." He traced their route on the map through the mini-gorges of the Daning to where they had landed the helicopter. "We parked the machine here and then walked up this slight elevation to the col. What do you notice?"

Preston looked at the map, studying the contour lines and trying to relate the topography of the grid-sheet to the features which they had observed on the ground.

"Come on!" Bradman urged him. "Look at the spot

heights! I checked them, by the way, against the altimeter readings."

Suddenly Preston understood. "The col!" He said. "The spot height marked for the col, is that what you mean?"

"Exactly. Work it out and you'll see that the col is exactly 190 metres above the Sandouping river-level."

"Oh my God!" Preston at last grasped the full implications. "It's going to be flooded, and the water is going to spill down into the Hidden Valley, fill up the saucer, at least to the 200 metre level. So goodbye pandas!"

"Right!" Bradman said quietly. "And if the word gets out, they know perfectly well there will be an international outcry . . ."

"There's no way they're going to let a few pandas prevent them flooding the valley," said Preston. "This isn't America and besides, who is going to believe us? You go back to the States and announce you've seen a bunch of pandas where there aren't supposed to be any and the first thing the Chinese Government will do is put out an official disclaimer! How are you going to prove that you're right and that they're wrong? People will think you're a nut. Where's the evidence? Where are the photographs? Where's the film?"

"Here." Bradman unpacked the bag which they had deposited in Preston's bungalow earlier that day. "Lesson number one," he chortled, holding the cassettes in his hand, "is never leave your film in your camera when you're passing through hostile terrain. Lesson number two is, when someone asks you to open your camera, make one hell of a fuss before you allow them to destroy the blank tapes! That way they may just possibly forget to search the rest of your bags!"

Still smiling, Bradman slipped one of the cassettes into Preston's player.

"Maybe we will win that prize at Cannes after all," said Preston as they watched the pandas poking around the fire to discover – perhaps for the first time in their lives – that though it was pretty, it was also hot!

"Look at those little cubs rolling around by the trees

there!" Bradman added. "This footage has got to be unique."

They spent the night copying the tapes and working out their strategy for the next steps.

"I'm pulling out of here tomorrow," Bradman said. "There are people back in the States who have to see this! Maybe I can even get the President to intervene! I'll give it everything it takes! All my money, all my time. Hell, Preston, I've never done anything more important in my life!" Bradman paused and looked at Preston appraisingly. "I'm going to need your help too, you know."

"What can I do? The Chinese aren't going to listen to me, they aren't going to listen to any of us now."

"There's another way. It may not work, but it's worth a try."

"What's that?"

"Let's work the showbiz connection: Go and see Lilly Wu," Bradman urged. "Show her the tapes! Tell her what's happening! Ask her to help! If Wu will listen to anyone, he'll listen to her. And if he won't listen, maybe there are other people who will. We have to keep trying!"

Ben Bradman was gone by lunch-time the next day. Preston, no less anxious to depart, had nevertheless to ensure that colleagues would be able to cover for him during his absence.

"Better to take a holiday now," Horst Klarfeld had advised sympathetically, "while things are quiet. It will be different later on when they've filled the dam and are running tests on the turbines."

11

Lilly Wu looked at her notes.

"15.35 hours. Za-Za walks uphill", she read, "and sits in bamboo patch, barely visible among the stems, about 25 metres from the observer. She eats fargesia shoot. Standing up, she reaches forward and breaks off a second shoot, then she strips off sheath and eats as she sits.

"15.40. She snorts and honks, having sensed the observer, but she continues to forage.

"15.45. Abruptly, she walks from the bamboo into a clearing and, her nose raised high as if sniffing, she faces the observer, who sits quietly at ten metres. Then, bobbing her head up and down, she honks and snorts in agitation for 30 seconds before retreating to 19 metres."

For a few minutes, Lilly continued her reading, then closed the note-book and stood up. The panda, still 19 metres away, blinked as though registering her movement, but otherwise seemed unperturbed. She watched placidly, still chewing on the bamboo stem, as Lilly quickly packed up her things in a tote bag, before heading down the steep trail which led to her camp on the rugged, east-facing slope of the Choushuigou valley.

She walked quickly, ducking under the overhanging vegetation and occasionally forcing aside obstructions with a quick, deft movement of her outstretched left hand. Once, when a frond swung back and caught her across the face, she grimaced with annoyance.

When she reached the trail and was able to look down at the tents below, Lilly Wu paused in mid-stride. The sense of dissatisfaction, almost of disillusion, which she had been experiencing recently had less to do with the physical setting – in spite of the inevitable hardships she rejoiced in the beauty of the mountains – than with the nature of the research at Wolong. For years now scientists had been patiently tracking the movement of the pandas. If she had filled one note-book with the kind of observations she had made that morning, she had filled a hundred. Apart from visual sightings, there was the digital radio-log recording the movement of animals who had been trapped and tagged and released back into the wild with small radio-transmitters planted on a collar round their necks. The Wolong team had studied feeding strategy as well as activity patterns. They had studied the population dynamics of the Giant Panda, as well as its social behaviour. Several books had already been written by Chinese or foreign experts, and several more were in the course of preparation, describing every aspect of the panda's daily life, including courtship and mating, gestation and maternity, the interaction between mother and young and just about any other topic which seemed relevant. A huge movement, almost an industry, had grown up around that famous black and white animal. And yet, Lilly Wu asked herself sharply, what was the reality? What did all this effort add up to? As she stood there, looking down into the valley, which had been her home for half her working life, she felt the tears trickling down her cheeks.

"Let's face it," she was speaking out loud, though there was no-one to hear her. "It's too late, it's far too late!"

When she reached her camp, she was not a little surprised to find Preston Murphy waiting for her.

"I hope you don't mind me barging in like this," Preston said. "I need to talk to you."

For a moment, she didn't recognise him. But when she heard his voice, the clipped almost prim New England accent somehow softened by a touch of Irish blarney, her heart – literally – gave a leap. Assisi was half a world away yet the memory of those magic autumnal days in Umbria had stayed with her. More than once, in the solitude of the forests, she had found herself thinking of the tall handsome American who for one strange improbable evening had held her in his arms.

"Preston!" She wiped her eyes with the back of her hand. "What are *you* doing here?"

"Hello, Lilly." Oh God, thought Preston, can this really be true? She was even more beautiful than he remembered. He held out his hands and pulled her gently to him.

"I've been thinking about this moment ever since I last saw you."

Her lips found his and for a moment they stood together, embracing passionately. Then she drew back, smiling, "I'm on duty at the moment . . ."

The evening was beginning to draw in. They lit a fire and sat down in front of it.

"They've got a loud speaker rigged up on top of the dam and everyone stopped work the first time they played your latest hit! You didn't tell me you were famous!"

Lilly shrugged her shoulders and laughed. "You never told me you liked Chinese music."

"I didn't until I heard you sing. As far as I'm concerned you can keep Streisand and Madonna!"

"Don't you think, Preston," Lilly lifted a boiling billy off the fire and poured the water into a pot, "that you ought to tell me why you're really here." As she passed him a cup of tea, her fingers brushed his hand.

Preston spent the next half hour giving a detailed account of the visit which he and Ben Bradman had made to the secret valley above the head-waters of the Daning River.

"We have films too," he concluded. "You may need them, otherwise they may not believe you . . ."

"Frankly, Preston, I find the whole thing incredible. And I tell you, my father would never have permitted such a thing to happen!"

"I've looked at the files." Preston wasn't going to give up now. "Three Gorges has been your father's pet concern right from the beginning. His imprint is stamped on every block of concrete and on the blade of every turbine. But maybe it's not too late for him to change his mind. Once your father is convinced that the wrong decision has been taken, he can convince the others. If any man can unscramble this mess, he can!"

Lilly's jaw jutted and her eyes flashed. "Maybe we've

been fooled by old men for too long. Or I'm a fool for listening to you."

As they were getting the tents ready for the night, he said to her: "It's funny. I've been glancing at my father's Chinese diaries. Haven't had time to read them properly yet. Dad speaks of a young Chinese lad he met in Chungking during the war. They seem to have become close friends. He was called Wu Canping, too. Did you ever hear your father mention anyone called Murphy? Of course, there are thousands of Murphys just like there are thousands of Wus, I suppose."

A frown crossed Lilly's brow. "I do remember my father once talking about an American he had known during the war. It was the day of Chou En Lai's funeral. Mother was away – she always seemed to be away, that was part of her job – so Dad had no one to talk to but me. We went to the funeral together, just the two of us. Dad was almost the only member of the Politburo to attend; the others tried to ignore Chou's death. They wanted him buried quietly with the minimum of fuss. But somehow the word got out and half a million people gathered in the streets of Beijing to pay their last respects. When we got home, Dad wanted me to sit with him, wanted me to listen while he talked. He told me about how he had first met Chou En Lai in Chungking during the war, how his career had really begun after that. I remember him saying there were two people he respected during those days. One was Chou, the other was this American who had given him his first job. Mind you, I never heard him mention his wartime work with the Americans except on that one occasion." Lilly Wu laughed. "That's understandable, isn't it? When I was growing up, the Americans were the arch-enemy. Men who were on the way up like my father didn't go around boasting about their one-time close association with Uncle Sam!"

Preston was scarcely listening. He was staring at Lilly Wu as though in her he could see something of himself.

"The man your father talked about was my own father, Lilly. I'm sure of that." As he spoke, he was conscious of

254

the bond between them, and of the links between this young Chinese woman and the father he had never known.

That night she came to his tent and lay down beside him on the hard ground-sheet.

"People write to me asking for my photograph, they listen to my songs. In the schools, in the universities, there are Lilly Wu societies. They think I'm a modern Chinese woman." She paused, then – still holding him – added: "But I've never made love before."

He ran his hand over her breasts. They were so small, he thought, so delicate. She sat up to pull her tunic over her head, then in one swift movement removed the khaki drill trousers which she had been wearing all day.

"Come into my sleeping bag," he said. "There's plenty of room. Quickly, you'll be cold!" Her hair, still smelling of the smoke from the camp fire, was in his face. He remembered how he had first seen her on the road to Assisi with her hair blowing in the wind. Her body was flat against his.

"Are you sure you want to do this? I don't want to do anything you don't want to do."

She put a finger on his lips: "This is not an exercise in Marxist dialectic."

"I love you, Lilly." He took her hand and held it. "Somehow I feel I've known you for years."

"Shush. Please kiss me, Preston."

Her lips tasted of salt and smoke, her body was hard yet pliable. She had never made love before yet she seemed to know all there was to know.

Later, much later, she said to him: "Please you remember me when you go back to America."

"America! How do you know I'm going back?"

She shook her head in the darkness, still clinging to him. "You have your work, I have mine."

He was hurt, offended. "I don't see why . . ."

She realised she had upset him and sought to make amends.

"My darling," she nibbled his ear in a playful, kittenish way, the way she had seen it in the movies from Hong Kong

255

which sometimes played in Chengdu, "you were wonderful." She drew out the vowel-sounds in a passable imitation
of a southern drawl.

He took her then roughly, almost angrily. She screamed
when she climaxed, arched her back and banged her head
hard against the ground.

Three days later, after travelling down by bus from Wolong
to Chengdu, Lilly Wu saw her father in the grand office
which the Sichuan provincial government made available
for visiting dignitaries and – in Minister Wu's case – native
sons.

"Ah, the famous star!" There was a hint of irony in Wu's
voice as he embraced his daughter. "To what do I owe this
signal honour?"

She didn't beat about the bush. "Father, I've come on a
serious matter."

Wu raised an eyebrow. "How can I help?" He held his
hands in a self-deprecating manner. "The Vice-Premier
has very little power. Better to be an official at the provincial
level. Then you can really get things done!"

For the next 20 minutes, Wu Canping listened in silence
as his daughter retold the story which Preston Murphy had
related to her. She left out none of the salient facts though
she was studiously vague about Preston's visit to the camp-
site, leaving Wu to suppose that their encounter had taken
place not in the solitude of the mountains but down in the
valley in the crowded well-chaperoned surroundings of the
Wolong Nature Reserve headquarters, where international
visitors were frequently received.

"Have you seen the film?" asked Wu.

"Preston left me a copy."

"Have you brought it with you?"

"Yes, I thought you would want to have it."

"Thank you." Wu took the cassette from her and put it
away in a desk-drawer. "I'm sorry," he said heavily. "Even
if everything you say is true, there is nothing I can do. The
decision to build the Super-Dam has been taken at the
highest level. It has been confirmed and reconfirmed by the

256

Politburo. Even I cannot reverse that decision now, and, frankly, I wouldn't want to."

"Why?" Her initial amazement had turned to fury.

"Because people are more important than animals," Wu replied coolly. "That dam will bring prosperity to China, above all to Sichuan. The great ships will come up the Yangtze into the very heart of this province. Chungking will overtake Shanghai as China's biggest port! I have been dreaming about this for 40 years. Nothing can stop it now. Certainly not a few pandas."

"I don't believe what I'm hearing!" Lilly spat out the words.

Wu tried to humour her, just as he had tried to humour her when she was a small child throwing tantrums at home because she couldn't get her sums right. "We'll mount a rescue operation if we have to. We'll move a few pandas to the zoos in Beijing and Shanghai." He tried to put his arm around her shoulder.

Lilly Wu pulled away. "Zoos are not the answer! As you very well know!" She paused, looked at her father as though seeing him clearly for the first time. "Are you even sure the dam's safe?"

Wu Canping drew back sharply.

"Be careful, Lilly, be very careful not to meddle in matters which are not your concern!"

She refused to be brow-beaten. "Who I talk to is my business, no-one else's! If you have the slightest suspicion the dam's not safe, the project should be scrubbed."

Wu sighed. "We may have a policy of openness now in China, but there are still limits. The fact that you are my daughter makes it even harder for me."

He pressed a buzzer on the desk and a guard entered and saluted.

"Miss Wu is to be escorted back to Wolong," Wu Canping instructed. "She is to stay there until further notice."

As the guard grasped Lilly firmly by the elbow to escort her from the room, Wu turned back to the papers on his desk. For a few minutes he tried to concentrate on the documents in front of him but then, with a gesture of irritation, he thrust them aside. His thoughts raced backwards and forwards, as one memory crowded out another. So Preston Murphy had followed in his father's footsteps, had he? How much did Preston know? How much did he suspect?

He picked up the telephone.

"Wong," he shouted, "I want Murphy out of the country by the week-end. Put him on the plane to Hong Kong and make sure he doesn't come back!" He didn't wait for a reply.

The sun dropped low across the plain and still Wu sat at his desk meditating on the strange coincidences that had brought Oliver Murphy's son and his own daughter together whilst he, for a host of reasons, was actively concerned to keep them apart. A pity. He liked the sound of young Preston. If the circumstances had been different, he would have looked forward to meeting him. It was plain as a pikestaff from the way she spoke that Lilly had taken a shine to him. Perhaps, one day . . .

When he left his office for the day, he gave the cassette to the guard.

"Take this to Security," he ordered. "Tell them to destroy it."

258

12

As the plane took off from Hong Kong's Kai Tak airport, climbing steeply and banking quickly out to sea, Preston Murphy leaned his head back against the seat, closed his eyes and sighed audibly. Christ, what a balls-up! To be kicked out of China with barely 24 hours' notice and no chance to explain or defend himself! And, to endure the sanctimonious preachings of Sammy Wong! Preston could feel a hot flush returning to his face as he recalled Wong's lecture: "First, you make unauthorised visit to prohibited zone, Mr Murphy. Second, you make unscheduled trip to Wolong with no prior notice of your intention. Third, with your reckless and uncontrolled behaviour you insult traditional Chinese purity! Are you not aware, in any case, of laws of our country in this matter?"

For a moment, Preston hadn't realised what Wong was talking about. "You can't be serious . . ." he said but Wong cut him short by thrusting into his hand a copy of the relevant section of China's penal code.

"Article 43," he snapped: " 'No sexual relationship between unmarried persons.' Article 58: 'No Chinese woman may have sexual relationship, including marriage, with foreigner except by express permission of the State.' "

"You bastard!" Preston protested. "You people were spying on us all the time!"

The engine-note changed as the Pan-Am jumbo reached its cruising altitude. Cautiously, Preston opened his eyes to see a stewardess advancing on him with a message in her hand.

"Mr Murphy?"

"That's me."

"This was waiting for you at the check-in desk, but they forgot to give it to you. Sorry about that!" He opened the telex:

PLEASE REPORT FOR PERSONAL INTERVIEW
WITH MR WILMERS ON ARRIVAL IN NEW YORK
STOP GRAVEST CONCERN HERE RE YOUR
RECENT ACTIVITIES STOP FULLEST EXPLA-
NATIONS WILL BE REQUIRED ENDS.

He crumpled the message and stuffed it in the ash-tray of
the arm-rest. What was Wilmers, that tough old bastard,
going to say when Preston told him, first of all, that he had
been goofing off looking for pandas and, to make matters
worse, had ended up by boffing the Minister for Energy's
daughter?

"Oh God!" Preston groaned out loud.

"Can I help you sir?" A passing stewardess, noticing his
pallor offered the comfort of a hot moist face-towel, rolled
up like a pancake.

If the depths of Preston's gloom occurred over the China
Sea somewhere between Hong Kong and Tokyo, there was,
by the time the Jumbo began its descent for a re-fuelling
stop in Anchorage, Alaska, an unexpected lightening in his
mood. Beating a rapid retreat from his Sandouping bungalow, Preston had emptied the contents of his safe and had
removed, besides his passport and other personal documents, the parcel containing his father's diaries which had
arrived a few days earlier. For a moment, he had debated
whether to leave them for the Consortium to dispatch with
the rest of his consignment but, on reflection, he had
decided against it. First, his luggage might get lost. Second,
any interesting-looking documents he left behind might be
scrutinised or confiscated by the Chinese. Third, and most
important, since up till then he had only had time to glance
at the material, he had promised himself that he would
study those diaries more fully the moment he got back from
Wolong.

As it turned out, Colonel Oliver Murphy's Chinese journals proved to be the most riveting reading-matter that
Preston could have imagined choosing for a long plane
journey. As the hours passed, he became ever more deeply
immersed in his father's narrative.

260

The politics behind it all fascinated him. Those Chung-king years were the beginning of a long comedy of errors as far as the US-China relationship was concerned. The antics of SACO, and especially the descriptions of Commodore Miles and his various wild stratagems, also made gripping reading. But most intriguing of all was his father's account of his dealings with Wu Canping. It was clear that Wu had played a crucial role in his father's Chinese existence. He had not only served as batman-cum-general factotum; he had been Murphy's eyes and ears in a city where, if you weren't Chinese or at least Chinese-speaking, you were as good as blind and deaf; more than that, Wu's actions at a critical moment had very possibly saved Murphy's life.

"I didn't know it then," Preston read, "but it seems that all the time that I was delirious during that long journey back up the Yangtze after the raid on the Japs at Yichang, Wu was there at my side, keeping me from going under. I'm told he barely slept throughout the whole of that time. When our boat was half-swamped by a tidal wave and everyone else was looking after number one, making sure they didn't get washed down-stream, Wu somehow got me ashore. And when at last they took me to the military hospital in Chungking, for the first week, while I was recovering from the delirium, he refused to leave my bedside. As a matter of fact, Mary Cartwright, one of the nurses whose special charge I appear to be, has been slightly put out by his persistence . . ."

Later, as he was nearing the end of the first volume, Preston took out his pen and made some notes.

"Murphy befriends Wu," he wrote. "Wu imprisoned and tortured by Tai Li. Why? Was Wu actually working for Communists? If so, what was/is his relationship with Soong? That must be the key question."

A few pages further on, he had the answer: "November 11th, 1944," he read. "Visited Charlie Soong's magnificent villa outside Chungking today to see how Wu Canping was getting on. Poor chap! Tai Li really gave him a terrible going-over. They put him on the Aeroplane for three days and it wasn't until Charlie Soong intervened on the express

261

orders of the Generalissimo (that was a result of Mary's plea to Madame Chiang), that those Chinese devils released him. He was more dead than alive when they cut him down. He'd lost half his teeth, most of his ribs were broken, and one of his kidneys had been seriously damaged by the beating which he had received. Soong got him out of there. As a matter of fact, he read the riot act to Tai Li, charged him with overstepping the bounds, told him that the Generalissimo was extremely displeased – that, I gather, is the gist of what transpired.

"Charlie Soong wasn't there the day I went up to his villa. Wu let me in and I could tell straight away that something funny was going on. I'd expected that he'd be glad to see me. But instead of greeting me like an old pal, Wu looked extremely ill at ease. Physically he seemed to have recovered amazingly quickly from the effects of his imprisonment. He was still a bit pale and bruised, but you could see that he had an iron constitution, and was well on the way towards a total restoration of health, if not beauty. Mentally, however, it was a different story. It was quite clear to me that Wu was embarrassed, almost frightened, at being seen in Charlie Soong's villa. What's more, it was obvious that he wasn't simply there as a supernumerary servant, to be added to Soong's already large household staff as soon as he got better. He was smartly dressed in a suit and tie, almost as though Charlie Soong had taken him on as a private secretary. As far as I was concerned, Wu deserved nothing better and I wished Soong every good fortune with him. I'd have given Wu a reference myself if Soong had asked . . ."

Preston stared at the page, at the neat paragraphs penned in black ink in his father's handwriting. There it was, he thought. For 40 years or more, Wu had been playing both sides. Who could tell where his true allegiance lay? He had risen to the very pinnacle of the Chinese Communist Party. Once you were Vice-Premier, there was only one place left to go, the Premiership itself. Yet, whatever bonds there were between Wu and the Party, seemed to be balanced or even outweighed by the debt Wu had owed to Charlie

Soong. Soong had sprung Wu from gaol. Had Soong also provided the seed corn which enabled Wu, as he rose to power first in Sichuan, then at the national level, to reap such a rich harvest? He remembered how David Burns, the *New York Times* correspondent in Beijing, had reported his impression that Wu and Soong seemed already to know each other when they met that day at the press-conference in Beijing. You bet they did! Charlie Soong – Sir Charles, as he now was – must have been laughing all the way to the bank. Whatever investment he had made in young Wu Canping's future had paid off a thousandfold. How much did Soong stand to make when the big ships, Soong-owned or, at least, Soong-financed, began to reach Chungking?

For a few minutes, Preston dozed. It had been a long flight, and the material he had been reading had not only been mentally absorbing; it had unleashed an exhausting tumult of emotions. For the first time in his life, he felt that he was beginning to make his father's acquaintance. More important still, he liked what he saw.

With only a few minutes to go before landing, Preston opened the second volume of the diaries, the one which detailed Murphy's Washington existence, his visit to Wake Island with President Truman and subsequent mission to Peking, before continuing with the anguish and humiliation of the return to America and the dark days of disgrace. Some instinct made him turn to the end first and there it was! Under the entry for 4 December, 1950 – one of the last in the volume – he read:

"There are still some bright sparks amid the prevailing gloom. I've finally turned in my report on the Three Gorges Project to the US Army Corps of Engineers who commissioned it so many years ago. I've also sent a copy to the Bureau of Reclamation. The Corps and the Bureau seem to be involved in a dispute as to whose turf China is. Typical bureaucratic behaviour! Instead of cooperating, they spend all their time fighting each other!

"I phoned General Vogel and told him the document was on its way and that he probably wouldn't like it when he read it. The Corps is basically gung-ho for action and to

263

hell with the cost! Give them an untamed river and they want to throw a dam at it! Which is why Three Gorges is so irresistibly appealing to them. Biggest project in the world! But it just won't work. Given the geology and topography of the site, any structure higher than 180 metres is going to be unsafe. What's more, no-one seems to be talking about the seismic problem. Yet the fact of the matter is that China is one of the most earthquake prone countries in the world. You've got the Japan Pacific tectonic plate pushing deep down on one side and the Indian subcontinent plate pushing up from below; hence the Himalayas. When I was in Chungking during the war I picked up all the seismic data I could lay my hands on and I annexed the relevant papers to my report . . .

"Part of me, of course, deeply regrets that I was forced finally to reach a negative conclusion about the project. I can remember so clearly even now the day I first saw the potential dam-site just above the little village of Sandouping. Any engineer has to be grabbed by the idea of helping to build the largest dam in the history of civil engineering! But there is such a thing as conscience too and I could not, in conscience, knowing what I know, have recommended that the project go ahead or that American resources, whether technical or financial, be devoted to helping the Chinese bring it to fruition. We've got Murphy's Law; but we are going to have to do without Murphy's dam!"

As the plane touched down, Preston put the diaries away in his briefcase. If he had begun the long flight from Hong Kong in a mood of despair, he ended it with a sense of exhilaration. He realised that there was one overwhelming priority – to find, somewhere, a copy of his father's report and to make its conclusions public. If his father's judgement about the dam had been valid almost 40 years ago, why should it not be valid today?

But there was something else besides, something which – at least on a personal plane – was just as important. Preston knew now with total conviction that there was no way his father could have been a traitor, a Communist agent. No way the Oliver Murphy he had been reading about, the

264

man who had taken part in Commodore Miles's mad raid against the Japanese gunboats at Yichang, who had wooed and won Nurse Cartwright, and whose love for his wife and family informed every entry on the later pages of his journal, could have ended up as a shabby suicide.

13

"What the hell do you think you are playing at?" Wilmers shouted as soon as Preston entered the room. "For fifteen years we've worked our asses off building up a position in China. Now you just throw it all away. The firm's been kicked out of the country, thanks to you. We've just received the official notification." He flung a telex onto the desk. "What's more, they're refusing to pay us any completion fees. I want explanations now, Murphy, and they had better be good!" The bulky president of Wilmers and Friendly glowered behind his desk.

Preston took a deep breath, marshalling his thoughts.

"The pandas . . ."

"Fuck the pandas!" Wilmers banged furiously on the desk. "I don't give a damn about them and nor does anyone else. You can keep that for your Assisi weirdos . . ."

At first Preston let him rant on hoping that the storm would blow itself out. But it didn't. Wilmer's face reddened and his language grew increasingly foul.

"It's not just the pandas," Preston finally interrupted. "*The dam isn't safe*. This firm ought not to be associated with it. As a matter of fact, I'm not 100 per cent convinced that the original design was sound either, regardless of any extension. Frankly, I don't believe we looked at the seismic data properly."

"What fucking data are you talking about?" Wilmers roared. "The only data we have are the data the Chinese themselves provided. Are you suggesting that they're fool enough to build a dam in a high-risk zone?" He stood up abruptly and walked over to a filing cabinet. Pulling out a sheaf of papers, he thrust them at Preston.

"Take a look at those figures," he urged. "There are *no* seismic problems in the Sandouping area. These records go back 200 years; as a matter of fact, the Chinese have

266

been measuring earthquakes a great deal longer than that. For Christ's sake, face the facts. The largest quake which ever occurred within 500 miles of Sandouping *never exceeded 5.6!* Hell, we get tremors like that all over the United States, but that never stopped us building dams anywhere we goddam pleased!"

Preston took the papers from Wilmers and spread them on the top of the desk. The bottom of each page was stamped with the seal of the Sichuan Provincial Government's Department of Energy and Water Resources. Next to the seal were inscribed the words: "Certified authentic translation of records held by the Department." There was a scribbled, illegible signature above the data, as well as a further official-looking stamp.

Looking at the documents, Preston experienced a growing sense of uncertainty.

"When Wilmers and Friendly evaluated these data they were working on the basis of the original design specifications. But the extra 20 metres could be crucial. I've looked at the geology. There's no solid anchor-rock. They had to grout and fill all the way. Even a small earthquake could damage an unsound structure, maybe destroy it."

Wilmers looked at him scornfully. "You're fired, Murphy, as of now. It may take us months, it may take us years to retrieve our position in China, but whatever happens, I don't want you around to mess things up for us again. I want you out of here by tomorrow."

Wilmers picked up the data-sheets, put them back in the filing-cabinet and locked the door. Preston noticed that he slipped the key under the blotter on his desk.

Preston ate dinner alone that night in the restaurant of the UN Plaza Hotel where he was staying. In spite of his long journey, he felt keyed-up, tense. Despite the evidence, he was convinced that there was something rotten in the current state of affairs, something that didn't add up. Why, for example, did Wilmers have those seismic data neatly lined-up like that? It was almost as though he had expected to be challenged on them.

Later, Preston went swimming in the hotel's pool on the

35th floor. As he thrashed up and down, he could see the lights of the surrounding sky-scrapers, and, in the distance, the traffic on East River Drive.

He had done 48 lengths out of a planned 60 when he remembered that he still had his own set of keys to the Wilmers and Friendly offices. Tomorrow, no doubt, he would be required to turn them in, but tomorrow – as the lady put it – was another day.

He dressed quickly, went down to the lobby and caught a cab to Madison and 65th. Wilmers and Friendly had offices at the top of a modern chrome and glass building. Before entering the foyer, Preston stood on the pavement outside, craning his neck back to see whether there were any lights still burning. He had a perfectly legitimate reason for needing to visit the place after hours – he was supposed to be clearing his desk – but, even so, it was better to be prepared.

He showed his I.D. to the night-guard, took the elevator to the 26th floor and, a minute or two later, entered his room. It had been some months since he had last had an assignment in New York. Though the office was still nominally his, it had been used in his absence by various birds of passage and he had to spend some little time sorting out the extraneous bric-à-brac and identifying his own files.

He worked for half-an-hour or so, then, leaving a pile of papers in the middle of his desk and the light on in his room, he walked down the carpeted corridor to the office at the end which was occupied by the President of Wilmers and Friendly. It was the work of a moment to find the filing-cabinet key where Wilmers had left it, and to remove the data-sheets which he'd seen earlier that day. There was a photo-copy machine in the corridor outside.

Half an hour later, Preston left the building and headed once more for his hotel.

He didn't see Jim Wilmers the next day. When he enquired, he was told to address any questions to the personnel department. It was hardly a glorious exit to a career which, at one stage at least, had been full of promise.

Once or twice, as he carted his cardboard boxes to the

elevator Preston passed erstwhile colleagues only to be made painfully aware by their reaction that he might as well have come down with AIDS. Only the receptionist, a cheerful black girl, seemed ready to show him any sympathy.

"You really screwed up, didn't you, Preston? I'm sorry to see you go."

"Thanks, Bettie." Preston gave her a kiss on the cheek. He felt suddenly tired. "Did I screw up? Maybe yes, maybe no." He looked around. "By the way, is Bill Friendly in today? I'd like to say good-bye to him at least."

Bettie's smile froze. "Didn't you know? Bill's in hospital, up at the Medical Centre on East 70th." The receptionist lowered her voice. "It's terminal. Cancer of the throat."

Preston visited the hospital at lunchtime that day. He had to wait half an hour in an antiseptic lobby plastered with NO SMOKING signs before being shown into the private room and, when he did finally enter, he was shocked by Friendly's appearance.

"Don't tire him." The nurse left them alone.

"Bill, it's great to see you!" Preston pulled up a chair beside the bed.

"What the hell are you doing here, Preston? You're meant to be in China." Friendly managed a barely audible croak.

For the next several minutes Preston brought Friendly up to date with developments on the Three Gorges Project. Even though Friendly didn't, couldn't, say very much, for the first time since his arrival in New York, Preston had the sense that someone understood what he was saying. He spoke rapidly, almost as though he feared that Friendly might die on him before he got to the end of the story.

"I don't believe the dam is safe," he concluded. "Certainly not in its present configuration. Wilmers showed me some seismic data, called me a scare-monger, accused me of disloyalty to the firm and sacked me on the spot."

Bill Friendly nodded weakly. "You could be right, Preston. Hell, you just could be right. You know, I can't understand what Wilmers is playing at, either." It cost him a great deal of effort to get the words out. He paused, fighting for breath. "Did you give the tapes to Professor Zheng?"

When Preston nodded, Friendly leaned his head back on the pillow and closed his eyes with relief.

"Thank God!" he murmured. "Zheng is a good man. He'll pick up any anomalies, you can be sure of that."

"You knew there was something wrong too, didn't you?"

"They're all in it together." The dying man was now clearly exhausted with the effort of talking. "Wu, Soong, Wilmers too, perhaps. I started raising questions, just like you have. I'm sure that's why Friendly pulled me out of China – not for this" - he pointed a frail finger at his throat. Friendly put out his hand and, with sudden strength clutched Preston's arm. "Don't give up. Don't give up now. There are too many lives at stake. Take this. It will help you understand." He leaned over to his bedside table, picked up a thick volume which had the appearance of a scientific textbook and thrust it with trembling hand at his visitor.

There were tears in Preston's eyes as the nurse came back into the room and ushered him away.

Preston took the 8 p.m. shuttle from La Guardia to Washington National Airport. He checked in at the Mayflower, had dinner in the hotel restaurant, then settled down in his room to read the book which Friendly had given him as a parting present.

It was *The Social and Environmental Effects of Large Dams*, by E. Goldsmith and N. Hilyard, and published by the Wadebridge Ecological Centre in England. On the cover of the book Friendly had scribbled the words, "See chapter 9".

As soon as he turned to the relevant pages, Preston realised the reason for Bill Friendly's note. The authors of the book had, under the section headed "Dams, Earthquakes and Failures", collected an impressive array of evidence to support the hypothesis that pressure applied to sometimes fragile geological structures by the vast mass of water impounded by a big dam, could – and often did – give rise to earthquakes.

Preston studied with particular care some of the passages which Friendly had underlined. Thus, on page 107, he read: ". . . by 1969 the relationship between large dams and earthquakes came under renewed scrutiny, especially after the Fourth World Congress on Earthquake Engineering in Santiago, Chile, in January of that year. At the conference a French seismologist, Professor Jean Pierre Rothé, at that time, Secretary-General of the International Association of Seismology and Physics of the Earth's Interior, presented a paper entitled 'Manmade Earthquakes' in which he showed that the earthquakes referred to above – and a few less important ones as well – were definitely caused by the impoundment of reservoirs . . ."

Four case histories followed and Preston noticed that Friendly had in each instance underscored the crucial passage.

"Good God!" He was suddenly struck by the horrendous implications of what he was reading. What the authors were suggesting was (1) that earthquakes could actually be triggered by the impoundment of water in a dam and (2) the greater the seismic strains already present in a region, the greater was the likelihood that the impoundment of massive volumes of water behind a dam would lead to a quake.

He looked at the last of the underlined quotations: ". . . as Rothé puts it, when he builds dams, man plays the role of the sorcerer's apprentice: in trying to control the energy of the rivers, he brings about stresses whose energy can be suddenly and disastrously released . . ."

Preston pushed the book aside. He understood now why Friendly had wanted him to deliver the computer-disk to Professor Zheng in Xian. The data on that disk would have included any changes in seismic activity in the Sandouping region during the initial period of impoundment. Of course, if the historical level of seismic activity was low – as the records which Wilmers had shown him seemed to indicate – then the likelihood of a major earthquake being triggered by water-pressure, or occurring spontaneously, was perhaps insignificant. But what if those historical records were wrong? What if, contrary to what Wilmers had indicated, the Sandouping area was an important epicentre? Every day, every hour that passed might be vital. When he left, the water had already passed the 180 metre level. How much further could it rise before calamity struck?

He looked at his watch and saw that it was already past midnight. He set the alarm and turned out the light. He smiled grimly to himself in the darkness. If his father's report on the Three Gorges Dam still existed, in whatever form and in whatever location, he would find it . . .

"Hi, this is Debbie! How can I help you?"

"Good morning, Debbie. Is that the Office of History?"

"It is indeed, Sir."

Sitting in his hotel bedroom, with the telephone in his hand and his breakfast tray on the table in front of him, Preston came straight to the point: "My name is Preston Murphy. In the early fifties my father wrote a report about a potential dam-site on the Yangtze River in China and filed it with the US Army Corps of Engineers. He'd been working for the Corps during the war. I'm trying to trace that report."

"I'll see if I can direct you to one of the specific historians. One moment, please, Sir."

Thank God, Preston thought, for the Freedom of Information Act. It had changed the whole mentality of government officials. In the old days they used to clip articles from the *New York Times* and stamp secret all over them. Now, even the most sensitive files were accessible if someone came forward with a *bona fide* request.

"I'm going to transfer you to Dr Frank Bellairs. He probably knows more about the Corps' involvement in China than anyone else we've got here at Fort Belvoir."

A few seconds later a deep confident voice came on the line. "Can I help you?"

Once again Preston explained what he was looking for. When he had finished, Dr Bellairs sounded more than a little sceptical. "I didn't think the Corps was that heavily involved in the Three Gorges Project. Let me dig around. I'll call you back."

An hour later, the telephone rang, "As I thought," Dr Bellairs said, "the Corps' involvement on the Three Gorges

Project seems to have been minimal. I've looked in the 3-volume official history of the US Army Corps of Engineers activities in the China-Burma-India theatre during World War II. There's no mention of any Corps' interest in construction projects on the Yangtze, though it had some navigation concerns. As a matter of fact, historically speaking, the Corps' activities throughout the whole of China tended to be on the navigation rather than on the dam-building side." Bellairs paused. "Your father was in Chungking during the war, was he?"

"Yes."

"Who was he with?"

"SACO, actually."

"Oh, I see," Dr Bellairs seemed to hesitate. "That could explain things. Anything to do with SACO tends to have been deep-sixed. There aren't many units in the US Army who want to admit they were mixed up with Chiang Kai Shek's gangsters. Certainly not the Corps. Try the *Notary Engineer*, that's the monthly journal of the Society of Military Engineers, or else go and have a look through the back numbers of *Engineering Newsrecord*. That's published by McGraw Hill. They'll have the microfilm in the Library of Congress. Better still, talk to the Bureau of Reclamation. Their involvement with the Three Gorges Project was much more substantial than the Corps'. Your father's report could have been copied to them and there's just a chance they might still have it given their on-going interest in the project."

"As a matter of fact, he *did* copy it to them," Preston remembered.

"There you go, then." Dr Bellairs wished him luck as he hung up.

At 12 noon, having made an appointment by telephone, Preston Murphy entered the office of a large, elderly negro called Homer Coleman who was chief of the US Bureau of Reclamation's Division of International Activities. Coleman's office was situated on the seventh floor of the Department of Interior's massive C Street building and was decorated with photographs of engineering projects, at home and abroad, upon which the Bureau of Reclamation had been engaged over the years.

"That's Jackson Lake Dam," Coleman told him, following his gaze. "Near the headwaters of the Snake River in North-West Wyoming. Those are the Grand Teton mountains behind. Great fishing! And that – " he pointed to another photograph " – is Itaipu, in Brazil. Biggest in the world until the Three Gorges came along."

"I know," Preston grimaced. "I was down there myself."

Coleman poured them both some coffee from a pot which stood beside his desk. He looked at Preston appraisingly, as though wondering how much it was safe – or sensible – to tell him. Finally, he seemed to make up his mind.

"I'm going to tell you something, Preston, which I guess I'm the only person to know. I remember when your father died. I was in the Bureau at the time. I knew about his report. As a matter of fact, I read it or at least the summary. But then, the day after his death, word came down from the top that all copies of the Murphy Report were to be destroyed as being the product of a Communist spy. Those McCarthy fuckers could destroy a man and all his work overnight."

"So what happened?"

"I thought about the instruction for a couple of days, and I thought about your father. And then I decided what the hell, I wouldn't destroy the report, I'd archive it."

Preston's heart skipped a couple of beats. "Archive it . . . ?"

"I added it to the John Savage file. Savage was one of the Bureau engineers with an interest in China and a great collection of papers upon the subject."

"Where is the archive now?" Preston could feel his excitement increasing by the minute.

"In 1972, as part of its policy of decentralisation, the Bureau reviewed all the files which were held in Washington. A good many of the records were shipped to a depository in Denver. But the John Savage archive was handed over *in toto* to the University of Oregon."

"Is it still there?"

"As far as I know, yes." Coleman stood up and held out his hand. "Just one thing, Preston, if you ever do find the Murphy Report, don't say I rescued it from oblivion." He laughed: "I've only got another two years before my retirement and I've got my eye on a nice little place in Louisiana."

At 9 o'clock the following morning when the doors of Oregon University's School of Engineering opened for business, Murphy joined the gaggle of students heading for the library. The John Savage collection of papers was catalogued under geology and his father's monograph rated a separate entry.

The Three Gorges Dam Project in the Upper Yangtze Valley: a preliminary feasibility study, by Colonel Oliver E. Murphy (Rtd), he read.

Jackpot! thought Preston, as he filled in the order slip.

"You'll have to read it here," the freckle-faced girl behind the desk smiled prettily at him. A few minutes later she called out his number and Preston went back to the desk to pick up a large brown envelope tied up in some faded ribbon.

"I guess you are the first person to have asked for this one in quite a few years."

For the next hour, he sat with his back to the wall, his father's report spread out on the desk in front of him. Once or twice he took notes and, occasionally, nodded his head in approval, as though by some peculiar inversion of chronology, his father's judgements confirmed his own.

"Darn right!" he muttered as he read Murphy senior's analysis of the topography at Sandouping. But the clincher came later, when Murphy senior turned to the earthquake risk. "It might be argued," Preston read, "that the probability of a large earthquake occurring in the Upper Yangtze is so small that it can be safely ignored. As an engineer, I should be only too delighted if this were the case. Unfortunately, the seismic records which I obtained during my stay in Chungking indicate that this is not so. Attached as Annexe A to this report are the historical data of seismic events recorded in Sichuan province for a period of almost

275

100 years prior to World War II. I have the utmost faith in the accuracy of these data. We must remember that the Chinese have been measuring earthquakes and other seismic phenomena longer than any other nation. They virtually invented the science, and given the immense damage that earthquakes have caused in that country, it is not surprising that they continue to devote substantial resources to the business of earthquake measurement and prediction. A quick glance at the records shown in Annexe A reveals that seismic episodes exceeding 6.0 on the Richter scale occurred on average once every 28 years over the period. Though data as to the intensity of these earthquakes is lacking (what we would today call the Mercalli factor), it is a fair bet that at least in some instances the epicentre was located in the Upper Yangtze valley and more specifically in the area of the Three Gorges."

Holding his breath as though he feared that the precious manuscript might suddenly disintegrate before his eyes. Preston turned to the end of the report. For a moment he stared uncomprehendingly at the sets of figures shown in the Annexe. The form and presentation of the data, even the periods covered, were exactly the same as the ones in the table Jim Wilmers had shown him the other evening in New York. He opened his briefcase and took out the photocopy he had made in the Wilmers and Friendly office. No doubt about it, he thought. Both tables were the same. How on earth could his father draw one set of conclusions and all the experts reach another, quite different judgement?

He began to check the figures. And then, suddenly, he let out a long, low whistle, causing the student at the next desk to frown in annoyance.

14

"Shit, man, that's unbelievable!" Ben Bradman pounded the clenched fist of his right hand onto the plain pinewood table which graced the terrace of his mountain hideaway. From where he sat he could look out at the spectacular valley which the Benjamin Bradman foundation had acquired 15 years earlier to provide a refuge for wildlife of every kind and, for such was Bradman's dearest ambition, an eventual home for the giant panda as its prospects of survival in mainland China dwindled beyond the point of no return. Normally, the sight of the firs and hemlocks rising up the slopes of the far mountains, interspersed with luxuriant thickets of high-altitude bamboo, delighted the energetic film-star. He was monarch of all he surveyed, and he liked what he saw. Today, however, anger and amazement were the emotions uppermost in his mind.

"How the hell do they think they can get away with it?"

"They *have* got away with it," Preston reminded him quietly. He had telephoned Ben Bradman from a call-box in Eugene the previous day and, following his instructions, had driven north on US 5 up through Portland and across the Columbia River into the wild country of the Olympic Peninsula where the states of Oregon and Washington met. The trail from Graves Creek Range station snaked up along the Quinault river and the hike up to Bradman's retreat had taken Preston the best part of six hours.

"Tell Bill Leicester you're coming up to see me," Bradman had advised over the phone. "He's the National Park ranger. Strictly speaking, my spread is not in the park but he keeps an eye on things here too when I'm away."

As it turned out, the ranger had accompanied Preston on the first leg of the climb up to White Creek basin where the rain-forest began to thin out at the entrance to the valley.

"There's no place like it," Leicester told him. "You've got one of the densest populations of mountain lions – cougars – anywhere in the world. You've got 14,000 Roosevelt elks, that's the largest herd anywhere. Down there on the coast," he gestured towards the west, "you've got beaches full of sea lions and out in the ocean in the offshore waters there are packs of killer whales."

Around noon they had seen a black bear hugging a cottonwood and when they stopped for lunch, where a log bridge crossed the Quinault, Preston had been thrilled to see 50-pound chinook salmon hurtling rock falls on their way upstream to spawn and die.

Soon after that, the guide had turned back leaving Preston to cover the last few miles alone. It was late afternoon when he arrived at the log cabin, and by the time he had finished his detailed account of the latest developments, evening was drawing in. They moved indoors to sit in front of the fire.

"I still can't believe what I'm hearing," said Bradman. "Okay, so they're not bothered about a few old pandas, but risking the lives of millions of people living downstream . . ." He went over to a mahogany roll-top desk and pulled out a bunch of press-clippings. "Look at these!" He spread them on the table. "My people faxed them in today. Your friend Lilly Wu seems to be singing up a storm."

One of the articles was by David Burns: "Until her songs were banned by government decree, as they now have been, Lilly Wu's voice could be heard wherever music is played in China – and that includes not only the public places like the railway stations, the building sites, the workers' cafeterias, but also – and increasingly – the transistor radios and the cassette recorders which have become so much a feature of the new 'open' China . . ."

Towards the end of his piece, Burns speculated as to whether the "Save the Panda" movement which Lilly Wu had inaugurated would be successful: "It would be nice to believe," Burns wrote, "that Lilly's campaign will turn back the forces of progress and lead either to the abandonment of the Three Gorges Dam or at least to a scaling down of

278

the project back to its original size. Such an outcome is in fact quite unlikely. The threat to the snail-darter (whatever that is!) might have blocked the construction of a dam in the Tennessee Valley. But China is not the United States. Powerful interests are ranged here behind the Super-Dam. They include Sir Charles Soong whose equity participation in the Three Gorges project exceeds 4 billion US dollars. The viability of that investment almost certainly depends on the transportation prospects offered by the Super-Dam. Soong will be able to run his largest tankers and his grandest passenger-vessels from Shanghai thousands of miles up the Yangtze to Chungking and possibly even further. Ironically, the same powerful interests include Lilly Wu's own father, Wu Canping. Forty years ago Wu Canping made his name in Sichuan. He was the man appointed by Chou En Lai soon after the Liberation to improve navigation of the Upper Yangtze. Sichuan has been his power base ever since as indeed it has for so many of China's present leaders. Whatever affection Wu may feel for his remarkable daughter, he will never let sentiment hold sway over hard-headed commercial and political interest. As a matter of fact, it seems that the reverse is the case. The story here is that Wu himself personally ordered Lilly Wu to be confined to Wolong, under a kind of house-arrest. That she has now defied his orders and gone underground, probably in Shanghai or Wuhan or Nanking, only makes the present situation the more poignant . . ."

"What's the matter? Aren't you feeling well?" Ben Bradman was looking at Preston in concern.

"I didn't know she'd been arrested."

"Every good cause needs a martyr. This could just tip the balance." As he spoke, the light on the telefax machine inside the cabin began to flash. Bradman let out a yell and raised both hands to the mountains opposite. He waved the paper in the air.

"They're going to let us air-lift a maximum of 50 pandas out of danger. The project is to be coordinated jointly by the Chinese government and the World Wildlife Fund. They want me out there soonest!"

"That's great, Ben," said Preston "But if you go in there now and rescue the pandas, you take the pressure off."

"Pressure off what?"

"The pressure to cancel, or modify, the dam."

"Jesus, man. Are you suggesting we should tell the Chinese 'no'?" Then Bradman's face softened. "Look, Preston, you do your thing; I'll do mine. Maybe things will work out for both of us. What do you say?" When Ben Bradman smiled that wide, disarming, boyish smile, Preston Murphy found it impossible not to agree.

"Her full name is Sunshine Falls on Mountain Peak," Bradman explained. "I call her Sunshine for short. She has a doctorate from Berkeley, actually."

"Are there many of you up here?" Preston asked the tall stately woman, who had arrived silently out of the darkness and who had proceeded, quickly and efficiently, to cook them a meal.

"Around 20. We're a distant branch of the Sioux Indians. We're going to guard the animals when they arrive." She looked affectionately at the film-star.

"You bet they are!" Bradman laughed. "Anyone who goes after a panda on this reserve will end up with an arrow between his shoulder blades!"

While they ate, Preston told his story again. Sunshine, whose mental stature was clearly on a par with her physical attributes, seemed to be fascinated by the details.

"How can you be so sure that the data which the Chinese government had itself provided, were fake?" she asked.

By way of reply, Preston zipped open a side-pocket of his ruck-sack and laid two sheets of paper side by side on the table.

"Here are the fake data as given to Wilmers and Friendly by the Chinese; here are the real data – from my father's report. What do you notice about the two sets of figures?"

"Search me! They're different, that's all I notice." Bradman's forte was clearly not the balance sheet.

It took Sunshine about twenty seconds. "Your father's data showed that in 1932 an earthquake with a magnitude of 6.6 on the Richter scale was recorded and another one – magnitude 5.7 – in 1934, with a third – magnitude 6.0 – in 1935. The official Chinese figures, as relayed to Wilmers, give values respectively of 4.4, 3.8, and 4.0 – in other words, *each figure has been reduced to two-thirds of the true value.* And that is true for any other figure that you look at. Your father's data of course only go up as far as 1950, so we have no means of knowing for sure that the Chinese data *after* 1950 are also faked. But if you look at the pattern it's pretty obvious that they are . . ."

Later that night, when Bradman and Sunshine had disappeared into the recesses of the cabin to make Whoopee or whatever, Preston decided to telephone Beijing.

David Burns was about to sit down for lunch in his home in the Hutong not far from Tiantan, the Temple of Heaven, when the call came through. The line was good, apart from the occasional crackle which he put down to atmospheric interference. When his wife motioned to him to come to the table because his food was getting cold, he waved her impatiently away.

"You're quite sure about this?" he asked.

"Quite sure." Preston gave him chapter and verse.

"What do you want me to do? I'm a journalist, not a hero."

"Find Lilly Wu," Preston urged him. "Tell her the facts. Try to get hold of Zheng too. Tell him what I've told you. He'll know what to do."

"For Christ's sake, Preston. This is China. You can't expect Zheng to charge around like Ralph Nader." Then Burns added: "There's not much time, you know. The Chinese have increased the rate of impoundment since you left. They've virtually shut off the whole river-flow in the Yangtze so as to be sure they're ready for the Inauguration. The water-level is nudging 190 metres at the moment and they expect it to hit the 200-mark within the next ten days.

"Lilly Wu's campaign has a lot of support and these new facts will help. But at the present time I don't see any sign of a cave-in. Why don't you talk to the World Bank? The Bank still has a lot of leverage. They've got other loans in

China. A helluva lot of loans. And in any case, if the dam fails, how are the Chinese going to pay back the money? That's going to worry the Bank even if nothing else does."

"I'll call Harry Christiansen first thing in the morning."

When he woke next day, Preston found that Bradman had already gone, leaving a note speared to the table with a sheath-knife.

"Checked out," it read. "See you in China."

"Frankly, Mr Murphy," said Harry Christiansen with barely disguised irritation, "I'm not sure I follow you. When the Bank appraised the Three Gorges loan, we did so on the basis of all the available evidence, and that included the seismic data. Even if the Chinese, somewhere along the line, have falsified the figures – which I find wildly implausible – someone would have picked this up at the feasibility stage. What about Wilmers and Friendly for Christ's sake? Are you suggesting that they would have slipped up like that? I don't believe it!"

"That's just what I am suggesting," Preston interjected. "That's why I'm not working there any more."

"Then just who are you working for, Mr Murphy?" By now Christiansen's tone was downright hostile.

"I believe a terrible mistake is being made," Preston said. "The World Bank can't afford that mistake, any more than the Chinese can. Sir Charles Soong may have taken over the last tranche of financing, but there's over 10 billion dollars of World Bank money tied up in the Three Gorges project. The Bank's reputation in every sense – financial as well as moral – is at stake here."

There was a long silence at the other end. Finally Christiansen said, "Can you get hold of your father's report? The original, the one you saw in the archives? We'll contact the seismology people at Menlo Park out there on the Coast. I'll call in Haroon Tarzieff, the old boy President Mitterrand appointed his adviser on natural disasters. If they can't come, we'll fax them the data and have a teleconference. But I'm not going to move until I see the papers."

"Thank you, Mr Christiansen. I appreciate your cooperation." He looked at his watch. It would take him three or four hours to hike back to his car, another four to reach Eugene. "Can you have someone call the Dean of the Engineering Faculty at Oregon University. If the document is going to be removed, even temporarily, from the John Savage archive, the University will have to give its permission."

"I'll call him myself." The World Bank's Senior Vice-President seemed at last to be getting the message.

The pretty freckle-faced girl seemed puzzled when Preston stopped at her desk later that afternoon. "Yeah, the Dean called me earlier today to tell me it was all right to release the file. As a matter of fact, someone already came for it." She popped a wad of Juicy Fruit into her mouth.

"What the hell!" There was an irritated stir in the reading room at Preston's outburst. "You mean it's not here any longer?"

"Nope." The girl had the grace to stop chewing for a moment, and showed him the entry in the book. "I logged it out at 2.30 today."

He could feel the ground slipping beneath his feet. "Did the guy have an I.D.?"

The girl shook her head. "Didn't ask to see it. The Dean had called me in person."

Preston looked at the signature. "S. L. Tan," he read. There was an address next to the name.

"Do you have a register of students and faculty?"

"Sure we do."

There was no S. L. Tan in the book, of course.

"What did he look like, this Mr Tan? Can you tell me that?"

By now, the girl was so concerned that she actually removed the gum and put it in the ash-tray. "Have I done something wrong?"

"Just tell me what he looked like."

"Dark haired, spectacles, around 25, I'd say."

"Was he Chinese?" Preston urged.

"Well, he sure as hell wasn't a Puerto Rican!"

"Oh my God," Preston groaned inwardly. How could he have been so stupid, so unbelievably stupid? Why did he imagine, just because he was ringing Burns at home, that the line would be secure?

The librarian was looking at him anxiously. "Are you okay? Do you want to sit down for a minute?"

Preston pulled himself together, and gave her his card. "If you see Mr Tan again, call this number, day or night."

The girl smiled at him suggestively, but Preston wasn't in the mood.

Five minutes later, he was talking to Harry Christiansen's secretary at the World Bank.

"I'm afraid Mr Christiansen's in a meeting and he can't be disturbed."

"It's urgent. A matter of life or death, actually. Or it could be."

When Christiansen at last came to the phone, he was clearly annoyed, and when Preston told him that the crucial report was no longer in the archive, he had given a hollow cynical laugh. "I talked to Jim Wilmers since we last spoke, Mr Murphy. Frankly, he didn't give too good an account of you and your recent behaviour. I gather you screwed up in China in a fairly major way. Are you quite sure there ever was a report? I rather doubt it."

"Jesus Christ!" Preston shouted into the phone. "Of course I'm sure. I read the damn thing myself."

"Sorry." There was a note of finality in Christiansen's tone. "You'll have to do better than that. I'm not going to call a meeting of experts to review evidence which doesn't exist. All bets are off, Mr Murphy, is that clear?"

After Christiansen had hung up on him, Preston felt as near despair as he had ever been in his life before.

15

"I've been rereading the diaries. There's a passage where father says he's just about finished his report on the dam, he's going to mail the carbons and keep the fair copy in the safe. Do you think, just conceivably, it could still be there?"

"Have a look, son. The safe's still in the attic. Here's the key." Mrs Mary Murphy sighed. Delighted as she was to be receiving a surprise visit from Preston, she was also worried. In her experience Preston normally demonstrated a sang-froid that bordered on indifference. Now he was rushing around like a scalded cat and had lost his job into the bargain.

Ten minutes later, Preston returned crestfallen and cobweb-covered to the sitting-room.

"Nothing. I know what the report looked like and it wasn't there."

"Perhaps he took it with him that night . . ."

"Who could have wanted..?" Preston began. And then he answered his own question: "Wu Canping, of course! He'd asked dad all those questions about his report when they were going up the river to Canton . . ."

Mrs Murphy nodded emphatically, her handsome features suddenly marked by a look of disgust.

"I disliked Wu the first time I met him – and I was right. He incriminated your father in his so-called confession. What arrant nonsense! Fancy calling Oliver Murphy a Communist! Oliver was bitterly opposed to Chiang and his band of gangsters but that didn't make him a Communist. Then, later on, when your father met Chou in Beijing, Wu falsified the transcripts and leaked the doctored texts. He put words into Oliver's mouth which Oliver would never have said."

Preston let his mother get it out of her system. For years she had shut her mind to those dreadful days, but now the stopper had been pulled and the memories were flooding back.

At last he said softly: "Wu may have needed his report, if only to suppress it. He may have given a false confession under torture and been involved in other trickery for reasons we may never comprehend. But I'll tell you something I give him credit for, mother – his daughter, Lilly. I think I'm in love with her. One day I hope to marry her!"

"Oh, Preston!" Mary Murphy rose from her chair and for a second he thought she was going to strike him so intense was her anger.

"Never," she hissed. "How could you even think of it?"

From where he sat Preston could see the framed photograph which had been taken when President Truman visited Wake Island in the Pacific to talk to MacArthur. On the tarmac, waiting in full combat uniform to greet the Commander-in-Chief, stood the great General himself with – or so it had always seemed to Preston – a look of smug self-confidence on his face. On the steps of the plane, directly behind the President, wearing civilian clothes and carrying a briefcase, was his father. In the past, Preston had never been able to look at that picture without a feeling of confusion but now the doubts, the uncertainties had disappeared.

"I'm sorry, mother. I'm truly sorry." He could see that she was still trembling with rage and shock. "I don't believe Wu was involved in dad's death."

"Then who was? You say Wu may have wanted to suppress Oliver's report. Why not suppress the author at the same time?"

"I believe it was someone else, mother," Preston replied quietly. "I know what I'm looking for, but I need proof."

"I hope to goodness you're right. I could never forgive you otherwise."

That evening, when they were sitting together in strained silence over the remnants of supper, Mary Murphy suddenly said: "Tell me about Lilly Wu, Preston . . ."

Later still, as they cleared things away, she asked him: "What are you going to do?"

286

It was a question Preston had been asking himself all day.

"I'm going back there, mother."

"Will they let you in?"

"I'll find a way."

It was ironic, Mary Murphy thought as she got into bed that night, how history had a habit of repeating itself.

16

Most evenings David Burns returned home on foot from his cramped second-floor office in Jianguomenwei, not far from the British Embassy. Unless he was delayed for some reason, it took him about half an hour of rapid walking before he finally turned off the main thoroughfare and entered the dark narrow road, lined on both sides by bare grey walls and pungent with the aroma of a hundred evening meals being cooked in the hidden inner courtyards of the Hutong.

On the whole, the chief hazard on this, the last leg of his nightly journey, was not vehicular traffic, which tended to stick to the main arteries, but cyclists taking the short cut from Tien An Men to the Temple of Heaven or, as often as not, kitchen debris which the residents of the area tended to dispose of by the simple method of tipping it over the wall into the street. When he had first moved into the area, Burns had written a colourful piece for the *New York Times* Sunday magazine, illustrated with his own photographs. "In Europe's mediaeval cities," he had begun, "the cry 'gardez-loo' warned the passer-by to watch out for buckets of water, or, worse still, chamber-pots being emptied onto the street below. Living here as I do in the very heart of one of the world's most populous cities, and walking home each night along these unlit narrow streets, I find – just like those city-dwellers of the Middle Ages – that I have to look up as well as down. Still, it's better than being run over by a car . . ."

He was halfway down the street with not much more than 100 yards to go before he reached the door of his house when he heard a truck swing into the alley behind him. He turned to see the vehicle blocking the whole width of the road and even scraping the walls and doors as the driver accelerated.

There was no pavement to provide refuge, no doorway

he could step into. With the truck 50 yards away and closing fast, Burns in desperation tried the nearest door. Locked! He sprinted to the next only to find that this too was barred against him. By now the noise of the truck, contained within the tunnel of walls, was deafeningly loud. He fumbled in his pocket for his key as he ran. There was just a chance he could make it to the sanctuary of his own home. If he hadn't tripped on the skin of a discarded melon – it was the season of melons, the peasants had been wheeling their heavily laden hand-carts into the city all month – he might have made it. Or if he hadn't stopped to try the other doors along the street, he might have reached his own. As it was, the truck – going around 40 miles an hour – hit him in the back, spinning him round and knocking him to one side. As he fell, Burns twisted his body sideways in a desperate attempt to avoid the blaring, belching monster. The off-side front wheel crushed his torso and the rear wheels with their patched and thread-bare tyres pulverised his head and lower abdomen.

Ya Mei had just returned home herself when she heard the commotion in the street outside. She was the first to reach him and even she, with all her medical experience, was aghast at the extent of his injuries.

"Oh David, David," she wept as she cradled his shattered head in her arms. He died on the way to hospital.

17

When he first ran the disk which Preston had brought to Xian, Zheng had concluded that the data were so out of line with what he would normally have expected to see that there must have been some basic fault in the instrumentation itself. Somehow the network of tilt-meters and gravity meters had thrown up the wrong results or else the instruments had been wrongly calibrated. So he had sent the disk over to his colleague in the Engineering and Computer Science department of Xian's Jiaotong University for checking. That afternoon he had received the disk back with a note advising him that the data had been verified for internal consistency and that no flaws had been detected. Equally, the projections and predictions thrown up by the model appeared to be error-free.

Zheng passed a hand across his brow. Was this the reason why old Bill Friendly had been so anxious to get the disk to him? Did Friendly suspect that something fishy was going on down there at Sandouping, something which involved not merely the distortion of the historical evidence, but the manipulation of current data as well?

As a new set of figures came up on the VDU, Zheng drew in his breath with a sharp hiss. It was suddenly blindingly clear what had happened. The whole area upstream of the dam was experiencing a series of seismic spasms and the computer indicated, without the shadow of a doubt, a clear correlation between the volume of the water as it built up behind the dam and the frequency and intensity of the spasms. How long would it be before the spasms triggered an earthquake? And how severe would that earthquake be? The records indicated that the area had never experienced a shock exceeding 5.6 on the Richter scale. But Zheng no longer had any confidence in the official data. The numbers appearing on the screen in front of him would, just by themselves, have been enough to give him pause. The spasms or fore-shocks were already running around 4 or 5 on the Richter scale and that was just for starters! More alarming still was the telephone call he had received that morning from an American journalist in Beijing. Burns had warned him that any prediction of the seismic future based on information supplied through official sources was likely to be a long way wide of the mark! Add on one-half to the base data, Burns had advised, and run the tape again!

Zheng was doing just that as he sat there. He swore under his breath as the screen flashed. The numbers were going off the scale: 8.9 was meant to be the maximum possible earthquake recorded only once before in the history of the world! But now the computer, adjusted for bias, was predicting a quake magnitude of 9.1!

Feverishly, Zheng continued to punch the buttons on the keyboard in front of him. Where was the mega-quake going to occur? The last quake of anything approaching that magnitude had taken place in the sea east of Japan.

He had to wait a few seconds while the computer digested his request. The screen went blank as the lines of figures disappeared, to be replaced, seconds later, by a multi-colour map of China. The main geographical features – coastal outline, principal rivers, mountain ranges – were represented on the map. Superimposed were the areas of predicted seismic intensity, colour-graded according to the Mercalli scale. The map showed, therefore, not only where the epicentre of an earthquake would be, and the magnitude of the shock; it also indicated how that quake would be actually experienced – in terms of felt intensity - throughout the whole of China.

He swore again, this time out loud, as a pulsating blob came up in the very centre of the screen. There was no doubt about it! The mega-quake was going to occur somewhere in the Upper Yangtze region, probably within 100 miles of the Three Gorges dam! Sandouping, Yichang, even Wuhan – all these places would experience the shock at maximum intensity: up to 12 on the Mercalli scale!

He pressed ENTER and waited while the little red diode

flickered to indicate that the three giga-byte brain located in the university's central facility was properly engaged. Then, as the diode light went out, a box appeared in the top right hand corner of the screen:

PROBABLE TIME OF OCCURRENCE 28 SEPTEMBER 1989 TO 2 OCTOBER 1989. MODAL VALUE SHOWN FOR 1 OCTOBER 1989.

Zheng gazed blankly at the screen. It couldn't be! It just couldn't be! 1 October 1989! The fortieth anniversary of the Liberation! The day the great dam itself would be inaugurated!

Zheng switched the machine off. He felt utterly shell-shocked. Thank God there was still time! And thank God, too, that – since Tangshan – the emergency procedures had been worked out!

As he reached for the telephone on his desk to start the wheels turning, the door of his room burst open and a squad of soldiers entered.

"Zheng Fushun?" one of them shouted at him.

"I am a Professor at the University, please address me by my correct title." Though his heart was pounding, Zheng tried to retain his professional dignity. As he stood there, surrounded in his own office by gesticulating guards, his mind harked back 15 years. Was the Great Proletarian Cultural Revolution about to begin all over again? Were the Red Guards going to rampage through the streets? Would they put a dunce's cap on his head, spit at him and kick him?

"Come with us!"

There was no-one in the corridor outside, no-one to see him hustled into the car which had been parked by the door of the Institute of Seismology. And there was no-one that evening at the entrance of Xian's Great Wild Goose Pagoda to observe how four soldiers frog-marched their prisoner into the building and up the circular staircase which rose like a filament up through the massive seven-storey brick structure, completed over 13 centuries earlier to house the

292

collection of sutras which the famous Tang monk, Xuanzhuang, had brought back to China from India.

Did they know he was not only Professor at the University but also the President of Xian's Historical Society, Zheng wondered? Did they know he could tell them the history of every lintel and pedestal in the famous pagoda, read the inscriptions and the calligraphy? He began to speak but they silenced him roughly, pushing him up the narrow stairs ahead of them. There was a platform on the top floor, with four arched doorways facing north, south, east and west, doorways which, on a fine day, provided an unrivalled view of the great city of Xian and of the countryside beyond.

Professor Zheng Fushun stood silhouetted in one of the archways of the topmost floor of the Great Wild Goose Pagoda looking north over the Walled City. Ahead of him he could see the great South Gate and, beyond that, the sloping roofs of the Bell Tower and the Drum Tower. Far away to the north-east he could dimly discern the tumulus which housed the mortal remains of China's first emperor, Qin Shi Huang, and, beyond that, the plain where they had found the terracotta army. He shook his head sadly. What a pity that he would never be able to confirm his theory about the empty pit!

"Jump, Zheng Fushun! Jump now, or we'll push you out!"

He tried to plead with them then, but they closed in on him with the butts of their rifles raised, ready to bludgeon him if he resisted. "You're making a mistake," he shouted, desperate to be understood. "There will be a great catastrophe, a catastrophe a thousand times worse that Tangshan! We have to stop it!"

The first blow struck him high on the left cheek-bone, splintering his glasses.

18

Sir Charles Soong smiled benignly at his guests and raised his glass. "Ladies and Gentlemen, the Queen!"

He pushed his chair back and rose to his feet whilst the others followed suit.

"The Queen! God bless her!" The tall candles, set in their superb candelabra down the middle of the long mahogany table which Soong had purchased at Sotheby's in London for a small fortune three years earlier, flickered as the company toasted the Sovereign in the traditional manner. Down at the far end of the room, Sir David Wilson, KCMG, the Governor of Hong Kong and the Queen's representative, returned the compliment. As a senior official working for Britain's Foreign and Commonwealth Office Wilson had participated in the painstaking negotiations which had led, on 26 September, 1984, to the initialling of the draft Agreement on the Future of Hong Kong. That agreement provided that by 1997 Britain would withdraw from the administration of the colony in favour of China. In the meantime, a complicated series of arrangements was to be made. It was perhaps inevitable that Sir David, as one of the few men who understood all the details of the fine print, should have been appointed Governor during the transitional period. He was a slim, tough man, now in his middle-fifties, a diplomat of the old school who was firmly, yet good-humouredly, determined to ensure that, if Britain stuck to her side of the Agreement, the Government of the Chinese People's Republic would stick to theirs.

Rising to his feet, Sir David Wilson turned first to his hostess. "Lady Soong! Sir Charles! Ladies and Gentlemen! I give you a toast – to 1997!"

It was neatly done. The Lion could not formally salute the Dragon – not yet, anyway, with two-thirds of a decade still to run before the hand-over – but there were plenty of coded expressions which were well understood around the Colony. It was a matter of some satisfaction to Sir David that men like Charles Soong had made it clear that they fully intended and expected to stay in Hong Kong under the new regime. Indeed, Sir Charles – as everyone knew – was already preparing to expand his empire into mainland China itself long before the crucial date of 1997, a kind of "reverse takeover" as the local wags put it!

Lady Soong smiled sweetly at the Governor as, the toasts completed, he resumed his seat next to her. She was a tall, elegant woman, with jet black lacquered hair which contrasted with her pale, almost translucent skin. Pinned to the high collar of her dress was the magnificent diamond brooch which Richard Burton had once given to Elizabeth Taylor, while on the fingers of her left hand she wore a set of ruby rings which had once been the Maharani of Jaipur's most cherished possession. Everyone knew that, for all practical purposes, the real seat of power in Hong Kong was not Government House, where the Union Jack still gamely flew on the flagpost outside the front door; it was Sir Charles Soong's massive villa – colloquially known as White House East – set high up on Prince Consort Road just below Victoria Peak. But precisely because these facts of life were so well understood, Lady Soong had no need to stand on her dignity.

"How good of you to honour us with your presence tonight, David! And how well Natasha is looking!" She gave a quick smile down the table to where, at the far end, Lady Wilson was engaged in conversation with the host.

"How delightful to be here," Sir David purred. "What a splendid group of people you have here tonight! Has Sir Charles known Mr Nakamura long?" The question sounded innocent-enough, but it was in fact a matter of considerable interest to the Governor to note that Japanese tycoons like Nakamura, rather than pressing home a frontal attack on the industrial and commercial bastions of modern China, were taking the Hong Kong route and piggy-backing as it were on the ever-expanding activities of men like Soong. How ironic it would be, Wilson reflected, if Charlie Soong

– that great manipulator of men, the taipan of all the taipans – were to find himself out-gunned in the end by a man like Nakamura!

Lady Soong had learnt long ago not to reply to direct questions which concerned her husband's business activities, so she was studiously vague in her answer. "Mr Nakamura looks after our business in Japan, and I believe he's involved with my husband on the Yangtze dam. Everyone's making such a fuss about it at the moment."

"Ah?" The Governor's eye-brows arched with interest. He nodded towards the middle of the table where Ben Bradman sat, resplendent in a white tuxedo. "That's why your film-star is in Hong Kong, isn't it? Isn't he masterminding the great rescue – Operation Noah? All good box office stuff, I suppose." There was something in the tone of the Governor's voice which indicated that, as far as he was concerned, there were other priorities in this overcrowded part of the globe than rescuing a few pandas from oblivion.

"Exactly," Lady Soong nodded and then, moving her pearly lips to the Governor's ear, whispered, "He's even brought his girlfriend with him. Apparently she's a Red Indian princess called Sunshine! I've never had one of those to dinner before!" She have a sudden girlish giggle. "Charles is tickled pink by the whole thing. He's rustling up all the planes he can find, including a couple of old Sunderland flying-boats which haven't been in the air for about 20 years! He's going to pilot one himself! Of course, he knows that part of the world like the back of his hand . . ."

Later that evening, when the Governor and Lady Wilson had been driven off in their Rolls-Royce back to their residence, Sir Charles and Lady Soong entertained their house-guests in the library.

Ben Bradman sat in a deep leather arm-chair opposite his host, balancing a large balloon-glass of brandy on his knee. "I don't know how to begin to thank you, Sir

296

Charles." He drew on his cigar and puffed the smoke luxuriously towards the distant ceiling.

"Negotiation, dear boy! Everything is a matter of negotiation! You people assumed that the Chinese would agree to an international rescue operation merely because, if they didn't, the pandas would drown. But things are not as simple as that. You've got to understand the mentality. I doubt, frankly, whether the Chinese government cares one way or another about the survival of the panda. Most other animals have long since been obliterated in China, I'm afraid! But the Chinese government realises very well that the so-called international community cares. Bodies like the World Wildlife Fund and the people behind them are desperately anxious that the giant panda should continue to browse on bamboo shoots, if not in the mountains of Sichuan, then at least in the mountains of Washington State!"

Sir Charles Soong's sleek features beamed with satisfaction as he recalled the coup which would, in one fell swoop, both endear him to international do-gooders, like Ben Bradman and the environmentalists, and ensure that the return of the Soong dynasty to mainland China after an absence of over 40 years would be greeted with general rejoicing. "How did I do it, you may ask?"

"I bloody well do ask!" Bradman swirled the brandy in his glass.

Sir Charles Soong looked at his wife. "You must be tired, my dear?"

"Tell the story, Charles. I'll try not to nod off!"

"Another drink?" Soong refilled Nakamura's glass and topped up his own for good measure. For the next few minutes Soong gave his guests a clear succinct account of the famous Xian incident of December 1936 when the Young Marshal briefly held Chiang Kai Shek captive. Most of the guests, of course, knew the story in outline. It was one of the classics of modern Chinese history. But Soong gave it his own personal slant.

"I actually piloted the plane which carried Madame Chiang to Xian and which brought the Generalissimo and his party back to Chungking. The reason Young Marshal

297

let Chiang go was quite simple. Chiang had accepted his terms. Chou En Lai and the Communists had already agreed. Once the Generalissimo had given his assent as well, there was no further reason to keep him."

Soong paused, looked around the room and then asked, rhetorically; "Why did Chiang agree to the eight-point plan which in essence meant allowing the Communists to share in government? To save his skin? That was certainly part of it. Even more to the point, the Young Marshal offered Chiang, who was as avaricious as they come, a bribe he simply couldn't refuse!"

Soong milked the situation for all it was worth. "Five months before Chiang's visit to Xian, some peasants, digging an irrigation ditch not far from the great mound which is the mausoleum of Qin Shi Huang, came across a small sunken pit, in which there were 20 life-size terracotta figures in an almost perfect state of preservation. The famous terracotta army was first discovered not in 1974, *but almost 30 years earlier*! Scholars have always been puzzled about why the fourth pit was empty. Well, I can tell you the reason. The Young Marshal heard of the discovery and he offered the figures to Chiang in a gesture which, as he saw it, was designed to put the seal on the agreement which he thought he had reached with the Generalissimo. We loaded those 20 terracotta statues into the plane and when the Young Marshal came down to the airport to say goodbye, we loaded him in as well!" Soong chuckled at the memory. "The idea that the Young Marshal came with us of his free own will was utter nonsense. Chiang invited him on board the plane so he could see how well we had stowed the treasures, Tai Li – that old scoundrel – pulled the door shut, I gave the thumbs up sign and away we went!"

Ben Bradman found it hard to see what Soong was driving at. "So Chiang got the statues and later on you inherited or otherwise acquired them from Chiang. And now, you've offered to give back those 20 terracotta figures to the Chinese government in exchange for their permission to rescue up to 50 pandas with a free pardon for the sins and iniquities of the Soong family thrown in, is that right?"

"Absolutely right!" By now the smile on Soong's face stretched from ear to ear.

"But why should they play ball?" Bradman protested. "Hell! They've got a whole army of statues. Why should they care about an extra 20 or so figures from pit number four which turns out not to have been empty at all?"

Sir Charles Soong rose to his feet, like a conjuror preparing for his final, most spectacular trick. "I'll show you why."

As he led his guests down the long marble corridor towards the entrance to his private museum, he talked in hushed, almost reverent tones.

"Qin Shi Huang made the country, you know, 23 centuries ago. He built the roads, standardised the weights and measures and created the administrative system for the empire; he reformed the army and built the Great Wall of China. With his wife and concubines, he occupied the very pinnacle of power for 23 years." Soong waited while the small party gathered round him, then – savouring the drama of the moment – he flung open the doors to reveal the richly illuminated display within.

"You see here", he said, "the terracotta figures which were dug up in 1936 in Xian." He raised his hand and pointed. "The figure in the middle is the First Emperor himself. See the prominent nose, the large eyes, the chest of a bird of prey! That is the great Qin Shi Huang. The woman on his immediate right is the first empress. The other figures are the real life-size representations of the courtiers and concubines who attended him."

One by one, as though visiting a shrine, they followed Soong into the room to gaze at close quarters at a treasure unique not only in historical terms but also in the sheer artistry of the sculpture. Though every figure was in its way fascinating, though each courtier and concubine seemed to have a separate life and breath, their eyes were inevitably drawn – time and again – to the stern visage of the Emperor. Somehow, he dominated the room, his fierce eyes focussed on the middle distance as though he was still commanding his armies in battle.

It was Bradman who at last broke the spell. "And you agreed to give that lot back for a few pandas!"

"Indeed I did. Besides," Sir Charles positively oozed satisfaction, "the Chinese government has agreed to have me back as well!"

Later, after his guests had gone to bed, Soong returned – alone – to the room where the terracotta statues were displayed. He switched on the lights and gazed with satisfaction at the group of figures. What perfect craftsmanship!

A few weeks from now these very pieces would be on show in the Great Hall of the People in Beijing. Thousands, millions of awe-struck Chinese would file past them as now they filed past the embalmed body of Chairman Mao. For the first time in history, men and women and children would be able to look upon the likeness of the man who first made China great! And written up there in big bold letters – red on gold – would be the words: "DONATION OF SIR CHARLES SOONG TO THE CHINESE PEOPLE"!

19

Ben Bradman had no objection to sharing the spotlight with Sir Charles Soong. On the contrary, he was the first to recognise that the whole-hearted involvement of the Hong Kong financier in Operation Noah had transformed the exercise from a slightly amateurish affair mounted by so-called "international environmentalists" (with the dubious acquiescence of the Chinese government) into a fully-fledged rescue effort whose professionalism was not open to question. Soong brought with him not only his cheque book (though that was certainly important); he brought his entrepreneurial zeal and his knowledge of how to get things done in an Asian context. More important still, as the President and Chairman of Cathay Pacific Airlines, Soong was able to throw into the pot all the administrative and logistic resources that were needed. The fact that Soong saw this as one more step towards achieving his ultimate goal of the total merger of Cathay Pacific with CAAC, China's national airline, was – as far as Ben Bradman was concerned – neither here nor there.

Two days after the dinner in Soong's mansion, a small armada of aircraft converged on the air-strips and air-fields of China's Hubei and Sichuan provinces. Half-a-dozen sea-planes, one of them from Soong's personal fleet and piloted by the tycoon himself, touched down on the lake beside the dam. The sea-planes, together with the helicopters provided both by Bradman's China Air Tours and – at the last minute – by the Chinese Army, spear-headed the rescue, flying three or four times a day from Sandouping up through the Yangtze and Daning gorges, to the now almost totally flooded mountain valley.

While Soong master-minded the evacuation from his forward base at Sandouping (he had immediately struck up an easy working relationship with Sammy Wong), Bradman flew on virtually every sortie himself, taking with him the necessary experts and equipment. It was not the first time, of course, that such an operation had been mounted. At the end of the fifties the construction of the Kariba dam on the Zambesi had resulted in the flooding of an area the size of Wales. Desperate attempts had to be made to rescue animals which ranged from the largest of the land mammals – elephants and rhinos – to the tiniest vervet monkey marooned on the topmost branches of a tree. And there had been similar operations, since Kariba, in other parts of the world where the construction of dams, large or small, threatened to obliterate the fauna and flora of a given area. For all of these earlier rescue operations, it had been possible to use boats as well as planes. Equally important, there were corridors of land down which animals could be driven to safety provided they could be guided in the right direction. As far as Operation Noah was concerned, such favourable circumstances did not obtain. The nature of the terrain, the fact that the hidden valley of the pandas was virtually inaccessible except by helicopter or sea-plane, meant that the manoeuvres were both difficult and hazardous.

As often as not, Sunshine would come with him and Bradman was glad of that. That first day, when they had appeared like valkyries from behind the mountain-range to swoop down on the valley, she had gazed impassively at the spectacle below. There seemed to be pandas everywhere. Driven out of the bamboo groves and thickets by the rising waters, they had climbed up onto the higher ground, where the vegetation was in any case sparse, and where, even if they escaped drowning, they faced certain death from starvation.

"Why just 50? Why don't you save them all?" Sunshine found it hard to understand the half-a-loaf approach which characterised Operation Noah.

"That's not the deal. The Chinese are counting every last one of those animals." Bradman laughed sardonically. "Maybe they think the ones we leave behind will learn to grow gills!"

It took them a week in all to reach their quota and,

without Sunshine's help, they might have spent a great deal longer. Whereas the American scientists who had flown in with Bradman to help in this animal Dunkirk spent hours stalking their targets before, finally, taking aim with the tranquilliser-gun, the Indian woman seemed to have a natural affinity with the animals. She moved quickly and silently among the rocks and somehow managed to track down and immobilise her quarry in half the time it took anyone else. It was almost as though the animals were ready to surrender, but only on their own terms and only to someone – like Sunshine – who understood what those terms were.

One day, when Bradman was flying the helicopter downriver back to Sandouping, he turned round to see ominous signs of movement behind him as a half-drugged panda struggled to rise to its feet. A Chinese soldier on board had already drawn his gun preparing to shoot the animal before it caused the machine to crash, when Sunshine shouted, "Don't shoot!"

She vaulted into the back of the helicopter, to grab the animal – quite literally – by the scruff of its neck and then, talking to it quietly in the language of her people, she succeeded in settling it down once more. Within minutes, the giant panda lapsed back into unconsciousness.

"Hell! I thought only Crocodile Dundee could do that!" Bradman exclaimed.

Sammy Wong smiled as he handed the message over to Sir Charles Soong. "CHINESE GOVERNMENT ACCEPTS US GOVERNMENT OFFER OF ASSISTANCE IN FLYING PANDAS OUT. TWO C130S AUTHORISED LAND YICHANG."

"That is good news, yes?" On purely practical grounds, Wong was glad to see the end of Operation Noah. With the Three Gorges Dam now complete and with the reservoir behind it already filled almost to the brim, he had a week of intensive work ahead of him before Sandouping would be ready for the Great Inauguration. For months now the most precise plans had been drawn up covering not only all the practical questions – which Head of State would sleep in which guest-house, who would have breakfast with whom before the Opening, who would host the reception after-wards – but also the details of the ceremony itself.

For some reason Wong decided to brief Soong personally about the forthcoming event:

"The Politburo has indicated that you are to be a Guest of Honour, together with the visiting Heads of State and Government. In fact, you will be asked to take your place with Vice-Premier Wu in the special box which we are constructing for those who have the closest association with the project. You will have a superb view, because we are placing the box in the very centre of the dam, right above the spill-way! It is envisaged that Vice-Premier Wu will actually push the button, but you will be standing alongside him as he does so."

Wong nodded towards the massive ugly bulk of Big Tu, Soong's personal bodyguard, and added, smiling in his most innocent manner. "Big Tu will of course be able to accompany you at all times."

20

The rescue of the pandas inevitably caught the world's imagination. Journalists and cameramen flooded into China from the four corners of the earth. "It's like the Nixon visit all over again except the pandas are prettier!" they joked.

The news desks were only too delighted. As a story, it had all the best ingredients: furry animals; splendid scenery, which included mountains and gorges, helicopters and sea-planes; and a cast of characters which could have come straight out of a novel and which featured a real-life film-star, namely Ben Bradman, as well as his magnificent live-in lover, Sunshine, the Red Indian princess.

Because they were a lecherous bunch at the best of times, the gentlemen of the press and television took a particular interest in Sunshine. When they weren't filming the rescue of the pandas, they pursued the statuesque Red Indian woman, determined to photograph her, if not naked, then at least partially unclothed. The long awaited pay-off came one day when Sunshine, taking a break from her other duties, stripped to the buff and plunged into the waters of the lake. Whether or not she appreciated the sheer delight her action caused among the sex-starved cameramen and reporters was not clear, since she remained impassive throughout the performance. When one of the journalists shouted a greeting to her as she was drying herself on the bank, she look up and – miraculously – smiled.

"Enjoy yourselves, fellers!"

They loved her for it.

When they weren't training their tele-photo lenses on Sunshine's generous contours, the media circus got a good deal of mileage out of Sir Charles Soong. He had dug out his famous red kerchief and an old flying helmet and goggles and seemed only too happy to be christened the "Yellow Baron" and to have his wartime exploits rehashed on the

305

front pages of a thousand newspapers. Veteran Soong-watchers admired the bravura of the performance. In the interviews he gave to the press, Soong always managed to hint, without ever saying so in so many words, that he had been the vital go-between in the negotiations which had led to the Chinese government's eventual agreement to Operation Noah. At the same time, he lost no opportunity of stating, publicly and emphatically, his hope that the reconciliation of historic differences could now be considered to be complete.

"He's going for broke!" commented John Robinson in a story he telexed to the Hong Kong-based *Far Eastern Review*. "Under the accords signed by London and Beijing, the reintegration of Hong Kong into mainland China is not meant to occur until 1997. Sir Charles Soong is determined to ensure that, long before then, his own empire, whose flagship is the famous Rowlands-Soong conglomerate, is accorded a privileged position by the People's Republic. In other words, he wants to have a head-start on the opposition. Swires and Jardine Matheson and other firms of that ilk are still thinking about 1997 and how it will affect them. Soong has already made up his mind. He is thinking about 1990, not 1997!"

The same John Robinson organised one Sunday morning a small memorial meeting for David Burns, the *New York Times* Beijing correspondent whose unfortunate death had saddened all those who had known him and his work over the years.

"David was the doyen of all the China specialists," Robinson told them in his short address. "He came with Richard Nixon in 1972 and he stayed. If any journalist deserved to be here today, David Burns did. I myself am not convinced his death was an accident," he shrugged and there was a catch in his voice, "but I don't suppose we shall ever know the truth. That's just the way things are in this country."

If the world's news desks were pleased by the panda story, they were even more pleased at the thought of all the money they were saving. They were, in a sense, getting two stories for the price of one. With the inauguration of the

Three Gorges Dam only days away, the reporters who had already gathered in Sandouping could simply be told to stay put. As the last of the pandas flew out to their overseas sanctuary in the giant C130s belonging to the US Air Force whose use President Bush had personally authorised, the first of the international guests began to fly in.

Wearing dark glasses so as to make herself less recognisable, Lilly Wu walked briskly down Shanghai's Nanjing Road towards the waterfront, then turned right to follow Zhongshin Road East along the banks of the Huangpu River. In the old days this famous street was known as the Bund. It was Shanghai's Wall Street as well as the location of the great trading houses – such as Rowlands, Jardine Matheson, Sassoons and the Hong Kong and Shanghai Banking Corporation – which had helped make the city into the financial leviathan of Asia. The solid façades of the old buildings still remained, but for the most part they had been taken over by the State. And the activity along the Bund was no longer as frenetic as it had been in Shanghai's heyday. Whereas in the past the wide avenue would have been full of beggars and hawkers and black marketeers mingling with coolies and seamen from the ships anchored on the waterfront, today life proceeded at a more orderly pace. Trolley busses ran down the centre of the street which once would have been jammed by Chicago-style Oldsmobiles, trams, mule-carts and rickshaws; and disciplined groups of Tai-Chi fanatics occupied the pavements where, in days gone by, merchants and bankers would congregate to do business.

That morning in particular Lilly Wu needed space – and time to think. The success of Operation Noah, widely reported in the Chinese press, had taken the steam out of her underground Save The Panda movement. And, truth to tell, Lilly had disliked her role as a quasi-revolutionary. A few minutes earlier, in the back-room of a shabby tea-house, not far from the university, she had broken the news to a little group of friends and allies:

"I am a biologist and a singer. If you want to start a revolution, you must find someone else . . ."

Time to think . . . time to be alone . . . Solitude was, of course, a rare commodity in modern-day China. In a land of one billion people it was hard to be unobserved. Even in the mountains, Lilly reflected ruefully, there was always someone watching. As she headed for the one peaceful place she knew in Shanghai, the famous Yu Garden a mile or two down the Bund, she found herself thinking about Preston Murphy, and wishing she could feel his arms around her at this moment.

Marco Polo, 700 years earlier, had taken a different route, following the Old Silk Road through Iran and Afghanistan to enter China across the High Pamirs. It had taken the great Venetian a year or more to negotiate, first, the mountains of the "Roof of the World", then the blinding heat of the Gobi desert before finally arriving in Xanadu where the legendary Kublai Khan held sway. Preston Murphy, like Marco Polo coming from the West, had been able to profit from the newly-opened Karakoram highway which permitted the intrepid traveller to make his way up from Gilgit, in Pakistan, to the towering Khunjerab pass – 4,800 metres – and thence on to Kashgar, that dusty desert town which was the first main staging-post on the Old Silk Road within the borders of China.

Though he still had a valid Chinese visa in his passport, Preston had felt certain that he would find himself barred from entering the country if he tried any of the usual routes, such as by air to Beijing, or over-land from Hong Kong to Canton. The Karakoram highway, on the other hand, offered more than a sporting chance that he would be able to re-enter the People's Republic without his name flashing up on the computer of the immigration authorities. High tech hadn't yet reached the Himalayas!

By the time he reached Kashgar he had been on the road a week. He checked into the dilapidated Renmin Hotel and spent the next two days sitting in the lobby watching the hot sand blow in from the surrounding desert. When, finally, he found a seat on a plane to Urumqi with a half-promise of an onward connection to Shanghai, his nerves were stretched to breaking point. Even in Sinkiang, an "autonomous region" about as far removed from the central administration in Beijing as it was possible to be, preparations were already being made for the Grand Opening. Once, as he sat biting his nails, Preston watched a programme on a flickering colour TV devoted entirely to the construction and forthcoming inauguration of the Three Gorges Dam. Some of the honoured guests, he learned, had indeed already arrived. The longer he delayed, the greater grew his sense of anxiety and foreboding.

While in Kashgar, Preston tried unsuccessfully to contact David Burns and Professor Zheng. This failure served to increase his suspicion that the telephone call he had made from the United States to David Burns's home had been an act of great folly. Lilly Wu seemed to be his last hope. In his heart of hearts, however, he was not so sanguine about the prospects of finding her – it was a bit like looking for a noodle in a soup-tureen. Some noodle! And, even if he was able to track her down he was not convinced that Lilly Wu would in fact be able to work the political miracle he was hoping for.

On Preston's second evening in Kashgar, the hotel's television carried reports that Lilly Wu was about to step down from her leadership of the Chinese Save The Panda movement since an effective international rescue operation was now under way. For the time being, the famous scientist-singer was still in hiding, probably in Shanghai, but her reappearance was confidently predicted . . .

With over 700 foreign students of many different nationalities and of all ages registered at Shanghai University, Preston assumed – correctly – that his presence on campus would not excite much interest. To all intents and purposes, he could have been part of some exchange-deal, some cultural/academic programme linking the United States and China. If his image was "preppy" rather than "hippy", well, that was where it was at, nowadays.

After a morning spent in fruitless enquiry, he received a first important lead when a friendly Chinese graduate stu-

309

dent admitted that Lilly Wu had been seen on campus recently and suggested that the best way to contact her was via the "radical" group which had sponsored her visit. He had been kind enough to indicate the run-down tea-house in the immediate neighbourhood where the radicals were often to be found.

As luck would have it, Preston missed Lilly's dramatic renunciation of a specifically political future by approximately 30 minutes. He was, however, able to establish his credentials with the group and to prove to their satisfaction that his interest in their erstwhile leader was entirely benevolent.

"Where do you think she was going?" Preston asked, frustrated beyond measure by his failure to pin down his elusive quarry. They laughed at him. One of them said: "Do you know how many people there are in Shanghai? Fifteen or twenty million, perhaps more. How do you think you can find her?" Then he had relented. "She told me she was going to Yu Garden. If you're lucky, you may find her there."

As she walked round the most perfect classical Chinese garden to be found in Shanghai, as she admired the pavilions and corridors, the lotus ponds with goldfish swimming in them, the bridges and winding paths, trees and shrubs – all forming a part of a single unifying theme – Lilly Wu felt suddenly overwhelmed by a sense of peace and inner tranquillity. She knew she had made the right decision. She had told them the truth. She was not cut out to be a revolutionary leader. Her inspiration lay in nature rather than in political slogans.

She walked up to the top of Rockery Hill and looked down at the magical garden spread out below. It covered only 5 acres in the heart of the Old Chinese City, yet that small area contained a whole universe. What inspired artists they must have been, Lilly thought, to have created this paradise. The very names of the pavilions said it all: Hall for Heralding Spring; Hall for Watching Swimming Fish; Tower of Vitality; Tower of Lasting Clearness . . .

310

At first the dark glasses and sophisticated clothes had confused him – the last time he had seen her she had been dressed for the mountains – but when she removed her spectacles for a moment to contemplate the garden's exquisite pattern and balance, Preston's heart gave a great bound of relief.

"Thank God I've found you," he said.

They lay in bed together in his room on the ninth floor of the Peace Hotel. Through the open window came the sounds of the street and waterfront. Preston heard the deep blast of a hooter as one of the big ships, which he had seen earlier that day tied up at the wharf, put out into the wide muddy Huangpu River which connected the great port of Shanghai with both the Yangtze and the Yellow Sea. The noise jerked him back to reality.

"Tomorrow morning, first thing." he said, "you must talk to your father. You have to persuade him to give the order to open the spillways immediately so as to lower the level of water behind the dam and lessen the pressure on the underlying geological strata. There may still be an earthquake but its magnitude could be reduced and that may make all the difference. What's more, if they go back to the old design, to the 180 metre level, all the pandas still up there in the Hidden Valley can be saved!"

"How so?" Lilly Wu sat up in bed draping a sheet modestly across her small girlish breasts.

"The lake will drop below the level of the pass. That means the water will eventually seep away in the Hidden Valley and things will be the same as they were before."

She shook her head. "It would take too long. The vegetation would never recover, not soon enough anyway. The pandas would starve."

"Then we'll drill a tunnel in the base of the col and let the water out! Call your father, Lilly," he urged her quietly, "call him now!"

21

Preston stood on tip-toe on the wooden chair and gazed gloomily out of the high barred window of his prison cell. How could he have been so blind! He had persuaded Lilly to contact her father believing that Wu would be able to cut the Gordian knot. And what had Wu done? Had them thrown into jail as soon as they arrived at Sandouping in the military aeroplane which he had so kindly despatched to fetch them!

A few hundred feet away he could see the great concrete structure towering massively above the building in which he had been incarcerated. The sun's first rays caught the crest as he watched and he was able to distinguish clearly the canopy and ceremonial platform which had been erected above the spill-way. A few hours from now the dignitaries would gather in their alloted seats . . .

As he stood there, he sensed a tremor beneath his feet, a faint but perceptible vibration which lasted perhaps four seconds. Christ! thought Preston. It's happening! He was too late anyway! The strain had already built up to breaking point . . .

A moment later he heard the bolts of the cell being drawn back and an elderley Chinese gentleman with several front teeth missing entered the room.

"It is high time we met, though I should have preferred the circumstances to be different." Wu Canping gestured with his hand at the prison walls. "I've had some experience of prison myself and I know it is not entirely pleasant. Believe me, we shall release you as soon as we can."

Preston sat down abruptly on the hard narrow bed where he had just spent a restless night, while China's Vice-Premier sat on the cell's one wooden chair facing him.

"You have to understand, Mr Murphy," Wu continued, "that we all of us act according to our lights. Your father believed that, because of the earthquake risk, no dam should be built across the Yangtze, though, as an engineer, he was fascinated by the prospect. He wrote a report to that effect and I, as you already suspect, did my best to have that report suppressed."

He held up his hand to stop Preston interrupting. "You have seen something of our country, Mr Murphy. You have seen the poverty in which, even today, millions of our people live. We need the energy, we need the power, we need the economic benefits that the Three Gorges Dam will bring us! You say there is a risk. I say, there is a risk in everything and it is for us, the people of China, to decide finally whether that risk is worth taking! You want to make that decision for us and that is not acceptable."

"You can't make a correct decision based on phoney data!" Preston at last managed to protest. "Why don't you ask Professor Zheng in Xian? He'll tell you the truth!"

"Zheng is dead," Wu replied icily. "An unfortunate accident."

"You had him killed, you mean," Preston flashed back. "Just as you had my father killed. That's what some people think, at least."

Preston's last accusation seemed to sting Wu to the quick.

"I had no part in your father's death," he said sharply. "I can assure you of that."

As Wu spoke Preston experienced a great sense of relief. Something in Wu's voice convinced him that the man was telling the truth.

"What about the false confession? What about the faked transcripts?" he asked quietly.

"Soong's doing. I never made any confession to Tai Li." Wu touched his mouth involuntarily. "Soong fabricated the whole thing, implicating your father. As for the transcripts, Soong asked for them and I sent them to him. He doctored the text. He twisted Murphy's words to incriminate him. McCarthy needed a victim – the China Lobby needed a political boost. Your father was the ideal candidate. I'm sorry, Preston. I don't suppose you'll ever understand."

"Perhaps I understand more than you think. I read my father's diaries . . . And the murder? Are you telling me that Soong was responsible for that too?"

"Not Soong in person but one of his men acting on Soong's instructions."

"How do you know?"

"Big Tu signed a declaration when he visited Beijing with Soong. I had him followed. He still has family in China . . . there were other inducements as well."

"Big Tu?"

"The bodyguard. The large man with a pock-marked face and cauliflower ears . . ."

Wu's words, and the images he conjured up, suddenly unlocked the gates of Preston's subconscious memory. Now he realised why, that day in Beijing, he thought he had seen Big Tu before somewhere . . . Out of the mists of time, Preston remembered first the curiosity, then the fear. He remembered the powerful acrid smell of the large Chinese man who had clapped his hand over his mouth to prevent him from crying out as the car sped off in the direction of Connecticut Avenue . . .

"Why are you telling me this now?" he asked.

"Lilly has told me you wish to get married. She cares for you a great deal . . ."

"Then let us out for God's sake," Preston implored him. "Let us out now. Didn't you feel the tremor half an hour ago? I didn't take you for a fool. That could be the beginning."

Wu smiled. "It takes more than a tremor to destroy a dam!" He stood up and banged on the cell door.

For most of the next two hours Preston stood on the chair by the window staring out. Across the way, he could hear the music blaring from the ubiquitous loudspeakers as China prepared to greet a new dawn. For the first time, he felt a quick spurt of fear. The building in which he was held prisoner was, he calculated, adjacent to the power-houses set at the foot of the dam. Everyone else in Sandoup-

314

ing would be up there on the hill-side, watching the spectacle. But he – and Lilly Wu, if they were holding her in
the same place – would be first in line if the dam broke.

22

The big stars had all been assigned seats in the front row of the stalls. Bush, Thatcher, Gorbachov, Kohl – and half a dozen other political heavy-weights – were ushered to the special stand which had been erected on the northern escarpment of the Yangtze some 20 minutes before the official ceremony was to begin. Most of the men were hatless and, as a result, found themselves squinting in the bright light of the noon-day sun. Only Mrs Thatcher, dressed in a navy blue suit with a matching broad-brimmed hat which kept the glare from her face, seemed entirely at ease.

"It's really a *British* project, Denis," she reminded her husband. "After all, the Crown Colony of Hong Kong has played a crucial role in the financing. I recommended Soong for his knighthood . . ." She pointed to the Hong Kong tycoon who had just arrived with the official party.

"Who's the guy with Charlie Soong?" President Bush, who was seated next to her on the other side, asked the Prime Minister.

Mrs Thatcher suppressed an inward groan. Why didn't American Presidents do their homework? And Bush had once been US envoy to Beijing!

"That is Wu Canping, George. He's responsible for energy. My people were telling me last night that this has been his pet project for the last 40 years. The town we are all staying in – Sandouping – was once a small fishing village where Wu grew up."

Martial music blared from a cluster of loudspeakers which had been fastened to the lock-gates and a formation of Chinese fighter planes flew overhead. As they did so, the flotilla of boats – junks, sampans, ferry-boats – hooted and whistled. At 12 noon precisely, China's top leader, Deng Xiaoping, looking fit and well, mounted the poinsettia-bedecked dais which had been set up just opposite the VIP

316

stand and began to pronounce the discourse which would mark China's true coming of age as a modern nation.

"He lies about his age," whispered Bush. "He looks about 90 but really he's 110!"

Mrs Thatcher managed a grimace. Even Ronnie's jokes had often fallen flat as far as she was concerned.

Pulling out a pair of heavy black spectacles from the breast pocket of his grey tunic and placing them on his nose, Deng addressed the battery of microphones in front of him.

"On this very day, 40 years ago," he began, "our great leader Mao Tse Tung stood before the masses who had gathered in front of the Tien An Men gate in Beijing and proclaimed the founding of the Chinese People's Republic. Today, therefore, we celebrate our 40th anniversary as a nation. We have come a long way since then and this great dam which we now inaugurate in the presence of our distinguished guests can be seen as a gigantic milestone, commemorating a heroic past and pointing towards a yet more glorious future . . ."

Mrs Thatcher nudged her husband whose eyes were beginning to close. "Just jet lag, dear," he said.

As Deng droned on, Wu motioned to Soong that the moment had come for the button-pushing party to take its place on the raised platform in the middle of the dam. Soong boarded the Jeep, followed by Big Tu. The last person to clamber in, breathing heavily from the exertion, was Herr Horst Klarfeld, representing the construction interests involved.

"If China has come a long way, so have you, Wu Canping, wouldn't you say?" At this moment of supreme triumph, Soong could not resist the temptation of reminding Wu, none too subtly, of how it had all begun.

Wu kept his eyes fixed on the far bank and said nothing.

"Come now, admit it!" Soong was clearly nettled by Wu's silence.

Wu gave a short, tired sigh. "I've paid all my debts, you know that." Out of the corner of his eye he could see that

317

Big Tu, sitting immediately behind them, was listening to the conversation . . .

Sir Charles Soong drew in his breath sharply. When he looked at Wu Canping, he still saw the young man he had pulled – more dead than alive – from Tai Li's dungeon. "That's not the way . . ." he began.

Wu lifted a warning finger. "Enough is enough. If you try to squeeze any more out of me, I'll return the compliment."

"You have no hold over me."

"Indeed I have. I have Big Tu's signed deposition. I had him followed that night you came to my house in Zhongnanhai. Tu took advantage of his evening off to visit an aged mother who still lives in Beijing. Imagine that! He may work for you, Charles, but he wants to protect her too." Wu gave a mirthless laugh.

Sir Charles Soong pretended he didn't understand. "Deposition about what?"

"About Murphy's murder. You had him killed didn't you? Even after forty years, you wouldn't want that known, would you? It would be bad for the Soong image, yes? Of course there are some people, like Murphy's son for example, who would be pleased to know the truth."

As they reached the platform, Wu Canping turned to look Sir Charles Soong straight in the eyes. He gave a wide, malicious smile.

Soong had gone pale. He glanced nervously at Big Tu as they climbed the steps onto the dais. How much truth was there in what Wu had said? Was he bluffing? He would have trusted Big Tu with his life . . .

The best course of action, he decided, was to behave as though the conversation had not taken place at all. He walked over to the edge to stare down at the massive spillway and at the power-house, far below.

"Look at this, Wu," he said. "Isn't this something?"

The two of them stood together at the railing, gazing into space.

"I've paid all my debts," Wu repeated. "But I'm not sure you've paid all yours, Charles. Murphy was my friend. You had him killed. That was never part of the agreement."

318

"Murphy!" Soong could hardly believe his ears. "All that's past history. Besides, it was an accident. Big Tu made a mistake . . ."

"Big Tu doesn't make that kind of mistake."

Soong tried to move aside but it was too late. With one swift, precise movement, Big Tu grabbed him from behind and held him fast. One enormous hand twisted Soong's arm behind his back to the point of breaking, the other was clamped firmly across his mouth.

When Klarfeld sought to intervene, Wu shouted roughly: "Shut up! This has nothing to do with you!"

A mile away, they could hear the amplified voice of Deng Xiaoping as he neared the end of his peroration. The light on the dais glowed green. Wu pressed the button labelled "SPILLWAY" and, as he did so, the sluice-gates opened and a torrent of water burst through the dam beneath them to cascade with unbelievable force down the giant ramp. The spray and the spume covered the platform, reducing visibility to a few feet while the roar of the water made intelligible communication virtually impossible.

"Do it, Tu," Wu shouted above the noise. "Do it. Now!"

Big Tu pushed Soong forward to the very edge of the dam. For one long second he allowed Soong to contemplate the boiling cauldron below . . .

"A regrettable accident, Klarfeld, I'm sure you would agree?" Wu smiled as they drove back the way they had come. "Fortunately Mr Nakamura will be a very competent successor."

The German was pale and shaken but he took the point quickly. "*Ja, sehr gut!* Nakamura is a very fine man. Will certainly manage Rowland-Soong investments in correct fashion . . ."

They felt the first shock as a gentle, see-sawing motion. Deng's amplified oratory was halted in mid-stream as the electrical systems were disrupted. For a few seconds he continued gamely, his high-pitched sing-song voice struggling to compete against the cries of alarm from the spectators, crowded onto the lock-gates and the dam's abutments.

The British Prime Minister kept her face resolutely to the front while a line of school-day Latin went through her mind. *Etiam si labitur orbis, impavidum ferient ruinae.* Should be *impavidam*, of course, she thought. Trust Horace not to get the gender right!

The second shock followed forty seconds later and this time there was no mistaking its severity. The gigantic wall of the dam vibrated like a taut drum. On the south side, where all the grouting and filling had had to be done to secure the dam to the rock, two or three small land-slips occurred as the geological formations adjusted to the vast subterranean pressures exerted upon them. The whole episode lasted less than a minute but for those present it seemed like an eternity.

"Holy cow! I think we should be getting out of here," said Bush.

Denis Thatcher sensed the prospect of an early, if unforeseen, conclusion to the proceedings. "Lead on, Macduff," he exclaimed cheerfully, seizing the Prime Minister's arm.

Some 80 miles to the west, where the Yangtze River passed through Wuxia, or Witches Gorge, the gigantic rock statue known as Shennu or Goddess Peak seemed to rock on its base as the first shock hit it. To the passengers crowded on the deck of the ferry-boat, *Sichuan Star*, which happened to be passing through the Gorge at the time, the spectacle of the Goddess in motion, as it were, seemed to be nothing short of miraculous. Some of them cried out, others – responding to urges which 40 years of secularisation had not wholly suppressed – prostrated themselves on the deck, hands outstretched in supplication and the echoes of ancient prayers on their lips.

For most of them those prayers were the last words they ever spoke. Seconds later the largest earthquake ever to occur in China, or – as some would say later – ever to occur in the world, since it was thought to have exceeded 8.9 on

320

the Richter scale, took place, its epicentre being somewhere near the western end of Wuxia Gorge.

The captain of the *Sichuan Star* shouted a warning as he saw the first avalanche of rocks crash into the gorge half-a-mile ahead. Then, transfixed, he raised his arm and pointed: "The Goddess!" he screamed. "The Goddess is falling! Look out!" Realising the danger, he swung the wheel hard to port, looking vainly for a place of refuge amid the sheer towering cliffs.

The tidal wave, over 200 feet high, came round the bend at 80 miles an hour, caught the ferry-boat amidships and tossed it high into the air, as a terrier might toss a rat. With each curve and bend of the Gorges, the *tsunami* gathered speed. Its curling crest seemed to lap the very summit of the mountains. As it passed, it destroyed whole villages, sweeping away peasants as they worked in the terraced fields and stripping the sides of the Gorges bare of all vegetation.

Two miles from Sandouping, as the Gorges began to widen out, the force of the *tsunami* seemed to be marginally diminished. The lake, which had been created behind the dam, acted as a buffer absorbing and cushioning some of the impact. But the bore was still travelling at well over 60 miles an hour when it came round the final bend. Those who witnessed the sight and lived to tell the tale were prepared to swear that it was still 80 to 100 feet high.

Most of the VIPs had time to scramble to safety when they saw the wave coming. They were the lucky ones. Prime Minister Thatcher and President Bush, General Secretary Gorbachov and Chancellor Kohl wasted no time in following Deng Xiaoping (who moved with surprising agility) up the shoulder of the hill until they were out of harm's way.

Wu Canping saw the wave when the Jeep was still half a mile from the Yangtze's north bank.

"Mother of Mao! Faster, faster!" he shouted at the driver. Once before in his life he had witnessed the effects of a tidal wave on the Yangtze . . .

Horst Klarfeld, crouched in the back of the now hurtling

321

vehicle, offered his own variation on the theme. *"Schnell! Schnell!"* he urged, then he screamed . . .

Watching from the barred window of his cell, Preston could see the earthquake strike the dam. As the long seconds passed and as the whole of creation seemed to be pulsating as though driven by a giant pneumatic drill, he held his breath, waiting for the first crack to appear in the concrete structure, the first spurt of water, the trickle which would be followed by a flood and then . . .

By God, she's holding, he thought! Scanning the face, he could see no signs of leakage. He was still gazing up at the giant structure when the ceiling of his prison cell, quite literally, crashed in. It was a jerry-built affair, anyway, put up on a temporary basis like the other site-buildings. A clump of concrete narrowly missed Preston's head, and the dust of the collapsing building unsighted him for a time. When it cleared, he saw there was a gaping hole by the door.

Preston shouldered his way through into the rubble-strewn corridor. The place was deserted. The guards had fled at the first shock. As he started his search he heard a cry for help. It seemed to come from a room half-way down the corridor. Seizing a metal beam from among the debris, Preston ran forward and battered the door in front of him with a strength born of desperation. She was lying in the corner of the room, with her leg trapped beneath a pile of bricks. Preston heaved the obstacles aside, pulled the groaning woman to her feet and, without pausing to examine the extent of her wounds, slung her over his shoulder and carried her outside.

For a moment, he gazed wildly around, trying to make up his mind what to do. He could try the road which led up from the power-house towards the village. But that might take too long. Every second counted. It was a question of gaining the high ground as rapidly as possible. He looked at the sheer shoulder of rock to which the dam had been anchored. Could he, conceivably, scramble up there with Lilly on his back?

Seconds later, Preston began to climb . . .

When the giant wave hit the top of the dam it seemed as though the earth itself had been shattered, cracked like an egg. The noise was stupendous, unbelievable, the roar of a thousand armies clashing. For a time it seemed as though night had fallen. The sheer mass of water momentarily blotted out the sun.

The spectators crowding on the lock-gates or on the crest of the dam itself stood no chance. They had nowhere to run and nowhere to hide. Some tried desperately to cling to the masonry or steel-work but the wave swept them away like so much debris. Those who were not dead already, perished as they fell into the void.

The *tsunami* caught the Jeep in which Wu Canping and his party were travelling when it was still fifty yards from shore. Three of the occupants – Big Tu, Klarfeld and the driver – died immediately, swept with the vehicle into the abyss. Wu was luckier. By some fluke, the wave threw him not over the edge of the dam but into the deep groin between the face of the dam and the cliff.

Altogether Wu fell some two hundred feet, bouncing from ledge to ledge. He would have fallen still to his certain death, if he had not been ricocheted off a boulder to be wedged in a funnel of rock half-way down the cliff face. He lay there, bruised and battered, but alive . . .

The water crashed around them as Preston climbed with Lilly clinging desperately to his back. The whole of creation seemed to be careering past. Rocks and boulders poured over the lip of the dam as the earth and rock-fill extension which the Chinese had added at the last minute gave way before the overwhelming onslaught of the *tsunami*.

Looking down Preston could see that the building in which he and Lilly had been imprisoned only minutes earlier had been entirely swept away. A dozen sampans, which had avoided the main force of the wave (the remaining vessels had simply disappeared), had been smashed to matchwood on the shore. Bodies, both human and animal, had been sprayed like paint over the landscape and that, Preston knew, was just the beginning because the *tsunami* would have thundered on downstream carrying all before it. And if the dam itself broke ...

Twice Preston lost his footing and almost fell. And once, as the drenching cascade reached a peak, Lilly was wrenched from his back to end up clinging one-handed to the leather belt of his trousers.

"Christ!" Preston exclaimed. "We're never going to make it." He could feel himself tiring ...

Barely conscious, Wu heard the sounds of someone clambering up the cliff below him. He opened his eyes. "Help," he shouted feebly ...

Wu Canping was one of the luckier victims of the great Yangtze *tsunami*. Others did not escape so lightly. The loss of life was great, not only among those gathered together at the dam-site for the inaugural ceremonies, but downstream as well. In Yichang, for example, the nearest town, there was no time to sound the alarm and over five thousand people lost their lives in the flood. And scores of fishermen were drowned as their sampans were swamped by the turbulent Yangtze.

23

"The wheel comes full circle, then?" Wu Canping smiled benevolently as he looked around the table which had been curtained off for them in the Sandouping canteen. "I saved your father, Preston, last time a tidal wave hit the Yangtze. This time you saved me. You must be proud of your son, Mrs Murphy?"

"Of course I'm proud of him. Any mother would be," Mary Murphy replied sharply. She was prepared to believe the evidence that Wu had never sought to harm Colonel Oliver Murphy in any way and that Soong himself had been responsible for her husband's death but that still didn't mean she had to become the man's best friend overnight. Okay, so Preston was going to marry his daughter . . .

"In any case," she continued in the same frosty tones, "a lot of people lost their lives because you Chinese wouldn't listen to what Oliver said. He believed a dam should never be built here because of the earthquake risk."

"Excuse me, Mrs Murphy." Wu was prepared to give as good as he got, "The fact is that the dam *didn't* fail. It experienced the worst earthquake, the worst *tsunami* that could be imagined, yet it's still there. So who was right, your husband or me?"

Preston had to act as a kind of umpire in what was fast developing into a ding-dong battle. "You have to admit," he turned to his prospective father-in-law, "that you'll never rebuild the extension. The tidal wave did a neat job in creaming off the top-layer."

Wu conceded at least that point with good grace. "Agreed," he said. "Nobody's going to go back to the 200-metre level . . . not in my lifetime anyway."

"Not in the pandas' lifetime either," Lilly Wu intervened. "We reckon there must be over a thousand animals up there in the Hidden Valley. As far as I'm concerned, this is the population that counts for us now. Not Wolong. Not Washington State."

"You're right, my dear. We must never forget about the pandas, must we?"

Preston thought he detected a patronising note in Wu's remark and he put his arm round Lilly defensively. "Never underestimate your daughter, Wu. One day Lilly and her friends may decide that the old men have been around long enough! She gave up a political career once, but she may still be tempted . . ."

Wu laughed, a shade uncomfortably. "Will she have time for politics once she's married?"

Later when they had almost finished their meal, Mary Murphy – mellower, now, and more at ease with her surroundings – started to reminisce about the war-time years in Chungking. "Chiang's people were corrupt through and through. I thought Charlie Soong had a spark of good in him when he interceded with Tai Li on your behalf, Wu, but I realise now, that this was all part of his long-term cunning . . ." She laughed. "You're sure he's not going to be washed up somewhere downstream with his red kerchief round his neck? After all, you escaped, Wu, didn't you?"

Wu exchanged a quick glance with Sammy Wong across the table and permitted himself the faintest glimmer of a smile. "Dead as a dodo, I can assure you," he said. "To tell you the truth, Mrs Murphy, there was quite a lot of internal opposition in China to the rehabilitation of the Soongs. Leaving aside the personal factors, such as Soong's involvement in the murder of your husband, Soong's death was quite convenient for all of us . . ."

"Particularly", Wong interjected, beaming broadly, "now that Soong-Rowlands' investment is complete and Soong's treasures have arrived in Beijing!"

"My, what a cynical lot you all are!" Mary Murphy exclaimed, good-humouredly.

The wedding took place in the sitting-room of Sammy Wong's villa overlooking the lake. The sun shone from a cloudless sky. With the towering majesty of the dam in front of them and the spectacular backdrop of the Yangtze Gorges, the place looked like a Cecil B. De Mille film set.

Sammy Wong, in his role as civilian authority, presided over the brief simple ceremony. Wu Canping, still limping from the bruising he had received but otherwise intact, gave his daughter away. His present to Lilly was an autographed photograph of Chou En Lai.

"Oh, father!" Lilly threw her arms around his neck. "I know how much that photograph means to you! I'm so thrilled to have it! Look, Preston." Preston looked at the picture curiously. It showed the Chinese leader in, probably, his early forties, standing in front of some archaeological remains.

The unexpected arrival that morning of Lilly Wu's mother, Wang Wen-Chuan (who had managed to absent herself from her interpreting duties at an international congress of opthalmologists meeting in Canton) completed the family grouping.

When the service was over and they had signed the book, Sammy Wong poured out glasses of Mao Tai for the assembled company.

"Good luck to you both!" He raised his glass. "*Canpei! Here's health!*"

They drank to that. Then Preston turned to his mother. "Thanks for coming, mother. It means a lot to us."

There were tears in her eyes. "I wouldn't have missed it for the world," she said. As she spoke, she had a sudden vision of herself as a young woman, in a nurse's uniform, standing beside a tall, handsome American.

Preston sensed instinctively the direction of her thoughts. "Absent friends!" As her son raised his glass for a second time, Mrs Murphy's face broke into a warm, radiant smile.

Half a mile away the newly repaired lockgates of the great Three Gorges Dam opened to permit the passage of a crowded ferry-boat on its way up through the Yangtze Gorges to Chungking.

"You can't beat old news." Preston unfolded the week-old copy of the *International Herald Tribune*, Asian edition, and spread it on the table in front of him. "You can get it in Beijing the same day. I thought Beidaihe was meant to be the favourite resort of the Politburo."

"The Politburo doesn't need the *Tribune* to know what's going on," Lilly said.

They were sitting over a late breakfast on the terrace of Beidaihe's Summer Palace Hotel, gazing out – in approved honeymoon fashion – at the gentle swell of the China Sea.

"Maybe not," Preston commented, taking his eyes off the scenery and opening the paper. "But listen to this."

" 'The mystery of the Soong treasures continues to deepen,' " he read. " 'A week ago considerable consternation was caused in official circles by the discovery that the terracotta statues of China's First Emperor, Qin Shi Huang, and his entourage, which had been presented to the People's Republic by the late Sir Charles Soong, the eminent Hong Kong financier, were fake. Though their antiquity was meant to exceed two-thousand years, tests revealed that the statues had probably been "created" within the last several months. The fraud came to light when a cleaner in the Great Hall of the People, where the pieces were being displayed prior to their removal for permanent exhibition in Xian, accidentally broke the outstretched arm of one of the Emperor's concubines. Examining the damage, the curators of the exhibition were surprised to find that the inner moulding was made out of a sort of *papier mâché*, a technique certainly not known at the time of the Qin dynasty. Analysis, moreover, revealed that the *papier* in question, turned out to be a recent copy of the *South China Morning Post!* ' "

"Not the *Herald Tribune!*"

Preston smiled. "Here comes the good bit: 'Though Sir Charles Soong, who was drowned in the Three Gorges catastrophe, is clearly not available to answer questions, the Hong Kong Government, in the person of Sir David Wilson, has gone out of its way to answer the official enquiries which have been put to it by Beijing. The fact of the matter is that the Soong bequest is seen in some circles as part of a complex deal involving the expansion of certain

328

Hong Kong-based enterprises forming part of the Rowlands-Soong empire into mainland China itself, even before the crucial 1997 date. If that bequest now turns out to be fatally flawed, as they say, the whole situation may have to be reviewed.

" 'When the fakes were first discovered, most people assumed that Soong had simply done a swap. That the Qin statues existed in his personal collection was in fact known at least to his immediate circle as well as to certain privileged guests who graced the dinner table of the Soong mansion, known as White House East, on Hong Kong's famed Victoria Peak. What subsequently surprised everyone, however, including the Governor of Hong Kong, was that the Qin "originals" which were still to be found in Soong's private museum under the care of his widow, Lady Soong, were also fake, though in this case testing using the chemoluminescence method indicated that the items had been made between 50 and 60 years ago . . .' "

As Preston continued with the story, Lilly Wu's almond-shaped eyes widened with astonishment. "You've lost me now, Preston. Why should Soong have *fake* statues in his own collection? I could understand he might want to cheat by having copies made and then sending the copies to Beijing instead of the originals, but why would he make copies of copies, if you see what I mean?"

"I do indeed see what you mean." Preston nodded. "But I'm not sure I have the answer. Maybe Soong himself was conned for a change."

He passed the paper over to Lilly and spent the next few minutes trying to puzzle out whatever hidden meaning there might be in the story which he had just read.

"Show me the photo again, please, Lilly. The photo your father gave you as a wedding present. I've got an idea."

Lilly opened her bag and took out a small faded photograph, showing the former Chinese Premier, Chou En Lai, standing beside an earthenware jar over twice his height.

"Read me the inscription written on the back again."

" 'To my good friend Wu Canping,' " Lilly dutifully obliged. "That's Chou's signature, too."

"What's written at the bottom there?" Preston asked.

"It's difficult to make out. The writing's faded."

"Try."

"I'm pretty sure that this is also Chou En Lai's handwriting. I think it says something like: 'This photograph was taken by the Young Marshal in 1936 . . . !' "

As she spoke, Preston jumped to his feet and hugged her.

"That's it, Lilly! It has to be! Everything falls into place. Chou was there, Chiang was there, Soong was there, the Young Marshal was there . . ."

Two days later, with Lilly Wu sitting beside him in the meeting-room on the first floor of the Xian Hotel, Preston Murphy went over the ground again. His audience this time included experts and officials both from Beijing and from Xian itself. Though he had made considerable progress in Chinese over the last few months, Preston spoke in English, relying on Lilly to provide any necessary translation.

"I pay tribute", Preston began, "to the late Professor Zheng, once President of the Xian Historical Society. It is not up to me to speculate on the causes of the Professor's tragic death. I would merely recall on this occasion my belief that Zheng, too, was – before he died – elaborating a theory to explain the mystery of the empty pit, that is to say, Pit Number 4, and that theory was, I suspect, very similar to my own. Indeed, it was the account Zheng gave me of the Xian incident that provided me with the crucial clue." Preston paused and poured himself a cup of tea from the painted thermos in front of him.

"Get on with it," Lilly whispered. "The transport is already waiting for us."

"Of course." Preston had his audience where he wanted them. "When Professor Zheng and I had lunch together, soon after I first arrived in China, at the Huaqin Hot Springs outside Xian, where as you know Chiang Kai Shek was captured by the Young Marshal's troops, he told me that Chou En Lai himself had visited Xian to participate in the negotiations which ultimately led to the Generalissimo's release. It is known that Chou had several talks with Chiang though neither Chou nor Chiang ever revealed the content of those discussions. We do, however, know that Chiang was released and that he flew back to Chungking in the company of his wife, Madame Chiang, the former Mayling Soong, and a young pilot of the Chinese Air Force, Mayling's nephew, Charlie Soong. The Young Marshal came to see them off at the airport, then – to general surprise – flew off into captivity."

Preston looked around the room. On the walls hung scroll-paintings depicting a country of fruit and flowers, of bearded sages walking on delicate arched bridges over graceful lily-strewn ponds. "The Generalissimo, as we all know, was a thief on a grand scale." There was a rumble of disapproval. "The museums of Taiwan today are still full of the treasures which he removed from this country. He was a passionate collector and I believe that, as part of a three-way deal between Chou En Lai, the Young Marshal and himself, Chiang was offered a sweetener which he couldn't possibly refuse. Is it inconceivable, my friends," – Preston seemed almost to be challenging them to disagree with him – "that the terracotta army, or at least the statues in Pit Number 4, were discovered not in 1974, but in 1936? Professor Zheng told me that the irrigation works were actually begun at that time . . ."

"But, surely," the Curator of National Antiquities, a man who looked as dusty and as dry as some of the artefacts he was responsible for, intervened: "The treasures which the renegade scoundrel, Chiang Kai Shek, carried away with him to Chungking, the treasures which Soong eventually inherited or otherwise acquired, were fake. That's what the Hong Kong authorities have officially informed us. Soong had his own collection of Qin statues copied and then sent the copies to Beijing. But in fact, as we now know, the 'originals' in Soong's possession were no more authentic than the copies he had made. You're not suggesting, Mr Murphy, that the Shaanxi peasants working in the fields in 1936 actually uncovered a load of fakes which very conveniently happened to be buried there?"

Preston smiled. "Of course not. The treasures of Pit Number 4 were real treasures all right. But they weren't the treasures which Chiang carried away. My belief is that the Young Marshal 'did a Soong', if you like. There are plenty of people around even today who know how to make and bake a terracotta statue. You only have to look at the quality of the replicas being hawked for sale outside the museum or in the streets of Xian today ..."

"Wait a moment!" The curator of National Antiquities held up his hand to interrupt. "If, as you suggest, the Young Marshal 'did a Soong' and had the originals copied, then *where are the originals?* Are they still in China? Are they still in Xian? You seem to know the answer to so many questions, Mr Murphy, can you help us with this one too?"

"I was coming to that ..." Preston ignored the heavy irony.

An hour later, as they stood in fror' of the great funerary urns in the prehistoric village of Banpo some ten miles outside Xian, Preston held up the photograph to the light.

"Chou states that this photograph was taken by the Young Marshal in 1936. Where were they? Probably in Xian. That is surely a reasonable assumption, since they were both known to have been here at the time of Chiang's capture. Look at the picture, ladies and gentlemen, and you will see that Chou is standing in front of a large urn. In fact," Preston pointed to one of the large funerary objects, "it is clear that Chou is standing in front of this particular urn at Banpo. The prehistoric village of Banpo was, of course, discovered in the early thirties by the Young Marshal's archaeologists. These giant funerary urns which we are now looking at were then, as now, a distinctive feature of the site.

"A few months ago, when I came here with Professor Zheng, I learned one fascinating detail. In prehistoric times, people who had contagious diseases were simply buried alive in these giant urns. It may not have been the most humane way of dealing with the problem, but it was certainly effective. Zheng also told me that the Young Marshal, as war-lord of this region, had given the strictest instructions that these urns were never to be unsealed, presumably on the grounds that deadly germs – or pathogens – might still be lurking. Am I right, sir?" Preston turned to address the Curator.

"Quite right." The old man replied in a quavering voice. "These urns have never been opened since the Young Marshal first issued his edict."

"You'd agree, then, wouldn't you, that they'd make a very convenient hiding-place?" Even Hercule Poirot, Preston thought to himself, couldn't have managed the *coup de théâtre* with any more aplomb.

It took the workmen over three hours to prise off the lid of the giant urn in front of which Chou En Lai had had his picture taken in December 1936. The medical authorities of Xian insisted that the interior be thoroughly fumigated and disinfected before any inspection of the contents could be made. Someone had tipped off the press and television as well to the fact that the famous Lilly Wu was in town, not to give a recital but to witness the discovery or rather the rediscovery of the treasures of Qin. By the time they were finally ready a substantial crowd of onlookers had gathered.

"You take a look first." Preston had insisted that the Curator from the National Museum of Antiquities should do the honours. They held the ladder for him and passed him a flashlight as he rather shakily reached the top. For several long minutes the curator stood there on the top of the ladder, bending down and peering with the aid of the flashlight into the deep recesses of the urn.

"What do you see? Do you see anything?" they called up to him.

April Fool! thought Preston for a moment. Maybe the little grey cells have led us right up the garden path. He stepped forward to steady the ladder as the old man climbed back down.

"Well?" The man's face was expressionless. He looked

as though he was in a trance. "What did you see?" they asked him again.

"I saw a man with the face of an eagle," the Curator finally replied, choking with emotion, "the face of an eagle, the body of a lion . . ."

"You were terrific." Lilly snuggled closer to him in the wide double-bed on the 12th floor of the modern Xian Hotel. "You had them eating out of your hand. But something still puzzles me. If Chou En Lai knew about the terracotta statues all along, knew about the Young Marshal's trick, why did he never say anything? If father hadn't given me the photograph, and if you weren't as clever as Agatha Christie and Georges Simenon rolled into one, none of us would have been any the wiser."

"That's not quite true. Zheng was on the right track, poor chap."

Earlier that day, they had driven past the Great Wild Goose Pagoda and Preston had again felt a surge of remorse for the part he had unwittingly played in Zheng's death. If there was consolation to be found anywhere, it lay in the fact that the Chinese authorities had, without any admission of complicity or liability, made a substantial *ex gratia* payment to Zheng's widow, enough to keep her in relative comfort for the rest of her life. They had done the same for David Burns's wife, as well.

"You didn't answer the question about Chou."

"Either Chou didn't know about the Young Marshal's trick," Preston replied at last, "and it was just a coincidence that he had his photo taken at Banpo. Or he did know but deliberately kept the knowledge to himself apart from leaving that one obscure clue. Right up to the time of Chou's death in 1976 and long beyond it, I suppose, Qin Shi Huang was still officially regarded as the supreme example of a reactionary, renegade feudal despot, a man tyrannical enough to insist that thousands of his wives and concubines be buried alive with him when he died. What do you think the rampaging Red Guards would have done to those statues if they had discovered them? Smashed them into fragments, for sure. Even today, there are people – as I understand it – who question the rehabilitation of Qin Shi Huang and they're not all believers in Women's Lib! It takes the courage of a man like Deng to face them down. Who knows – perhaps the guy who broke the arm of the statue in the Great Hall of the People, the fake statue as we now know – did so accidentally on purpose . . ."

"You're suggesting that Chou believed the best way of keeping the Qin treasures safe was to say nothing and to allow them to remain hidden for future generations to discover?"

"It's possible." Preston remembered the words he had read in his father's Chinese diaries. "My father believed that Chou was the most intelligent man he had ever met."

"My father thought so too. Still does." She was silent for a time. Then she said, "Remember when we were in the mountains, I told you about what it was like in Beijing at the beginning of 1976, when Chou died. The Gang of Four hoped the country would forget him. There was almost no official mourning. Yet three months later, at the Qing Ming Festival when the dead are remembered, more than 10,000 wreaths were placed on the heroes' monument in Tian An Men Square in honour of the late Premier. By the end, the pile of wreaths rose fifty feet above the ground until the Gang of Four decided enough was enough and sent in men to tear them down. I went there one morning with my father soon after the wreckers had been. There were still a few wreaths scattered on the ground. I picked one up and read the inscription. Father took the wreath home that day. He still has it."

"What did the inscription say?"

She hesitated a moment, collecting her thoughts. " 'He left no inheritance,' " she began, " 'he had no children, he has no grave, he left no remains. His ashes were scattered over the mountains and rivers of our land.' "

While Lilly Wu lay on her back with her hands behind her head staring at the ceiling, Preston walked over to the window. The crowds which had thronged the square in front of the hotel earlier in the day had disappeared. Directly

335

below him, an old man was standing beneath a street-lamp,
practising Tai-Chi.